Flouting convention, flirting with danger...

Caroline, Diana and Elizabeth Copeland are faced with a challenge...a new guardian who is determined on marriage—to one of them! But these three sisters aren't afraid to discard the rules of Regency Society. They're equally determined to take their futures—including potential husbands—very much into their own hands....

The Copeland Sisters:

THE LADY GAMBLES
November 2011

THE LADY FORFEITS
December 2011

THE LADY CONFESSES
January 2012

He introduced himself.
"I am Dominic Vaughn, Earl of Blackstone."

Caro felt a tightness in her chest as she realized this man was a member of the *ton,* a man no doubt as arrogant as her recently acquired guardian. "If that is meant to impress me, *my lord,* then I am afraid it has failed utterly."

He raised dark brows. "I believe it is the usual custom at this point for the introduction to be reciprocated."

Her cheeks burned at the intended rebuke. "If you have spoken to Mr. Butler, then you must already know that my name is Caro Morton."

He looked at her shrewdly. "Is it?"

Her gaze sharpened. "I have just said as much, my lord."

"Ah, if only the saying of something made it true," he mused.

That tightness in Caro's chest increased. "Do you doubt my word, sir?"

"I am afraid I am of an age and experience, my dear Caro, when I doubt everything I am told until proven otherwise."

CAROLE MORTIMER

The Lady Gambles

TORONTO NEW YORK LONDON
AMSTERDAM PARIS SYDNEY HAMBURG
STOCKHOLM ATHENS TOKYO MILAN MADRID
PRAGUE WARSAW BUDAPEST AUCKLAND

Recycling programs
for this product may
not exist in your area.

ISBN-13: 978-0-373-29666-8

THE LADY GAMBLES

www.Harlequin.com

Printed in U.S.A.

Author Note

Welcome to the first in the trilogy featuring the Copeland sisters! Caroline, Diana and Elizabeth Copeland, eager to escape their new guardian's unacceptable marriage plans, decide to leave the comfort and safety of their home in Hampshire for the first time and embark on exciting, and separate, adventures in London.

They certainly find adventure—and danger—and most importantly of all, the men destined for each of them, and by doing so begin the biggest adventure of their lives: love.

The sisters are totally different in temperament, of course, but all are feisty and brave. And I do believe I fell in love with each and every one of the heroes during the writing of this trilogy. I hope you do, too.

Enjoy!

Available from Harlequin® Historical and
CAROLE MORTIMER

The Duke's Cinderella Bride #960
The Rake's Wicked Proposal #969
The Rogue's Disgraced Lady #975
Lady Arabella's Scandalous Marriage #987
†*The Lady Gambles* #1066

Other works include:

Harlequin Historical Undone ebooks

At the Duke's Service
Convenient Wife, Pleasured Lady
†*A Wickedly Pleasurable Wager*

*The Notorious St. Claires
†The Copeland Sisters

*Carole Mortimer also writes for Harlequin Presents!
Don't miss her next book, coming soon!*

Prologue

April 1817—Palazzo Brizzi, Venice, Italy

'Have I mentioned to either of you gentlemen that I had thought of offering for one of Westbourne's daughters?'

Lord Dominic Vaughn, Earl of Blackstone, and one of the two gentlemen referred to by their host, Lord Gabriel Faulkner, found himself gaping inelegantly across the breakfast table at the other man in stunned disbelief. A glance at their friend Nathaniel Thorne, Earl of Osbourne, showed him to be no less surprised at the announcement as he sat with his tea cup arrested halfway between saucer and mouth.

Indeed, it was one of those momentous occasions when it seemed that time itself should cease. All movement. All sound. Indeed, when the very world itself should simply have stopped turning.

It had not, of course; the gondoliers could still be heard singing upon their crafts in the busy Grand Canal, the pedlars continued to call out as they moved along the canal selling their wares, and the birds still sang a merry tune. That frozen stillness, that ceasing of time, existed only between the three men seated upon the balcony of the Palazzo Brizzi, where they had been enjoying a late breakfast together prior to Blackstone and Osbourne's departure for England later today.

'Gentlemen?' their host prompted in that dry and amused drawl that was so typical of him, one dark brow raised mockingly over eyes of midnight blue as he placed the letter he had been reading down upon the table top.

Dominic Vaughn was the first to recover his senses. 'Surely you are not serious, Gabe?'

That mocking dark brow was joined by its twin. 'Am I not?'

'Well, of course not.' Osbourne finally rallied to the occasion. '*You* are Westbourne!'

'For the past six months, yes.' The new Earl of Westbourne acknowledged drily. 'It is one of the *previous* Earl's daughters for whom I have offered.'

'Copeland?'

Westbourne gave a haughty inclination of his dark head. 'Just so.'

'I—but why would you do such a thing?' Dominic made no effort to hide his disgust at the idea of one of their number willingly sacrificing himself to the parson's mousetrap.

The three men were all aged eight and twenty, and had been to school together before serving in Wellington's army for five years. They had fought together, drunk together, eaten together, wenched together, shared the same accommodations on many occasions— and one thing they had all agreed on long ago was the lack of a need to settle on one piece of succulent fruit when the whole of the basket was available for the tasting. Gabriel's announcement smacked of a betrayal of that tacit pact.

Westbourne shrugged his wide shoulders beneath the elegance of his dark-blue superfine. 'It seemed like the correct thing to do.'

The correct thing to do! When had Gabriel ever bothered himself with acting correctly? Banished to the Continent in disgrace by his own family and society eight years ago, Lord Gabriel Faulkner had lived his life since that time by his own rules, and to hell with what was correct!

Having inherited the extremely respected title of the Earl of Westbourne put a slightly different slant on things, of course, and meant that London society—the marriage-minded mamas especially—would no doubt welcome the scandalous Gabriel back into the *ton* with open arms. But even so…

'You *are* jesting, of course, Gabriel.' Osbourne felt no hesitation in voicing his own scepticism concerning their friend's announcement.

'I am afraid I am not,' Westbourne stated firmly. 'My unexpected inheritance of the title and estates has left the future of Copeland's three daughters to my own tender mercies.' His top lip curled back in self-derision. 'No doubt Copeland expected to see his three daughters safely married off before he met his Maker. Unfortunately, this was not the case, and as such, the three young women have become my wards.'

'Are you saying that you have been guardian to the three Copeland chits for the past six months and not said a word?' Osborne sounded as if he could barely believe it.

Westbourne gave a cool inclination of his arrogant head. 'A little like leaving the door open for the fox to enter the henhouse, is it not?'

It was indeed, Dominic mused wryly; Gabriel's reputation with the ladies was legendary. As was his ruthlessness when it came to bringing an end to those relationships when they became in the least irksome to him. 'Why have you never mentioned this before, Gabriel?'

The other man shrugged. 'I am mentioning it now.'

'Incredible!' Osborne was still at a loss for words.

Gabriel gave a hard, humourless grin. 'Almost as incredible as my having inherited the title at all, really.'

It was certainly the case that it would not have occurred if the years of battle against Napoleon's armies had not killed off Copeland's two nephews, the only other possible inheritors of the title. As it was, because Copeland only had daughters and no sons, the disgraced Lord Gabriel Faulkner had inherited the title of Earl of Westbourne from a man who was merely a second cousin or some such flimsy connection.

'Obviously, the fact that I am now the young ladies' guardian rendered the situation slightly unusual, and so I had my lawyer put forward an offer of marriage on my behalf,' Westbourne explained.

'To which daughter?' Dominic tried to recall whether or not he had ever seen or met any of the Copeland sisters during his occasional forays into society this past two Seasons, but drew a complete blank. He did not consider it a good omen that none of the young women appeared to be attractive enough to spark even a flicker of memory.

Westbourne's sculptured mouth twisted wryly. 'Never having met any of the young ladies, I did not feel it necessary to state a preference.'

'You did not!' Dominic stared at the other man in horror. 'Gabriel, you cannot mean to say that you have offered marriage to *any* one of the Copeland chits?'

Westbourne gave a cool smile. 'That is exactly what I have done.'

'I say, Gabe!' Osbourne looked as horrified as Dominic felt. 'Taking a bit of a risk, don't you think? What if they decide to give you the fat and ugly one? The one that no other man would want?'

'I do not see that as being a problem when Harriet Copeland was their mother.' Westbourne waved that objection aside.

All three men had been but nineteen when Lady Harriet Copeland, the Countess of Westbourne, having left her husband and daughters, had tragically met her death at the hands of her jealous lover only months later. The woman's beauty was legendary.

Dominic grimaced. 'They may decide to give you the one that takes after her father.' Copeland had been a short and rotund man in his sixties when he died, and with little charm to recommend him, either—was it any wonder that a woman as beautiful as Harriet Copeland had left him for a younger man?

'What if they do?' Westbourne relaxed back in his chair, his dark hair curling fashionably upon his nape and brow. 'In order to provide the necessary heir, the Earl of Westbourne must needs take a wife. Any wife. Any one of the Copeland sisters is capable of providing that heir regardless of her appearance, surely?' He shrugged those elegantly wide shoulders.

'But what about—I mean, if she is fat and ugly, surely you will never be able to rise to the occasion in order to provide this necessary heir?' Osbourne visibly winced at the unpleasantness of the image he had just portrayed.

'What do you say to that, Gabe?' Dominic chuckled.

'I say that it no longer matters whether or not I would be able to perform in my marriage bed.' Westbourne picked up the letter he had set aside earlier to peruse its contents once again with an apparent air of calm. 'It would appear that my reputation has preceded me, gentlemen.' His voice had become steely.

Dominic frowned. 'Explain, Gabriel.'

That sculptured mouth tightened. 'The letter I received from my lawyer this morning states that all three of the Copeland sisters—yes, even the fat and ugly one, Nate…' he gave a mocking little bow in Osbourne's direction '…have rejected any idea of marriage to the disreputable Lord Gabriel Faulkner.'

Dominic had known Gabriel long enough to realise that his calm attitude was a sham, and that the cold glitter in those midnight-blue eyes and the harsh set of his jaw were a clearer indication of his friend's current mood. Beneath that veneer of casual uninterest he was coldly, dangerously angry.

A fact born out by his next statement. 'In the circumstances, gentlemen, I have decided that I will shortly be following the two of you to England.'

'The ladies of Venice will all fall into a decline at your going,' Osbourne predicted drily.

'Perhaps,' Gabriel allowed dispassionately, 'but I have decided that it is time the new Earl of Westbourne took his place in London society.'

'Capital!' Osbourne felt no hesitation in voicing his approval of the plan.

Dominic was equally enthusiastic at the thought of having Gabriel back in London with them. 'Westbourne House in London has not been lived in for years, and must resemble a mausoleum, so perhaps you would care to stay with me at Blackstone House when you return, Gabriel? I would welcome your opinion, too, on the changes I instructed be made at Nick's during my absence.' He referred to the gambling club he had won a month ago in a game of cards with the previous owner, Nicholas Brown.

'I should have a care in any further dealings you might have with Brown, Dom.' Gabriel frowned.

An unnecessary warning as it happened; Dominic was well aware that Nicholas Brown, far from being a gentleman, was the bastard son of a peer and a prostitute, and that his connections in the seedy underworld of England's capital were numerous. 'Duly noted, Gabe.'

The other man nodded. 'In that case, I thank you for your invitation to stay at Blackstone House, but it is not my intention to remain in town. Instead, I will make my way immediately to Shoreley Park.'

An occurrence, Dominic felt sure, that did not bode well for the three Copeland sisters...

Chapter One

*Three days later—Nick's gambling club,
London, England*

Caro moved lightly across the stage on slippered feet
before arranging herself carefully upon the red-velvet
chaise, checking that the gold-and-jewelled mask covering her face from brow to lips was securely in place,
and arranging the long ebony curls of the theatrical wig
so that they cascaded over the fullness of her breasts
and down the length of her spine, before attending to
the draping of her gold-coloured gown so that she was
completely covered from her throat to her toes.

She could hear the buzz of excitement behind the
drawn curtains at the front of the small raised stage, and
knew that the male patrons of the gambling club were
anticipating the moment when those curtains would be
pulled back and her performance began.

Caro's heart began to pound, the blood thrum-
ming hotly in her veins as the introductory music

began to play, and the room behind the drawn curtains fell into an expectant silence.

Dominic hesitated at the entrance of Nick's, one of London's most fashionable gambling clubs, and one of his favourite haunts even before he had taken possession of it a month ago.

Newly arrived back from Venice that afternoon, he had decided to visit the club at the earliest opportunity, and as he handed his hat and cloak over to the waiting attendant, he could not help but notice that the burly young man who usually guarded the doorway against undesirables was not in his usual place. He also realised that the gambling rooms beyond the red-velvet curtains were unnaturally silent.

What on earth was going on?

Suddenly that silence was bewitchingly broken by the sultry, sensual sound of a woman singing. Except that Dominic had given strict instructions before his departure for Venice that in future there were to be no women working—in *any* capacity—in the club he now owned.

He was frowning heavily as he strolled into the main salon, seeing at once the reason for the doorman's desertion when he spotted Ben Jackson standing transfixed just inside a room crowded with equally mesmerised patrons, all of them apparently hearing only one thing. Seeing only one thing.

A woman, the obvious source of that sensually seductive voice, lay upon a red-velvet *chaise* on the stage, a tiny little thing with an abundance of ebony hair that cascaded in loose curls over her shoulders and

down the length of her slender back. Most of her face
was covered by a jewelled mask much like the ones
worn in Venice during carnival, but her bared lips were
full and sensuous, her throat a pearly white. She wore
a gown of shimmering gold, the voluptuousness of her
curves hinted at rather than blatantly displayed, and the
more seductive because of it.

Even masked, she was without a doubt the most sensually seductive creature Dominic had ever beheld!

The fact that every other man in the room thought
the same thing was evident from the avarice in their
gazes and the flush to their cheeks, several visibly lick-
ing their lips as they stared at her. A fact that caused
Dominic's scowl to deepen as his own gaze returned
to that vision of seduction upon the stage.

Caro tried not to reveal her irritation with the man
who stood at the back of the salon glowering at her,
either by her expression or in her voice, as she brought
her first performance of the evening to an end by slowly
standing up to move gracefully to the edge of the stage
as she sang the last huskily appealing notes.

It did not prevent her from being completely aware
of that pale and disapproving gaze or of the man that
gaze belonged to.

He was so extremely tall that even standing at the
back of the salon he towered several inches over the
other men in the room, his black superfine tailored to
widely muscled shoulders, his white linen impeccable
and edged with Brussels lace at his throat and wrist.
His fashionably styled hair was the colour of a raven's
wing, so black it almost seemed to have a blue sheen.

His eyes, those piercingly critical eyes, were the pale colour of a grey silky mist, and appeared almost silver in their intensity. He had a strong, aristocratic face: high cheekbones, a straight slash of a nose, firm sculptured lips, and a square and arrogantly determined jaw. It was a hard and uncompromising face, made more so by the scar that ran down its left side, from just beneath his eye to that stubbornly set jaw.

His pale grey eyes were currently staring at Caro with an intensity of dislike that she had never encountered before in all of her twenty years. So unnerved was she by his obvious disdain that she barely managed to maintain her smile as she took her bows to the thunderous round of applause. Applause she knew from experience would last for several minutes after she had returned to her dressing-room at the back of the club.

It was impossible not to take one last glance in the scowling man's direction before she disappeared from the stage, slightly alarmed as she saw that he was now in earnest conversation with the manager of the club, Drew Butler.

'What is the meaning of this, Drew?' Dominic asked icily under cover of the applause for the beauty still taking her bows upon the stage.

The grey-haired man looked unperturbed; as the manager of Nick's for the past twenty years, the cynicism in his tired blue eyes stated that he had already seen and done most things in his fifty years, and was no longer disturbed by any of them, least of all by the disapproving tone of the man who had become his employer only a month ago. 'The patrons love her.'

'The patrons have neither drunk nor gambled since that woman began to sing some quarter of an hour ago,' Dominic pointed out.

'Watch them now,' Drew said softly.

Dominic did watch, his brows rising as the champagne began to flow copiously and the patrons placed ridiculously high bets at the tables, the level of conversation rising exponentially as the attributes of the young woman were loudly discussed, along with more bets being placed as to the chances of any of them being privileged enough to see behind the jewelled mask.

'You see.' Drew gave an unconcerned shrug as he turned back to Dominic. 'She's really good for business.'

Dominic shook his head impatiently. 'Did I not make it clear when I was here last month that this is to be a gambling club only in future, and not a damned brothel?'

'You did.' Again Drew remained completely unruffled. 'And as per your instructions the bedchambers upstairs have remained locked and unavailable to all.'

A gentleman, an earl no less, owning a London gambling club of Nick's reputation was hardly acceptable to society. But it had been a matter of honour to Dominic, when Nicholas Brown had challenged him to a game of cards the previous month for ownership of Midnight Moon, the prize stallion kept at Dominic's stud at his estate in Kent. In return, Dominic had demanded that Nicholas put up Nick's as his own side of the wager and obviously Dominic had won.

Owning a gambling club was one thing, but the half-a-dozen bedchambers on the first floor, until recently available to any man who had wished for some privacy with…whomever, were totally unacceptable; Dominic drew the line at being considered a pimp! As such, he had ordered a ban on women—all women—inside the club, and the bedrooms upstairs to be immediately closed off. With the exception of the mysterious young woman, who had so recently held the club's patrons enthralled—and not just with her singing!—those instructions appeared to have been carried out.

Dominic's mouth compressed. 'I believe my instructions were to dispense with the services of all the… ladies working here?'

'Caro ain't—is not, a whore.' Drew visibly bristled, his shoulders stiffening defensively.

Dominic frowned darkly. 'Then what, pray, is she?'

'Exactly as you saw,' Drew said. 'Twice a night she simply lays on the *chaise* and sings. And the punters drink and gamble more than ever once she leaves the stage.'

'Does she bring a maid or companion with her?'

The older man looked amused. 'What do you think?'

'What do *I* think?' Dominic's eyes had narrowed to icy slits. 'I think she is a disaster in the making.' He scowled. 'Which gentleman has the privilege of escorting her home at the end of the evening?'

'I does.' The doorman, Ben Jackson, announced proudly as he passed them on his way back to his vigil at the entrance to the club, his round face looking no less cherubic for all that his nose had obviously been broken more than once. His ham-sized fists did not come amiss in a brawl, either.

Dominic raised sceptical brows. '*You* do?'

Ben beamed contentedly, showing several broken teeth for his trouble. 'Miss Caro insists on it.'

Oh, she did, did she?

Ben Jackson could make grown men quake in their boots just by looking at them, and Drew Butler was a cynic through and through, and yet *Miss Caro* appeared to have them both eating out of her delicate little hand!

'Perhaps we should continue this discussion in your office, Drew?' Dominic turned away, expecting rather than waiting to see if the older man followed him, his impatience barely held in check. Nevertheless, he still managed to greet and smile at several acquaintances as he moved purposefully towards the back of the smoke-filled club to where Drew's office was situated.

He barely noticed the opulence of that office as Drew followed him into the room before closing the door behind him and effectively shutting out the noise from the gaming rooms. Although Dominic did spot a decanter of what he knew to be a first-class brandy, and he swiftly poured himself a glass and took an appreciative sip before offering to pour one for the manager, too.

The older man shook his head. 'I never drink during working hours.'

Dominic made himself comfortable as he leant back against the front of the huge mahogany desk. 'Well, who is she, Drew? And where is she from?'

The manager shrugged. 'Do you want my take on her or what she told me when she came to the back door asking for work?'

Dominic's gaze narrowed. 'Both.' He took another sip of his brandy, giving every appearance of studying the toe of one highly polished boot as the other man began to relate the young woman's tale of woe.

Caro Morton claimed to be an orphan who had lived with a maiden aunt in the country until three weeks ago, the death of the elderly lady leaving her homeless. Consequently she had arrived in London two weeks earlier with very little money and no maid or companion, but with a determination to make her own way in the world. Her intention, apparently, had been to offer herself as companion or governess in a respectable household, but her lack of references had made that impossible, and so she had instead been driven to begin knocking on the back door of the theatres and clubs.

Dominic looked up sharply at this part of the story. 'How many had she visited before arriving here?'

'Half a dozen or so.' Drew grimaced. 'I understand she did receive several offers of…alternative employment along the way.'

Dominic gave a humourless smile as he easily guessed the nature of those offers. 'You did not feel tempted to do the same when she came knocking on the door here?' He had no doubt that Miss Caro Morton was a young woman most men, no matter what their age, would like to bed.

The older man shot him a frowning glance as he moved to sit behind the desk. 'My lord, I happen to have been happily married for the past twenty years, with a daughter not much younger than she is.'

'My apologies.' Dominic gave a slight bow. 'Very well.' His gaze sharpened. 'That would appear to be Miss Morton's version of her arrival in London; now tell me who or what *you* think she is.'

Drew looked thoughtful. 'There may have been a maiden aunt, but somehow I doubt it. My guess is she's in London because she's running away from something or someone. A brutish father, maybe. Or perhaps even a cruel husband. Either way she's far too refined to be your usual actress or whore.'

Dominic eyed him speculatively. 'Define refined?'

'Ladylike,' the older man supplied tersely.

Dominic looked intrigued; a woman of quality attempting to conceal her identity would certainly explain the wearing of that jewelled mask. 'And you do not think that actresses and whores are capable of giving the impression of being ladylike?'

'I know they are,' Drew answered. 'I just don't happen to think Caro Morton is one of them.' His expression became closed. 'Perhaps it would be best if you were to talk to her and decide for yourself?'

That the manager felt a fatherly protectiveness towards the 'refined' Miss Caro Morton was obvious. That the doorman, Ben Jackson, felt that same protectiveness was also apparent. If she really were a runaway wife or daughter, then Dominic felt no such softness of emotions. 'I fully intend doing so,' he assured the other man drily as he straightened. 'I merely wished to hear your views first.'

Drew looked concerned. 'Are you intending to dismiss her?'

Dominic gave the thought some consideration before answering. There was no doubting Drew Butler's claim that Caro Morton's nightly performances were a draw to the club, but even so she might just be more trouble than she was worth if she really were a runaway wife or daughter. 'That will depend upon Miss Morton.'

'In what way?'

He raised arrogant brows. 'I accept that you have been the manager of Nick's for several years, Drew. That you are, without a doubt, the best man for the job.' He smiled briefly to soften what he was about to say next. 'However, that ability does not give you the right to question any of my own actions or decisions.'

'No, my lord.'

'Where is Caro Morton now?'

'I usually ensure that she has a bite to eat in her dressing-room between performances.' Drew's expression challenged Dominic to question that decision of *his*.

Remembering the girl's slenderness, and the pallor of her translucent skin, Dominic felt no inclination to do so; from the look of her, that 'bite to eat' might be the only food Caro Morton had in a single day.

'I'd like to be informed if you decide to let her to go. She has wages owing to her,' Drew defended as Dominic looked surprised.

She also, Dominic decided ruefully as he agreed to the request before leaving the office, had the cynical club manager wrapped tightly about her tiny little finger, and no doubt the older man would offer her his assistance in finding other employment should Dominic decide to let her go.

Deciding for himself who or what Miss Caro Morton was promised to be an interesting experience. It was a surprising realisation for a man whose years in the army, and the two years since returning to England spent evading the clutches of every marriage-minded mama of the *ton*, had made him as cynical, if not more so, as the much older Drew Butler.

Caro gave a surprised start as a brief knock sounded on her dressing-room door. Well, not a dressing-room as such, she allowed ruefully, more a private room at the back of the gambling club that Mr Butler had put aside for her use in between her performances.

A room that he had assured her was completely off-limits to any and all of the men who frequented Nick's…

She stood up slowly, nervously making sure that her robe was securely tied about her waist before crossing the tiny room to stand beside the locked door. 'Who is it?' she asked warily.

'My name is Dominic Vaughn,' came the haughty reply.

Just like that, Caro *knew* that the man standing on the other side of the locked door was the same man who had looked at her earlier with those disdainful silver-coloured eyes. She was not sure why or how she knew that, she just did. There was an arrogance in the deep baritone voice, a confidence that spoke of years of issuing orders and having them instantly obeyed. And he was obviously now expecting her to obey him by unlocking the door and allowing him inside…

Her hands clenched in the pockets of her robe, the nails digging painfully into the palms. 'Gentlemen are not allowed to visit me in my dressing-room.'

A brief silence followed her statement, before the

man replied with hard impatience, 'I assure you that my being here has Drew Butler's full approval.'

The manager of Nick's had been very kind to Caro this past week, and, what's more, she knew that she could trust him implicitly. But having a man approach her dressing-room in this unexpected way and simply stating that Mr Butler approved of his being here and expecting her to believe his claim was not good enough. 'I am sorry, but the answer is still no.'

'I assure you, my business with you will only take a few moments of your time,' came the irritated response.

'I am in need of rest before my next performance,' Caro insisted.

Dominic's mouth firmed in frustration at this woman's stubborn refusal to so much as open the door. 'Miss Morton—'

'That is my final word on the subject,' she informed him haughtily.

Drew had claimed that Caro Morton was 'ladylike', Dominic recalled with a narrowing of his eyes. He could hear that quality himself now in the precise diction of her voice. A subtle, and yet unmistakable authority in her tone that spoke of education and refinement. 'You will either speak to me now, Miss Morton, or I assure you there will be no "next performance" for you at Nick's.' Dominic stood with his shoulder leaning against the wall in the darkened hallway, arms folded across the broad width of this chest.

There was a tiny gasp inside the room. 'Are you threatening me, Mr Vaughn?' There was a slight edge of uncertainty to her voice now.

'I feel no need to threaten, Miss Morton, when the truth will serve just as well.'

Caro was in something of a quandary. Having fled her home two weeks earlier, sure that she would find employment in the obscurity of London as a lady's companion or governess, instead she had found herself being turned away from those respectable households, time and time again, simply because she did not have the appropriate references.

Everything in London had been so much more expensive than Caro had imagined it would be, too. The small amount of money she had brought with her, saved over the months from her allowance, had diminished much more rapidly than she had imagined it would, leaving her with no choice, if she were not to return to an intolerable situation, but to try her luck at the back door of the theatres. She had always received compliments upon her singing when she'd entertained after dinner on the rare occasions her father had invited friends and neighbours to dine. Those visits to the theatres *had* resulted in her receiving several offers of employment—but all of them were shocking to a young woman brought up in protected seclusion in rural Hampshire!

She owed her present employment—and the money with which to pay for her modest lodgings—completely to Drew Butler's kindness. As such, she was not sure that she could turn Dominic Vaughn away from her dressing-room if for some reason the older man really had approved the visit.

Her fingers shook slightly as she took her hands from the pockets of her robe to slowly turn the key in the

lock, only to step back quickly as the door was immediately thrust open impatiently.

It *was* the silver-eyed devil from earlier! He looked
even more devilish now as the subdued candlelight illu-
minating the hallway threw that scar upon his cheek
into sharp relief and his black jacket and white linen
only added to the rawness of the power that seemed to
emanate from him.

Caro took another step backwards. 'What is it you
wished to speak to me about?'

Dominic deliberately schooled his expression to
reveal none of the shock he had felt as he looked at
Caro Morton for the first time without the benefit of that
concealing jewelled mask. Or the ebony-coloured wig,
which had apparently concealed her own long and glori-
ously golden curls. Those curls now framed sea-green,
almond-shaped eyes, set in a delicate, heart-shaped face
of such beauty it took his breath away.

An occurrence, if she were indeed a disobedient
daughter or—worse—a runaway wife, that did not
please him in the slightest. 'Invite me inside, Miss
Morton,' he demanded dictatorially.

Long-lashed lids blinked nervously before she
arrested the movement and her pointed chin rose
proudly. 'As I have already explained, sir, I am resting
until my next performance.'

Dominic's mouth hardened. 'Which I understand
from Drew does not take place for another hour.'

The slenderness of her throat moved convulsively,
drawing his attention to the bare expanse of creamy-
white skin revealed by the plunging neckline of her
robe. His hooded gaze moved lower still, to where the
silky material draped down over small, pointed breasts.

Her waist was so slender that he was sure his hands could easily span its circumference. He also privately acknowledged, with an unlooked for stirring of his arousal, that his hands could easily cup her tiny breasts before lowering to the smooth roundness of her bottom and lifting her against him for her to wrap those long, slender legs about his waist…

Caro found she did not much care for the way Dominic Vaughn was looking at her. Almost as if he could see beneath her robe to the naked flesh beneath. Her cheeks became flushed as she straightened her shoulders determinedly. 'I would prefer that you remain exactly where you are, sir.'

That silver gaze returned to her face. 'My lord.'

She blinked. 'I beg your pardon?'

He introduced himself. 'I am Lord Dominic Vaughn, Earl of Blackstone.'

Caro felt a tightness in her chest as she realised this man was a member of the *ton*, a man no doubt as arrogant as her recently acquired guardian. 'If that is meant to impress me—*my lord*—then I am afraid it has failed utterly.'

He raised dark brows as he ignored the sarcasm in her tone. 'I believe it is the usual custom at this point for the introduction to be reciprocated?'

Her cheeks burned at the intended rebuke. 'If, as you claim, you have spoken to Mr Butler, then you must already know that my name is Caro Morton.'

He looked at her shrewdly. 'Is it?'

Her gaze sharpened. 'I have just said as much, my lord.'

'Ah, if only the saying of something made it true,' he jeered.

That tightness in Caro's chest increased. 'Do you doubt my word, sir?'

'I am afraid I am of an age and experience, my dear Caro, when I doubt everything I am told until proven otherwise.'

There was no doubting that the cynicism and mockery of this man's expression gave him a world-weary appearance, and that scar upon his left cheek an air of danger, but even so she would not have placed him at more than eight or nine and twenty. Not so much older than her own twenty years.

Nor was she his 'dear' anything! 'How very sad for you.'

Not the response Dominic had expected. Or one he wanted, either; the wealthy and eligible Earl of Blackstone did not desire or need anyone's pity. Least of all that of a woman who hid her real appearance behind a jewelled mask and ebony wig.

Could Butler's assessment of her be the correct one? Had this young woman run away to London to hide from possibly an overbearing father, or a brutish and bullying husband? She was of such a tiny and delicate appearance that Dominic found the latter possibility too distasteful to contemplate.

Whatever the mystery surrounding this woman, he was of the opinion that neither he, nor his gambling club, was in need of the trouble she might bring banging upon the door. 'Are you even of an age to be in a gambling club, Caro?'

She looked startled. 'My lord?'

'I simply wondered as to your age.'

'A gentleman should never ask a lady her age,' she retorted primly.

Dominic slowly allowed his gaze to move from the top of that golden head, over the slenderness of her body, the delicacy of her tiny wrists and slender hands, to the bareness of her feet, before just as slowly returning to her now flushed and slightly resentful face. 'As far as I am aware, *ladies* are always accompanied by a maid or companion; nor do they cavort upon the stage of a gentlemen's gaming club.'

Her little pointed chin rose once more. 'I do not cavort, my lord, but simply lie upon a *chaise*,' she bit out tartly. 'I also fail to see what business it is of yours whether or not I have a maid or companion.'

Dominic glanced into the room behind her, noting the tray on the dressing table, with its bowl of some rich and still-steaming stew and a platter of bread beside it, a plump and tempting orange upon another plate, obviously intended as her dessert. No doubt that 'bite to eat' Butler had mentioned providing for her.

'I appear to have interrupted your supper,' he acknowledged smoothly. 'I suggest that we finish this conversation later tonight when I, and not Ben, act as your escort home.'

Her eyes widened in alarm before she gave a firm shake of her head. 'That will not be possible, I am afraid.'

'Oh?'

This was not a man used to receiving no for an answer, Caro realised ruefully as she took in the glittering arrogance in those silver eyes beneath one autocratically raised brow. And her lack of maid or companion was easily explained—if she had felt inclined to offer this man any explanation, which she did not! To have brought either maid or companion with her when she fled Hampshire two weeks ago would have placed them in the position of having abetted her in that flight, and she was in enough trouble already, without involving anyone else in her plight.

'No,' she reaffirmed evenly now. 'It would hurt Ben's feelings terribly if he were not allowed to walk me home. Besides,' she added as his lordship would have dismissed that excuse for exactly what it was, 'I do not allow gentlemen I do not know to escort me to my home.' A man she had no wish to know, either, Caro could have added.

Mocking humour glittered briefly in those pale grey eyes. 'Even if Drew Butler were to vouch for this gentleman?'

'I have yet to hear him do so. Now, if you will excuse me? I wish to eat my supper before it becomes too cool.' Caro's attempt to close the door in Dominic Vaughn's face was thwarted by the tactical placing of one of his booted feet against the door jam. Her eyes flashed a warning as she slowly reopened the door. 'Please do not force me to call upon Ben's help in having you removed from the premises.'

A threat that did not seem to bother the arrogant Dominic Vaughn in the slightest as he continued to smile down at her confidently. 'That would be an... interesting experience.'

Caro eyed him uncertainly. Ben was as tall as the earl, and obviously more heavily built, but there was an underlying air of danger lurking beneath this man's outward show of fashionable elegance. An aura of power that implied he could best any man against whom he chose to pit the strength of those wide shoulders and tall, lithely muscled body. Besides which, Caro very much doubted that the Earl of Blackstone had received that scar upon his face by sitting comfortably at home by his fireside!

She forced the tension from her shoulders as she smiled up at him. 'Perhaps we might defer discussing your offer to escort me home until after I have spoken to Mr Butler?'

And perhaps, Dominic guessed, this young lady would choose to absent herself without so much as bothering to talk to Drew Butler. 'I will be waiting outside for you when you have finished your next performance.'

The irritated darkening of those beautiful sea-green eyes told him that he had guessed correctly. 'You are very persistent, sir!'

'Just anxious to acquaint myself with one of my own employees.'

She gasped, those sea-green eyes wide with alarm. 'Your…? Did you say *your* employee?'

Dominic gave an affirmative nod, and took great pleasure in noting the way the colour drained from the delicacy of her cheeks, as she obviously realised he did indeed **have** the power to ensure she never performed at Nick's again. 'Until later then, Miss Morton.' He bowed elegantly before returning to the gaming rooms, a smile of satisfaction curving his lips.

Chapter Two

'I would prefer to walk, thank you.' It was a little over two hours later when Caro firmly dismissed even the idea of getting inside Dominic Vaughn's fashionable carriage as it stood waiting outside Nick's—a man Drew Butler had confirmed to Caro was not only the Earl of Blackstone, but also the man who had recently taken ownership of the gambling club at which they were both employed. That aside, she had no intention of placing herself in the vulnerable position of travelling alone in his carriage with him!

'As you wish.' He indicated for the driver of the carriage to follow them, his raven-black hair now covered by a fashionably tall hat, and a black silk cloak thrown about those widely muscled shoulders.

Caro shot him a sideways glance from beneath her unadorned brown bonnet, only a few of her golden curls now showing at her temples and nape. The brown gown she wore beneath her own serviceable black cloak was equally as modest in appearance, with its high neckline and long sleeves.

She had bought three such gowns when she'd arrived in London two weeks ago, this brown one, another in a dull green, and the third of dark cream, having very quickly realised that the few silk gowns she had brought to town with her stood out noticeably in the genteelly rundown area of London where she had managed to find clean and inexpensive lodgings. And being noticed—as herself, rather than as the masked lady singing at Nick's—was something she dearly wished to avoid.

To say that Dominic had been surprised—yet again!—by Caro Morton's appearance on joining him a few minutes ago would be an understatement. In fact, it had taken him several seconds to recognise her beneath that unbecoming brown bonnet that hid most of those glorious golden curls, and the equally unfashionable cloak that covered her from neck to ankle, so giving her every appearance of being a modest and unassuming young lady of meagre means.

That dark modesty of her clothing opened up a third possibility as to why Caro Morton was living alone in London and so obviously in need of work in order to support herself. Her slender hands were completely bare of rings, but that did not mean she was not one of those starry-eyed young ladies who, during the years of war against Napoleon, had abandoned all propriety by eloping with their unsuitable soldier beau before he marched off to battle, only to find themselves widowed within weeks, sometimes days, of that scandalous marriage having taken place.

No matter what the explanation, there was certainly

very little danger of any of the patrons of Nick's recognising this drably dressed young woman as the ebony-haired siren whose seductive performance had so easily bewitched and beguiled them all so completely twice this evening.

Himself included, he readily admitted.

'Perhaps you would care to enlighten me as to why an unprotected young woman should choose to work in one of London's fashionable gambling clubs?'

It was a question she seemed to have been expecting as her expression remained cool. 'For the money, perhaps?'

Dominic scowled. 'If you must work, then why did you not find more respectable employment? You have the refinement to be a lady's maid, or, failing that, to serve in a shop.'

'How kind of you to say so,' she returned oversweetly. 'But one needs references from previous employers to become either of those things. References I do not have,' she added pointedly.

'Perhaps because you have never worked as a lady's maid or served in a shop?' he pressed.

'Or perhaps I was just so inadequate at both those occupations that I was refused references?' she suggested tartly.

Dominic gave an appreciative smile at her spirited answer. 'So instead you have chosen to put yourself in a position where you are ogled by dozens of licentious men every night?'

Caro came to an abrupt halt, her own humour fading at the deliberate insult, both in his tone and expression, as he paused beside her in the flickering lamplight and allowed that silver gaze to rake over her critically from her head to her toes. 'It appears that I needed no references for that,' she informed him with chilling hauteur.

Dominic knew that it really was none of his concern if she chose to expose herself to the sort of ribald comments he had been forced to listen to following her second performance this evening, when the bets as to who would eventually become her lover and protector had increased to a level he had found most unpleasant. And yet... 'Do you have so little regard for your reputation?'

Her cheeks became flushed. 'The jewelled mask I wear ensures my reputation remains perfectly intact, thank you!'

'Perhaps.' Dominic's jaw tightened. 'I am surprised you did not consider a less...taxing means of employment.'

She looked puzzled. 'Less taxing?'

He shrugged. 'You are young. The comments of your numerous admirers this evening are testament to your desirability. Did you not consider acquiring a single male protector, rather than exposing yourself in this way to the attentions of dozens?'

Caro felt the flush that warmed her cheeks. 'A protector, my lord?'

'A man who would see you housed and suitably clothed in exchange for the pleasure of your...company,' he elaborated.

Caro's breath caught in her throat, that flush covering the whole of her body now as she realised that the earl was suggesting she should have taken a lover when she arrived in London rather than 'singing for her supper' at Nick's.

A lover!

When Caro's father had been so averse to any of his three daughters appearing in London society that he had not even allowed any of them to have so much as a Season, but instead had kept them all secluded at his estate in Hampshire. Had ensured his daughters were so overprotected that Caro had never even been alone with a young gentleman until now.

Although that description was hardly appropriate in regard to the arrogant Dominic Vaughn; that scar upon his otherwise handsome face, and the mockery that glittered now in those narrowed silver-coloured eyes, proclaimed him to be a gentleman in possession of a cynicism and experience that far exceeded his calendar years...

'I believe it would not be merely my *company* that would be of interest in such an arrangement, my lord.' She arched pert blonde brows.

Dominic was beginning to wish that he had never broached this particular subject. Indeed, he had no idea why he was taking such an interest in the fate of this particular young woman. Perhaps his sense of chivalry was not as dead as he had believed it to be? 'Surely the attentions of one man would be preferable to being undressed, mentally at least, by dozens of men, night after night?' he bit out harshly.

Her gasp was audible. 'You are attempting to shock me, sir!'

Yes, he was. Deliberately. 'I am attempting to stress,

madam, how foolishly you are behaving by repeatedly placing yourself in such a vulnerable position.'

Her eyes widened indignantly. 'I assure you, sir, I am perfectly capable of taking care of myself. I am in absolutely no danger—' Dominic put an end to this ridiculous claim by the simple act of pulling her effortlessly into his arms and taking masterful possession of the surprised parting of her lips.

He did it as a way of demonstrating the vulnerability of which he spoke. As a way of showing Caro how easily a man—any man—could take advantage of her delicacy. How the slenderness of her tiny body was no match for a man bent on stealing a kiss. Or worse!

He curved that willowy body against his much harder one as he took possession of the softness of those parted lips. With deliberate sensuality, his tongue swept moistly across her bottom lip before exploring farther, his hands moving in a light caress down the slenderness of her back before cupping her bottom and pulling her even more firmly against him as that marauding tongue took possession of the hot cavern of her mouth. Thrusting. Jousting. Demanding her response.

Nothing in Caro's previous life, not the twenty years spent in seclusion in Hampshire, or these past two weeks in London, had prepared her for the rush of sensations that now assaulted her and caused her to cling to Dominic Vaughn's wide and powerful shoulders rather than faint at his feet.

She was suffused with a heart-pounding heat, accompanied by a wild, tingling that began in her breasts, causing them to swell beneath her gown and the tips to harden so that they felt uncomfortable and sensitised as they chafed against her shift, that heat centring, pooling between her thighs, in a way she had never imagined before let alone experienced. She—

'What ho, lads!'

'Don't keep her all to yourself, old chap!'

'Give us all a go!'

Caro found those hard lips removed from her own with a suddenness that made her gasp, the earl's hands hard about her waist as those silver-coloured eyes glittered down at her briefly before he put her firmly away from him. He turned and bent the fierceness of that gaze upon the three young gentlemen walking slightly unsteadily towards them.

Caro staggered slightly once released, knowing herself badly shaken by the searing intensity of Dominic Vaughn's kiss—a punishing, demanding assault upon her lips and senses that in no way resembled any of her previous youthful imaginings of what a kiss should be. There had been none of the gentleness she had expected. None of the shy thrill of emotions. Only that heart-pounding heat and the wild tingling in her breasts and thighs.

Emotions not reflected in the hard intensity of his lordship's expression as he signalled to his coachman and groom that he was as in control of this present situation as he had obviously been whilst kissing her!

The young gentlemen had come to an abrupt and wary halt as they suddenly found themselves the focus of Dominic's glittering silver gaze, the three of them backing up slightly at the chilling anger they obviously recognised in his expression, that savage slash of scar running the length of his left cheek adding to the impression of impending danger.

'We meant no offence, old chap,' the obvious ringleader of the trio offered in mumbled apology.

'A little too much to drink, I expect,' the second one excused nervously.

'We'll just be on our way.' The third member of the group grabbed a friend by each arm before turning and staggering back in the direction they had just come.

Leaving a still-trembling Caro to the far from tender mercies of Dominic Vaughn!

That trembling increased as he turned the focus of his glowering attention back on to her. 'I believe you were assuring me that you are perfectly capable of taking care of yourself and that you believe yourself to be in absolutely no danger from any man's unwanted attentions?'

Caro felt a shiver run the length of her spine as she looked up into that harshly forbidding face; no wonder those three young gentlemen had decided that retreat was the best and safest course of action. She felt like retreating herself as she recalled how demanding and yet arousing that firmly sculptured mouth had felt against her own...

Her shoulders straightened determinedly. 'You kissed me deliberately, my lord, purely in an effort to demonstrate your superior strength over me.'

His nostrils flared as that silver gaze raked over her. 'In an effort to demonstrate how *any* man's strength would be superior to your own—even those three drunken young pups who just ran away with their tails between their legs.'

Caro raised a haughty brow. 'You exaggerate, sir—'

'On the contrary, Miss Morton,' he snapped coldly, 'I believe myself to be better acquainted than you with the lusts of my own sex.' His mouth twisted in distaste. 'And if I had not been here to protect you just now then I guarantee you would now find yourself in an alley somewhere with your skirts up about your waist whilst one of those young bucks rutted between your thighs and the other two awaited their turn!'

Caro felt herself pale and the nausea churn in her stomach at the vividness of the picture he painted. A vividness surely designed to shock and frighten her— and succeeding? Those three young gentlemen had obviously over-imbibed this evening, and were feeling more than a little playful, but surely they would not have behaved as shockingly as the earl suggested?

She looked at him in challenge. 'Then it is a pity that there was no one here to protect me from your own unwanted attentions, was it not?'

Dominic drew in a swift breath at the accusation. In the circumstances, it was a perfectly justified accusation, he allowed fairly. He had meant only to teach a lesson, to demonstrate her vulnerability by taking advantage of her himself. Instead he had found he enjoyed the honeyed taste of her as he explored the heat of her mouth, as well as the feel of her slender curves pressed against his much harder ones. To the extent that he had taken the kiss far beyond what he had originally intended.

He straightened, the expression in his eyes now hidden behind hooded lids. 'I meant only to demonstrate how exposing yourself on a stage night after night has left you open to physical as well as verbal abuse.'

'You are being ridiculous,' she dismissed briskly. 'Neither am I a complete ninny. It was for the very reason of protecting my reputation that I donned the mask and wig at Nick's. Indeed, I doubt that anyone would ever recognise the woman I am now as the masked and ebony-haired woman who sings in a gambling club each evening.'

There was some truth in that; Dominic had barely recognised Caro himself when she had joined him earlier. Even so... 'The fact that you are masked, and your own blonde curls hidden beneath those false ebony tresses, would, I am afraid, only protect your identity as far as the bedroom.'

Her throat moved convulsively as she continued to look up at him proudly. 'My...identity?'

Dominic gave an exasperated sigh. 'Your voice and manner proclaim you as being a lady—'

'Or a disgraced lady's maid,' she put in quickly.

'Perhaps,' Dominic allowed tersely. 'I have no idea what your reasons are for taking the action you have—and I doubt you are about to enlighten me, are you?'

Her mouth firmed. 'No.'

'As I thought.' He gave an abrupt nod. 'Of course, the simplest answer to this predicament would be for me to simply terminate your employment. At least then I would not feel honour bound to take responsibility for your welfare.'

She gave an inelegant snort. 'That would only solve the problem for *you*, my lord; *I* would still need to find the means with which to earn my own living.'

She was right, Dominic allowed sourly. But there was another alternative... He could offer to become her protector himself—his enjoyment of their kiss earlier proved that his senses, at least, were not averse to the idea. And no doubt, with a little coaching as to his physical preferences, Caro would be more than capable of satisfying his needs.

But in the ten years since Dominic had first appeared in town he had never once taken a permanent mistress, as many of his male acquaintances chose to do, preferring instead to take his pleasures whenever and with what women he pleased. He had no wish to change that arrangement by making the spirited and outspoken Caro Morton his mistress.

'Of course, if you were to decide to terminate my employment then you would leave me with no choice but to seek the same position elsewhere.' She shrugged those slender shoulders. 'Something that should not prove too difficult now that the masked lady has, as you say, gained something of a...male following,' she added.

It was a solution, of course. Except at Nick's, whether the chit was aware of it or not, Caro at least had the protection of the attentive Drew and Ben. And, apparently, now Dominic himself. 'If it is only question of money—'

'And if it were?' Caro had immediately bristled haughtily.

His mouth thinned. 'In those circumstances I might perhaps see my way clear to advancing you sufficient funds to take you back to wherever it is you originate from.'

'No!' Those sea-green eyes sparkled up at him rebelliously. 'I have no intention of leaving London yet.'

Dominic was unsure as to whether Caro's vehemence was due to his offer to advance her money, or his suggestion that she use that money to take herself home, so he decided to probe further. 'Is the situation at home so intolerable, then?'

She attempted to repress a shudder and failed. 'At present, yes.'

Dominic studied her through narrowed lids, noting the shadows that had appeared in those sea-green eyes, and the pallor of her cheeks. 'That remark would seem to imply that the situation may change some time in the future?'

'It is to be hoped so, yes,' she confirmed with feeling.

'But until it does, it is your intention to remain in London, whether or not I continue to employ you at Nick's?'

Her mouth set firmly. 'It is.'

'You are very stubborn, madam.'

'I am decisive, sir, which is completely different.'

Dominic sighed heavily, not wishing to send Caro back to a situation she obviously found so unpleasant, but also well able to imagine the scrapes this reckless young woman would get herself into, if she were once again let loose to roam the streets of London seeking employment. 'Then I believe, for the moment, we must leave things as they are.' He looked away. 'Shall we continue to walk to your lodgings?'

Caro shot him a triumphant glance. 'We have been standing outside them for some minutes, my lord!'

Dominic gave her an irritated scowl before glancing

at the house behind them. It was a three-storied building so typical of an area that had once been fashionable, but which was no longer so, and as such had fallen into genteel decay. Although the owner of this particular lodging had at least attempted to keep up a veneer of respectability, the outside being neat and cared for, and the curtains at the windows also appearing clean.

He turned back to Caro. 'In that case it remains only for me to bid you goodnight.'

She gave an abrupt curtsy. 'My lord.'

'Miss Morton.' He nodded curtly.

Caro gazed up at Dominic quizzically as he made no move to depart for his waiting carriage. 'There is no need for you to wait to leave until you are assured I have entered the house, my lord.'

He raised an eyebrow. 'In the same way you were in "absolutely no danger" earlier on?'

Her cheeks coloured prettily. 'I find your manner extremely vexing, my lord!'

'No more so than I do your own, I assure you, Miss Morton.'

Caro had never before met anyone remotely like Dominic Vaughn. Had never dreamed that men like him existed, so tall and fashionably handsome, so aristocratic. So arrogantly sure of themselves!

Admittedly her contact with male acquaintances had been severely limited before she came to London, usually only consisting of the few sons of the local gentry, and occasionally her father's lawyer when he came from London to discuss business matters.

Even so, Caro knew from Drew Butler's respectful attitude towards the earl earlier this evening, and the hasty departure of those three young gentlemen just minutes ago, that Dominic Vaughn was a man whose very presence demanded respect and obedience.

Except, after years of having no choice but to do as she was told, Caro no longer wished to obey any man. Not least of all the guardian she had so recently acquired...

She flashed the earl a bright meaningless smile before turning to walk to the front door of her lodgings, not even glancing back to see if he still watched as she quietly let herself inside with the key the landlady had provided for Caro's personal use when she had taken the rooms two weeks ago.

She waited several heartbeats before daring to look out through the lace-covered window beside the front door. Just in time to see the earl climbing inside his carriage before the groom closed the door behind him and hopped neatly on to the back of the vehicle as it was driven away.

But before it did so Caro saw the pale oval of Dominic Vaughn's grimly set face at the carriage window as he glanced towards where she stood hidden. She moved away quickly to lean back against the wall, her hands clutched against her rapidly beating heart.

No, being kissed by the Earl of Blackstone had been nothing at all as she imagined a kiss would be.

It had been far, far more exciting...

'So, where did you get to last night, Dom?' Nathaniel Thorne, Earl of Osbourne, prompted lazily the following evening, the two men lounging in opposite wing-chairs beside the fireplace in one of the larger rooms at White's.

'I was…unavoidably detained.' Dominic evaded answering his friend's query directly. The two men had arranged to meet late the previous evening, an appointment Dominic obviously had not kept as he had instead been occupied with seeing Caro Morton safely delivered back to her lodgings. For all the thanks he had received for his trouble!

Nathaniel raised a blond brow. 'I trust she was as insatiable as she was beautiful?'

'Beautiful—yes. Insatiable? I have no idea.' In truth, hours later, Dominic still had no idea what to make of Caro Morton, of who and what she was. He had taken the trouble, however, to send word to Drew Butler to continue feeding her, as well as arranging for Ben Jackson to escort her home at the end of each night's work; Caro might have no care for her own welfare, but whilst she continued working for Dominic, he had every intention of ensuring that no harm befell her.

'Yet,' Nathaniel drawled knowingly.

Both of Dominic's parents had died years ago, and he had no siblings, either, making Nathaniel Thorne and Gabriel Faulkner the closest thing he had to a family; the years they had all spent at school together, and then in the army, never knowing whether they would survive the next battle, had made them as close as brothers. Even so, Dominic could have wished at that moment that Nathaniel did not know him quite as well as he did.

Thankfully he had the perfect diversion from his lack of appearance the night before. 'I received a note from Gabriel today. He expects to arrive in England by the end of the week.' He lifted his glass of brandy and took an appreciative sip.

'I received one, too,' Nathaniel revealed. 'Can you imagine the looks on the faces of the *ton* when Gabe makes his entrance back into society?'

'He reaffirmed it was his intention to first go to Shoreley Park and confront the Copeland sisters,' Dominic reminded him.

Osbourne snorted. 'We both know that will only take two minutes of his time. By the time Gabriel returns to town, past scandal or not, I have no doubt that all three of the silly chits will be clamouring to marry him!' Nathaniel made a silent toast of appreciation to their absent friend.

It was a fact that Gabriel's years of banishment to the Continent and the army had in no way affected his conquests in the bedchamber; one look at that raven-black hair, those dark indigo eyes and his firmly muscled physique, and women of all ages simply dropped at Gabriel's feet. Or, more accurately, into his bed! No doubt the Copeland sisters would find themselves equally as smitten.

'What shall we do with the rest of the night?' After the dissatisfaction he had felt at the end of the previous evening, Dominic knew himself to be in the mood to drink too much before falling into bed with a woman who was as inventive as she was willing.

Nathaniel eyed him speculatively. 'I have heard that there is a mysterious beauty currently performing at Nick's…'

As close as the three men were, Dominic knew that some things were best kept to oneself—and his meeting with Caro Morton the previous night, his uncharacteristic, unfathomable sense of protectiveness where she was concerned, was certainly one of them! Although Dominic could not say that he was at all pleased that she was already so great a source of gossip at the gentlemen's clubs after only a week of appearing at his.

He grimaced. 'I believe the only reason she is considered such a mystery is because she wears a jewelled mask whilst performing.'

'Oh.' The other man's mouth turned down. 'No doubt to hide the fact that she's scarred from the pox.'

'Possibly,' Dominic dismissed in a bored voice, having no intention of saying anything that would increase his friend's curiosity where Caro was concerned.

Nate sighed. 'In which case, I believe I will leave the choice of tonight's entertainment to you.'

That choice involved visiting several gambling clubs before ending the evening at the brightly lit but nevertheless discreet house where several beautiful and accomplished ladies of the *demi-monde* made it only too obvious they would be pleased to offer amusement and companionship to two such handsome young gentlemen.

So it was all the more surprising when those same two gentlemen took their leave only an hour or so later, neither having taken advantage of that willingness. 'Perhaps we should have gone to view the mysterious beauty at Nick's, after all.' Osbourne repressed a bored yawn. 'Scarred from the pox or not, I doubt I could find her any less appealing than the ladies we have just wasted our time with!'

Dominic frowned, knowing that to demur a second time would definitely incur Nate's curiosity. 'Perhaps we are becoming too jaded in our tastes, Nate?' he murmured drily as he tapped on the roof of the carriage and gave his driver fresh instructions.

The other man raised a questioning brow. 'Do you ever miss the excitement of our five years in the army?'

Did Dominic miss the horror and the bloodshed of war? The never knowing whether he would survive the next battle or if it was his turn to meet death at the end of a French sword? The comradeship with his fellow officers that arose from experiencing that very danger? He missed it like the very devil!

'Not to the point of wanting to renew my commission, no. You?'

Osbourne shrugged. 'It is a fact that civilian life can be tedious as well as damned repetitious.'

Dominic felt relieved to know that he was not the only one to miss those years of feeling as if one walked constantly on the knife edge of danger. 'I am told that participating in a London Season often resembles a battlefield,' he mused.

'Do not even mention the Season to me,' the other man groaned. 'My Aunt Gertrude has taken it into her head that it is high time I took myself a wife,' he explained at Dominic's questioning look. 'As such she is insisting that I escort her to several balls and soirées during the next few weeks. No doubt with the expectation of finding a young woman she believes will make me a suitable Countess.'

'Ah.' Dominic began to understand his friend's restlessness this evening; Mrs Gertrude Wilson was Osbourne's closest relative, and one, moreover, of whom he was extremely fond. She reciprocated by taking a great interest in her nephew's life. To the point, it seemed, that she was now attempting to find him a wife. Reason enough for Dominic to be grateful for his own lack of female relations! 'I take it that you are not in agreement with her wishes?'

'In agreement with the idea of shackling myself for life to some mealy-mouthed chit who has no doubt been taught to lie back and think of king and country when we are in bed together? Certainly not!' Osbourne barely suppressed his shiver of revulsion. 'I cannot think what Gabriel is about even contemplating such a fate.'

It was a fact that all three gentlemen would one day have to take a wife and produce the necessary heir to their respective earldoms. Fortunately, it seemed that Osbourne, at least, was as averse to accepting that fate as Dominic was. Although there was no doubting that Mrs Gertrude Wilson was a force to be reckoned with!

Dominic's humour at his friend's situation faded, his mouth tightening in disapproval, as the two gentlemen stepped down from his carriage minutes later and he saw that Ben Jackson was once again absent from his position at the entrance to Nick's; obviously they had arrived in time for Nathaniel to witness Caro Morton's second performance of the evening.

However, the sound of shouting, breaking glass and the crashing of furniture coming from the direction of the main gaming room as they stepped into the spacious hallway of the club in no way resembled the awed silence Dominic had experienced on his arrival the previous evening.

Especially when it was accompanied by the sound of a woman's screams!

Chapter Three

Caro had never been as frightened in her life as she was at that moment. Even with Ben and two other men standing protectively in front of her, and keeping the worst of the fighting at bay, it was still possible for her to see men's fists flying, the blood freely flowing from noses and cut faces as chairs, tables and bottles were also brought into play.

In truth, she had no idea how the fighting had even begun. One moment she had been singing as usual, and the next a gentleman had tried to step on to the stage and grab hold of her. At first Caro had believed the second gentleman to step forwards was attempting to come to her aid, until he pushed the first man aside and also lunged towards where she had half-risen from the *chaise* in alarm.

After that all bedlam had broken loose, it seemed, with a dozen or more men fighting off the first two with fists and any item of furniture that came readily to hand.

And through it all, every terrifying moment of it, Caro had been humiliatingly aware of Lord Dominic Vaughn's dire warnings of the night before…

'Care to join in?' Osbourne invited with glee as the two men stood in the doorway of the gaming room still hatted and cloaked.

Dominic's narrowed gaze had taken stock of the situation at a glance. Thirty or so gentlemen fighting in earnest. Several of the brocade-covered chairs broken. Tables overturned, and shattered glasses and bottles crunching underfoot. Drew Butler was caught in the middle of it all as he tried to call a halt to the fighting. And on the raised stage, Ben Jackson stood immovable in front of where a head of ebony curls was just visible above and behind the *chaise*.

'Head towards the stage,' Dominic directed Osbourne grimly as he threw his hat aside. 'If we can get the girl out of here, I believe the fighting will come to an end.'

'I sincerely hope it does not!' Nathaniel grinned roguishly as he stepped purposefully into the mêlée.

Most of the gentlemen fighting seemed to be enjoying themselves as much as Osbourne, despite having bloody noses, the occasional lost tooth and several eyes that would no doubt be black come morning. It was the three or four gentlemen closest to Ben Jackson, and their dogged determination to lay hands on Caro as she crouched down behind the *chaise*, that concerned Dominic the most. Although to give Ben his due, he had so far managed to keep them all at arm's length, and even managed to shoot Dominic and Osbourne an appreciative grin as they stepped up beside him.

At which point Caro Morton emerged from behind the *chaise* and launched herself into his arms. 'Thank goodness you are come, Dominic!'

Osborne grinned knowingly at the spectacle. 'You take the girl, Dom; this is the most fun I've had in years!' He swung a fist and knocked one of the men from the stage with a telling crunch of flesh against teeth.

At that moment Dominic was so angry that he wanted nothing more than to break a few bones for himself. A satisfaction he knew he would have to forgo as Caro's arms tightened about his neck, a pair of widely terrified sea-green eyes visible through the slits in the jewelled mask as she looked up at him.

Dominic's gaze darkened as he saw that her gold gown was ripped in several places. 'Did I not warn you?' Dominic's voice was chilling as he pulled her arms from about his neck and swung off his cloak to cover her in it before bending down to place his arm at the back of her knees and toss her up on to his shoulder as he straightened.

'I— What— Put me down this instant!' Tiny fists pummelled against his back.

'I believe now would be as good a time as any for you to learn when it is wiser to remain silent,' Dominic rasped grimly as several male heads turned his way to watch jealously as he carried her from the stage and out to the private area at the back of the club.

The last thing that Caro had needed in the midst of that nightmare was for Lord Dominic Vaughn to tell her 'I told you so'. She had already been terrified enough for one evening without the added humiliation of being thrown over this man's shoulder as if she were no more than a sack of potatoes or a bail of straw on her father's estate!

Caro struggled to be released as soon as they reached the relative safety of the deserted hallway. 'You will put me down this instant!' she instructed furiously as her struggles resulted only in her becoming even more hot and bad-tempered.

'Gladly.' Dominic slid her unceremoniously down the hard length of his body before lowering her bare feet on to the cold stone floor.

'I do not believe I have ever met a man more ill mannered than you!' Caro looked up at him accusingly even as her flustered fingers tried to secure the engulfing cloak about her shoulders and hold the soft silk folds about her trembling body.

'After I have tried to save you from harm?' His voice was silky soft as those silver eyes glittered down at her in warning.

'After you have manhandled me, sir!' Caro was unrepentant as she tried to bring some semblance of order to the tangled ebony curls, all the time marvelling at how the jewelled mask and ebony wig had managed to stay in place at all. 'Your own anger a few minutes ago seemed to imply that you believe *I* am to blame for what just took place—'

'You *are* to blame.'

'Do not be ridiculous!' Caro gave him a scornful glance. 'Every woman knows that men—even so-called gentlemen—will find any excuse to fight.'

She might very well be in the right of it there, Dominic acknowledged as he remembered Osbourne's glee before he launched himself into the midst of the fighting. But that did not change the fact that this particular fight had broken out because Caro had refused to see the danger of flaunting herself night after night before a roomful of intoxicated men.

As it was, Dominic had no idea whether to beat her or kiss her senseless for her naïvety. 'I have a good mind to take out the cost of this evening's damages on your backside!' he grated instead.

Her eyes widened and her cheeks flushed a fiery red even as her chin rose in challenge. 'You would not dare!'

Dominic gave a disgusted snort. 'Do not tempt me, Caro.'

Caro gave up all attempt to bring order to those loosely flowing locks and instead removed the jewelled mask in order to glare at him. 'I believe you are just looking for an excuse to beat me.'

Dominic stilled, his gaze narrowing searchingly on her angrily defiant face. Just the thought of some nameless, faceless man ever laying hands on this delicately lovely woman in anger was enough to rouse Dominic's own fury. Yet at this particular moment in time, he totally understood the impulse; he badly wanted to tan Caro's backside so hard that she would not be able to sit down for a week! 'I assure you, where you are concerned, no excuse is necessary,' he growled.

'Oh!' she gasped her indignation. 'You, sir, are the most overbearing, arrogant, insulting man it has ever been my misfortune to meet!'

'And you, madam, are the most stubborn, wilfully stupid—'

'*Stupid?*' she echoed furiously.

'*Wilfully* stupid,' Dominic repeated unrepentantly as he glared back at her.

Caro had never been so incensed. Never felt so much like punching a man on his arrogant, aristocratic nose!

As if aware of the violence of her thoughts those sculptured lips turned up into a mocking smile. 'It would be most unwise, Caro.' His warning was silkily soft and all the more dangerous because of it.

Sea-green eyes clashed with silver for long, challenging moments. A challenge she was almost—almost!—feeling brave enough to accept when an amused voice broke into the tension. 'I came to tell you that Butler and his heavies have thrown out the last of the patrons and are now attempting to clean up the mess, but I can come back later if now is not a convenient time…?'

Dominic was standing directly in Caro's line of vision and she had to lean to one side to see around him to where a tall, elegantly dressed man leant casually against the wall of the hallway. His arms were folded across the width of his chest as he watched them with interest, only the ruffled disarray of his blond and fashionably long hair about the handsomeness of his face to show that he had only moments ago been caught up in the thick of the fighting.

'I believe our earlier assessment of the…situation to have been at fault, Blackstone.' The other man gave Dominic an appreciative smile before turning his dark gaze back to pointedly roam over the unblemished, obviously pox-free skin of Caro's beautiful face.

It was a remark she did not even begin to understand, let alone why he was looking at her so intently! 'To answer your earlier question, sir—I believe Lord Vaughn and I have finished our conversation.'

'Not by a long way.' One of Dominic's hands reached out, the fingers curling about Caro's wrist like a band of steel, as she would have brushed past him. 'I trust not too many heads were broken, Osbourne?'

The blond-haired man shrugged. 'None that did not deserve it.' He straightened away from the wall. 'Care to introduce me, Blackstone?' A merry brown gaze briefly met his friend's before he looked at Caro with open admiration.

'Caro Morton, Lord Nathaniel Thorne, Earl of Osbourne,' Dominic said coldly.

'Your servant, ma'am.' Lord Thorne gave an elegant bow.

'My lord.' Really, did every man she met in London have to be a lord and an earl? she wondered crossly as she pondered the ridiculousness of formally curtsying to a gentleman under such circumstances.

'If you were thinking of leaving too now all the excitement is over, Osbourne, then by all means do so,' Dominic said. 'I fear I will not be free to leave for some time yet.'

His gaze hardened as he glanced down pointedly at Caro Morton, his mouth thinning as those sea-green eyes once more stared back at him in silent rebellion.

She broke that gaze to turn and smile graciously at the other man. 'Perhaps, if you are leaving, I might prevail on you to take me with you, Lord Thorne?'

To all intents and purposes, Dominic recognised

impatiently, as if she were a lady making conversation in her drawing room! As if a fight had not just broken out over who was to share her bed tonight. As if Dominic's own property had not been destroyed in that mêlée.

As if she were not standing before two elegant gentlemen of the *ton* dressed only in a ripped gown, and with her ebony wig slightly askew!

Dominic gave a frustrated sigh. 'I think not.'

Those sea-green eyes flashed up at him with annoyance before Caro ignored him to turn once again to Nathaniel. 'I would very much appreciate it if you would agree to escort me home, Lord Thorne.' A siren could not have sounded or looked any more sweetly persuasive!

Dominic easily read the uncertainty in his friend's expression; a gentleman through and through, Osbourne never had been able to resist the appeal of a seeming damsel in distress. Seeming, in Dominic's estimation, being a correct assessment in regard to Caro Morton. The woman was an absolute menace and had become a veritable thorn in Dominic's side since the moment he'd set eyes upon her.

'I am afraid that is not possible,' Dominic answered smoothly on the other man's behalf.

Those delicate cheeks flushed red. 'I believe my request was made to Lord Thorne and not to *you*!'

Dominic allowed some of the tension to ease from his shoulders, aware that he had been in one state of tension or another since first meeting her. 'Lord Thorne is gentleman enough, however, to accept a prior claim, are you not, Osbourne?'

Osbourne's eyes widened. As well they might, damn

it; Dominic had as good as denied all knowledge of this woman earlier tonight, a denial that had been made a complete nonsense of the moment Caro had launched herself into his arms and, in her agitation, called him by his given name.

Hell and damnation!

'I believe you were quite correct in your assertion earlier, Blackstone,' Osbourne's drawled comment interrupted Dominic's displeasing thoughts. 'Personally I would say exquisite rather than beautiful!'

Dominic nodded irritably. 'Just so.'

'That being the case, Blackstone, I believe I will join Butler and Ben and enjoy a reviving brandy before I leave. My respects, Miss Morton.' Osbourne gave a lazy inclination of his head before leaving the two of them alone.

Caro blinked at the suddenness of Lord Thorne's departure. 'I do not understand.' Neither did she have any idea what tacit agreement had passed between the two men in the last few moments. But something most certainly had for the gentlemanly Lord Thorne to have just abandoned her like that.

Dominic released her wrist before stepping away from her. 'You should go to your room now and change. I will be waiting in Drew Butler's office when you are ready to leave.'

Caro frowned. 'But—'

'Could you, for once, just do as I ask without argument, Caro?' The scar on Dominic's cheek showed in stark relief against his clenched jaw.

She looked up into that ruthlessly hard face, repressing a shiver of apprehension as she saw the dangerous glitter in those pale silver eyes. Of course—this man had already told her that he held her responsible for the occurrence of the fight and the damages to his property, and he had also threatened to take out the cost of those damages on her backside!

Never, in all of her twenty years, had Caro been spoken to in the way the arrogant Dominic Vaughn spoke to her. So familiarly. So—so…intimately. A gentleman should not even refer to a lady's bottom, let alone threaten to inflict harm upon it!

Her chin rose haughtily. 'I am very tired, my lord, and would prefer to go straight home once I am dressed.'

'And I would prefer that you join me in Butler's office first so that we might continue our conversation.'

'I had thought it finished.'

'Caro, I have already been involved in a brawl not of my making, and my property has been extensively damaged. As such, I am really in no mood to tolerate any more of your stubbornness this evening.' His hands had clenched at his sides in an effort to control his exasperation.

'Really?' She arched innocent brows. 'My own patience with your impossible arrogance ended some minutes ago.'

Yes, Dominic acknowledged ruefully, this young woman was undoubtedly as feisty as she was beautiful. To his own annoyance, he had also spent far too much time today allowing his thoughts to dwell on how delicious Caro's mouth had tasted beneath his the night before.

'Would you be any more amenable to the suggestion if I were to say please?'

She eyed him warily, distrustfully. 'It would be a start, certainly.'

He regarded her for several seconds before nodding. 'Very well. I insist that you join me in Butler's office shortly so that we might continue this conversation. Please.'

A second request that was intended to be no more gracious than the first! 'Then I agree to join you in Mr Butler's office shortly, my lord. But only for a few minutes,' Caro added firmly as she saw the glitter of triumph that lit those pale silver eyes. 'It is late and I really am very tired.'

'Understandably.' He gave a mocking bow. 'I will only require a few more minutes of your time this evening.'

That last remark almost had the tone of a threat, Caro realised worriedly as she made her way slowly to her dressing-room to change. And for all that she had so defiantly told Dominic Vaughn the previous evening that she would simply seek employment elsewhere if he chose to dismiss her, after this evening's disaster she could not even bear the thought of remaining in London without the protection of Drew and Ben.

She had been completely truthful the evening before when she'd assured Dominic that she had every intention of returning home as soon as she felt it was safe for her to do so. Unfortunately, Caro did not believe that time had come quite yet...

Dominic made no attempt to hide his pained wince as he looked at the dull green gown Caro was wearing when she joined him in Drew's office some minutes later; it was neither that intriguing sea-green of her eyes, or of a style in the least complimentary to her graceful slenderness. Rather, that unbecoming colour dulled the brightness of her eyes to the same unattractive green, and gave the pale translucence of her skin an almost sallow look. The fact that the gown was also buttoned up to her throat, and her blonde curls pulled tightly back into a bun at her nape as she stood before the desk with her hands demurely folded together, gave her the all appearance and appeal of a nun.

Dominic stood up and stepped lithely around the desk before leaning back against it as he continued to regard her critically. 'You appear none the worse for your ordeal.'

Then her appearance was deceptive, Caro acknowledged with an inner tremor. Reaction to the horrors of this evening's fighting had begun in earnest once she had reached the safety and peace of her dressing-room, to the extent that she had not been able to stop herself trembling for some time. It had all happened so suddenly, so violently, and the earl's rescue effected so efficiently—if high-handedly—that at the time, Caro had not had opportunity to think beyond that.

She was still shaking slightly now, and it was the reason her hands were clasped so tightly together in front of her; she would not, for any reason, show the arrogant Dominic Vaughn any sign of weakness. 'I did not have opportunity to thank you earlier, my lord, for your timely intervention. I do so now.' She gave a stiff inclination of her head.

Dominic barely repressed his smile at this show of grudging gratitude. 'You are welcome, I am sure,' he replied. 'Obviously it is going to take several days, possibly a week, to effect the repairs to the main salon—'

'I have no money to spare to pay for those repairs, if that is to be your next suggestion,' she instantly protested.

Dominic looked at her from underneath lowered lids, seeing beyond that defiant and nunlike appearance to the young woman beneath. Those sea-green eyes were still slightly shadowed, her cheeks pale, her hands slightly trembling, all of those things evidence that Caro had been more disturbed by the violence she had witnessed earlier than she wished anyone—very likely most especially him—to be aware of.

He found that he admired that quality in her. Just as he admired her pride and the dignity she'd shown when faced with a situation so obviously beyond her previous experience.

Did that inexperience extend to the bedchamber? he could not help but wonder. After her initial surprise the previous evening, she had most definitely returned the passion of his kiss. But then afterwards she had appeared completely unaware of the danger those three young bucks had represented to her welfare.

Just as she had seemed innocent of the rising lusts of the men who returned night after night to watch her performance at Nick's. Perhaps an indication that she was inexperienced to the vagaries of men, at least?

Caro Morton was fast becoming a puzzle that Dominic found himself wishing to unravel. Almost as much, he realised with an inward wince, as he wished to peel her out of that unbecoming green gown before exploring every inch of her delectably naked body...

'It was not,' he answered. 'I was merely pointing out that Nick's will probably have to be closed for several days whilst repairs and other refurbishments are carried out. A closure that will obviously result in your being unable to perform here for the same amount of time.'

She looked at him blankly for several moments, and then her eyes widened as the full import of what he was saying became clear to her. She licked suddenly dry lips. 'But you believe it will only be for a few days?'

Dominic studied her closely. 'Possibly a week.'

'A week?' Her echo was distraught.

Alerting him to the fact that she was in all probability completely financially reliant upon the money she earned each night at the gambling club—her clothes certainly indicated as much! It also proved, along with her determination to remain in London 'for the present', that her situation at home must be dire indeed...

'There is no reason for you to look so concerned, Caro,' he assured her. 'Whether you wish it or not, for the moment, it would appear you are now under my protection.'

Her eyes went wide with indignation. 'I have absolutely *no* intention of becoming your mistress!'

Any more than it was Dominic's wish to take her—or any other woman—as his mistress...

His parents had both died when he was but twelve years old. Neither had there been any kindly aunt to take an interest in him as there had with Nathaniel. Instead Dominic's guardianship had been placed in the hands of his father's firm of lawyers until he came of age at twenty-one. During those intervening years, when he was not away at school, Dominic had lived alone at

Blackstone Park in Berkshire, cared for only by the impersonal kindness of servants.

It would have been all too easy once he reached his majority, and was at last allowed to manage his own affairs, to have been drawn into the false warmth of affection given by a paid mistress. Instead, he had been content with the friendship he'd received from and felt for both Gabriel and Nathaniel. He knew their affection for him, at least, to be without ulterior motive. The same could not be said of a mistress.

'I said protector, Caro, not lover. Although I am sure that most of the gentlemen here tonight now believe me to already have that dubious honour,' he pointed out.

She stiffened at the insult in his tone. 'How so?'

'Several of them witnessed you throwing yourself into my arms earlier—'

'I was in fear of my life!' Two indignant spots of colour had appeared in the pallor of her cheeks.

Dominic waved a dismissive hand. 'The why of it is not important. The facts are that a masked lady is employed at my gambling club, and tonight that lady threw herself into my arms with a familiarity that was only confirmed when she called out my name for all to hear.' He shrugged. 'Those things are enough for most men to have come to the conclusion that the lady has decided on her protector. That she is now, in all probability, the exclusive property of the Earl of Blackstone.'

If it were possible, Caro's cheeks became even paler!

Chapter Four

For possibly the first time in her life, Caro was rendered bereft of speech. Not only was it perfectly shocking that many of the male members of society believed her to be the exclusive property of Lord Dominic Vaughn, but her older sister, Diana, would be incensed if such a falsehood were ever related to her in connection with her runaway sister, Caroline!

Caro had left a note on her bed telling her sisters not to worry about her, of course, but other than that she had not confided her plan of going to London to either Diana or her younger sister, Elizabeth, before fleeing the family home in Hampshire two weeks ago, before their guardian could arrive to take control of all their lives. A man none of the Copeland sisters had met before, but who had nevertheless chosen to inform them, through his lawyer, that he believed himself to be in a position to insist that one of them become his wife!

What sort of man did that? Caro had questioned in outraged disbelief. How monstrous could Lord Gabriel

Faulkner, the new Earl of Westbourne, be that he sent his lawyer in his stead to offer marriage to whichever of the previous earl's daughters was willing to accept him? And if none chose willingly, to *insist* upon it!

Never having been allowed to mix with London society, none of the Copeland sisters had any previous knowledge of their father's heir and second cousin, Lord Gabriel Faulkner. But several of their close neighbours had, and they were only too happy to regale the sisters with the knowledge—if not the details—of his lordship's banishment to the Continent eight years previously following a tremendous scandal, with talk of his having settled in Venice some years later. Other than that, none of the sisters had ever heard or seen anything of the man before being informed that not only was he their father's heir, but also their guardian.

They had all known and accepted that a daughter could not inherit the title, of course, but it was only when their father's will was read out after his funeral that the three sisters learnt they were also completely without finances of their own, and as such their futures were completely dependent upon the whim and mercy of the new Earl of Westbourne.

But as the weeks, and then months, passed, with no sign of the new earl arriving to take possession of either the Shoreley Hall estate, or to establish any guardianship over the three sisters other than the allowance sent to them by the man's lawyer each month, they had begun to relax, to believe that their lives could continue without interference from their new guardian.

Until, that is, the earl's lawyer had arrived at Shoreley Hall three weeks ago to inform them that the new Earl of Westbourne was very generously prepared to offer marriage to one of the penniless sisters. An offer, the lawyer had informed them sternly, that as their guardian, the earl could insist—and indeed, would insist—that one of them accept.

Diana, the eldest at one and twenty, was half-promised to the son of the local squire and so was safest from the earl's attentions. Elizabeth, only nineteen and the youngest of the three, had nevertheless declared she would throw herself on the mercy of a convent before she would marry a man she did not love and who did not love her. Caro's plan to avoid marrying the earl had been even more daring.

Desperate to bring some adventure into her so far humdrum existence, Caro had decided she would go to London for a month, perhaps two, and seek obscurity as a lady's companion or governess. And when Lord Gabriel Faulkner arrived in England—as his lawyer had assured them he undoubtedly would once informed of their refusal of his offer—then Diana, incensed by the disappearance of one of her sisters, would reduce the man to a quivering pulp with the cutting edge of her legendary acerbic tongue, before sending him away with his cowed tail tucked between his legs.

A month spent in London, possibly two, should do it, Caro had decided as she excitedly packed her bag before creeping stealthily from the house to walk the half a mile or so to the crossroads where she could catch the evening coach to London.

None of Caro's plans had worked out at she had expected, of course. No respectable household would employ a young woman without references, nor the dress shops, either, and the small amount of money Caro had brought with her had been seriously depleted, as instead of being taken into the warmth and security of the respectable household of her imaginings, she was forced to pay a month in advance for her modest lodgings.

In fact, until Drew Butler had taken pity on her, allowing her to sing at Nick's, Caro had feared she would have to return home with her own tail between her legs, before the earl had even arrived in England, let alone been sent on his way by the indomitable Diana!

Dominic had been watching Caro's expressive face with interest as he wondered what her thoughts had been for the past few minutes. 'You know, you could simply put an end to all this nonsense by returning from whence you came,' he said persuasively.

A shutter came down over that previously candid sea-green gaze, once again alerting Dominic to Caro's definite aversion—maybe even fear?—of returning to her previous life. Once again he wondered what, or who, this beautiful young woman was running away from.

And what possible business was it of his? Dominic instantly rebuked himself. None whatsoever. And yet he could not quite bring himself to insist that Caro must go home and face whatever punishment she had coming to her for having run away in the first place.

What if it were that bullying father she was running away from? Or the brutish husband? Either of whom would completely crush the spirit in Caro that Dominic found so intriguing…

She shook her head. 'I am afraid that returning to my home is not an option at this point in time, my lord.'

He raised dark brows. 'So you have already informed me. And between times, is it your intention to continue turning my hair prematurely grey as I worry in what scrape you will next embroil yourself?'

'I do not see a single grey hair amongst the black as yet, my lord.' Amusement glittered in those sea-green eyes as she glanced at those dark locks.

'I fear it is only a matter of time.' Dominic pulled a rueful face, only to then find himself totally enchanted as she laughed huskily at this nonsense. He realised, somewhat to his dismay, that he was as seriously in danger of falling under this woman's spell as Butler and Ben—and possibly Osborne—so obviously were.

It was a spell Dominic had no intention of succumbing to. Bedding a woman was one thing; allowing his emotions to become engaged by one was something else entirely. It was about time he changed his tactics; if he couldn't persuade Caro to leave London by simply asking her, he would have to try a more direct approach…

Caro took an involuntary step back, her eyes widening warily, as Dominic rose slowly to his feet, his movements almost predatory as he moved around the desk to cross over to the door and slowly turn the key in the lock.

'So that we are not disturbed,' he murmured as he moved so that he now stood only inches away from her.

She moistened suddenly dry lips as she tilted her head back so that she might look up, fearlessly, she hoped, into that arrogantly handsome face. 'It is time I was leaving—'

'Not quite yet, Caro,' the earl murmured huskily as one of his hands moved up to cup the side of her face and the soft pad of his thumb moved across the pouting swell of her bottom lip.

'I— What are you doing, my lord?'

'You called me Dominic earlier,' he reminded her huskily.

Caro's throat moved convulsively as she swallowed. 'What are you doing, Dominic?' she repeated breathlessly.

He shrugged those broad shoulders. 'Endeavouring, I hope, to show you there could be certain…benefits to becoming my mistress.'

Caro's knees felt weak just at the thought of what method this man intended using to demonstrate those 'benefits'. She so easily recalled the feel of that hard and uncompromising mouth against her own the night before, the feel of his hands as they ran the length of her spine to cup her bottom and press the hardness of his body intimately into hers. 'This is most unwise, my lord.'

He made no answer as he moved to rest back against the edge of the desk, taking her with him, those strange, silver-coloured eyes fixed caressingly upon Caro's slightly parted lips, the warmth of his breath stirring the tendrils of hair at her temples.

Dominic was standing much too close to her. So close that she could feel the heat of his body. So close that she was aware of the way that he smelt; the delicate spice of his cologne, and a purely male smell, one that appeared to be a combination of a clean male body and musky heat, uniquely his own.

Caro made every effort to gather her scattered senses. 'Dominic, I have no intention of allowing you to—oh!' she gasped as he encircled her waist and pulled her in between his parted legs, her thighs now pressed against him, as her breasts were crushed against the firm muscles of his chest. She placed her hands upon his shoulders with the intention of pushing him away.

'I think not,' Dominic murmured as he realised her intention, his arms moving about her waist to hold her more tightly against him, quelling her struggles as he looked to where her hair was secured in that unbecoming nunlike bun. 'Remove the pins from your hair for me, Caro.'

She stilled abruptly. 'No!'

'Would you rather that I did it?' He quirked dark brows.

'I would rather my hair remain exactly—oh!' She gave another of those breathless gasps as Dominic reached up and removed the pins himself. It was a breathless gasp that he found he was becoming extremely fond of hearing.

'Better.' He nodded his approval as he reached up to uncoil her hair and allow it to cascade in a wealth of golden curls over her shoulders and down the length of her spine. 'Now for the buttons on this awful gown—'

'I cannot possibly allow you to unbutton the front of my gown!' Caro's fingers clamped down over his, even as she glared up at him.

Dominic found himself smiling in the face of this

display of female outrage. 'It has all the allure of a nun's habit,' he said drily.

'That is exactly what it is supposed to—' Caro broke off the protest as she saw the way those silver eyes had narrowed to shrewdness.

'Do…?' Dominic finished softly for her. 'As no doubt the wearing of that unbecoming bonnet was designed to hide every delicious golden curl upon your head?'

'Yes,' she admitted.

He shook his head as he resumed unfastening the buttons on the front of her gown. 'It is a sacrilege, Caro, and one I am not inclined to indulge.' He folded back the two sides of her gown to reveal the thrust of her breasts covered only by the thinness of her shift above her corset.

Caro had no more will to protest as she saw the way those silver eyes glittered with admiration as Dominic gazed his fill of her. Indeed, she found she could barely breathe as she watched him slowly raise one of his hands to pull aside that gauzy piece of material and bare her breast completely. Her cheeks suffused with colour as, even as she watched, the tiny rose-coloured nub on the crest of her breast began to rise and stiffen.

'You are so very beautiful here,' he said huskily, the warmth of his breath now a tortuous caress against that burgeoning flesh. He looked up at her enquiringly. 'I wish to taste you, Caro.'

She found herself mesmerised by the slow flick of Dominic's tongue across his lips. Mesmerised and aching, the tip of her breast deepened in colour as it became firmer still. In anticipation. In longing, she knew, to feel that hot tongue curling moistly over it.

Where had these thoughts come from? Caro wondered wildly. How was it that she even knew the touch of Dominic's lips and mouth against her breast would give her more pleasure than she had ever dreamt possible? Woman's intuition? A legacy of Eve? However Caro knew these things, she surely could not allow Dominic to—

All thought ceased, any hope of protest dying along with it, as he gave up waiting for her answer and instead lowered his head to gently draw the now pulsing tip of Caro's breast into the heat of his mouth. His hand curved beneath it at the same time as he laved that aching bud with the moist heat of his tongue, and sending rivulets of pleasure into her other breast and down the soft curve of her abdomen to pool between her thighs.

Caro was filled with the strangest sensations, her breasts feeling full and heavy under the intimacy of Dominic's ministrations, the muscles in her abdomen clenching, that heat between her thighs making her swell and moisten there. She discovered she wanted to both squeeze her thighs together and part them at the same time. To have Dominic touch her there and ease that ache, too.

Her back arched instinctively as his hand moved to capture her other breast, the soft pad of his thumb now flicking against that hardened tip in the same rhythm with which he drew on its twin.

Dominic's lovemaking had been intended as a way of showing Caro that she did not belong here in London, that she was no match for him or other experienced men of the *ton*. Instead he was the one forced to recognise that he had never tasted anything quite so delicious as her breast, the nipple as sweet as honey as he kissed her there greedily, the hardness of his erection pulsing in his pantaloons testifying to the strength of his own arousal.

He drew back slightly to look at that pouting, full nipple, stroking his tongue across it before moving slightly to capture its twin, drawing on it hungrily before looking up at her flushed face and feverishly bright eyes. 'Tell me how you wish me to touch you, Caro,' he murmured against her swollen flesh.

Her fingers dug into his shoulders. 'Dominic!' she groaned a throaty protest.

He took pity on her shyness. 'Do you like this?' He swept his thumb lightly over that pouting nipple.

'Yes!' she gasped, shuddering with pleasure.

'This?' He brought his mouth down to her breast once more, even as he allowed his hand to fall to her ankle and push her gown aside and began a slow caress to her knee.

'Oh, yes!'

'And this?' Dominic ran his tongue repeatedly over that swollen nipple even as his hand caressed higher still to weave a pattern of seduction along her inner thigh, the heat of her through her drawers, her dampness, telling him of her arousal.

Nothing in Caro's life had prepared her to be touched with such intimacy. How could it, when she had never realised that such intimacies existed? Such achingly pleasurable intimacies that she wished would never end.

'I would like you to touch me in the same way, Caro,' Dominic encouraged gruffly.

She swallowed hard. 'I—' She broke off her instinctive protest as someone rattled the door handle in an effort to open the locked door.

'My lord?' Drew Butler sounded both disapproving and concerned at this inability to enter his own office.

Dominic turned his head sharply towards the door. 'What is it?'

'I need to speak with you immediately, my lord.' The other man sounded just as irritated as Dominic.

He scowled his displeasure as Caro took advantage of his distraction to extricate herself from his arms before turning away to begin fastening the buttons of her gown with fingers that were shaking so badly it took her twice as long as it should have done. What had she been thinking? Worse, how much further would she have allowed these intimacies to go if not for Drew's timely intervention?

'Caro—'

'Mr Butler requires your attention, my lord, not I!' Caro protested, her cheeks aflame.

Dominic's gaze narrowed in concern on her flushed and disconcerted face, knowing, and regretting, being the obvious cause of her discomfort. He had not meant things to go so far as they had. As for demonstrating to Caro how ill equipped she was to withstand the advances of the gentlemen of the *ton*, Dominic knew full well that *he* had been the one seriously in danger of overstepping that line! 'Caro—'

'Mr Butler requires you, my lord,' she reminded him.

Dominic stood up impatiently to stride over to the door and unlock it, his expression darkening as the other man's gaze instantly slid past him to where Caro stood with her back towards the door. Dominic deliberately stepped into the other man's line of vision. 'Yes?'

Speculative blue eyes gazed back at him. 'There is… something in the main salon I believe you should see.'

Dominic frowned. 'Can it not wait?'

'No, my lord, it cannot,' Drew stated flatly.

'Very well.' He nodded before turning to speak to Caro. 'It appears that I have to leave you for a few minutes. If you will be so kind as to wait here for me—'

'No.'

Dominic's eyes widened. 'No?'

'No.' Caro rallied, still embarrassed by the intimacies she had allowed this man, but determined not to allow that embarrassment to render her helpless. She carefully lifted her cloak and bonnet from the chair she had placed them on earlier. 'Mr Butler, is Ben available to escort me home now?'

'Yes, he is.'

'I would prefer that you wait for me here, Caro,' Dominic insisted firmly.

She met his gaze unflinchingly. 'And I would prefer that Ben be the one to accompany me to my lodgings.'

A nerve pulsed beside that savage slash of a scar on Dominic's left cheek. 'Why?'

Caro looked away as she found she could not withstand the probing of that narrowed silver gaze. 'I would simply prefer his company at this time, my lord.'

'Drew, could you wait outside for a moment, please?' Dominic did not even wait for the man's compliance before stepping back into the room and firmly closing the door behind him.

'I have nothing more to say to you, my lord—'

'Dominic.'

Caro gasped. 'I beg your pardon?'

The earl gave a graceful shrug. 'You did not seem to have any difficulty calling me Dominic a few minutes ago,' he reminded her wickedly.

Caro's cheeks burned with mortification as she recalled the most recent circumstances under which she had called this man by his first name. 'I do not even wish to think about just now—'

'Do not be so melodramatic,' Dominic interjected. 'Or perhaps, on consideration, it is the hideousness of my scars you would rather not dwell upon?' His voice hardened even as he raised a hand to his scarred cheek.

'I trust I am not so lily-livered, my lord,' Caro protested indignantly. 'No doubt you obtained that scar during the wars against Napoleon?'

'Yes.'

She nodded. 'Then it would be most ungrateful of me—of any woman—to see your scar as anything less than the result of the act of bravery it undoubtedly was.'

Dominic was well aware that some women found the scar on his face unsightly, even frightening. He should have known that the feisty Caro was made of sterner stuff. 'I will endeavour to conclude my business with Butler as quickly as is possible, after which I will be free to escort you home. No, please do not argue with me any further tonight,' he advised wearily as he saw that familiar light of rebellion enter those sea-green eyes.

'You are altogether too fond of having your own way, sir.' She frowned her disapproval at him.

And his efforts to frighten this young woman into

leaving London had only succeeded in alarming himself, Dominic recognised frustratedly. 'And if I once again add the word please?'

'Well?' she prompted tartly as he added nothing further.

Dominic found himself openly smiling at her waspishness. '*Please*, Caro, will you wait here for me?' he said drily.

Her chin remained proudly high. 'I will consider the idea whilst you are talking to Mr Butler.'

Dominic shot her one last exasperated glance before striding purposefully from the room. He forgot everything else, however—kissing and touching Caro, her response to those kisses and caresses, his own lack of control over that situation—the moment he entered the main salon of the club and saw a bloodstained and obviously badly beaten Nathaniel Thorne lying recumbent upon one of the couches there...

Chapter Five

'Dominic, why—?'

'Not now, please, Caro,' he cut in as he sat broodingly across from her inside the lamp-lit coach.

Not that the lamp was really necessary, dawn having long broken, and the sun starting to appear above the rooftops and chimneys of London, by the time they had delivered Nathaniel safely to his home. The two of them had remained long enough to see him settled in his bedchamber and attended by several of his servants before taking their leave.

Caro had given a horrified gasp earlier when she'd ventured from Drew's office and entered the main salon of the club to see a group of men standing around Lord Thorne as he lay stretched out upon one of the couches, with blood covering much of his face and hands and dripping unchecked on to his elegant clothing.

Not that Dominic had spared any time on the pallor of her cheeks or her stricken expression as he'd turned and seen her standing there. 'Someone take her away from here!' he had ordered as Caro stood there, simply too shocked to move.

'Dom—'

'Stay calm, Nate.' His voice softened as he spoke soothingly to the injured man, some of that softness remaining in his face as he turned back to Caro. 'It really would be better for all concerned if you left, Caro.'

'I'll take her back to my office,' Drew offered before striding across the room to take a firm hold of her arm and practically drag her from the room.

She barely heard the older man's comforting words as he escorted her to his office before instructing Ben to remain on guard outside the door. Caro had paced the office for well over an hour whilst the two men obviously dealt with the bloody—and Caro sincerely hoped not too seriously injured—Nathaniel Thorne.

Dominic had grimly avoided answering any of her questions when he'd finally arrived to escort her home. Caro had gasped in surprise as he had thrown his cloak over her head just as she was about to step outside. 'What are you doing?'

He had easily arrested her struggles to free herself. 'Continue walking to the coach,' he had instructed.

Caro had thrown that cloak back impatiently as soon as she'd entered the carriage, any thought of further protest at Dominic's rough handling of her dying in her throat as she saw Lord Thorne reclining upon the bench seat opposite, the dressings wrapped about both his hands seeming to indicate that he had received the attentions of a doctor since she had seen him last. His face had been cleansed of the blood, revealing his many cuts and bruises, injuries that could surely only have been inflicted by fists and knives.

Caro felt herself quiver now as she remembered the full extent of those numerous gashes and bruises, and the imagined violence behind them. 'How—?'

'I am in no mood to discuss this further tonight,' Dominic rasped, the attack on Nathaniel having been a brutal awakening, a timely reminder that there was no place for a vulnerable woman like Caro in his world.

Sea-green eyes gazed back at him reproachfully. 'But why would someone do such a thing to Lord Thorne?'

'I should have realised that asking you for silence, even for a few minutes, was an impossibility.' Dominic sighed heavily. 'The simple answer to your question is that I do not know. Yet,' he added grimly. But he had every intention of discovering who was responsible for the attack on Nathaniel and why.

Caro flinched. 'He appeared to be badly injured...'

Dominic nodded curtly. 'He was beaten. Severely. Repeatedly. By four thugs wielding knives as well as their fists.' He knew more than most how strong a fighter Nathaniel was, but the odds of four against one, especially as they had possessed weapons, had not been in his friend's favour.

She gasped as her suspicions were confirmed, one of her hands rising to the slenderness of her throat . 'But *why*?' She appeared totally bewildered.

Nathaniel had remained conscious long enough to explain that he had been set upon the moment he'd stepped outside the club earlier, the wounds on his hands caused both from the blows he had managed to land upon his attackers, and defensively as he'd held those hands up in front of him to stop the worst of the knife cuts upon his face. Once he'd fallen to the ground, he had not stood a chance against the odds, as he was kicked repeatedly until one of those blows had caught him on the side of the head. After which he knew no more until he awoke to stagger back inside the club and ask for help.

Considering those odds of four against one, Dominic was sure that if murder had been the intention, then Nathaniel would now be dead. Also, his purse had still been in his pocket when he'd regained consciousness, the diamond pin also in place at his throat, so robbery was not the motive, either. From that Dominic could only surmise that the thugs had achieved what they had set out to do, and that the attack had been a warning of some kind.

But a warning to whom exactly…?

The words of caution Gabriel had given Dominic before he'd left Venice, in regard to Nicholas Brown, the previous owner of Nick's, had immediately come to mind. Dominic was well aware of the other man's violent reputation; while publicly Brown behaved the gentleman, privately he was known to be vicious and vindictive, his associates mostly of the shady under-world of London's slums. Also, the other man had been most seriously displeased to lose Nick's in that wager to Dominic.

No, the more thought he gave to the situation—when Caro allowed him the time to think about it, that was—the more convinced he became that Nicholas Brown was somehow involved. That tonight's attack might not been meant for Nathaniel at all…

Dominic had left for Venice only days after winning the wager that had cost Brown his gambling club, only returning back to London two days ago, a fact that would no doubt have reached the other man's ears as early as yesterday. As such, it would have been all too easy for the four thugs lying in wait outside the club to have assumed that the gentleman leaving alone, long after the last patron had left, with his face hidden by both the darkness and the hat upon his head, was Dominic himself.

He had discussed the possibilities briefly with Drew, the older man having agreed that his previous employer was more than capable of sending some of his paid thugs to attack Dominic. Except those thugs had not dealt the lethal blow to the man they had attacked. Drew had offered the possibility that it might not have been a case of mistaken identity at all; that Brown could well be deliberately hurting people known to be associated with Dominic, as both a threat and a warning, before later extracting his revenge from Dominic himself.

Dominic gave a grimace as he anticipated Caro's reaction to what was to be the subject of their next conversation. 'I have no idea as yet. But in view of the fact that the attack occurred outside Nick's, it has been decided that, for the next few days at least, all of us associated with the club should take the necessary precautions.'

Caro stared across at him blankly. 'But surely *I* am in no danger? No one except you, Lord Thorne, Drew Butler, and Ben Jackson has even seen the face of the masked lady singing at Nick's. That is the reason you threw your cloak over me when we were leaving the club earlier!' she realised suddenly, looking shocked.

He nodded grimly. 'It is not my intention to frighten you, Caro.' He frowned darkly as she obviously became so. 'But, until we know more, Drew and I are agreed that the masked lady must disappear completely, whilst at the same time every precaution taken to ensure the safety of Caro Morton.'

'Perhaps I might go to stay with Mr Butler and his family?'

'Drew and I dismissed that possibility,' Dominic explained. 'Unfortunately, Drew and his family share their modest home with both his wife's parents and his own so there is simply no room.'

'Oh.' Caro frowned. 'Then perhaps I might move to the obscurity of an inexpensive hotel—'

The earl gave a firm shake of his head. 'A hotel is too public.'

She sighed her frustration with this situation. 'Is there any real danger to me, or is this just another way for you to ensure that it is impossible for me to do anything other than return from "whence I came"?'

Dominic looked at her thoughtfully. 'Would you even consider it if I were to suggest it?'

'No, I would not,' she stated firmly.

'No,' Dominic conceded flatly. In truth, it was no longer an option; if Brown really were responsible for tonight's attack, there was also every possibility he was already aware of Caro's identity as the masked lady. He undoubtedly had informers and spies everywhere. As such, Caro returning to her home unprotected could put her in more danger than if she were to remain in

London. 'Drew and I have come up with another solution.'

Caro eyed him warily. 'Which is…?'

'That I now escort you to your lodgings, where you will pack up your belongings and return to Blackstone House with me.' Not an ideal solution, he allowed honestly, but one that more easily enabled him to ensure her safety. The fact that she would at the same time be all too available to the desire he was finding it more and more difficult to resist was something he had tried—and failed—not to think about.

No wonder Caro stared at him so incredulously!

He raised an eyebrow. 'If you choose to accompany me to Blackstone House, then I will do all in my power to ensure your stay there is a temporary one. If it appears that it is to be longer than two, or possibly three days, then I will endeavour to find alternative accommodations for you. In any event, my offer of protection is one of expediency only. A desire, if you will, not to find one, or more, of my employees dead in a doorway during the next few days.'

Caro felt her face grow pale. 'You truly do believe those thugs will attack again?' She was totally confused as to what she should do. She had managed her escape from Hampshire easily enough, but she knew her older sister well enough to realise that Diana would not allow that situation to continue for long. That, despite Caro's letter of reassurance, once Diana had ascertained she was nowhere to be found in Hampshire, then her sister would widen her search, in all probability as far as London.

Diana's wrath, if she should then discover Caro living

in the household of a single gentleman of the *ton* would, she had no doubt, be more than a match for this arrogant man!

She shook her head. 'Surely Mr Butler did not agree with this plan?'

'On reflection Drew agreed with me that at the moment your safety is of more importance than your... reputation.' Dominic's mouth twisted derisively.

She shook her head. 'I simply cannot—'

'Caro, I am grown weary of hearing what you can or cannot do.' He sat forwards on the seat so that their two faces were now only inches apart, his eyes a pale and glittering silver in the weak, early morning sunlight. 'I have told you of the choices available to you—'

'Neither of which is acceptable to me!'

He gave her a hard smile. 'Then it seems you must choose whichever you consider to be the lesser of those two evils.'

Caro understood that Dominic was overset concerning the injuries inflicted upon his friend this evening, and the damage also caused to his gambling club before the attack, that he was genuinely concerned there might be another attack on those working or associated with the gambling club. But having already suffered twenty years of having her movements curtailed out of love and respect for her father, she had no intention of being told what she could or could not do, either by her guardian, or a man she had only met for the first time yesterday. 'And if I should refuse to do either of those things—go home or accompany you?'

Dominic had admired this young woman's courage from the start. Appreciated that feistiness in her, her lack of awe, of either him or his title, as well as her willingness to disagree with him if she so chose. But at this moment he could only wish she was of an obedient and compliant nature! 'It is late, Caro—or early, depending upon one's perspective.' He sighed wearily. 'In any event, it has been a very long night, and as a consequence perhaps it would be best if we waited until later today to make any firm decision one way or the other?'

She nodded. 'Then we are in agreement that once you have returned me to my lodgings I will remain there until we are able to talk again?'

Caro had all the allure of a prim old maid in that unbecoming brown bonnet that once again hid most of her hair, Dominic decided dispassionately. In fact, she looked nothing at all like the delicious, half-naked woman he had made love to earlier. Which was perhaps as well, given the circumstances! Dominic had thought to teach her a lesson earlier, and instead he had been taught one—that at the very least, Caro Morton was a serious danger to his self-control.

'We are not agreed at all,' Dominic contradicted, making no effort to continue arguing with her, but instead tapping on the roof of the carriage and issuing instructions to his groom to drive directly to Blackstone House. 'I will send to your lodgings for your things later today,' he informed her.

'You—'

'Caro, I have already assured you that should my enquiries take longer than those two or three days, then I will make other arrangements for you; let that be an end to the matter,' he said as he relaxed back in his seat, one dark brow raised in challenge.

A challenge she returned. 'It is seriously your intention to introduce me—even temporarily—into your household?'

'Seriously,' Dominic said.

She gave a disgusted snort. 'As what, may I ask?'

'Should any ask for an explanation—' his tone clearly implied that there were few who would dare ask the Earl of Blackstone for an explanation concerning any of his actions! 'then I will suggest that you are my widowed and impoverished cousin—so many young women were left widowed after Waterloo. That you are newly arrived from the country on the morning coach, with the intention of staying with me at Blackstone House whilst I arrange a modest household for you in London.'

'Without clothes or a maid?' Caro scorned.

Dominic shrugged unconcernedly. 'An impoverished widow cannot afford to employ a maid until I arrange for one, and your trunk will be delivered later today.'

She eyed him impatiently. 'Does the Earl of Blackstone even have a widowed and impoverished cousin?'

'No.'

'Do you have *any* cousins?'

'No.'

She eyed him quizzically. 'Any family at *all*?'

'Not a single one.'

Caro could not even imagine a life without her two sisters in it. Admittedly she had put a distance between them now, but it had been done in the knowledge that she could return to them as soon as Gabriel Faulkner had been convinced by Diana that none of the Copeland sisters had any intention of ever marrying him.

'Do not waste any of your pity on me.' Dominic's tone was laden with warning as he obviously saw that emotion in her expression. 'Having witnessed the complications that so often attend having close family members, I have come to regard my own lack of them as being more of a blessing rather than a deprivation.'

Could that really be true? Caro wondered with a frown. Could Dominic really prefer a life derelict of all family ties? A solitary life that allowed for only a few close friends, such as Lord Thorne?

She was given no more time to dwell on that subject or any other as the coach came to a halt, a glance outside revealing a large town house in an obviously fashionable district of London. Mayfair, perhaps. Or St James's? Whatever its location, Blackstone House was a much grander house than any she had ever seen before.

Shoreley Hall was a rambling red-bricked house that had been erected for the first Earl of Westbourne in the sixteenth century. It had been built upon haphazardly by succeeding earls until it now resembled nothing more than a rambling monstrosity surrounded by several thousand acres of rich farmland.

In contrast, Dominic Vaughn's home was of a mellow cream colour, four storeys high, with gardens all around covered in an abundance of brightly coloured spring flowers, the whole surrounded by a high black wrought-iron fence.

'Caro?'

She had been so intent on the beauty of Blackstone

House, so in awe of its grandeur, that she had not noticed that one of the grooms had opened the door and folded down the steps, and was now waiting for her to alight. 'Thank you.' She accepted the aid of the young man's hand as she stepped down on to the pavement, Dominic's obvious wealth making her more than ever aware of her own drab and unfashionable appearance.

Vanity, her sister Diana would have called it. And she would have been right. But that did not make Caro feel it any less!

Again, she was allowed no more time for protest as Dominic took a firm hold of her arm to pull her along beside him as he ascended the steps up to the front of the house. The door opened before they reached the top step—despite it being barely past dawn—by a footman in full livery. If he was in the least surprised to see his employer accompanied by a drably clothed young woman he introduced as his cousin, Mrs Morton, then the man did not show it.

The inside of Blackstone House was even grander than the outside, if that were possible—the floor of the entrance hall a beautiful mottled green-and-cream marble, with four alabaster pillars either side leading to the wide staircase and up to a gallery that surrounded the whole of the first floor. High above them, suspended from a domed and windowed ceiling, a beautiful crystal chandelier glittered and shone in the sunlight. Caro had every expectation that the rest of Dominic's home would be just as beautiful.

'Would you take Mrs Morton up to the Green Suite, Simpson?' Dominic ignored Caro's awestruck expression as he turned to address the butler who had now appeared in the entrance hall. 'And provide her with whatever refreshment she requires.' He turned away with the obvious intention of passing her into the care of the servants.

'My lord!'

He was frowning slightly as he turned. 'What is it now?'

She nervously ran the tip of her tongue across her lips before answering him. 'I—you recall my trunk will not be arriving until later today…'

Dominic's frown deepened at this further delay. 'I am sure that Simpson will be only too happy to provide you with anything that you require.' He nodded abruptly to the attending butler before turning on his heel and striding down the hallway to where his study was situated at the back of the house.

Dominic needed time in which to think. Time, now that both he and Caro were safely ensconced in Blackstone House, in which to try to make some sense of everything that had occurred during these past few hours.

And unfortunately, he recognised darkly, he was unable to think in the least bit clearly whilst in Caro Morton's company…

It was Caro's indignation at the abruptness of Dominic's departure that helped her through the next few minutes, as she was shown up to a suite of rooms on the first floor, that indignation not in the least mollified by the delightful private sitting room that adjoined the spacious bedchamber. Both rooms were decorated in a warm green and cream—the reason it was named the

Green Suite, no doubt!—with cream furniture in the sitting room and a matching four-poster in the bed-chamber, the latter surrounded by the same beautiful cream-brocade curtains that hung at the huge windows overlooking the front of the house and the square beyond.

Yes, it was all incredibly beautiful, she acknowledged once she had been left alone with warm water in which to wash, and a maid had delivered a pot of fresh tea to revive her flagging spirits. But the beauty of her surroundings did not change the fact that she should not be here.

Running away to London and posing as Caro Morton in order to avoid her guardian's marriage proposal was one thing, but chancing the possibility of ever being found out as Lady Caroline Copeland was something else entirely, and had certainly never entered into any of her hastily made plans.

It was not a part of her plans now, either. Just because Dominic had chosen to bring her here, supposedly for her own protection, did not mean that she had to remain. As such, she would escape at the first opportunity—

'I would seriously advise against it...'

Caro was so surprised to hear the softness of Dominic's voice behind her that she almost dropped the cup she had been nursing in her hands. As it was, some of the hot tea tipped and spilled over her fingers as she turned to find him lounging in the open doorway of the sitting room. 'Advise against what, may I ask?' she demanded crossly even as she placed the cup back in its saucer before inspecting her scalded fingers.

'What have you done now?' The concern could be

heard in the deep timbre of Dominic Vaughn's voice as he threw something down on a chair before striding across the bedchamber towards her.

She turned to glare at him at the same time as she clasped her hands tightly together behind her back. 'What have *I* done? *You* were the one who startled me into spilling my tea!'

'Let me see your hands.' Those silver eyes glowered down at her even as he reached behind her to easily pull her hands apart before bringing them both forward for his minute inspection.

Caro's protest died in her throat as she saw how pale and tiny her hands looked as he cradled them gently in his much larger ones. He was also standing far too close to her, she realised a little breathlessly, the light from the candelabra giving his hair that blue-black sheen as he bent over her so attentively, his strong and handsome face appearing all savagely etched hollows and sharp angles in the candlelight.

'Why are you here, Dominic?'

'Why?' He could no longer remember the reason why as he felt his response to the way she spoke his name so huskily; his chest felt suddenly tight, his arousal stirring, rising, inside his pantaloons. 'It was certainly not with the intention of hurting you,' he murmured ruefully as he lifted her hand to sweep the moistness of his tongue soothingly over that slightly reddened skin, even as he looked up and held her gaze captive.

'I—it was an accident.' Her lips were slightly parted as she breathed shallowly.

'One that would not have happened if I had not

startled you,' he apologised ruefully as he continued to stroke his tongue against her silky soft skin.

The slenderness of her throat moved convulsively. 'I—I believe my hand is feeling better now, my lord.' But she made no effort to release her fingers from either Dominic's hand or the attentions of his lips and tongue.

She tasted…delicious, he recognised achingly as he placed delicate kisses between each individual finger, a combination of lightly scented soap and the natural saltiness of her skin, the trembling of her hand as he held it gently in the palm of his an indication of the pleasure she felt from his caressing attentions.

Dominic's thighs ached now, throbbed, his arousal more engorged and swollen just from the eroticism of kissing Caro's fingers than he had ever known it to be under the ministrations of the most accomplished of courtesans.

She had removed her bonnet and cloak since he'd last seen her, several golden curls having escaped the confinement of the pins designed to keep them in place, those curls shining like the clearest gold in the mellow candlelight. Her eyes had grown dark and misty, her cheeks slightly flushed, the full swell of her lips slightly parted as if waiting to be kissed.

She snatched her hands from his now before stepping back, her eyes wide with alarm. 'I believe we are already agreed that I have no intention of ever becoming your mistress, my lord.'

Dominic drew in several deep and controlling breaths as he acknowledged he had once again fallen under the sensuous spell of this woman. A woman who refused to tell him anything about herself other than her name—and he suspected even that was a fabrication!

He gave a slight shake of his head as he straightened. 'It would appear, Caro, because Butler and Jackson make no effort to hide their admiration of you, that you are under the misapprehension that every man you meet must necessarily be as smitten as they are,' he drawled mockingly.

Caro's cheeks flushed a fiery red at the accusation. 'Of course I am not—'

'Perhaps that is as well.' He looked down the length of his arrogant nose at her with those pale and glittering eyes. 'I assure you, my own jaded tastes require a little more stimulation than the touch of a woman's fingers—moreover, a woman with an eye for fashion that would surely make even a nun weep!' That silver gaze raked over her critically.

Caro had no idea why, but she felt that he was being deliberately harsh with her. Not that this green gown was not as unbecoming as the brown one she had worn the night before, because she knew that it was. But that had been the purpose in buying them, had it not? Besides, Dominic had not seemed to find her gown so awful when he'd made love to her earlier! 'I chose my gowns to suit myself, my lord, and not you,' she said calmly.

'Your choices are deplorable.' His top lip curled. 'I will arrange for a dressmaker to visit you later today. Hopefully she will have some suitable day dresses already made that can easily be altered to fit you, but you will also need to choose some materials for an evening gown or two.' He scowled. 'If I must have you as a guest in my home for the next few days, then I can at least ensure you are a decorative one.'

'I am your unwilling guest, remember?'

Dominic shrugged. 'Your reasons for being here are not important—what is far more pressing is not having the delicacy of my senses constantly offended by your drab appearance, even for the short time you will reside here!' He was being deliberately cruel, he knew. Because he had not cared earlier, or even a few minutes ago, how unbecoming Caro's gown was, or even who she might be; he had only been interested in the alluring curves of the silken body he knew lay beneath that gown.

Those sea-green eyes sparkled up at him angrily now. 'You are offensive, sir!'

He looked completely unaffected by her annoyance. 'If you choose to find the truth offensive, then who am I to argue?' He turned to walk over to the door, coming to a halt halfway across the room as the garment he had thrown on the chair earlier drew his attention. 'In view of your earlier reticence, it occurred to me that you might feel uncomfortable asking Simpson to find you something suitable in which to sleep, and so I brought you this.' He indicated the white robe draped across the chair.

The thought was a kind one, Caro acknowledged— the offhand method of bestowing that kindness was not! Any more than she appreciated having Dominic Vaughn arrange for a dressmaker to call on her here later today. 'I cannot possibly—' She broke off abruptly as she recalled this man's scathing comment earlier when she'd stated what she could and could not allow.

'I am afraid, where my gowns are concerned, that your "delicate senses" will just have to continue to be offended, my lord!'

He eyed her incredulously. 'You are saying you do not care for pretty gowns?'

Of course she liked pretty gowns—did she not secretly long for all the beautiful gowns she had left behind at Shoreley Hall? If only so that she could wear one of them to show Dominic Vaughn how fashionable she really was!

But she did not long for those pretty confections of silk and lace enough to agree to have a dressmaker attend her here—almost as if she really were about to become Dominic's mistress! 'Not at the moment, no,' she said mendaciously, only realising the error of answering so unguardedly as she saw the earl's eyes narrow shrewdly.

'And why is that, Caro?' he prompted slowly. 'Could it be because you believe yourself to be less conspicuous in those shabby gowns?'

She instantly bridled at the description. 'I will have you know that these gowns cost me several crowns.'

'Then it was money obviously wasted,' he drawled, before adding softly, 'I should warn you, Caro, that every attempt you make to hide your true identity from me only makes me more curious to learn exactly what or who it is you are hiding from…'

A shiver of apprehension quivered down her spine. 'You are imagining things, sir!' Her scorn sounded flat—and patently untrue—even to her own ears.

'We shall see,' Dominic said as he continued his

stroll to the doorway before looking back at her briefly. 'I trust you will bear in mind what I said to you earlier?'

She gave a weary sigh, as tired now as he had claimed to be earlier. 'You have said so many things to me tonight—to which nugget of wisdom do you refer?'

'I also seem to recall we have said a great many things to each other—and most of them impolite.' The earl's mouth twitched ruefully. 'But the advice I am referring to now is not to attempt to leave here without my knowledge. As I have said, it is not my wish to alarm you,' he added more gently as she visibly tensed. 'But, until I know more about the events of this evening, I cannot stress strongly enough your need for caution.'

Her throat moved convulsively as she swallowed. 'Truly?'

'Truly,' he echoed grimly.

Caro could only stand numbed and silent as Dominic closed the door softly behind him as he left, the walls of the bedchamber instantly seeming to bear down on her, making her their captive.

No—making her Lord Dominic Vaughn's unwilling captive…

Chapter Six

Caro awoke refreshed, a smile curving her lips as she felt the sun shining upon her face while she lay snuggled beneath the warmth of the bedclothes. That smile swiftly faded as she remembered exactly where she was. Or, more exactly, who owned the bed she had been asleep in. That arrogant, silver-eyed devil Lord Dominic Vaughn, Earl of Blackstone!

Her eyes opened wide and she looked about her in alarm as she tried to gauge what time of day it was. The sun had not been shining in the bedchamber when she'd finally drifted off to sleep earlier, and now it completely lit up and warmed the room, meaning that she must have slept for several hours, at least.

Sleeping during the day had seemed decadent to her a week ago, but she had quickly learned that it was impossible for her to do anything else when the gambling club did not open until—

No, Nick's would now not be opening at all for several days, according to Dominic, which meant she could not work there in the evenings, either. She had enough money for the moment, courtesy of Drew Butler having paid her when she'd arrived for work the previous evening. But how was she supposed to fill her time now, incarcerated at Blackstone House for several days at least?

Caro had always disliked the usual pursuits expected of women of her class; her embroidery work was nondescript, and she had no talent for drawing or painting. She rode well, but doubted she would enjoy the sedateness of riding in the London parks. Perhaps Dominic had a decent library she might explore? She had always liked to read—

What was she doing? she wondered with disgust; as she had realised earlier this morning, she was not to be a guest here, but held virtually as a prisoner, albeit in a gilded cage, until Dominic Vaughn deemed it was safe for her to leave.

She threw the bedclothes back restlessly and swung her legs to the floor before standing up, only to become instantly aware of the garment the earl had provided for her to sleep in. White in colour, and reaching almost down to her knees, with buttons from the middle of her chest to throat and at the cuffs of the long sleeves, the garment could only be one of Dominic's own silk evening shirts.

A sensuously soft and totally decadent gentleman's white silk evening shirt. A garment that, once it had slid softly over Caro's nakedness, had evoked just as sensuous and decadent thoughts of the gentleman it belonged to...

Caro dropped down upon the side of the bed as she

recalled the wickedness of her thoughts before she had drifted off to sleep. Of how those memories, of Dominic's lips and tongue upon her bared breasts earlier, had once again made her breasts swell and the strawberry tips to become hard and engorged, evoking a warm rush of moisture between her thighs that had sent delightful rivulets of pleasure coursing through her when she'd clenched them tightly together. She—

'You're awake at last, madam.' A young maid had tilted her head around the slightly opened door, but she pushed that door completely open now before disappearing back into the hallway for several seconds.

Long enough, thankfully, for Caro to climb quickly back beneath the bedclothes and pull them up to her chin before the maid reappeared carrying a silver tray she dearly hoped had some tea and toast upon it; she had not eaten for some time and just the thought of food caused her stomach to give an unladylike growl. She grimaced self-consciously as the smiling maid bustled about opening up the small legs beneath the tray before placing the whole across Caro's thighs above the bedclothes.

Not only was there tea and toast, Caro realised greedily, but two perfectly poached eggs and several slices of sweet-smelling ham. 'This looks delicious.'

'I'm sure it will be, madam.' The young girl bobbed a curtsy. 'His lordship surely has the best cook in London.'

Unfortunately Caro's appetite had suddenly deserted her. The maid's continual use of the title 'madam' was a timely reminder that she was supposed to be Dominic Vaughn's poor and widowed cousin, a deception that did not please her at all. She didn't want to be connected to Dominic in any way, even in a falsehood!

'Eat up, madam,' the maid encouraged brightly as she hovered beside the bed. 'The dressmaker has been waiting downstairs for quite some time already.'

The dressmaker Caro had told the earl she did not require. She should have known that the arrogant man would completely disregard her instruction. Just as she fully intended to disregard his!

She smiled up at the maid. 'What is your name, dear?'

'Mabel, ma'am.'

Caro nodded. 'Then, Mabel, could you please go downstairs and inform the dressmaker that there has been a mistake—'

'No mistake has been made, Caro,' Dominic drawled as he strolled uninvited into the bedchamber, crossing the room on booted feet until he stood beside the bed looking down mockingly at a red-faced Caro. That silver gaze raked over her mercilessly before he turned to the blushing young maid. 'That will be all, thank you.'

'My lord. Madam.' The young girl bobbed a curtsy to them both before hurrying from the room.

Caro wished that she might escape with her, but instead she once again found herself the focus of those chilling silver eyes as the earl stood tall and dominating beside the bed. And looking far too handsome, she thought resentfully, in buff-coloured pantaloons above black Hessians, a severe black superfine stretching the width of those wide shoulders, with a grey waistcoat and snowy white shirt beneath.

No doubt a white silk shirt similar to the one that she now wore as a nightgown!

'Impoverished widowed cousin or not, I do not believe that entitles you to enter my bedchamber uninvited, my lord,' Caro hissed when she at last managed to regain her breath.

Dominic could not help but admire how beautiful Caro looked with her golden curls loose upon the pillows and the pertness of her breasts covered only by the white silk of one of his own dress shirts, the nipples standing firm and rosy beneath the sheer material.

His jaw clenched now as he once again resisted the urge to push that material aside and feast himself on those firm and tempting buds. 'Eat up, Caro; the dressmaker does not have all day to waste while you laze about in your bed.'

Her cheeks coloured with temper. 'I distinctly remember telling you that I did not require the services of a dressmaker.'

'And I distinctly recall telling you that I refuse to see you dressed in one of those drab gowns a moment longer.' Dominic bent calmly to pluck a slice of ham from the plate upon the laden tray after making this announcement.

Caro found her gaze suddenly riveted upon his finely sculptured lips and the white evenness of his teeth, as he took a bite of the delicious-smelling ham, unsure if the moisture that suddenly flooded her mouth was caused by that mouthwatering ham or the unexpected sensuality of watching Dominic eat...

Those lips and teeth had been upon her breasts only

hours ago, the tongue he now used to lick his lips having swirled a delicious pattern of pleasure on her flesh.

She wrenched her gaze away from the earl's dangerously handsome face as the contents of the tray placed across her thighs rattled in rhythm with her trembling awareness. 'I fear I am no longer hungry.' Her fingers curled about the handles of the tray as she attempted to remove it.

'Careful!' Dominic Vaughn took the tray from her shaking fingers to lift it and place it on the dressing-table before turning back to face her, the sunlight shining in through the window once again giving his hair the blue-black appearance of a raven's wing as that silver gaze narrowed on her critically. 'Speaking as a man who prefers a little more meat on the bones of the women he beds, I do believe you need to eat more,' he finally drawled.

Her chin rose challengingly. 'Speaking as a woman who has no interest in your preferences regarding "the women you bed", I prefer to remain exactly as I am, thank you very much!'

Dominic gave an appreciative grin; Caro had obviously lost none of her feistiness in the hours since he last saw her.

They had been busy hours for him, as he first set some of his associates from the army ranks, now civilians, the task of investigating Nicholas Brown's dealings over the past few days, before dispensing with his own household and estate business, and then returning to Nathaniel's home to see how his friend fared. Dominic's mouth tightened grimly as he thought of the other man's discomfort and obvious pain.

'Before you dismiss the dressmaker so arbitrarily, I believe you should be made aware that when your things were brought from your lodgings earlier, I instantly instructed one of the maids to consign all of the gowns inside into the incinerator,' he announced with satisfaction.

Caro gasped. '*All* of them?'

'All.'

Her startled gaze moved to the chair where she had placed her green gown earlier, only to find that chair now empty apart from her underclothes. And if the earl had indeed sent all her other gowns to be burned, then he must have included the three fashionable gowns Caro had brought to London with her two weeks ago. She turned back to him accusingly. 'You had no right to touch my things!'

'You were refusing to replace them.' Dominic gave an unapologetic shrug. 'It seemed easier to leave you with no choice in the matter rather than continue to argue the point.'

Her eyes sparkled indignantly. 'And I suppose I am now expected to go down to the seamstress dressed only in my shift?'

It was a pleasant thought, if an impractical one, Dominic accepted. 'She will come up here to you, of course. With, I might add, two gowns at least that you should be able to wear immediately.' He had personally instructed the dressmaker to bring a gown of sea-green and another of deep rose, the one reminding him of Caro's eyes, the other the tips of her breasts when they were aroused.

'Have you received word on how Lord Thorne fares?'

Dominic's thoughts of the anticipated changes to Caro's appearance completely dissipated at this reminder of the attack on one of his two closest friends. Not that he would ever forget that first moment of seeing Osbourne covered in blood in the early hours of this morning.

How could he, when it was such a stark reminder of the last memories Dominic had of his mother sixteen years ago?

He moved away from the bed to stand in front of one of the picture windows, his back to the room, his hands clasped tightly together behind his back as he fought back those memories. Memories that had returned all too vividly after Caro had questioned him concerning his family...

He breathed in deeply before answering. 'I have done better than that; I have been to see him.' He went on to explain that Nathaniel's aunt, Mrs Gertrude Wilson, having learnt that her nephew had suffered injuries and was confined to his bed, had wasted no time in having her own physician visit him, and fully intended removing Osbourne to her own home in St James's Square later this afternoon. An occurrence that aided Dominic's determination to ensure the future protection of his friend.

Dominic hoped to have some news later today concerning the enquiries into last night's attack, but if those enquiries should prove unhelpful, then he had plans of his own for later this evening that may give him some of the answers, if not all of them.

'And?' Caro prompted with concern as Dominic fell broodingly silent.

'And the physician has discovered he has two cracked ribs to go with his many cuts and bruises.'

Caro knew by the harshness of the Dominic's tone that he was far from happy at this news of his friend's condition. 'I am sure that he will recover fully, my lord.'

He did not look in the least comforted by her reassurances. 'Are you?'

'He is otherwise young and healthy,' Caro nodded. 'Now if—if you would not mind, I should like to get out of bed now.' She had not had time to deal with her morning ablutions before her bedchamber was invaded, first by the maid, and then Dominic Vaughn, and that need was becoming more pressing by the moment.

He raised dark brows. 'I was not aware I was preventing you from doing so?'

'You know very well that your very presence here is preventing me from getting out of bed.'

He gave a disbelieving laugh. 'You have flaunted yourself in a gambling club for this past week, in front of dozens of men, but now take exception to my seeing you clothed in one of my own shirts?'

Caro gave a pained frown. 'The gown I wore at those performances covered me from neck to toe.'

'And titillated and aroused the interest of your audience all the more because of it!'

Had it titillated and aroused this man's interest? she wondered breathlessly. Obviously something had, if his passion earlier this morning was any indication. A passion she had responded to in a way that still made her blush. 'Then it would seem the sooner I am clothed in one of my new gowns, the better it will be for everyone.'

His gorgeous mouth curved into a pleased smile.

'You are sufficiently recovered from your previous outrage to now accept the new gowns?'

Caro bristled. 'I believe it is more a case of having little choice in the matter when you have had all of my own gowns burned. I should become a prisoner of this bedchamber rather than just the house if I did not accept the new gowns, would I not?'

He winced. 'You are not to be a prisoner here, Caro, only to take the precaution of being accompanied if you should decide to go about.'

'I do not even know where "here" is!' she snapped caustically.

'Blackstone House is in Mayfair,' he elaborated. 'And as soon as you are dressed, and the seamstress has gone about her business, I will be only too happy to take you out for a drive in my carriage.'

'Accompanied by the maid I do not have?' she came back derisively.

'We are believed to be cousins, Caro,' he reminded her drily. 'Making such a fuss about the proprieties would be a nonsense.'

'In that case, if you would send the dressmaker up to me now I should very much like to go out for a drive.'

Her tone, Dominic noted ruefully, was almost as imperious as Osbourne's Aunt Gertrude's. Further evidence, if he should need it, that Caro Morton was a woman used to instructing her own servants and having those instructions obeyed. Because she was, in fact, a lady of quality?

He crossed the room to once again stand beside the bed. 'Have you considered the possibility, Caro, that I might be more…amenable, if you did not constantly challenge me?'

'I have considered it, my lord—and as quickly dismissed it.' Her expression was defiant as she glanced up at him. 'It goes completely against my nature, you see.'

Dominic could not prevent his throaty chuckle as he looked down at her admiringly. No, he never found himself bored in Caro's company, even when he was not making love to her! 'I will arrange for the carriage to be brought round in an hour's time.' He gave her a brief bow before taking his leave.

Caro did not move for several minutes after he had left the bedchamber, still slightly breathless from the transformation that had overcome his austere features when he laughed. Those silver eyes had glowed warmly, with laughter lines fanning out at their sides, the curve of those sculptured lips revealing the white evenness of his teeth. Even that savage scar upon his cheek had softened. The whole rendered him so devastatingly handsome that just looking at him had stolen her breath away…

'Relax, Caro,' Dominic drawled softly as she sat tensely beside him as he controlled the reins of his curricle, his two favourite greys stepping out lively in the sun-dappled park. 'By this time tomorrow, all of society will be agog to know who was the beautiful young lady riding in the park with Blackstone in his curricle.' And she looked every inch a lady of quality in her rose-coloured gown and matching bonnet, with several golden curls framing the delicate beauty of her face, and her hands covered in pale cream gloves.

'How disappointed they will be when they learn it is only your impoverished and widowed cousin up from the country,' she came back tartly. 'And the last thing I desire is to become the talk of London society,' she added with a delicate shudder.

It was rather late for that, when to Dominic's certain knowledge the male members of the *ton*, at least, had been avidly discussing the masked woman who had sung at Nick's for the past week! Not that any of those men would recognise the blonde woman sitting so demurely beside him in his curricle as the same masked and ebony-haired siren who had entertained them so prettily at Nick's; several of those gentlemen had already greeted Dominic as they passed in their own carriages, with no hint of recognition in their gazes as they'd glanced admiringly at the golden-haired beauty at his side.

'A beautiful woman, impoverished or otherwise, is always a source of gossip amongst the members of the *ton*,' he said.

Caro glanced at him beneath long golden lashes, noting how easily he kept the two feisty greys to a demure trot as he drove his elegant curricle through the park. She had also noted the admiring glances sent his way by all of the ladies in the passing carriages, before those covetous glances had shifted coldly on to Caro, no doubt due to the fact she was the one sitting beside the eligible Earl of Blackstone in his carriage.

Wearing a beautiful gown, and being driven through a London park in a fashionable carriage, with a wickedly handsome man at her side, had long been one of Caro's dreams. But in those girlish dreams the man had been totally besotted with her, something she knew Dominic would never be with regard to her.

Admittedly, the circumstances under which they had first met had been less than ideal, but if Lady Caroline Copeland and Lord Dominic Vaughn, Earl of Blackstone, had met in a fashionable London drawing room, he would certainly have behaved more circumspectly towards her.

Except she was not, at this moment, Lady Caroline Copeland, and the earl's casualness of manner towards her was reflective of that fact. 'I believe I would like to return to Blackstone House now, if you please,' she said stiffly.

Dominic glanced down at Caro, frowning slightly as he saw the way her lashes were uncharacteristically cast down. 'There is a blanket beside you if you are becoming chilled?'

'I am not in the least chilled; I would just prefer to leave now.' Her voice was huskily soft, but determined.

Dominic transferred both reins to his right hand before reaching down with his left to lift Caro's chin so that he might look into her face. Far from invigorating her, she seemed to have grown paler during the drive, and, unless he was mistaken, the glitter in her eyes was not due to her usual rebellion. 'Are you about to cry?' His voice sounded as incredulous as he felt.

'Certainly not!' She wrenched her chin out of his grasp and turned away. 'I merely wish to return home, that is all. To Blackstone House, I meant, of course,' she added awkwardly.

Dominic had known exactly what Caro meant. Strange, in all the years he had been the Earl of Blackstone, he had never particularly regarded any of his houses or estates as being his home—how could he, when all of them were a reminder of the parents who had both died when he was but twelve years old?

Or how, along with those memories, came the nightmare reminder of the part he had played in their deaths! Memories that were usually kept firmly at bay, but had haunted him this past few hours…

'Of course.' Dominic gave a curt nod before turning the greys in front of the curricle back towards Blackstone House. 'Perhaps you should go to your bedchamber and rest before dinner?'

'I am simply grown bored of driving in the park, Dominic; I am not decrepit!'

He gave an appreciative smile as Caro answered with some of her usual spirit, all trace of what he had thought were tears having disappeared as she glared up at him. 'I assure you, Caro, I would not have brought you out driving with me at all if I thought you decrepit.'

'Is that because only women you consider beautiful are allowed in your curricle?' she asked, regarding him with a scornful purse to her mouth.

Dominic dearly wished to kiss that expression from her lips. Damn it, he had wanted nothing more than to kiss her again since she had appeared downstairs earlier looking breathtakingly beautiful in the rose-coloured gown and bonnet!

'No woman, beautiful or otherwise, has ever been invited to accompany me to the park in my curricle before today,' he admitted after a moment of silence.

She eyed him curiously. 'Should I feel flattered?'

'Do you?' Dominic asked.

'Not in the least,' she said with a return of her usual waspishness. 'No doubt, as far as the gentlemen of the *ton* are concerned at least, it will only add to your considerable reputation if you are believed to have the ebony-haired masked lady from Nick's in your bed at night, and a golden-haired lady in your curricle by day.'

Dominic gave her a mocking glance. 'No doubt,' he agreed.

Caro's eyes flashed deeply green. 'You—Dominic, there is a dog about to run in front of the carriage!' She reached out to grasp his forearm, half-rising in her seat as the fluffy white creature ran directly in front of the hooves of the now-prancing greys, quickly followed by a young girl in a straw bonnet who seemed to have the same disregard for her own welfare as the dog as she narrowly avoided being trampled under the hoofs of the rearing horses before following the animal across the pathway, and on to the grass, and then running into the woodland in hot pursuit without so much as a glance at the occupants of the carriage.

It took Dominic several minutes to bring the startled greys back under his control, by which time the dog and the girl had both completely disappeared, leaving Caro with the startled impression that the young girl in the straw bonnet had looked remarkably like her younger sister, Elizabeth!

Chapter Seven

'Bring brandy into the library, would you, Simpson?'
Dominic instructed the butler as he kept a firm hold of
Caro's arm, unsure as to whether or not she might faint
away at his feet if he did not.

Admittedly, the near-miss in the park had been of
concern for several seconds, but even so he had been
surprised to see Caro so white and shaking after the
event. Damn it, she was *still* white and shaking!

His hand tightened on her arm. 'At once, if you
please,' he said to the butler briskly before taking Caro
into the library and closing the door against curious
eyes. He led her gently across the room and saw her
seated in the chair beside the fireplace.

Ordinarily, he would have been impatient with a
woman's display of nerves. But having already witnessed Caro's fortitude several times—when faced with
the ribaldry of three young bucks, in the midst of a
brawl, and then again when Osbourne had received a
beating by those four thugs—Dominic could only feel

concern that a minor incident, such as the one that had happened in the park just now, should have reduced her to this trembling state.

He moved down on to his haunches beside the chair in which she now sat, before placing one of his hands on top of her clasped and trembling ones. 'No harm was done, Caro. In fact,' he continued drily, 'I believe that young girl to be completely unaware of the near-accident that she caused.'

The young girl who had reminded Caro so much of her younger sister, Elizabeth...

For it could not really have been Elizabeth, could it? No, the young and ebony-haired girl in the blue gown and spring bonnet could not possibly have been Elizabeth, only someone who looked a little like her—because Elizabeth was safely ensconced at Shoreley Hall with their sister, Diana.

Caro had been reminding herself of that fact for the ten minutes or so that it had taken Dominic to drive the curricle back to Blackstone House—all the while shooting her frowning glances from those silver-coloured eyes, at what he obviously viewed to be her overreaction to the near-accident.

An assumption she dared not refute, for fear he would then demand an explanation as to what had really upset her.

She pulled both her hands from beneath his much larger, enveloping one. 'Do not fuss, Dominic. I assure you I am now perfectly recovered!'

Dominic straightened to step away and lean his arm casually upon the top of the mantel as he looked down at her; this caustic Caro was much more like the one he had come to know these past two days. 'I am glad to hear it.' He gave a mocking inclination of his head, giving away none, he hoped, of his own disturbed emotions with regard to the near-accident.

It was difficult, nearly impossible after all that had already happened this past twelve hours, for the incident not to have once again reminded Dominic of the carriage accident that had killed his mother sixteen years ago, and resulted in the death of his father, too, only days later. Especially when Caro had obviously been rendered so upset by it all.

'Ah, thank you, Simpson.' He turned to the butler as he entered to place the tray containing the brandy decanter and glasses down upon the table in the centre of the room.

'I trust Mrs Morton is feeling better, my lord?' The remark was addressed to Dominic, but the elderly man's gaze lingered in concern on Caro as she sat so white and still beside the fire.

She turned now to bestow a gracious smile upon the older man. 'I am quite well now, thank you, Simpson.' She continued to smile warmly as she removed her bonnet.

Dominic listened incredulously to the exchange—when, by all that was holy, had Caro managed to beguile his butler? An elderly man who was usually so stiffly correct he was in danger of cutting himself from the starch in his collar. 'That will be all, Simpson,' he dismissed the servant curtly.

Caro waited until the two of them were alone before speaking. 'I believe, Dominic, that you might find your servants were happier in their work if you were to treat them with a little more politeness.'

Brought to task by this little baggage, by damn! 'And what, pray, would *you* know about servants' happiness in their work?' Dominic decided to attack rather than defend, and was instantly rewarded with the flush that coloured her cheeks. 'Unless, of course, you were once a servant yourself?'

Her chin rose. 'And if I were?'

Then Dominic would be surprised. *Very* surprised! 'I will know the story of your past one day, Caro,' he warned softly as he moved to pour brandy into two glasses.

She eyed him coolly. 'I doubt you would find it at all interesting, my lord.'

He moved to hand her one of the bulbous glasses. 'Oh, I believe that I might...'

Rather than answer him, Caro took a sip of her brandy, her eyes widening as the fiery alcohol hit the back of her throat and completely took her breath away. 'My goodness...!' she gasped, her eyes watering as the liquid continued to burn a path down to her stomach.

Dominic eyed her with amusement. 'I take it that you have never drunk brandy before?'

She placed the glass carefully down upon the table beside her. 'It is dreadful stuff. Disgusting!'

'I believe it may be something of an acquired taste.' He took another appreciative sip.

Caro gave a delicate shudder, her stomach still feeling as if there were a fire lit inside it. 'It is not one I ever intend to acquire, I assure you.'

'I am glad to hear it,' he smiled. 'There is nothing so unattractive to a man as an inebriated woman.'

Caro wrinkled her nose delicately. 'Really? In what way?'

'Never mind. Would you care for some tea, instead?'

'That will not be necessary—oh. Do you play?' Caro had taken the time to glance about the comfortable library as the two of them talked, spotting the chess pieces set up on the table beside the window.

Dominic followed her line of vision. 'Do you?'

'A little,' she answered noncommittally.

His brows rose. 'Really?'

'You do not sound as if you believe me?' Her eyes sparkled with challenge.

He shrugged. 'In my experience, women do not usually play chess.'

'Then I must be an unusual woman, because I believe I play rather well.'

Dominic didn't doubt she was an unusual woman; she had been the source of one surprise after another since he had first met her.

'Would you care for a game before dinner?' she challenged lightly.

He grimaced. 'I think not. I was taught by a grand master,' he explained as Caro looked up at him enquiringly.

As the undisputed chess champion in her family and that included her father, she felt no hesitation in pitting her own considerable ability against Dominic Vaughn's or anyone else's. She was certainly a good enough player that she would not embarrass herself.

She stood up to cross over to the chess-table. The

pieces appeared to have been smoothly carved out of black-and-white marble, the table inlaid with a board of that same beautiful marble. She glanced back to where Dominic still stood beside the fireplace. 'Surely you cannot be refusing to play against me simply because I am a woman?'

'Not at all,' Dominic drawled. 'I simply prefer to play against an opponent I consider to be my equal in the game.'

Her eyes widened. 'How do you know I am not until we have played together?'

He quirked a brow. 'A game in the nursery with your nanny does not equip you to play a champion.'

Caro bristled. 'You are being presumptuous, sir!'

'Concerning your game or the nanny?'

'Both!' Caro was all too well aware how determined Dominic was to learn more of her past. 'But being a gentleman of the *ton*, perhaps you would find it more of a challenge if I were to propose a wager?'

He eyed her guardedly. 'What sort of wager?'

'Are you any further forwards in your enquiries concerning the attack upon Lord Thorne?'

Dominic's expression became even more cautious. 'I am hoping to receive news on the subject later today.'

'But you are not sure?' she pressed.

Dominic's mouth tightened. 'At this precise moment, no.'

Caro nodded briskly. 'In that case, if I win, I would like for you to find me other accommodation sooner rather than later.'

Those silver eyes narrowed. 'Why?'

'I do not have to state a reason, my lord, merely name a forfeit,' she pointed out primly. 'And if you win—'

'Should I not be allowed to choose your own forfeit for myself?' Dominic interjected softly, those silver eyes glittering in challenge.

She drew in a deep breath, not at all sure she had not ventured beyond her depth, after all; Dominic seemed utterly convinced that he would win any game of chess between them. But she could not back down now; she owed it to other females who played chess to defend their reputation against such obvious male bigotry! Besides which, she dearly wished to escape Blackstone House. And the disturbing Lord Dominic Vaughn... 'Name your forfeit, my lord.'

'Dominic.'

Her eyes widened. 'That is your forfeit?'

'That is only an aside request, Caro, and not the actual forfeit,' he said. 'I am sure you will not find it too difficult to do; you seem to have no trouble at all in calling me Dominic before launching yourself into my arms!' Those silver-coloured eyes openly laughed at her now beneath long dark lashes.

Caro's cheeks burned, not at all sure which occasion he was referring to—there had been so many, it seemed! 'Very well, name my forfeit...Dominic.'

He seemed to give the matter some thought. 'You will reveal something of your true self to me, perhaps?'

Caro looked at him warily. She knew of her own ability in playing the game of chess, but Dominic's self-confidence could not be overlooked, either; he was so obviously sure of his ability that he had not even attempted to dispute the forfeit she would demand of him if she were the victor. To agree to tell him something of her true self was not something she had ever intended doing, either now or in the future. But then, neither did she intend allowing him to win this game of chess… 'Very well, I agree.' She gave a haughty inclination of her head.

Dominic lounged back in his chair, his expression one of boredom as the game began, sure that he was wasting both his own time and hers by playing at all.

After only a few more moves in the game he knew that victory was not going to be so easily won. Caro's opening gambit had been an unusual one, and one Dominic had put down to her lack of experience in the game, but as he now studied the pieces on the board he saw that if the game continued on its current path, then she would have him in check for the first time in only three more moves.

'Very good,' he murmured appreciatively as he moved his king out of danger.

Caro could see that, instead of continuing to lounge back uninterestedly, she now had all of Dominic's attention. 'Perhaps we might play in earnest now?' Her heart did a strange leap as he looked up to smile across the table at her. A warm and genuine smile that owed nothing to his usual expression of mockery or disdain, and instead leant a boyish charm to the usual severe austerity of his face.

'I am looking forward to it, Caro,' he replied, his attention now fully on the chessboard.

The maid, Mabel, had come in and attended to the fire, and Simpson had arrived to light several candles whilst the game continued, but neither opponent had even been aware of their presence as they concentrated completely on the chessboard between them.

It had become more than a game of chess to Caro; it had come to represent the inequality of the relationship that currently existed between the two of them. An equality that would not have existed between Lord Dominic Vaughn and Lady Caroline Copeland, but which most definitely existed between Lord Dominic Vaughn and Caro Morton. As such, it had become more than a battle of wills to Caro, and she played like a fiend in her determination not to be beaten.

Something that Dominic was well aware of as he studied her flushed and determined face between narrowed lids. Her eyes were more green than blue in their intensity, and the flush added colour to her otherwise porcelain white cheeks and down across the full swell of her breasts. Those rosy tips were no doubt deeper in colour, too, and were perhaps swollen and begging for the feel of his—

'Check!' Caro announced with barely concealed excitement.

Dominic's attention was reluctant to return to the board rather than considering the taste of Caro's breasts. He moved his own piece out of danger.

Irritation creased Caro's brow before clearing again as she made another move. 'Check.'

Dominic studied the board intently for several seconds. 'I believe that we will only continue in this vein *ad nauseam*, and that this game, therefore, must be declared a draw.'

She eyed him mockingly. 'Unless you were to concede?'

'Or you were?'

She sat back in her chair. 'I think not.'

'Then we will call it a draw.' Dominic said. 'And hope that one of us will be the victor on the morrow.'

'We could play again now—'

'It is time for dinner, Caro,' he murmured after a glance at the clock on the mantel, surprised to learn that a full two hours had passed since they had began to play. Surprised, also, at how much he had enjoyed those two hours.

Caro did not talk as she played, but neither was the silence awkward or uncomfortable. More, despite the fact they were in opposition to one another, it had been a companionable and enjoyable silence. And he, Dominic, decided as the realisation caused him to rise abruptly to his feet, was not a man to be domesticated to his fireside by any woman. Least of all a woman who steadfastly refused to reveal anything of her true self to him!

'Does this mean that we both concede our forfeit or that neither of us does?' she asked.

Dominic's eyes narrowed as he glanced back to where Caro had now risen gracefully from the table. 'Stalemate would seem to imply that neither of us do,' he replied. 'As we are so late I suggest that neither of us bothers to change before dinner.'

'Oh, good.' She gracefully crossed the room on slippered feet as she confided, 'I am so ravenously hungry.'

Dominic found himself laughing despite his earlier uncomfortable thoughts concerning domesticity. 'Has no one ever told you that ladies are supposed to have the appetite and delicacy of a sparrow?' he drawled.

'If they did, then I have forgotten,' Caro retorted as

they strolled through the hallway and into the small candlelit dining room together, another fire alight in the hearth there to warm the room.

'I take it you are now, out of pure contrariness, about to show that you have the appetite and delicacy of an eagle.' Dominic pulled her chair back, lingering behind her a few seconds longer than was strictly necessary as he enjoyed the floral perfume of her hair.

Caro, in the act of draping her napkin across her knee, paused to give the matter some thought before answering. As far as she was aware, she had eaten nothing so far today. 'Perhaps a raven.' Not a good comparison, she realised with an inner wince, when the colour of Dominic's hair reminded her of a raven's wing...

Dominic was chuckling softly as he took his seat opposite hers at the small round table. Not so intimate that their knees actually touched beneath it, but certainly enough to create an atmosphere Caro could have wished did not exist.

She ignored Dominic to smile at Simpson as he entered the room with a soup tureen and began to serve their first course. It was a delicious watercress soup that Caro enjoyed so much that the butler served her a second helping.

'As I said, an eagle...' Dominic muttered so that only she could hear, wincing slightly, but not uttering a sound, as she kicked him on the shin beneath the table with one slipper-covered foot; no doubt it had hurt her more than it had hurt him!

He inwardly approved of the fact that she made no effort to hide her appetite; he had spent far too many evenings with women who picked at their food, and in doing so totally ruined his own appetite. In contrast to those other women, Caro ate just as heartily of the fish course, and her roast beef and vegetables, all followed by some chocolate confection that she ate with even more relish than the previous courses.

So much so that Dominic found himself watching her rather than attempting to eat his own dessert. 'Perhaps you would care to eat mine, too?' He pushed the untouched glass bowl towards her.

Her eyes lit up, before she gave a reluctant shake of her head. 'I really should not...'

'I believe it is a little late for a show of maidenly delicacy,' Dominic teased as he placed the bowl in front of her before standing up to pour himself a glass of the brandy Caro had so obviously disliked earlier. He sat down again to study her as he swirled the brandy round in the glass, easily noting the colour in her cheeks. 'I was commenting on the subject of food, of course...'

That colour deepened. 'If you are going to start being ungentlemanly again—'

'I was not aware that in your eyes I had ever stopped?' Dominic said, raising dark, mocking brows.

Perhaps not, Caro conceded, but there had been something of a ceasefire during and since their game of chess. In fact, she had believed she had even seen a grudging respect in those silver-coloured eyes when the game had ended in a draw. 'What shall we do with the rest of the evening?' She opted for a safer subject.

'I, my dear Caro, am going out—'

'Out?' She frowned after a glance at the gold clock on the mantel. 'But it is almost eleven o'clock.'

He gave an inclination of his head. 'And if Nick's

were open, you would still have a second performance of the evening to get through.'

True. But having spent most of the day sleeping, Caro was not ready to retire to her bedchamber just yet. 'Are you going to see Lord Thorne? If so, perhaps I might come with you?'

'No, on both counts, Caro,' Dominic said; engrossed as he had been in their game of chess, and much as he had enjoyed his dinner, he had nevertheless been continually aware of the fact that the news he had been waiting for concerning Nicholas Brown had not been delivered, leaving him no choice but to now instigate his own plans for the evening. 'I have already visited Osbourne once today, and doubt that a second visit this late in the day would be welcome.' Mrs Gertrude Wilson would most definitely frown upon it! 'And where I am going tonight you definitely cannot follow.'

'Oh.'

Dominic quirked one eyebrow as he saw how flushed Caro's cheeks had become. 'Oh?'

Caro frowned her irritation, with her own naïvety as much as with Dominic Vaughn. Just because he kissed her whenever the mood took him did not mean that he did not have a woman he occasionally spent the night with. That he was not going out in a few minutes to spend the rest of the night in bed with such a woman!

Strange how much even the idea of that should seem so distasteful to her…

She had, Caro realised in dismay, enjoyed Dominic's company this evening. The verbal exchanges. The challenge of trying to best him at chess. Even the teasing in regard to her appetite. She now found it more than unpleasant to be made aware of the possibility he might be spending the rest of the night in bed with some faceless woman.

Which was utterly ridiculous!

She stood up abruptly. 'In that case, with your permission, I believe I will go back into the library and choose a book to read.'

It wasn't too difficult for Dominic to guess what Caro's thoughts had been during these last few minutes of silence: that she imagined it was his intention to spend the night in some willing woman's bed. Much as the idea appealed—it had been some time since Dominic had bedded a woman; those few unsatisfactory forays with Caro did not count when they had left him feeling more physically frustrated than ever—it did not actually enter into his plans for the rest of the night.

No, Dominic's immediate destination had absolutely nothing to do with bedding a woman and more to do with personally paying a visit to Nicholas Brown... 'Do not bother to wait up for me, Caro. I expect to be very late,' he said after he emptied the last of the brandy before placing the glass down upon the table.

Her cheeks were flushed with temper. 'As if I have any interest in what time it will be when—or even if— you should return!'

Dominic chuckled softly as he strolled over to the door. 'Sweet dreams, Caro.'

'As long as they are not of you then I am sure they will be!' she snapped.

He paused in the doorway to glance back at her. 'I very much doubt that I shall ever have the dubious pleasure of featuring in any young girl's dreams,' he said drily before closing the door softly behind him.

Dominic could not be sure, but he thought he might have heard the tinkling sound of glass shattering on the other side of that closed door...

Chapter Eight

It was some hours later when Dominic finally returned to Blackstone House, and he could not help smiling slightly as the attentive Simpson opened the door for him as if it were three o'clock in the afternoon rather than the morning.

'Mrs Morton is in the library, my lord,' the butler advised softly.

Dominic came to an abrupt halt halfway across the marble entrance hall and turned back sharply. 'What the devil is she still doing in there?'

The butler turned from locking and bolting the front door. 'I believe she fell asleep whilst reading, my lord. She looked so peaceful, I did not like to wake her.'

Dominic felt no such qualms as he glanced in the direction of the library, his expression grim. 'Get yourself to bed, man. I will deal with Mrs Morton.'

'Very good, my lord.' The elderly man gave a stiff bow. 'I—I believe that Mrs Morton may have been upset earlier, my lord.' he added as Dominic walked in the direction of the library.

Dominic was slower to turn this time. 'Upset?'

'I believe she was crying, my lord.' Simpson looked pained.

What the hell! The last thing he felt like dealing with tonight was a woman's tears. Or, as was usually the case, having to guess the reason for those tears. Whatever could have happened to reduce the indomitable Caro to tears? Perhaps the danger he had warned her of had become all too real to her once she was left alone for the evening?

Whatever the reason it gave him a distinctly unpleasant sensation in the pit of his stomach to think of Caro alone and upset…

He could see the evidence of her tears on the pallor of her cheeks once he had entered the library and stood looking down at her as she lay curled up asleep in the wing-backed armchair beside the fire, the book she had been reading still lying open upon her knees.

He was also struck by how incredibly young and vulnerable she looked without the light of battle in her eyes and the flush of temper upon her cheeks. So young and vulnerable, in fact, that Dominic questioned how she could ever have survived her first week in London without falling victim to some disaster.

Not that he imagined for one moment that Caro would have succumbed quietly—she did not seem to do anything quietly!—but she wasn't physically strong enough to fight off a male predator, and her youth and lack of a protector would have made her easy prey for the seedy underworld of a city such as this one. As it was, he had no doubt that Caro had Drew Butler's visible protection to thank for her physical well being this past week, at least.

If Dominic had needed any reassurance that he had done the right thing in now placing Caro in his protection, then he had received it this evening when he'd visited Nicholas Brown at his home in Cheapside.

The bastard son of a titled gentleman and some long-forgotten prostitute, Brown, whilst now giving the appearance of wealth, had in fact grown up on the streets of London, and was as hardened and tough as any of the cut-throats that walked those darkened streets. A toughness he had taken advantage of by building himself a lucrative business empire that often catered to the less acceptable excesses of the *ton*; Nick's had been the more respectable of the three gambling clubs the man owned.

Within minutes of Dominic being admitted to Brown's house earlier, the other man had had the unmitigated gall to offer to allow the masked lady to sing at one of his other clubs, until such time as Nick's reopened. An offer Dominic had felt no hesitation in refusing on Caro's behalf!

Looking down at her now as she slept the sleep of the innocent, he could only shudder at the thought of her ever being exposed to the vicious and seedy underbelly of Nicholas Brown's world. At the same time Dominic feared that Brown, with his many spies in the London underworld, might already know that the young woman now staying with him and masquerading as his widowed cousin was that same masked lady...

Brown had not by word or deed revealed whether

or not this was the case, but the fact that the other man had denied hearing any gossip or rumours concerning the perpetrators of yesterday's attack on Nathaniel Thorne, when directly asked by Dominic, was suspicious in itself; Brown was a man privy to all the secrets of the London underworld.

Like the officer and soldier he had once been, Dominic had now only retreated in order to decide how best to deal with the villain.

But first he must see Caro safely delivered to her bed...

Dominic's expression softened as he picked the book up from her knee and placed it on the side table before bending down to scoop her up into his arms. She stirred only slightly before placing her arms about his neck and sighing contentedly as she lay her head down against his shoulder.

For all that she'd had such a hearty appetite earlier, she weighed almost nothing at all, and it was no effort for Dominic to carry her up the wide staircase to her bedchamber, to where the fire was alight, and candles were burning on the dressing table to light the room in readiness for when Caro retired for the night.

Dominic crossed the room to lay her down upon the bedcovers, having every intention of straightening and leaving her there, only to discover that he could not as her arms were still clasped tight about his neck. 'Release me, Caro,' he instructed softly. Her only answer was to tighten that stranglehold to the point that Dominic had to sit down on the side of the bed or risk causing her discomfort.

As he had absolutely no intention of having to remain

in this uncomfortable position for what was left of the night, he had no choice but to wake her. The Lord knew she was going to be indignant enough when she awoke and found he had carried her up to bed, without exacerbating the situation by giving into the temptation Dominic now felt to take off his boots, lie down beside her and then fall asleep with his head resting upon her breasts! 'Wake up, Caro,' he encouraged gruffly.

An irritated frown creased her brow and she wrinkled her nose endearingly before her lids were slowly raised and she looked up at him with sleepy sea-green eyes. 'Dominic?'

He raised mocking brows. 'Were you expecting someone else?'

Caro stilled, knowing by the candle lighting the room and the silence of the house that it must be very late. Which posed the question—what was Dominic doing in her bedchamber? More to the point, how did she come to be in her bedchamber? The last thing she remembered was sitting beside the fire in the library reading a book—

'You fell asleep and I carried you up the stairs to bed,' Dominic answered the puzzle for her.

Even if it did not provide the answer as to what he was still doing here! Or why her fingers were linked at his nape, and in doing so bringing his face down much too close to Caro's own?

She slowly unlinked those fingers, although her arms stayed about his shoulders. 'That was—very kind of you.'

He gave a hard smile. 'I am sure we are both aware that kindness is not a part of my nature.'

Caro could not agree. How could she, when he had saved her time and time again, from dangers she had not even been aware existed when she had left Hampshire to embark on what she had thought would be a wonderful adventure?

And in doing so, had left her two sisters, and everything in life that was familiar to her...

It was a fact that had been brought sharply home to Caro earlier today, when she had seen that young girl in the park who reminded her so much of Elizabeth. It did not matter that it had not actually been her sister; the familiarity, along with the game of chess she and Dominic had played earlier and which had so reminded her of the times she had played the board game with her father, had been enough to incite an aching homesickness once Caro was left alone, for both her home and family.

Dominic frowned as he saw the emotions flickering across her expressive face. 'Simpson seems to believe you have been...upset, whilst I was out this evening?'

That open expression immediately became a frown as she finally drew her arms from about his neck to push the curling tendrils of her hair back from her face. 'If I was, then I assure you, it had absolutely nothing to do with your own absence.'

This was more like the Caro he was used to dealing with! 'With what, then?'

She looked more cross than upset now. 'Does there have to be a reason?'

Where this particular woman was concerned? Yes. Most definitely. Dominic did not believe her to be the type of woman to give in to tears without good reason.

Just as her pride would not allow her to now reveal to him the reason for those tears. 'Perhaps you have found the events of the past few days more disturbing than you had first thought?'

'I believe they would have reduced any woman of sensitivity to tears,' she came back tartly.

And far too quickly for Dominic to be convinced that the excuse he had so conveniently given her was the true reason for Caro's upset. But he could see, by the stubbornness of her expression, that this was the only explanation she was about to give. 'I should leave you now and allow you to prepare for bed,' he rasped.

'You should.' Caro nodded agreement.

Still neither of them moved, Caro lying back against the pillows, Dominic sitting beside her on the bed looking so dark and handsome in the candlelight, the hard and handsome savagery of his face made to appear even more so with that jagged scar upon his cheek.

It was a ragged and uneven scar, as if the skin had been ripped apart. 'How did it happen?' Caro finally gave in to the longing she had felt to lightly touch that scar with her fingertips.

Dominic flinched but did not move away. 'Caro—'

'Tell me, please,' she encouraged huskily.

His mouth tightened. 'It was a French sabre.'

Caro's eyes widened before her gaze returned to the scar. 'It does not have the look of the clean stroke of a sword…'

Dominic gave a dismissive shrug, more than a little unnerved at the gentle touch of her fingertips against his ragged flesh. 'That is because I did not make a good job of it when I sewed the two sides together!'

Her eyes widened. 'You sewed the wound yourself?'

'It was a fierce battle, with many injured, and the physicians were too busy with my seriously wounded and dying men for me to trouble them over a little cut upon my face.'

'But—'

'Caro, it is late— What the—?' Dominic broke off, shocked to his very core, when she sat up to place her lips against the scar on his cheek. 'What on earth do you think you are doing?' He grasped hold of her arms to hold her firmly away from him as he glared down at her.

Caro ignored Dominic's anger and the firm grasp of his fingers upon her arms, too concerned—disturbed— by thoughts of the terrible wound he had suffered and then stitched himself. No doubt completely without the aid of the alcohol that would have numbed the pain but at the same time impaired his judgement. Just the thought of it was enough to make her shudder. 'War is barbaric!'

Dominic gave a ruefully bitter smile. 'So is tyranny.'

Reminding Caro that, although this man now gave every appearance of being a fashionable and dissolute man about town, he had admitted to being a soldier, an officer in charge of men, all of them fighting to keep England safe from the greedy hands of Napoleon.

Her gaze was once again drawn back to the scar upon his cheek. A daily reminder to him, no doubt, of the suffering and hardships of that long and bloody war. 'You were a hero.'

'Do not attempt to romanticise me, Caro!' Dominic stood up abruptly, a nerve pulsing in his tightly clenched jaw as he scowled down at her.

In doing so, he could not help but notice the way her breasts swelled over the top of her gown as she rested back on her elbows. Or how several enticing curls had come loose from their pins and now lay against the bareness of her shoulders. He acknowledged that at this moment his arousal was hard and throbbing, and that he wanted nothing more than to push her back against the pillows before ripping the clothes from her body and taking her with a fierceness that caused his engorged erection to ache and throb anew!

'I am not, nor will I ever be, any woman's hero,' he dismissed harshly.

Caro swallowed hard as she saw the fierce desire in those glittering silver eyes. She knew instinctively that Dominic was poised on the very edge of control; that one wrong word from her and he would in all probability lose it completely.

Caro, her emotions already so raw—from her fear during the brawl that had broken out at Nick's the previous night, the brutality of the attack against Lord Thorne that had followed, being whisked away by Dominic to the indulgent splendour of Blackstone House, and then that sighting earlier today of the young girl that had so reminded her of her younger sister—could not help but relish the very idea of Dominic losing the firm grip he was attempting to maintain upon his control.

She moistened her lips with the tip of her tongue. 'That scar upon your face says otherwise, Dominic.'

Dominic knew that women were more often than not repulsed by the ugly scar that ran the length of his face from eye to jaw; Caro had already assured him she felt no such repulsion. But then, Dominic already knew that she was unlike any other woman he had ever met…

He should leave. He needed to put distance between himself and Caro. Now!

And yet something in her expression held him back. The soft sea-green of her eyes, perhaps. The flush upon her cheeks. The pouting softness of her parted lips...

'You should tell me to go, Caro!' Even as he said the words Dominic was striding back to the bedside and pulling her roughly up on to her knees. He looked down at her fiercely. 'If it should transpire that you are a married woman—'

She gasped. 'I am not—'

It was all the encouragement Dominic needed as his mouth came down crushingly against hers and cut off further speech.

Caro felt on fire as his lips against hers gave no quarter, no gentleness, his arms like steel bands about her waist as he curved her body up into the uncompromising hardness of his, allowing her no time or chance for further thoughts as her fingers clung to the wide width of his shoulders.

Nothing else existed at that moment but Dominic. His lips hungry, his body hard and unyielding. His hands warm and restless as they caressed down the length of her spine before cupping her bottom and lifting her into him, a low growl sounding in his throat as he ground his thighs against her.

Caro seemed to melt from the inside out, as she felt the evidence of his desire pressing against her, so hard, so hot and pulsing, and inducing a reciprocal and aching heat inside her as her breasts swelled and between her thighs moistened. That heat increased, intensified as one of Dominic's hands cupped the full swell of one of her aching breasts before he pulled the material down and bared the fullness of that breast to his caress, capturing the hardened tip to roll it between fingers and thumb.

Caro groaned low in her throat as those caresses bordered on the very knife-edge between pleasure and pain, and rendering them all the more arousing because of it as she arched her breast into that caress even as Dominic's mouth continued to hungrily devour hers.

Her lips parted, invited, as Dominic ran his tongue moistly between them, gently at first, and then more forcefully as he thrust into the heat of her mouth in the same rhythm as he caressed the hard tip of her breast—

'No!' Dominic suddenly wrenched his mouth from hers, eyes glittering furiously as he straightened her gown before he put her away from him.

Caro felt dazed, disorientated, hurt by the suddenness of his rejection. 'Dominic—'

'I may be accused of many things, Caro,' he bit out harshly, hands clenched behind his back as though to resist more temptation. 'And I have no doubt that I am guilty of most of them.' His mouth twisted self-derisively. 'But, married or not, I do not intend to add seducing an unprotected female guest in my own home to that list, even when I am invited to do so!'

Could it be called seduction when Caro had been such a willing participant? When she still longed, ached, for the touch of Dominic's hands and mouth upon her? When just thinking of those things made her tremble in anticipation?

When his last comment showed that he was aware of all those things…

One glance at the savage fury on Dominic's hard and uncompromising face was enough to tell Caro that the moment of madness had passed. For him, at least... All that remained was for her to try to salvage at least some of her own pride. 'I did not invite you to seduce me, Dominic!'

His mouth thinned. 'You invite seduction with every glance and every word you speak.'

'That is unfair!' Caro gasped at the accusation. Yes, her body still ached with longing, but she had only to look at Dominic to see the evidence of his own hard arousal beneath his pantaloons.

'Is it?' Dominic's nostrils flared as his gaze raked over her mercilessly. This woman tempted him, seduced him, with just her presence. So much so that he did not believe he could be under the same roof with her for even one more night and retain his honour. 'Go to bed, Caro,' he instructed harshly. 'We will talk of this again in the morning.'

'I—what is there to talk about?' She looked confused.

Dominic's lids narrowed until his eyes were only visible as silver slithers. 'As I said, the morning will be soon enough—'

'I would rather we talked *now*!' Her eyes flashed in warning.

A warning that Dominic had no intention of heeding. Damn it, he had been a commissioned officer in the army for five years, had been responsible for the lives and discipline of the dozens of men under his command; the temper of one tiny woman did not concern or impress him. 'I have said the morning will be soon enough, Caro,' he repeated firmly.

Caro's cheeks flushed hotly. 'I am beginning to find your arrogance a little tiresome, Dominic.'

He gave a humourless smile. 'Then let us both hope that you do not have to suffer it for much longer.'

Caro sincerely hoped that meant his arrangements for her removal from Blackstone House were progressing as quickly as he had hoped they might; she really did not think she could bear to stay here with him for too much longer.

She sank back on the bed once Dominic had left her bedchamber and closed the door softly behind him; the tears that fell down her cheeks now were for a completely different reason than those she had shed earlier tonight.

What was it about Dominic Vaughn that made her behave so shamelessly? To the point that just now Caro had been practically begging for the return of his kisses, for his hands upon her breasts? Whatever the reason, she knew she was seriously in danger of succumbing to the temptation of those kisses and caresses if she remained at Blackstone house with him for much longer…

'Will Lord Vaughn be down soon, do you think, Simpson?' Caro enquired lightly of the butler at nine o'clock the next morning as she sat alone at the breakfast table, drinking tea and eating a slice of buttered toast.

What had remained of the night, once Dominic had left her bedchamber, had been long and restless for

Caro, as she'd tried to fall asleep but was unable to do so, her thoughts too disturbed after yet another incident of finding herself in the earl's seductive arms. All of those disturbing thoughts had come down to the simple fact that it was becoming nearly impossible for Caro to remain at Blackstone House, under Dominic Vaughn's protection.

'His lordship breakfasted and left the house some time ago, Mrs Morton,' the butler answered her question.

Caro's eyes widened. 'He did?'

'Yes, madam.'

Caro's heart sank. Much as she appreciated the grandeur of Blackstone House, and the attentiveness of the servants, the mere thought of having to idle away the morning here alone was unthinkable, reminding her as it did of the tediousness of the life she had been forced to lead at Shoreley Hall for the first twenty years of her life.

Strange, it had only been two weeks since she had come to London, and yet during that time—and despite some of the more *risqué* aspects of her behaviour!— Caro had come to enjoy having control over her own actions. So much so that she could no longer bear the thought of having her movements restricted in this way, least of all by a man whose emotions she could not even begin to understand…

She looked up to smile at the attentive Simpson as he stood ready to provide her with more tea or toast. 'Does his lordship have another carriage that I might use?' Caro held her breath as she waited to see if Dominic had acted with his usual efficiency and left instructions with the servants to restrict her comings and goings from Blackstone House.

The elderly man nodded. 'His lordship keeps four carriages for his use when in London, Mrs Morton.'

Caro's heart began to pound loudly in her chest. 'And do you suppose I might use one of these other carriages?'

The butler gave a courtly bow. 'If you wish, I am sure one can be readied for your use as soon as you have finished breakfast.'

Caro released her breath slowly, her features carefully schooled so as not to give away her inner feelings of elation; Dominic had not had the time—or, as was more likely, in his arrogance, he had decided he did not need to bother—to issue the instruction that Caro was never to leave Blackstone House unaccompanied.

Not that it was her intention to leave for good. She was not so foolish, and knew enough to believe Dominic when he'd warned of the danger that might be lurking outside these four walls—indeed, the attack on Lord Thorne was proof enough! But a drive in one of Dominic's own carriages, driven by his own servants, was surely safe enough?

'I do wish, Simpson,' she told the butler brightly. She stood up. 'In fact, I will go back upstairs this minute and collect my bonnet and gloves.' Caro hurried from the room to run lightly up the stairs, anxious to absent herself from Blackstone House before Dominic had the chance to return and prevent her from going.

Chapter Nine

Had Dominic ever been this angry in his life before?

He thought not; after all, until three days ago he had been in blissful ignorance of Caro Morton's very existence! Now, after years spent totally in control of his emotions, Dominic found himself the opposite; one minute aroused by her, the next enchanted, but more often than not, furiously angry. At this moment he was most definitely the latter as he had returned to Blackstone House at a little after ten o'clock, only to learn from Simpson that Caro had taken advantage of Dominic's absence and fled to heaven knew where. More insultingly, that she had made that escape in one of his own carriages!

Dominic paced the hallway as he waited for the return of that carriage so that he might learn where, exactly, the driver had taken her. And while he paced he listed all the ways in which he was going to punish Caro for her recklessness when he finally caught up with her. As he most assuredly would. He wanted an

explanation as to exactly what she had thought she was
doing by placing herself in danger in this way—

'I believe Mrs Morton has every intention of returning, my lord.' Simpson spoke diffidently, tentatively,
behind him, having been made aware several minutes
ago as to his employer's displeasure at finding Caro
gone.

Dominic turned sharply, gaze narrowed. 'And what
gives you that impression, Simpson?'

The other man gave a slight flinch at he obviously
heard his employer's continued displeasure. 'I took the
liberty, after our earlier conversation, of having one
of the maids to go upstairs and check Mrs Morton's
bedchamber.'

'And?' Dominic frowned darkly.

'All of Mrs Morton's things are just as she left them,
my lord.' The man looked relieved at being able to make
this pronouncement.

As far as Dominic was aware, all of her things now
consisted of only the few belongings left to her after
her other gowns had been consigned to the incinerator
and he did not believe Caro felt strongly enough about
any of them to return for them.

Just as Caro had felt no hesitation in leaving Blackstone House the moment Dominic's back was turned,
despite his warnings. That, perhaps more than anything
else, was what rankled, when Dominic's whole existence seemed to have been invaded by her in the three
days since they had met. Not a pleasant realisation for
a man who had long ago decided he would never allow
any woman, even the wife needed to provide his heir, to

dictate how he should live his life, let alone take charge of it in the way protecting Caro seemed to have done.

Nevertheless, the circumstances of the Nicholas Brown situation were such that Dominic could not—as he told himself he dearly wished to do—rid himself of that particular imposition just yet. The fact that Caro had not only attempted to leave Blackstone House unaccompanied this morning, but had succeeded, showed that one of them, at least, needed to have a care for her welfare.

Damn it.

Dominic gave a weary sigh as he answered his butler, 'I greatly admire your optimism, Simpson, but I am afraid in this instance I feel it is sadly misplaced. It would seem that Mrs Morton is dissatisfied with London society and has decided to return to her previous life.' He spoke with care, mindful of the fact that no matter what the household servants might think or say of this situation in private, publicly, at least, Dominic must continue to claim Caro as his widowed cousin.

The more Dominic considered her disappearance this morning, the less inclined he was to believe that she would have left without first saying her goodbyes to Drew Butler and Ben Jackson…and Dominic knew both those men were at Nick's this morning, overseeing the repairs.

'I believe I will go out again, Simpson.' Dominic collected up his hat and cane. 'If Mrs Morton should return in my absence…'

'I will advise her of your concern, my lord,' the older man assured as he held the door open attentively.

His concern? Dominic's feelings, as he climbed back

into his curricle, were inclined more towards wringing her pretty neck than showing her concern. A pleasure he continued to relish for the whole of the time it took to manoeuvre the greys through the busy London streets to Nick's.

He had been too hasty earlier, Dominic acknowledged as he entered the gambling club some half an hour later—now was the time he felt more angry than he ever had in his life before!

And, once again, Caro was the reason for that emotion.

As was usual at this time of day, the gambling club appeared closed and deserted from the outside, but almost as soon as Dominic had entered the premises by the back door he had been aware of the murmur of voices coming from the main salon. The deep rumble of Drew Butler and Ben Jackson's voices were easily recognisable, as was the lightness of Caro's laughter, but there was also a third male voice that Dominic found shockingly familiar.

The reason for that became obvious as Dominic stood in the doorway of the salon looking through narrowed lids at the four people seated around one of the tables: Drew Butler, Ben Jackson, Caro—and, of all people, the previous owner of the club, Nicholas Brown!

Admittedly, Drew and Ben were seated protectively on either side of Caro, with Brown sitting opposite. But that protection was completely nullified by the admiration gleaming in Brown's calculating brown gaze as he looked across the table at Caro beneath hooded lids.

The fact that the four of them appeared to be enjoying a bottle of best brandy, at only eleven o'clock in the morning, only increased his displeasure. 'I take it from your lack of activity, Drew, that all of the repairs have been completed?'

Caro gave a guilty start at the silky and yet nevertheless unmistakable sarcasm in Dominic's tone, and instantly saw that guilt reflected in the faces of at least two of the three men seated at the table with her. Drew Butler and Ben Jackson instantly rose to their feet and excused themselves before returning to the aforementioned repairs.

Only the relaxed and charming Nicholas Brown appeared unperturbed at the unexpected interruption as he turned to smile unconcernedly at the younger man. 'I am to blame for the distraction, I am afraid, Blackstone. After our conversation last night I felt I ought to come and see things here for myself. Finding the beautiful Mrs Morton here, too, has been an unexpected pleasure.' He turned to bestow a warm smile on her.

Caro blushed prettily at the compliment, although that colour faded just as quickly, and a shiver of apprehension ran the length of her spine, as she saw the dark scowl on Dominic's face as he looked across at her; his eyes were that steely grey that betokened banked fury, his cheekbones hard beneath the tautness of his skin, his mouth a thin and uncompromising line, and his jaw set challengingly. Although whether that displeasure was because of Nicholas Brown's admiration for her, or because Caro had so blatantly disobeyed his instruction earlier concerning leaving Blackstone House unaccompanied, she was as yet unsure.

Caro was inclined to think it might be the latter; after the way in which he had left her bedchamber so abruptly during the night after rejecting her, she could not think of any reason why he should be in the least upset by Nicholas Brown's attentions towards her. Although that man's comment, concerning the two men having spoken together last night, seemed to indicate that Dominic had been telling the truth when he'd claimed he was not going out with the intention of visiting a mistress.

'You must excuse my cousin, Brown. I am afraid she is fresh from the country, and unfamiliar with the dictates of London society that prevent her from venturing out without her maid,' Dominic bit out coldly as he strode across the room to stand beside the table where Caro and Brown now sat facing each other. Although a brief glance at the tabletop at least revealed that she had a half-drunk cup of tea in front of her rather than having joined the men in a glass of brandy. Dominic wondered with abstract amusement where in the gambling club Butler had managed to obtain the china cup, let alone the tea to put in it!

'I assure you, no apology is necessary, Blackstone,' Brown came back smoothly. 'Indeed, I find such independence of nature in a beautiful woman refreshing.'

Caro's cheeks had coloured at the rebuke in Dominic's tone. 'I had thought to offer my assistance to Mr Butler after you informed me of the damage that had occurred here.'

Dominic raised dark brows. 'And I had similarly expected you at Blackstone House when I returned.'

Caro raised her brows. 'You had already left the house when I came down for breakfast, and I did not relish the idea of spending the rest of the morning alone.'

'Perhaps I should withdraw and allow the two of you to continue this conversation in private?' Brown offered lightly.

Dominic's narrowed his gaze on the older man, not convinced for a moment by the innocence of the other man's expression. With his dark and fashionable clothes and politeness of manner, he gave every outward appearance of being the gentleman and yet he most certainly was not; it was well known that he would sell his mother to the highest bidder if it was found to be in his own best interests.

Nor was Dominic unaware of the significance of the older man's visit here so soon after their conversation about the attack on Nathaniel the evening before. It was only whether or not Brown knew of Caro's identity as the masked lady appearing at Nick's that was still in question...

Although Dominic could not attach blame to any young woman—including Caro—for being flattered by the older man's marked attention; at forty-two, with dark and fashionable styled hair, and a roguishly hand-some face, no doubt the rakish Nicholas Brown was enough to set the heart of any young woman aflutter.

'Not at all, Brown,' Dominic dismissed with a casual tone he was far from feeling as he took the seat that Drew Butler had recently vacated. 'My rebuke was only made to indicate my disappointment at not finding my cousin at home when I returned earlier.'

Caro glared at him beneath lowered lashes, knowing very well that his emotion had not been 'disappointment' at not finding her exactly where he had left her—he had been, and obviously still was, furious. 'I am to come and go as I please, I hope, my lord,' she said airily, choosing to ignore the retribution promised in Dominic's pale silver eyes for this open challenge to his previous instructions concerning her movements to and from Blackstone House.

'Not without your maid—'

'Perhaps we should, after all, discuss this later?' Caro interrupted what she was sure was going to be yet another verbal reprimand concerning the inadvisability of her having ventured out alone on to the London streets. 'I am sure that neither of us wishes to bore Mr Brown any further with the triviality of what is merely a family disagreement.'

'On the contrary, Mrs Morton, I find I am highly diverted by it.' The older man eyed them both speculatively.

It was a speculation that Caro did not in the least care for. 'You must forgive poor Dominic, Mr Brown.' She reached out to lightly rest her gloved hand on the back of Dominic's as it lay on the tabletop. 'I am afraid my widowed state has made him feel he has been placed in a position where he has to act the role of my protector. Much like an older brother, or perhaps even a father.'

Dominic was not fooled for a moment by the coy flutterings of silky lashes over those blue-green eyes, knowing from experience that she did not have a coy bone in her gracefully beautiful body. Nicholas Brown was just as aware of her insincerity, if the appreciative humour sparkling in the darkness of his eyes as he looked at her was any indication…

Dominic turned his hand over and captured Caro's gloved fingers tightly within his grasp. 'I assure you, my dear cousin, my feelings towards you have never been in the least fraternal *or* paternal.' He lifted her hand, his gaze easily holding her widened one captive as he slowly, and very deliberately, placed a kiss within her gloved palm. He then had the satisfaction of watching as the indignant colour warmed her cheeks.

'I see the way of things now…' Nicholas Brown gave an appreciative laugh as he rose elegantly to his feet. 'I hope I did not cause offence by any of my earlier comments, Blackstone?' His movements were languid as he straightened his cuffs beneath his expertly tailored black superfine.

Dominic's fingers tightened even more firmly about Caro's, preventing her from snatching her hand away, as he looked up at the older man challengingly. 'Not in the least, Brown. I can see that in future I shall have to make sure I remain constantly at Caro's side in order to provide her with suitable amusement.' His voice had hardened in warning over that last statement, a warning he knew the other man was fully aware of as that calculating brown gaze met his in shrewd assessment.

Caro was very aware that Dominic had been manipulating the conversation these past few minutes. And in a way that she did not in the least care for; after the things he had both said and implied, she believed that the handsome and charming Mr Nicholas Brown could come to only one possible conclusion concerning the Earl of Blackstone's relationship with his 'cousin'!

'Perhaps, if you have time, Mr Brown, you would care to come for a turn about the park with me before taking your leave?'

Dominic had the grim satisfaction in seeing Caro's triumphant expression turn to a wince as his fingers tightened about hers. 'I do not think that advisable, Caro,' he grated harshly. 'For one thing, it has turned a little chill.' His tone implied that it was going to get a lot chillier! 'I am afraid Caro and I must also go to another appointment, Brown,' he informed the other man distantly.

Nicholas Brown turned to give Caro a courtly bow before handing her his card. 'You have only to contact me if you should ever again feel a need for company during another of your jaunts about London, Mrs Morton.'

Nicholas Brown would only ever be allowed to accompany Caro anywhere over Dominic's dead body! Which, he allowed grimly, was a distinct possibility if she continued to behave so recklessly…

'You little fool!' Dominic's teeth were tightly clenched together as he returned from dismissing the carriage Caro had arrived in earlier, a nerve now pulsing in the hard set of his jaw, the scar upon his cheek once again a livid slash as he lifted her up into his curricle as if she weighed no more than a feather.

She bristled indignantly. 'I do not think there is any need—'

'Believe me, Caro, you do not want to hear what my

particular needs are at this moment in time.' He gave
her a silencing glare.

'You—' Caro's second protest was arrested in her
throat as Dominic urged his highly strung greys on to
what she considered to be a highly dangerous speed.
Not that she did not have every confidence that he was
in complete command of the sleek and powerful horses,
but she did fear for the safety of the occupants of the
other carriages who were driving at a more sedate pace
along the busy cobbled streets.

Streets that did not look in the least familiar... 'This
does not look like the way back to Blackstone House?'

If anything Dominic's jaw clenched even tighter.
'Possibly because it is not.'

'But—'

Dominic had turned and speared her with eyes that
glittered a pale and dangerous silver. 'Unless you wish
for me to stop the curricle this instant, and warm your
bottom to the degree that you will not be able to sit
down again for a week, then I urgently advise that you
not say another word for the duration of our journey!'

Caution was not normally a part of Caro's nature,
but she decided that in this instance it was perhaps
the wisest course; Dominic was angry enough at this
moment to actually carry out that scandalous threat!

That Dominic had been angry at finding her gone
from Blackstone House in his absence was in no doubt.
That he had been put to the trouble of seeking her out
had obviously not improved his temper. That he had
found her in the company of the charming Mr Nicholas
Brown only seemed to have added to that displeasure.

Why any of those things should necessitate Dominic

now behaving with the savagery of a barbarian, Caro had no idea. Neither did she think it sensible at this moment—indeed, it might be highly detrimental to her health—to question him further.

She looked about her curiously as Dominic turned the curricle on to one of the city's quieter residential streets, the wide arc of cream-fronted town houses along this tree-lined avenue nowhere near as magnificent as Blackstone House, but of a style that was nevertheless elegant as well as quietly genteel. She turned to Dominic with a guarded frown. 'Are we to go visiting?'

His mouth twisted scathingly. 'Hardly.'

'Then why are we here?'

They were here because Dominic had realised, after almost making love to her last night, that for Caro's sake, as well as his own, he could not allow her to remain within his own household for a single night longer. That having her so freely available to him at Blackstone House was a temptation he was finding it increasingly hard to resist. The only solution to that dilemma, he'd felt, was to move Caro to other premises as quickly as was possible. With the added security of being able to staff that establishment with men and women Dominic could trust to ensure that she did not repeat this morning's recklessness.

In fact, the sooner she was made aware that the oh-so-charming Mr Nicholas Brown was, in fact, the danger Dominic was attempting to protect her from, the better for them all!

Dominic brought the curricle to a halt in front of the three-storeyed terraced house he'd had prepared for Caro's arrival only that morning, allowing an immediately attentive groom to take hold of the horses before he jumped lightly down to the pavement. He moved around to the other side of the carriage to raise his hand with a politeness he was far from feeling. 'Caro?' he prompted tersely as she remained seated.

Caro's earlier puzzlement had obviously turned to wariness as she stubbornly refused to take his hand and step down from the curricle. 'What are we doing here, Dominic?'

Dominic was not a man best known for his patience, and what little he possessed had already been pushed to its limit this morning by this infuriating young woman. Neither did he care to explain himself in the middle of the street. 'Will you step down voluntarily, or must I employ other, perhaps less dignified, measures?'

Her eyes flashed the same sea-green as her gown. 'You did not seem to have the slightest thought for my dignity earlier when you made a show of me in front of Mr Brown!'

'It is my dignity I referred to now, and not your own.' Dominic eyed her quellingly.

'Then let me assure you that I have absolutely no intention of going anywhere with you until you have explained— Dominic...!' The last came out as a surprised squeak as he wasted no further time on argument but took Caro by the hand to pull her forwards on the seat before throwing her over one of his shoulders. 'How dare you? Put me down this instant!'

No, Dominic acknowledged grimly as he began to walk down the path towards the house, dignity certainly had no part in these proceedings!

Chapter Ten

It was a little difficult for Caro to take in the unfamiliarity of her surroundings when she was hanging upside-down over one of Dominic Vaughn's broad shoulders. Even so, she did manage to take note of the quiet elegance of the hallway once they were inside the house, and several doors leading off it to what were probably salons and a dining room.

Several servants stood just inside the hallway as the Earl of Blackstone calmly handed one of them his hat before he began to ascend the staircase with Caro still thrown over his shoulder.

'Not a word!' he warned softly as he obviously guessed she was about to voice another protest.

Caro clamped her lips together, her cheeks red with mortification as the servants below continued to watch the two of them until Dominic had rounded a corner to enter a long hallway. 'You will be made to regret this indignity if it is the last thing I ever do!' she hissed furiously.

He gave a scathing snort. 'If I could be sure that was the outcome, I might allow you that privilege!'

'You are despicable! An overbearing, arrogant bully—' Her flow of insults came to an abrupt halt as Dominic entered one of the bedchambers and tilted her forwards over his shoulder before throwing her unceremoniously down on to a bed. Caro barely had time to glare her annoyance up at him before she suffered the further indignity of having her bonnet tilt forwards over her eyes as she bounced inelegantly upon the mattress.

Her eyes glittered up at him furiously as she pushed the bonnet back into place. 'How dare you treat me in this high-handed manner?'

'How dare you completely disobey my instructions this morning and leave Blackstone House unaccompanied?' Dominic thundered, appearing completely unaffected by her indignation as he glowered down at her.

Her eyes narrowed in warning. 'I do not consider myself in need of your permission concerning anything I may, or may not, choose to do!' She drew in an angry breath. 'Neither does anything I have done this morning compare to your outrageous behaviour of just now.'

'I beg to differ.' He eyed her coldly, dark hair rakishly ruffled, although the rest of his appearance was as elegantly fashionable as always: perfectly tied neckcloth against snowy white linen, a deep grey superfine over a paler grey waistcoat and black pantaloons above brown-and-black Hessians.

His sartorial elegance made Caro even more aware of her own dishevelled appearance. Her sea-green gown was in disarray, rumpled from where she had been thrown down on to the bed, her hair even more so as she sat up to untie and remove the matching bonnet completely.

She gave an unladylike snort as she threw the bonnet aside. 'I do not believe you have ever begged for anything in your life.'

'No,' he acknowledged unrepentantly. 'Nor am I about to start now.'

'What are we doing here, Dominic?' Caro still felt agitated by the fact that he appeared to have carried her into the home of someone she did not even know; there was no way she could know the owner of this house when she was unacquainted with anyone in London except Dominic himself. And Drew Butler and Ben Jackson, of course. And now Nicholas Brown.

Dominic watched coldly as Caro tried unsuccessfully to tidy the waywardness of her curls. 'I am more concerned at this moment with the fact that your recklessness in going to Nick's this morning may result in much more serious repercussions than what you view as the indignity of being carried against your will into this house.'

Caro ceased fussing with her hair to look up at him scornfully. 'You are being ridiculous. There was no danger involved in my choosing to visit Mr Butler and Ben—'

'And Nicholas Brown?' Dominic's nostrils flared angrily. 'Do you believe yourself to have been in absolutely no danger from him, too?'

Her chin rose. 'Mr Brown was charming, and behaved the perfect gentleman in my company.'

Dominic gave a fierce scowl. 'Ben Jackson is more of a gentleman than Nicholas Brown.'

She eyed him haughtily. 'After your most recent behaviour, I am inclined to believe Ben to be more of a gentleman than you, too!'

Dominic's eyes narrowed to icy cold slits, his jaw clenching as he once again fought the battle to retain his usual control over his emotions, rather than letting them control him. It was a battle he had been destined to lose from the moment he'd walked into Nick's earlier and saw Caro calmly sitting down and drinking tea with the man he believed responsible for the attack on Nathaniel Thorne. As for being a gentleman, Brown was a man whose rakish handsomeness often occasioned him being invited into the bedchambers of married ladies of the *ton*, but who would nevertheless never be invited into the drawing room of one.

Dominic's teeth clenched so tightly together he heard his jaw crack. 'You have absolutely no idea what you have done, do you?'

She looked unconcerned. 'I merely exerted my free will—'

'To sit down and drink tea with the previous owner of Nick's.'

'Oh.' Caro looked momentarily nonplussed by this information, before rallying once again. 'I am sure I do not understand why, when you now own the club, that you should choose to hold that against him.'

'It is an ownership Brown relinquished to me with great reluctance,' Dominic grated pointedly.

'No doubt. Even so—'

'Caro, I know you to be an intelligent woman.' Dominic spoke with controlled impatience. 'I wish that you would now stop arguing with me long enough to use that intelligence.'

She eyed him warily. 'With regard to…?'

'With regard to the fact that only minutes ago you sat down and drank tea with the man I have every reason to believe is the very same man I have these past two days been attempting to protect you from.' Dominic's hands were now clenched at his sides.

Caro looked startled. 'You are referring to Mr Brown?'

'I am indeed referring to the man *you* think is a perfect gentleman.' Dominic's tone implied he knew the man to be the exact opposite of her earlier description of him. 'I believe him to be behind the attack on Nathaniel.'

Caro swallowed. 'Are you sure?'

Dominic's expression was grim. 'After this morning, yes!'

Caro began to tremble slightly, as the full import of what she had done began to sweep over her. She had found Nicholas Brown affable and charming, had flirted with him lightly, as he had flirted with her. She had even invited him to go walking with her! Admittedly that had been in response to what she had considered to be Dominic Vaughn's overbearing attitude, but that did not change the fact that she had made the invitation. And all the time, the man was a complete villain!

'If you truly know this for certain, then I do not understand why you did not instantly challenge him with the despicable deed?' Caro, uncomfortably aware of the severity of her error, decided to attack rather than defend, only realising her mistake as she noted the anger smouldering in the depths of Dominic Vaughn's ice-grey eyes once more flare into a blaze.

'I was an officer in the King's army, Caro, and a soldier does not confront the enemy before he has his own troops firmly in place and, more importantly than that, the civilians removed from harm's way.'

She gave a dismissive snort. 'Apart from myself, there were but the two of you present this morning.'

'And Brown's cut-throats were no doubt waiting outside in the shadows, eager to assist him if the need should arise.' Dominic looked down at her coldly. 'One of my dearest friends has already suffered a beating on my behalf, I was not about to see the same happen to you this morning, or indeed Butler and Jackson.'

Her eyes widened. 'You believe the attack on Lord Thorne to have been meant for *you*?'

'Only indirectly. It would appear that, for the moment at least, Brown is enjoying playing a cat-and-mouse game of inflicting harm on my friends rather than a direct attack upon me.'

'Then that is even more reason, surely, for you to have confronted him this morning?'

'Caro, it sounds distinctly as if you are accusing me of lacking the personal courage to confront him.' Dominic's tone was now every bit as glacial as his eyes.

It would be very foolish indeed of her to accuse him of such cowardice, when three nights ago she had personally witnessed him challenging those three young bucks well into their cups. When he had not hesitated to come to her rescue in the middle of a brawl. When she knew him to have been a gallant officer as the mark of that gallantry was slashed for ever upon his face.

But foolish was exactly how Caro felt at learning how mistaken she had been concerning Nicholas Brown's nature. Foolish, and embarrassed, to have been flattered by the attentions of the man she now knew him to be.

Her chin rose proudly. 'I would have thought you might, at the very least, have allowed him to see that you are aware of his guilt.'

Dominic gave a hard smile. 'Oh I am sure he is well aware of that fact.'

'How could he be, when apart from making such a show of implying our relationship is that of more than cousins, you were politeness itself?' Caro asked.

'The fact that I implied our relationship to be that of more than cousins, as you so delicately put it, was done with the intention of warning Brown, should he even consider the idea, of the inadvisability of harming one golden hair upon your head.' A nerve pulsed in Dominic's tightly clenched jaw. 'Which is not to say that I now feel that same reluctance myself.' The very softness of his tone was indicative of the depth of his anger.

Caro's trembling deepened as she realised too late her mistake in questioning Dominic when he was already so displeased with her; the grey of his eyes had become so pale and glittery that they glowed a shimmering silver, the scar standing out harshly in the tautness of his cheek, and his mouth had thinned to a dangerous line.

If those things were not enough to tell Caro of her mistake, then the purposeful look in his eyes as he moved to kneel on the bed beside her before pulling her roughly up against him and lowering his mouth to capture hers certainly did!

There was no gentleness in him as he ground his lips against hers before his tongue became as lethal as an arrow as it speared between her lips to thrust deeply into the heat of her mouth, and one of his hands moved to cup and then squeeze the fullness of her breast in that same remorseless rhythm.

Caro knew she should have been at the least frightened, if not repulsed, by the force of Dominic's passion, but instead she found herself filled with an aching excitement; her cheeks felt hot, her breasts full and aroused, and between her thighs became damp and swollen.

Dominic roughly pulled the bodice of her gown and chemise down to her waist and pushed the two garments down about her knees, before his mouth once again captured hers. His hand cupped firmly about one of Caro's exposed breasts and his fingers began to tweak and tug on the hardened nipple.

She forgot everything else but Dominic. Her neck arched invitingly as he finally wrenched his mouth from hers to lay a trail of fire down the column of her throat, her arms moving up over his shoulders and her fingers becoming entangled in the dark thickness of hair at his nape, as his head moved lower still and he drew one of those hardened nipples deep into the heat of his mouth.

Caro gave a choked gasp as there seemed to be a direct line of pleasure from Dominic's rhythmic tugging at her breast to the dampness between the bareness of her thighs, her movements becoming restless as she pressed into his hardness in search of some sort of relief for that throbbing and hungry heat.

Dominic had meant only to punish Caro for her disobedience, for her questioning his courage, but as he kissed and caressed her he instead found himself more aroused than he had ever been in his life before. So much so that he had not hesitated to pull down her gown and chemise and expose the silky paleness of her naked body to his heated gaze. Her breasts were high and firm, her waist narrow and flat, with a tiny thatch of enticing golden curls in the vee of her thighs.

He continued to lay siege to both her breasts with his lips, tongue and teeth as one of his hands gently parted those thighs before cupping her silky mound with his palm and allowing his fingers to explore the heat beneath. Caro was so hot and wet as he parted those sensitive folds to caress a finger along the heat of her opening, slowly, gently, circling but not yet touching the swollen nub nestled amongst those curls, in no rush to hurry her release, but instead savouring every low aching groan she gave as he caressed ever closer to that sensitive spot.

He touched her there once, lightly, feeling the response of that hard and roused little nubbin as it pulsed against his finger, hearing but ignoring Caro's low moan as he resumed caressing the swollen opening below, fingers testing, dipping slightly inside, and feeling the way her muscles contracted greedily about his finger even as she pushed her hips forward in an effort to take him deeper still. An invitation Dominic resisted as he continued to tease and torment her.

'Dominic, please!'

He raised his head slightly in order to look into Caro's flushed and reproachful face. 'Please what?'

Her eyes flashed deeply green and her fingers clenched on his shoulders. 'Do not tease me, Dominic.'

'Tell me precisely what you want from me, Caro,' he encouraged gruffly. 'You have only to issue an instruction and I will obey.'

Could she do that? Caro wondered wildly. Could she really tell Dominic plainly, graphically, what it was she required from him in order to give her relief from the heat threatening to consume her?

'Do you want some part of me inside the sweetness of you, Caro?' Dominic prompted softly as he seemed to take some little pity on her desperate silence.

'Yes!' she groaned achingly.

'Which part, Caro?' he pressed. 'My fingers? My tongue? My shaft?'

Oh, help! Those satisfying fingers? The hot and probing moistness of his tongue? His swollen arousal that she could clearly see hard and throbbing beneath his pantaloons? From not knowing what she needed, Caro now knew she wanted to experience having all three of those things inside her.

'Perhaps we should experiment? See which it is you like the best?' Dominic looked down at her nakedness with eyes that had become both dark and hungry as he once again swirled his fingers into the silky curls between her thighs to unerringly find and gently stroke against that secret part of her.

Caro felt the instant return of that earlier pleasure, stronger now, more demanding, as she instinctively began to move into those caresses, knowing she was poised on the brink of—Caro had no idea what she was poised on the brink of, she only knew that she wanted, needed it, with a desperation she had never known before.

She moaned again in her throat as one long finger probed her before slipping inside her heat. Deeper. Then deeper still. At last giving her some relief for that aching need as she moved her hips in rhythm with that finger as it thrust slowly in and out of her.

'Lie back upon the bed, Caro,' Dominic instructed throatily even as he eased her back against the pillows, continuing that slow and penetrating thrust inside her as he discarded her gown and chemise completely before moving to kneel between her legs to lower his head between her parted thighs.

Caro's hips jerked up from the bed at the first hot sweep of his tongue against her sensitised flesh, her fingers contracting, clutching at the bedclothes beside her, at the second sweep. She cried out, her neck arching her head back into the pillows, as unimagined pleasure ripped through her, Dominic thrusting a second finger deep inside her at the same time as he administered a third sweep of his tongue against that pulsing nubbin.

Caro became pure liquid heat. She felt as if she were on fire as wave after wave of pleasure radiated from deep between her thighs, only to surge through the whole of her body, each caress of his tongue and fingers creating yet another, deeper, swell of that mind-shattering pleasure.

Dominic watched Caro's face even as he continued to lave her with his tongue and slowly thrust with his fingers, knowing the exact moment she became lost in the throes of her climax; her eyes were a wide and stormy blue-green, her cheeks flushed, lips slightly parted, her breasts thrusting, the nipples hard as pebbles, her thighs a parted invitation as the nubbin pulsed beneath his tongue and she convulsed greedily about his thrusting fingers.

As he looked at her Dominic knew he had never experienced anything more beautiful, more physically satisfying, than watching Caro lost in the pleasure she felt from the touch of his mouth and hands. He found it more satisfying even than attaining that climax for himself.

He had been so angry with her earlier, so absolutely furious, not least because by behaving in that reckless way she had exposed her whereabouts to Nicholas Brown. But he did not want to dwell on that here and now, when Caro still quivered and trembled from the ministration of his lips and hands. Not with her all but naked beneath him, her only clothing now a pair of white silk stockings.

Besides, he had no answer as yet to his earlier question: fingers, tongue, or shaft?

Caro lay back weak and satiated against the pillows as she watched Dominic quickly strip off his boots, jacket, waistcoat, neckcloth and shirt, to reveal a hard and muscled chest covered in a light dusting of dark hair that disappeared beneath the top of his pantaloons. Pantaloons he now unfastened and pushed down and off equally hard and muscled legs to reveal the surging power of his engorged arousal.

Caro had never seen a naked man in her life before, but even so she was sure that Dominic was a physically well-endowed man. Her gaze rose to look at his face, and she swallowed convulsively as she saw the flush to his cheeks and the slightly fevered glow in those silver eyes as he wrapped a hand around that impressive length before moving forwards to rub it slowly against the opening between her thighs.

Caro felt herself quiver with each stroke of that hardness against her sensitivity, breathing heavily as she felt the return of that heat between her thighs. Surely she could not feel that pleasure again so quickly?

She could, Caro discovered only seconds later as Dominic continued to stroke that silky hardness against her own reawakened nubbin, her breasts becoming firm, nipples thrusting achingly even as she felt herself moisten in anticipation.

'Fingers? Tongue? Or shaft?' Dominic prompted gruffly even as he moved his hips forwards into her opening, one inch, two, before pulling back and starting again. One inch. Two. Three this time, before he pulled out and started again.

Caro had never experienced pleasure like this in her life before. Never imagined anything so exquisite as looking down at Dominic as he knelt between her parted thighs and slowly breached her, inch by glorious inch.

Each time Dominic thrust inside Caro she felt full and satisfied. Each time he pulled out again she felt bereft and empty. And each time he thrust inside her a little deeper she was sure she had reached her limit, that she had inwardly stretched and accommodated him as far as she was able. Until Dominic pulled out before thrusting even deeper inside her the next time.

Caro had been convinced when she first saw the size of Dominic's arousal that she would never be able to accommodate anything so large—

'Oh, my God!' Caro tensed suddenly, eyes wide with shock as she felt herself start to rip apart inside the moment Dominic took his weight on his arms to thrust forwards urgently with his hips so that he surged into her completely. It felt as if she were being torn in two as she finally took his whole length inside her.

'What the—!' Dominic froze above her, his face suddenly pale, his eyes glittering like opaque silver as he stared down at her incredulously.

'It is all right, Dominic,' Caro assured breathlessly. And, incredibly, it was, that first searing pain having now faded, and so allowing her to once again become aware of the pleasure of having his fullness completely inside her.

His face was grim. 'It most certainly is *not* all right!'

'I assure you that it is,' she encouraged softly. Dominic's arousal had looked hard and fierce earlier, but now that he was completely inside her Caro realised that fierce hardness was encased in skin of seductive and silky velvet. She moved her hips up, and then down again, the better to feel that sleek and velvety smoothness as it moved against her sensitive flesh.

'Do not move like that again, Caro, or I cannot be responsible for the consequences.' Dominic's jaw was clenched, his expression pained, a fine sheen of moisture upon his brow.

But of course Caro must move! How could she not move, when every part of her, every sensitised inch of her, cried out for the relief of having that pleasure-giving hardness stroking inside her?

Dominic had been stunned into immobility the moment he discovered Caro's innocence. 'Why did you not tell me?' His gaze was fierce as he looked down at the flushed beauty of her face, angry with himself at the moment rather than Caro, knowing he should have put a stop to this long before it had come to the point of his breaching her virginity.

And he had every intention of putting a stop to it now!

Dominic moved up and carefully away from her as he slowly disengaged himself, frowning as he saw Caro's wince of discomfort as he slipped from her obviously sore entrance. That frown turned to a dark scowl as he looked down and saw the blood smeared between her thighs as well as on him.

'Do not move,' he instructed harshly as he stood up to cross the room to the jug and bowl on the washstand, pouring some of the water from the jug into the bowl before moistening a cloth and cleaning Caro's blood from his own body before returning it to the bowl to rinse it in preparation for her. The water was cold, of course, but would hopefully be all the more soothing because of it.

Caro had watched Dominic beneath her lashes as he stood up to cross the bedchamber, completely uncon-cerned by his own nakedness, his movements gracefully predatory, like the sleek movements of a large jungle cat. He stood with his back towards her now, his shoul-ders wide, his back long and muscled, his buttocks a smooth curve above heavily muscled thighs and legs. If a man could be described as beautiful, then Caro knew that he could be called such.

The colour warmed her cheeks, however, when he returned to sit on the side of the bed and began to bathe between her thighs with a cool and soothing washcloth, his face a study of unreadable hauteur. Caro attempted to push those attentive hands away. 'There really is no need—'

'There is every need.' Dominic barely glanced up at her before continuing that studied bathing between her sensitive thighs.

Caro felt embarrassed, both by the intimacy of his ministrations, and the fact that their lovemaking had come to so abrupt an end once he'd been made aware of her innocence.

Surely there should have been more to it than that? A completion? A reciprocal pleasure? Dominic had certainly not shown signs of experiencing anything like the pleasure that Caro had.

All whilst in the bedchamber of house she had never visited before!

Caro moistened her lips, instantly aware of how swollen and sensitive they still were from the force of his kisses.

'Exactly where are we, Dominic?'

He looked at her briefly before turning away to place the cloth back in the bowl. 'I hope you are a little more comfortable now.' He stood up abruptly, his arousal already noticeably depleted. 'Perhaps I should send for a physician and he might give you some sort of soothing balm to apply—'

'I have no intention of being attended by a physician!' Caro's cheeks were hot with embarrassment as she imagined having to explain this situation to a third party. 'Dominic, is it possible I might become with child from—from what just occurred between us?'

Dominic closed his eyes even as he gave a groan of self-disgust. An innocent. Damn it, he had just deflowered a complete innocent!

Chapter Eleven

'It is very doubtful,' Dominic answered stiffly.

'But possible?'

'Perhaps,' he allowed abruptly.

Caro turned away. 'Whose house is this?'

Dominic looked down at her between narrowed lids, her cheeks flushed, her mouth slightly trembling as she pulled the sheet over her nakedness. It was a little late in the day for maidenly modesty, of course, but now was possibly not the right time for Dominic to allude to that fact.

'I do not believe that to be important at this moment—'

'I do.' There was a stillness about Caro now. A wariness that bordered on anger, perhaps?

He gave a humourless smile. 'You had made it obvious from the first that you did not wish to remain at Blackstone House, and last night it became just as obvious to me that the two of us could not continue to reside under the same roof any longer—'

'At which point in last night's proceedings did this become so obvious to you, Dominic?' Caro interrupted sharply. 'Perhaps at the point where you announced the inappropriateness of seducing a female guest in your own home?' Angry colour now heightened the delicacy of her cheeks.

Looking down at her, the warmth of their lovemaking still visible upon her body, Dominic knew that she had never looked lovelier: her eyes sparkled, her cheeks were flushed, her lips slightly swollen from the passion of their kisses, and the skin across her shoulders and the exposed tops of her creamy breasts was slightly pink from the abrasion of the light stubble upon Dominic's jaw.

That jaw hardened at the accusation he heard in her tone. 'If you are somehow meaning to imply that I brought you to this house in order to seduce you—'

'Did you not?' She stood up, her movements agitated as she held the sheet tightly to her breasts to pace the bedchamber.

'Do not be ridiculous, Caro.' Dominic's quickly rising anger was more than equal to her own. Damn it, he was the one who had been in complete ignorance of her innocence until a few minutes ago!

The signs had been there if he had cared to see them, Dominic instantly rebuked himself. Caro's naïvety concerning the interest of the men who had come to Nick's night after night just to see her. The frequent indications of her being a young lady of refinement. The often imperious manner that hinted at her being used to issuing orders rather than receiving them.

That Dominic was now assured he had not been

guilty these past three days of attempting to make love to a married woman or a member of the servant class was poor consolation when he had instead robbed a young woman of the innocence she should one day have presented to her husband.

'Ridiculous?' Caro now repeated softly, eyes gleaming as dark as emeralds. 'You strode into this house earlier as if you owned it—and perhaps that is because you do?' She didn't wait for Dominic to answer before striding across the bedchamber to throw open the wardrobe doors, her expression darkening as she saw the three pretty silk gowns hanging there. She turned to shoot Dominic a scathing glance. 'The previous occupant of this house appears to have been so hastily removed that she has left several of her gowns behind!'

'There was no previous occupant of this house—'

'All evidence to the contrary, my dear Dominic!' Caro was breathing hard in her agitation—she could only hope this anger served to hide the deep hurt she really felt.

It was humiliating enough that he had not even desired her enough to complete their lovemaking once he'd become aware of her innocence, but for him to have chosen to bring her to the house he had already owned, and where another woman had obviously been hastily removed, was a much more painful insult.

Dominic was well aware that at the moment Caro did not consider him her 'dear' anything; in fact, she looked more than capable of plunging a knife between his shoulder blades if one had been readily available.

Which, thank God, it was not… 'Look at the gowns more closely, if you please, Caro,' he ordered.

Her nose wrinkled delicately at the suggestion. 'I have no wish to—'

'Look at them, damn you!' Dominic demanded impatiently. 'Look at the gowns, Caro,' he repeated more evenly as he realised that it was himself he was angry with and not her. 'Once you have done so, you will see that they are the ones ordered for you yesterday.'

Caro eyed him uncertainly for several seconds before turning her attention back to the gowns hanging in the wardrobe, frowning as she realised they were indeed the ones ordered from the seamstress yesterday. Two days dresses, one of pale peach, the other of deep yellow. The third an evening gown of pure white silk and lace.

A purity Caro was all too aware she could no longer lay claim to…

'If you care to look in the drawers in the dressing table you will find your own undergarments and new nightgowns, too.'

Caro firmly closed the wardrobe door on the mockery of that white gown. 'All that proves is that you were sensible enough, after all, to remove the belongings of your mistress and replace them with my own.'

Dominic drew in a sharp breath, knowing that engaging in their usual verbal battle of wills was not going to help this already disastrous situation. And no matter what she might choose to think to the contrary, he had not brought her here with any intention of seducing her. The opposite, in fact. He had thought—hoped—that by removing her from Blackstone House, he would be removing her from his temptation. Instead of which he had merely exacerbated the situation by bringing Caro here and making love to her before he had even had chance to explain.

'Caro, I acquired ownership of this house only this morning.'

'Now who is being ridiculous?'

Dominic knew, for all that Caro was putting such a brave face on things, that she had to be keenly feeling the loss of her innocence. 'I can take you to the office of my lawyer, if you wish,' he spoke gently. 'I am sure he would be only too happy to show you today's date upon the transfer of the deeds, if that will help to convince you I am telling you the truth?'

Her chin rose. 'You not only bought this house this morning but somehow managed to engage all those servants downstairs, too?' A flush entered her cheeks as she obviously recalled the curious gazes of those servants earlier as he'd carried her through the entrance hall and up the stairs.

An impulse he now deeply regretted when it had resulted in him taking Caro's innocence... 'They are, one and all, men and women already known to me. Men who served under me in the army, and their wives, whom I knew could be trusted to protect you,' he admitted ruefully.

Her eyes glittered, whether with anger or tears, Dominic was unsure. 'Obviously they did not feel that protection was necessary when it applied to *yourself*!'

'Caro—'

'Do not touch me, Dominic!' Her warning was accompanied by a step away from him, the knuckles on her fingers showing white as she tightly gripped the bedcover about her nakedness. 'I believe, if this truly is to be my home for the immediate future, that I should like you to leave now.'

No more so than Dominic wished to remove himself, he felt sure. At this moment, all he wanted to do was walk away from Brockle House and forget he had ever met Caro Morton. Forget especially that he had taken her innocence.

'Perhaps on your way out you might ask for a bath and hot water to be brought up to me?' Caro requested stiltedly as Dominic pulled on his pantaloons and shirt before sitting on the side of the bed to pull on his boots.

Dominic inwardly winced at the thought of the soreness she must now be experiencing following their lovemaking. 'Please believe me when I tell you I did not plan for what happened here this morning—'

'Planned or otherwise, it is done now.'

There was so much sadness in her tone, that if that knife had been available, then Dominic believed himself to be capable of plunging it into his own heart at that moment. 'I cannot express how much I...regret what has happened.'

Caro looked up at him searchingly, not sure whether she felt reassured by Dominic's claim, or insulted by it. Their lovemaking had been a mistake, of course, a shocking error on both their parts. But even so... 'I had not believed you could possibly insult to me more than you already have; I was obviously wrong.' She turned her back on him to stare sightlessly out of the window into the square below. 'I require the bath and hot water to be brought up to me now, if you please, Dominic.'

Dominic stared at the proud set of Caro's bare shoulders for several long seconds before bending to pick up the rest of his clothes from the floor. 'I will call on you later this afternoon.'

She turned sharply. 'For what purpose?'

Dominic's heart sank at the suspicion he so easily read in her expression. 'For the purpose of checking that you have not suffered any feelings of ill health from this morning's...activity.'

Caro gave a humourless snort. 'As far as I am aware, we did not indulge in anything of an unnatural nature this morning.'

A flush warmed the hardness of Dominic's cheeks. 'No, of course we did not.'

'Then I fail to see why you might think I will suffer any ill health because of it?'

'Damn it, Caro—'

'I suppose if you think it more fitting, then I could perhaps swoon or have a fit of the vapours?' she continued scathingly. 'But only if you believe it absolutely necessary.' Her nose wrinkled. 'Personally, I have always believed that women who behave in that way, seemingly at the slightest provocation, to be complete ninnies.'

Even in the midst of what Dominic considered, at best, to be an exceedingly awkward situation, he could not help but admire her courageous spirit. She truly was a woman like no other he had ever met. What had just happened between the two of them could certainly not be termed a mere 'slight provocation'. In fact, Dominic felt sure that most women in her position would be either screaming obscenities at him or alternately demanding jewels and gowns, the latter as compensation for the loss of her innocence; Caro asked only for a bath and hot water in which she might bathe the soreness from her body.

Dominic gave a rueful smile. 'I, too, would prefer that you do not swoon or have a fit of the vapours.' That smile faded as he looked at her searchingly. 'You truly are unharmed from our encounter?'

He knew himself to have been severely provoked when he'd returned to Blackstone House earlier and found Caro gone. Even more so when he'd arrived at Nick's and found her happily engaged in conversation with Nicholas Brown—even now Dominic dreaded to think what might have befallen Caro if he had not been present when she had been foolish enough to suggest walking with him in the park! For her to then taunt him as she'd done regarding his own behaviour towards Brown had been more than Dominic's already frayed nerves had been able tolerate.

An intolerance that Caro had paid for with her innocence...

'I am as comfortable as might be expected in the circumstances.' Caro kept her chin proudly high even as she saw the way Dominic winced at her lack of assurances. In truth, it was her pride that now hurt more than her body.

Caro eyed him uncertainly now from beneath her lashes, still so very aware of how handsome he looked with the darkness of his hair rakishly tousled, and his shirt hanging loosely over his pantaloons, the buttons still undone halfway down his chest and revealing the hard and muscled flesh beneath. Hard and muscled flesh that Caro now knew more intimately than she did her own...

She gave a decisive shake of her head. 'We were both in error earlier. Let that be an end to it.'

Dominic continued to look at her searchingly for several long seconds. A scrutiny that Caro was determined to withstand without alerting him to how distressed she felt inside. And not by their lovemaking, as Dominic presumed, but because of the emotions which Caro feared had instigated her own part in that wild and wonderful lovemaking.

He frowned. 'I have your promise that you will stay well away from Nicholas Brown?'

'Such a promise is completely unnecessary, I assure you.' Caro's brow creased with irritation that Dominic, after revealing to her that Brown was the person behind the attack on Lord Thorne and consequently was the excuse for her own incarceration in this house, could for one moment think she had any interest in ever meeting the villain again!

Dominic wanted nothing more than to take Caro in his arms and smooth the frown from her brow and the shadows from her eyes. Even knowing of the physical discomfort she must now be suffering following their lovemaking, Dominic was not enough in control of his own emotions at that moment to be sure that he would be able to stop himself from making love to her fully if he were to touch her again.

He was a man who had enjoyed his first physical encounter at the age of sixteen. And there had been many women since that first time with whom he had enjoyed the same physical release. It was disturbing to realise that almost making love with Caro had been completely unlike any of those previous encounters. More sensuous. More out of control. With the promise of being more wildly satisfying…

'Caro—'

'Dominic!' Her eyes flashed in warning as she turned to face him, the control she had been exerting over her own emotions obviously at an end. 'In the past two days I have been caught up in the midst of a brawl, seen an innocent man beaten within an inch of his life, been deposited in your own household against my wishes, drunk tea with the man you assure me is responsible for that innocent man being beaten, been literally carried away and deposited in this house like a piece of unwanted baggage, before then being made love to. I should warn you, I am seriously in danger of resorting to behaving like that complete ninny I mentioned earlier, if you do not soon take your leave!' Her voice quivered with emotion, an emotion she masked by crossing the room to ring for the maid.

Still he hesitated. 'I should also like your promise that you will not attempt to go out alone again, now that you are aware of the danger.'

Could Caro make Dominic such a promise? What choice did she have? The only place she wished to go was back to Shoreley Hall in Hampshire, where she might be with her sisters and lick her wounds in private. Something she most certainly could not do, now that she and Nicholas Brown had met, when it might also result in her taking the danger that man represented back home with her…

In truth, what Caro most wanted at that moment was

the privacy to sit down and cry. To scream and shout, if necessary. And after doing those things she needed the peace and quiet in which to come to terms with the loss of her innocence and the wantonness of her own behaviour this morning in Dominic's arms.

She gave a cool inclination of her head. 'You have my promise. Now, do you not think your own time would not be better spent in dealing with Nicholas Brown, rather than in lingering here to extract superfluous promises from me?'

Dominic's eyes narrowed. 'Superfluous?'

She gave a tight smile. 'Of course it is superfluous, when I so obviously have nowhere else of safety to go.'

'Caro—' Dominic broke off what he was going to say as, after a brief knock, a maid appeared in the doorway in answer to Caro's ring. 'Your mistress requires a bath and hot water,' he instructed tightly. 'Immediately,' he added firmly as the maid seemed inclined to linger in order to satisfy her curiosity rather than be about her business. He waited until the woman had gone before turning back to Caro. 'My advice is that once you have bathed you then rest quietly—'

'Why is it, I wonder, Dominic, that when you offer advice it always has the sound and appearance of an order?' Caro eyed him with exasperation.

Dominic gave a weary sigh as he ran impatient fingers through his already tousled hair. 'Caro, this situation is already difficult enough—could we not at least try to behave in a civilised manner towards each other?'

Could they? Somehow Caro doubted that they could ever be completely civilised with each other; it seemed that whenever the two of them were together their emotions ran to extremes. Arrogance. Anger. Desire.

She sighed heavily. 'Perhaps when you return this afternoon our emotions will be less…fraught than they are now,' she allowed distantly.

Dominic certainly hoped that would be the case.

But somehow he doubted it.

Chapter Twelve

'I am afraid I cannot accurately describe any of the four men who attacked me.' Nathaniel Thorne lay propped up against the pillows in one of the bedchambers at his widowed Aunt Gertrude's house, his expression regretful as he gazed across to where Dominic stood in front of one of the long picture windows.

Dominic had been shocked by the worsening of his friend's appearance when he arrived at Mrs Wilson's home a few short minutes ago, and the elderly lady's young companion showed him into Nathaniel's bedchamber. His friend's face was extremely pale except for the myriad of brightly coloured bruises and cuts that, although they were starting to heal, still looked vicious and painful. The bandage about Nathaniel's broken ribs was visible at the unbuttoned collar of his loose white nightshirt.

Nathaniel shook his head. 'As I told you at the time, I had no sooner walked outside than I was set upon by those four men wielding knives, and fists that had the force of hammers. I was immediately too busy defending myself to take note of what any of them looked like.' He grimaced at his oversight.

In truth, Dominic had not held out much hope of Nathaniel being able to add any more light on this particular subject. Regrettably, his reasons for coming here were, in fact, as much self-interest as they were concern for Nathaniel. Much as he wished to assure himself of Osbourne's well being, Dominic had been even more in need of a diversion from his own company!

Having returned to Blackstone House earlier to bathe and change his clothes, Dominic had then found himself pacing his study, too restless, his thoughts too disturbed, for him to be able to even glance at the papers concerning estate business sitting on his desktop awaiting his attention.

How could it be any other when all he could think about was Caro's stolen innocence?

'What is it, Dom?' Nathaniel's softly probing concern was the first indication he had that he might have actually groaned his self-disgust out loud.

Dominic had believed, hoped, that he could talk to Nathaniel about his present dilemma with regard to Caro. Instead he had realised since coming here that, as close as the two men were, there was no way that he could confide his despicable deed to the other man. More importantly, that he could not speak about Caro in such a way with a third party. Even one of his closest friends.

Gabriel, Nathaniel, and Dominic had always been as close as brothers, but even so, Dominic knew that he could not reveal to one of those friends what had taken place at Brockle House that morning. Osbourne, quite rightly, could not help but consider the taking of Caro's innocence as being beneath contempt. The same contempt, in fact, that Dominic now felt towards himself...

The truth of it was that he had been suffused with feelings of helplessness when he'd discovered Caro had gone from Blackstone House this morning, but instead of feeling relieved when he found her at Nick's, he had instead been filled with anger to see her calmly sitting drinking tea with Nicholas Brown. So much so that Dominic had completely lost control of the situation once they'd reached Brockle House.

How Caro must now hate and despise him—

'Dom?'

He closed his eyes briefly before focusing on Osbourne. 'I believe it is time I left; I have no doubt tired you enough for one day,' he dismissed briskly as he stepped forwards into the bedchamber, ready to take his leave. 'Is there anything I might bring to make you more comfortable?'

Nathaniel winced. 'No, as usual my Aunt Gertrude appears to have everything well in hand.'

Dominic smiled slightly at his friend's affectionate irony. 'I did not see her when I arrived earlier.'

'She has been persuaded to go out visiting this morning.' The relief could be heard in Osbourne's tone. 'Between her over-attentiveness, and her companion's sharp tongue, I am not sure I will last out the week!'

Dominic would not have thought the quiet and gracious young lady who had shown him up to Osbourne's bedchamber capable of being sharp-tongued. 'I am sure you will manage, Nate.'

'I wish I had the same confidence.' His friend gave a shake of his head. 'Of all things, my aunt is talking of removing me to the country to convalesce once I am well enough to travel.'

The idea had merit, Dominic decided after only the briefest of considerations. Nathaniel would be removed from danger, at least, if he were safely guarded by the formidable Mrs Wilson at her country home. 'It sounds a reasonable plan to me.'

'It is not at all reasonable!' Nathaniel glared. 'The Season has barely begun and Aunt Gertrude is intending to subject me to the boredom of the country when I am in no condition to protest.'

'No hardship, surely, when she is also removing you from the avaricious sphere of all those marriage-minded mamas?' Dominic reasoned drily.

'As I have reached the age of eight and twenty without as yet falling foul of those marriage-minded mamas, I am reasonably optimistic that I will have no trouble continuing to resist the allure of their beautiful daughters.' Osbourne eyed Dominic curiously. 'Speaking of which… Was I hallucinating, due to the beating I had just taken, or did your angel accompany us home in your carriage two evenings ago?'

Dominic stiffened. 'My angel?'

He knew to whom Nathaniel referred, of course; although the last time he had seen Caro, she had, quite rightly, presented him with all the warmth of a porcelain statue…

'You know exactly to whom I am referring, Dom,' Nathaniel prodded ruthlessly.

Exactly, yes. 'Do I?'

'Do you have any idea how boring it is just lying here with nothing to do but think?' Nathaniel's scowl was disgruntled to say the least.

'If you must think, then perhaps you should give consideration to Gabriel's future rather than my own?' Dominic attempted to change the subject.

Osbourne brightened slightly. 'He should be arriving in England very shortly.'

Dominic shrugged. 'But with the intention of travelling immediately to Shoreley Hall, remember.' Fortunately. If informed, Gabriel would definitely have had something to say about the situation Dominic found himself in. 'I—'

'I am sure we are very grateful for the frequency of your visits, Blackstone, but the physician has assured me that my nephew is in need of rest rather than excessive conversation.' An officious Mrs Wilson bustled forcefully into the bedchamber to begin enthusiastically plumping up the pillows beneath Osbourne's head, obviously now returned from her visiting, and not at all pleased that Dominic was once again disturbing her nephew in his sickbed.

Dominic gave her a polite bow. 'I assure you I am just as concerned for Osbourne's welfare as you obviously are, ma'am. In fact, I was about to take my leave when you came in.'

'Oh, I say, Aunt—'

'We must all take note of Mrs Wilson, Nate, if you

are to make a full and speedy recovery,' Dominic drawled mockingly over his friend's protest.

The other man shot him a narrow-eyed glare that contained the promise of retribution for Dominic's defection at some later date. A glare that he chose to ignore as he smilingly took his leave. A smile that faded as soon as Dominic stepped from Mrs Wilson's home, as he acknowledged that he could no longer put off his return to Brockle House.

And Caro...

'Lord Vaughn is here to see you, Mrs Morton.'

Caro heard the butler's words, but did not immediately respond to them.

The first thing Caro had done, once Dominic finally left earlier that morning, was to strip the soiled sheets from the bed and attempt to remove the worst of the bloodstains with some of the cold water left in the jug; bad enough that she was aware of this tangible evidence of her lost innocence, without the whole household being made aware of it, too.

Although she doubted there could be much doubt in the minds of any of the servants Dominic had engaged at Brockle House, concerning the events of this morning!

To their credit, Caro could not claim there had been any evidence of that in the demeanour of any of the servants who'd brought in the bath and hot water some half an hour after Dominic's departure, their manner both polite and attentive as the fire was lit in the hearth before the footmen placed the bath in front of it and the water was poured in.

Caro had refused the offer of help from one of the maids, however, needing to be alone as she soaked in the bath and contemplated the events of the morning just past.

Not one of those thoughts had offered any comfort to the situation in which she now found herself. Caro knew, at the very least, that she should feel angry with Dominic for having taken her innocence and yet somehow she could not bring herself to do so. Perhaps because she knew herself to be just as responsible as he—if not more so—for what had happened?

She had wanted Dominic to make love to her this morning. Had desired him as much as he had desired her, to the extent that her chief emotion had been disappointment when he had brought an abrupt halt to their lovemaking. It was a shameless admission from a young woman who had been brought up to believe that women who behaved in such a way were wantons, no better than the prostitutes who roamed the streets of any large town or city.

As to how Caro now felt towards Dominic himself…

That was a question she had considered and then shied away from answering. Whatever her feelings towards him, it would be madness indeed for Caro to care anything for the Earl of Blackstone—a man who so obviously shunned all the softer emotions in life.

That Dominic had now returned, as he had said he would, made Caro all the more determined that he not become aware of her own inner confusion of emotions. 'Show him in, please,' she instructed the butler coolly as she stood up to receive him with the same formality to be found in the sunlit drawing room in which she sat.

* * *

One glance at Caro's coolness of expression and the dignified elegance of her body was enough to tell Dominic that, even if she had not recovered from this morning, she did not intend to reveal as much by her demeanour. Aware of the presence of the butler, Dominic greeted her formally. 'Mrs Morton.'

She gave a brief curtsy in response to his abrupt bow. 'How kind of you to call again so soon, Lord Vaughn.'

Dominic wasn't fooled for a moment by the politeness of Caro's greeting, aware as he was of the utter disdain in her expression. As aware, in fact, as he was of how lovely she looked in a gown of deep lemon, with the sun shining through the window behind her and giving her delicate curls the appearance of spun gold, her light and floral perfume tantalising his senses.

He waited until the butler had left the room and closed the door behind him before answering drily. 'A visit you obviously wish I had not made.'

Caro raised her light-coloured brows. 'On the contrary, I am merely curious as to why you bothered to have yourself announced when you are the owner of this house?'

Dominic frowned his irritation. 'I may own the house, Caro, but you are the one living here—'

'Temporarily.'

'As such,' Dominic continued firmly, 'it would have been impolite of me to simply walk in unannounced.'

Her smile was more bitter than amused. 'And politeness is to be between us from now on, is it?'

Dominic's mouth compressed as he walked farther into the room. 'It is to be attempted, yes.'

'How nice.' Caro resumed her seat upon the sofa, her hands folded neatly together to rest upon her thighs as she looked across at him serenely. 'In that case, would you care to take tea with me, Lord Vaughn?'

What Dominic would rather have was a return of the old Caro. The Caro who no more cared for polite inanities than he did and who opposed him at every turn. The same Caro who had defiantly assured him on numerous occasions that she would do exactly as she pleased, when she pleased. A Caro who, as far as Dominic could tell, was nowhere to be seen in this coolly self-possessed young lady who gazed back at him so aloofly.

'Or perhaps you would care for something stronger than tea?' she prompted distantly when Dominic made no answer, not betraying by word or expression how deeply his presence here disturbed her.

She had no idea how a woman was supposed to behave towards a man who only that morning had taken her innocence, but had afterwards made it patently clear how much he considered that action to have been a mistake. She was sure, given the circumstances, that she should not be quite so aware of how magnificently handsome he appeared in a superfine of deep blue, a paler waistcoat beneath, his linen snowy-white, with buff-coloured pantaloons above brown Hessians.

Although the expression in those silver-coloured eyes, and the hard tension in his jaw, showed he was far from as confidently relaxed as he wished to appear.

The coldness that now existed between the two of them was intolerable, Caro decided heavily. Not that it was her wish for either of them to allude to the events of earlier this morning—it was, in truth, the very last thing she wished to talk, or even think, about—but she found the polite strangers they were pretending to be just as unacceptable. So much so that her emotions were once again verging on the tearful.

She stood up abruptly to tug on the bell-pull. 'You would prefer brandy? Or perhaps whisky?'

A glass of either of those held appeal, Dominic acknowledged wryly. Except he doubted that even imbibing a full decanter of alcohol would numb the feelings of guilt that had beset him as he observed the changes in Caro. 'By all means order tea for us both.' He moved restlessly to stand over by the window as she spoke softly to the butler when he arrived to take her order.

He could have been the male guest in the drawing room of any female member of the *ton*, Dominic recognised with a frown. There was the same politeness, the same formality and stiffness of manner he could have expected to receive there. The sort of polite formality that had never existed between himself and Caro!

He drew himself up determinedly once the two of them were once more alone. 'Caro, it must be as obvious to you as it is to me that we need to talk.'

'What would you care to talk about, Lord Vaughn?' she prompted brightly as she resumed her seat on the sofa to look across at him with unreadable sea-green eyes. 'The weather, perhaps? Or the beauty of the gardens at this time of year? I am afraid, never having attended one, that I cannot talk knowledgably of the balls and parties given in the homes of the *ton*—'

'You will cease this nonsense immediately.' Dominic

could no longer contain his impatience with the distance yawning between them. 'I have no more wish to discuss the weather, the garden, or the doings of the *ton*, than I believe you do.'

She raised haughty brows. 'I thought I had just assured you that I would be only too happy to converse on either of the first two subjects—'

'If you do not stop this nonsensical prattling, Caro, then I will have no other recourse but to come over there and shake you until your teeth rattle!' Dominic's hands were clenched at his sides as he resisted that impulse, a nerve pulsing in his tightly set jaw as he glared across the room at her.

She visibly bristled. 'If you even attempt to do so, then I assure you *I* will have no other recourse but to take the letter opener from the table over there and stab you with it!'

Dominic gave an appreciative grin as his tension eased slightly. Better. Much better. Almost the Caro he was used to, in fact.

He waited until the tray of tea things had been placed on the low table in front of her, and the butler once again departed about his business, before speaking again. 'I had thought you might be interested in hearing how Lord Thorne fares this afternoon?' He strolled across to make himself comfortable in the armchair facing Caro as she sat forwards on the sofa to pour the two cups of tea.

She paused to look across at him. 'He is well, I hope?'

'Slightly better, yes. But, if I read the situation correctly, he is also being thoroughly suffocated by the kindness of his doting aunt, as well as browbeaten by the sharp tongue of her young companion.'

Caro smiled slightly at the image this conjured up of the rakishly handsome Lord Thorne being fussed over by one lady and rebuked by another. 'No doubt something he considers more tiresome than his injuries.' She handed Dominic his tea before picking up her own cup and saucer and settling back against the sofa.

There was a slight pause before Dominic spoke again. 'Caro, we should have had this conversation this morning, but...' He gave a shake of his head. 'Emotions were such that I did not feel the time was right—'

'I sincerely hope you do not intend plaguing me by enquiring again after my own health, Lord Vaughn!' Her eyes flashed deeply green as she looked across at him. 'I have already assured you that I am perfectly well and do not wish to discuss this subject further.' To her dismay her hand shook slightly as she concentrated on raising her cup to her lips and took a sip of the milky unsweetened tea in order to avoid meeting the probing of that silver gaze.

It was uncomfortable to sit here drinking tea together as if they were only casual acquaintances, but Caro knew she preferred even that to the humiliation of discussing the events of this morning. Just being in the same room as Dominic was enough to make her aware of the slight aches and soreness of the different parts of her body—all of them a physical reminder of their lovemaking earlier today.

As she had hoped, the bath she had taken had eased some of her discomfort. But it seemed there had been no soothing the slight redness to her breasts from the chafing of stubble upon Dominic's jaw as it rubbed against her tender flesh, or the slight soreness between her thighs every time she moved—a constant reminder of what had happened between them.

None of them were things Caro cared to discuss with Dominic!

Or things she should think of and dwell on, when he had already made it so clear that he considered their lovemaking to have been a mistake.

If only Caro were not still so aware of him. Of the way his silky dark hair had fallen rakishly over his brow. Of how the hand he now raised to push back those dark locks had this morning been entangled in the golden curls between her thighs—

'Would that we could dismiss it so easily.' Dominic's mouth had thinned with displeasure.

She frowned as she forced her thoughts back from those memories of carnal delight. 'I do not see why we cannot.'

Could Caro really be this innocent? Dominic wondered. If so, then it was even more important that they have this discussion. 'You were the one to mention earlier that there may be consequences from our actions this morning.'

She stilled. 'Consequences I recall you saying would be extremely unlikely.'

Dominic gave up all pretence of appearing in the least relaxed as he stood up to pace restlessly on the rug in front of the fireplace. Earlier, he had been too shocked by that proof of Caro's innocence, so befuddled by the intensity of his arousal, to be in any condition to think clearly, let alone have a rational discussion on the subject.

Even now, Dominic found himself in danger of wanting to make love to her again rather than talk, as they surely must. To kiss the vulnerability of her exposed nape, to touch and caress the firm swell of her breasts, to part the soft curls between her thighs as he stroked the sensitive nubbin there before throwing up her skirts and once again thrusting his arousal into the exquisite pleasure of her!

His hands clenched at his sides. 'Consequences I said *may* be a possibility,' he corrected stiltedly.

'I do not understand?'

'Much as it pains me, Caro, there is the possibility—remote, I do acknowledge—that merely by having penetrated you, you could become with child,' Dominic explained as she looked up at him blankly.

Caro's eyes widened and all the colour drained from her cheeks as the cup and saucer she was holding slipped from her fingers and tumbled to the floor.

Chapter Thirteen

Caro could only stare down numbly at the broken cup
and saucer as it was quickly surrounded by a rapidly
spreading pool of milky tea that threatened to wet her
satin slippers as well as the rug in front of the fire.

'Caro—'

'Ring for Denby, would you, Dominic?' Caro
grabbed a napkin from the tea-tray and fell down on to
her knees to wipe up the worst of the tea before starting
to gather up the shattered pieces of porcelain, grateful
to have this diversion as a means of avoiding answering
Dominic's previous statement.

Caro was not ignorant about how babies were made;
even if Diana, as the eldest, had not felt it her duty to
discuss such matters with her two younger sisters once
she considered them both old enough, it would have
been impossible to avoid knowing about such things,
when their father had often discussed the selective
breeding for the deer and other livestock at Shoreley

Hall with his estate manager in the presence of his three daughters.

She had simply chosen to believe—to the point of denial—that such a thing could not possibly come about from Dominic's brief penetration.

'Leave it, Caro.' He stepped forwards to take a grip of her arm and pull her effortlessly to her feet, maintaining that hold as he turned to speak to the butler who had entered the room. 'Denby, could you see that this is cleaned up whilst I take Mrs Morton outside for a refreshing walk in the garden?' Dominic's expression was grim as Caro appeared too dazed to respond with her usual aversion to being told what to do, but instead allowed him to guide her outside into the sunlit garden. In truth, he was unsure as to whether she might have collapsed completely if he had not maintained that steadying grip upon her arm. 'Caro, I realise the delicacy of this situation, but surely—'

'Not now, Dominic,' she managed to breathe. 'I—allow me a few minutes in which to think, if you please.' She stepped away from him, releasing his hold upon her arm before turning her back on him and walking over to gaze down into the murky depths of the fishpond.

She looked so delicate, Dominic realised with a frown, so very young and vulnerable, as she stood there so still and silent. Unseeing, too, he did not doubt, knowing from the stunned expression and the pallor of her face that her thoughts were troubled ones.

As troubled as Dominic's own. 'I have come here this afternoon to assure you, that if by some mischance you do find yourself with child, I will of course feel honour-bound to offer you my hand in marriage.'

'Marriage!' Caro appeared horrified by the mere suggestion of it as she turned to stare at him.

Dominic had always been aware that he would have to marry one day. As a means of providing an heir, if for no other reason. But, if he had given the matter any thought at all, then the future bride he had imagined for himself would be selected from one of the families of the *ton*, a young lady of gentleness and obedience. She would certainly not be a stubborn and forthright young woman who refused to so much as listen—worse, who wilfully went her own way no matter what advice was offered to her.

He took a deep breath. 'It is obvious to me, despite the circumstances under which we first met, that you were obviously brought up to be a lady.'

'Indeed?' Caro's tone was icy.

'And that for reasons of your own,' Dominic continued determinedly, 'you have chosen to temporarily separate yourself from your family. Luckily, no one but Butler and Jackson...' and possibly Nicholas Brown, he mentally acknowledged '...is aware that Caro Morton and the masked lady are one and the same person. It is regrettable that you ever associated yourself with a gambling den, of course, but it cannot be changed now—'

'I assure you, if I have any desire to change *anything* about my visit to London, then it is that I ever had the misfortune to meet *you*!' Caro informed him frostily.

Dominic's mouth tightened at the deliberate insult. 'Even so, if you should indeed find yourself with child, then I am prepared, in view of the fact that I know of your previous innocence, to accept my responsibility—'

'I would advise that you not say another insulting word.' Her eyes flashed in warning. 'With child or otherwise, I would never consider even the possibility of ever marrying you,' she continued scornfully. 'Not even if you were to go down upon your knees and beg me to do so!'

Dominic could never envisage any situation in which he would ever go down upon his knees and beg any woman to marry him, although the vehemence with which Caro dismissed the very notion of a marriage between the two of them was insulting rather than reassuring.

She gave a delicate shudder now. 'I knew you to be an arrogant man, *my lord*, but I had not realised you to be one so full of self-conceit, too!'

Dominic felt the angry tide of colour in his cheeks at this further added insult. 'These character faults of mine did not seem a hindrance to the desire you felt for me earlier today!'

Caro's own cheeks became flushed at this reminder of her response to his lovemaking. But having come to London in the first place in order to escape the possibility of her guardian—another Earl, no less—being able to somehow coerce her into marrying him, Caro could not help but feel slighted by Dominic's obvious aversion to the unwelcome possibility that he might have to take her as his own Countess.

'I believe we have both of us made our feelings in this matter clear, Lord Vaughn,' she dismissed. 'And this conversation is therefore at an end. It would be better if you did not lay hands upon me again!' Her eyes narrowed as she found Dominic was now standing far too close to her for comfort and about to take a grip upon her arm.

His eyes glittered down at her just as fiercely as his fingers closed around her arm. 'And if I should choose not to heed that advice?'

Caro's chin rose challengingly. 'Then you will leave me no choice but to punch you upon your arrogant chin!'

He gave a start of surprise, then the angry glitter began to fade from his eyes to be replaced by reluctant admiration as he gave a brief laugh. 'You are without doubt the most unusual woman I have ever encountered.'

Unfortunately for him, Caro's own anger remained just as intense as it had ever been. 'Because I choose to threaten you with something you would understand rather than womanly hysteria?'

'Exactly so.' His fingers relaxed slightly upon her arm, but he did not release her. 'Caro, I meant you no insult just now when I said that I am prepared to offer you marriage should there be a child—'

'Did you not?' She tossed her head. 'Am I to understand that you expect me to feel grateful, then, by your *honour-bound* offer? Flattered when you express how *regrettable* you consider this situation to be? Suggesting that, as you are completely assured of my innocence before today, I should be happy that you are prepared to *accept your responsibility* as the father of any baby I might produce in the next nine months?'

'You are twisting my words—'

'Indeed I am not,' Caro denied hotly, her anger deepening the more she thought about Dominic's so-called proposal of marriage. At the moment, she really did feel capable of punching him upon his arrogant chin! 'Please accept my assurances, Lord Vaughn, that if I did happen to find myself unfortunate enough to be carrying your child, you would be the very last man I would ever think of going to for assistance.'

Dominic looked down at her sharply. 'Who else should you go to but me?'

Caro might have behaved recklessly in coming to London in the first place, most especially by remaining to become a singer in a gentleman's gambling club, even more so by allowing the lovemaking with Dominic this morning to go as far as it had, but none of those things changed the fact that she was in reality Lady Caroline Copeland, and the daughter of an Earl. A woman, moreover, who was Dominic Vaughn's social equal. That he had no idea of her true identity was irrelevant—the man was arrogance personified!

'I am not without friends, sir.' Caro looked down the length of her nose at him—not an easy feat when she was so much shorter than he. 'Good and faithful friends, who would be true to me no matter what I have done.' Caro considered her two sisters to be her best friends as well as her family. As such, she had no doubt that both Diana and Elizabeth would stand beside her, no matter what the circumstances.

His top lip curled. 'And where have these friends been these past two weeks?'

Her chin rose. 'Exactly where they have always been.' There had been comfort for Caro in knowing that her two sisters would be waiting for her at Shoreley Hall whenever she should choose to return to them. No doubt with a severe reprimand from Diana for having run away at all, and a whispered urging from Elizabeth to relate her adventures once they were alone together, but nevertheless, Caro had no doubt that her sisters would stand beside her come what may.

Dominic scowled darkly as his hand once again took a firm grip upon her arm. 'Damn it, Caro—'

'No doubt, by tomorrow, I will be in possession of as many black-and-blue bruises as Lord Thorne!' Caro protested, knowing full well he wasn't hurting her, but the implication that he was would make him release her immediately.

'I apologise.' As she had predicted, Dominic did indeed let her arm go abruptly. 'Caro, put your stubborn pride aside for one moment, and just consider—'

'The honour of becoming your Countess?' she flung back at him derisively. 'I have considered it, my lord— and as just quickly dismissed it!' She eyed him with the disdain of a queen.

Dominic was fast losing patience with this conversation. In attempting to be honest with her and proposing marriage if she should find herself with child, it appeared he had only succeeded in insulting her. And nothing he had said since appeared to have in any way rectified that situation. It appeared, in fact, that he could not regain favour in her eyes no matter what he did or said.

Yet did he wish to regain favour in her eyes? Surely it would be better for both of them if he left things exactly as they were? It was unpleasant to feel the lash of her tongue and coldness of manner towards him, but the alternative would no doubt only result in another of those passionate encounters. Dominic still burned with desire for her, despite knowing how ill advised a repeat of this morning's activities would be.

Just to look at Caro was to remember the silky smoothness of her skin beneath his fingers. To remember the hard pebbles of her nipples being drawn into his mouth. The burning heat of her slick and yet tight thighs as she took him deep inside her... No, perhaps it would be much safer to foster this lack of accord between them!

'As you wish, Caro,' he said haughtily as he turned away to studiously straighten the shirt cuffs beneath his jacket.

Caro was absolutely incensed as he turned his back on her. 'I cannot imagine what I could have been thinking of this morning, allowing you to make love to me, when you are so obviously everything that I most despise in a man!'

He turned back sharply, nostrils flared. 'Just as your own rebellious and outspoken nature is everything that I most dislike in a woman!'

Caro eyed him coldly. 'Then we are agreed we do not care for each other?'

His jaw tightened. 'Indeed we are!'

She gave a cool nod. 'Then I will wish you good day, Lord Vaughn.'

Dominic eyed her with frustration. He had never met a woman who could bring him so quickly to anger. To impatience. To fury. But most especially to desire...

Logical thought told Dominic that if he wished to retain his sanity, then any future protection he provided for Caro's safety must necessarily be given from a distance. Just to be with her was playing the very devil with his self-control—

'Am I to remain a prisoner here, as I was at Blackstone House, until this danger from Nicholas Brown is over?' Caro interrupted Dominic's disturbing train of thought. 'Or am I to be allowed out for a carriage ride, at least?'

He refocused on her, his instincts telling him, for the sake of her own safety, to deny her even that small pleasure. However, that same instinct was quickly overridden by the memory of how flagrantly Caro had chosen to defy those same instructions only this morning and what the result of that defiance had been!

His mouth twisted. If he denied her, she'd likely find a way to disobey him, and then all hell would be let loose. Far better that he knew what she was doing at all times. 'I believe a carriage ride is permissible.'

'How kind!' Her sarcasm was unmistakable. 'And am I to take a maid with me on this carriage ride?'

'I do not believe that to be necessary unless you especially wish to do so. The grooms and coachmen here are also old comrades of mine,' he added before she had the opportunity to make another scathing comment. 'I trust in their ability to ensure that no harm befalls you.'

'*Further* harm, I think you mean?'

Dominic flinched as that verbal arrow of hers hit its mark. How he longed to take this rebellious woman into his arms. To kiss her into submission, if he could achieve her obedience in no other way. Yet at the same time he knew he should not, could not do either of those things. 'I will call on you again tomorrow—'

'I am sure there is no need to trouble yourself on my account,' she cut in.

Once again Dominic bit back his frustration, knowing how badly he had already handled this situation. 'I will take my leave, then.'

She nodded coolly. 'Lord Vaughn.'

There was nothing more for Dominic to do or say. Nothing he could do or say, it seemed, that would make things as they had once been between them.

Even if he did not know, could not completely comprehend, exactly what that had been…

Caro was filled with a raw restlessness once she was sure that the Earl had gone from the house, aware as she was of the rest of the afternoon and the long evening alone that now stretched before her. Tomorrow, too, in all probability, now that she had told Dominic it was unnecessary for him to call on her.

He should not have made her so angry! Should not have said those insulting things to her. Insults, Caro acknowledged ruefully, that she had more than returned.

How different things could have been, if instead of offering her marriage in that insulting manner, Dominic had first made a declaration of having fallen in love with her.

And if he had? Caro asked herself. What would her answer have been then to his marriage proposal? Would she have returned that declaration of love before accepting his marriage proposal?

The thought that she might have done both of those things was so disturbing to Caro that she found herself hurrying from the drawing room, pausing only long enough in the entrance hall to instruct Denby to have the coach brought round, before hurrying up to her bedchamber to collect her bonnet and pelisse. The afternoon seemed to have grown chilly since Dominic's abrupt departure…

Quite where she intended going on her carriage ride Caro had no idea, aware only that she had to escape the confines—the memories!—of Brockle House, if only for a short time.

She instructed the coachman to drive through the same park as yesterday—perhaps with the hope that she might once again catch a glimpse of the young girl with the dog that had so achingly reminded her of Elizabeth. But if that was her wish then she was disappointed, and after only a short time she was also a little tired of the curious glances being directed towards where she travelled in the black carriage so obviously bearing the crest of the Earl of Blackstone.

Feeling in need of sympathetic company, Caro knocked upon the roof of the carriage and instructed the coachman to take her to Nick's; Drew Butler and Ben had been delighted when she had called to see them this morning, so surely a second visit would not be too unwelcome?

But they had not gone far in that direction before Caro looked up and noticed a huge black cloud billowing up into the sky, her attention fixed on that black haze as she once again tapped on the roof of the coach. 'What is that about, Daley?'

'I believe it might be smoke, Mrs Morton,' he answered respectfully.

Smoke? If there was smoke then there must be a fire. And fire was a dangerous thing in a city the size of London. 'Perhaps we should go and see if we can be of any assistance, Daley?'

The middle-aged man looked uncertain. 'I doubt his lordship would approve, madam.'

Dominic.

Smoke?

Fire!

Quite why Caro was so convinced those three things were connected she had no idea—she only knew that she became more convinced of it by the second!

Chapter Fourteen

'You have to stop now, Drew; there is nothing more we can do,' Dominic instructed the man wearily.

The two men were blackened from head to toe from having several times entered the burning building before them, thick black smoke now billowing out of every doorway and window of the building even as the flames and sparks shot up through a hole in the burning roof.

Butler's eyes glittered wildly in his own soot-covered face. 'Ben is still in there!'

'There is nothing more we can do,' Dominic repeated dully, his own expression grim beneath the soot and grime as he stared up at the inferno that had once been Nick's.

'But—'

'He's gone, Drew.'

The older man's arms fell helplessly to his sides, his weathered face echoing the defeat both men felt as they could only stand now and watch the fire blaze out of control despite their own efforts and that of the men who had arrived a few minutes ago to help put it out.

The fire had been well under way when Dominic himself had arrived some half an hour or so ago. Nowhere near as fierce as it was now, of course, but even so he had quickly drawn a halt to Drew and Ben Jackson's efforts as they rushed in and out of the building salvaging what they could.

Unfortunately Ben had decided to return one more time to collect some personal belongings and the account books from the desk in Drew Butler's office.

He had not come out again…

Drew's hands clenched into fists at his sides. 'I'm going to kill the bastard!'

Dominic's jaw tightened. 'Brown?'

The older man's eyes blazed with fury as he turned. 'Who else?'

It was a conclusion that Dominic had come to himself the moment he saw the fire blazing and so easily recalled Brown's air of quiet satisfaction when he had left the gambling club earlier today.

Dominic had gone into the lion's den the evening before, with the intention of ascertaining whether Brown truly was the one responsible for the attack on Osborne. The slickness with which the other man had denied all knowledge of that attack—when he was a man known to boast that he was aware of everything that happened in what he regarded as being 'his city'—had seemed to indicate those suspicions were correct.

That Brown had himself arrived at the gambling club earlier today, supposedly to pay a visit on his old friends, Butler and Jackson, as well as the guarded conversation that had transpired between Brown and Dominic in Caro's presence, was simply a measure, Dominic was certain, of the other man's audacity.

A fire in that building, only hours after Brown's visit, was to Dominic's mind tantamount to a direct challenge…

He frowned darkly. 'The law will need evidence before they will agree to act.'

The older man gave a scathing snort. 'I don't need any evidence to recognise Brown had a hand in this.'

Neither did Dominic. 'Be assured, I feel exactly the way you do about this, Drew, but nevertheless I must seriously advise against taking matters into your own hands—'

'So I'm to sit back and let him get away with murder, am I?'

Dominic had already experienced one slight on his honour in the past two days; he was not about to suffer another one. He put his hand on the older man's arm. 'I am hoping you will trust me to ensure that will not happen.'

Drew barely seemed to hear him. 'I worked for the man for almost twenty years. Had my suspicions before this of what a low-down cur he could be, but—' He gave a disgusted shake of his head. 'Brown did this as surely as my name is Andrew Butler.'

Dominic drew his breath in sharply. 'And I have assured you that I will ensure he will be made to pay for his crimes—'

'Dominic! Drew! Oh, thank goodness you are both safe!'

Dominic turned just in time to catch Caro as she launched herself into his arms.

Caro had barely been able to comprehend the sight that had met her eyes as the carriage turned into the avenue and she saw the blazing remains of the club where she had worked until two evenings ago. The whole building was ablaze, with that heavy black smoke billowing everywhere, and dozens of men hurrying back and forth as they threw water upon the blaze to prevent it passing to the vulnerable neighbouring buildings.

Her relief when she spotted Dominic, standing to one side in conversation with Drew, had been immense. So much so that she had briefly forgotten her earlier disagreement with Dominic, and simply thrown herself into his arms out of the sheer relief of seeing him safe.

Her cheeks now felt hot—and not from the effects of the fire!—as she gathered herself together and extracted herself from Dominic's embrace before turning to face the older man. 'How good it is to see that you are unharmed, Drew—'

'Never mind that now, Caro,' Dominic was the one to answer her as he pulled her firmly back from the danger of the hot timbers now starting to fall from the top of the blazing building. 'Explain what you are doing here, if you please!'

She frowned up into his dark and disapproving face. 'I had gone out for a drive, as I told you I intended, when I saw the smoke...'

'And decided to investigate,' Dominic recognised with barely restrained violence. 'Did you not realise that by doing so you might have become caught up in the blaze yourself and possibly been injured?'

She waved an airy hand. 'I hope I have more sense than to have gone close enough so that—'

'And yet here you are!' Dominic glared down at her, very aware that she was as yet unaware of Ben Jackson's absence. That when she did realise he would have another crisis on his hands; Caro's affection for the gentle giant had been obvious from the first, and once she discovered that Ben had disappeared into the blazing building some minutes ago, and not returned, she was sure to react. In truth, Dominic had no idea which direction those emotions would take, tears and cries of anguish, or anger that her friend might have perished in the fire...

She gave a pained frown. 'I was concerned—'

'And now that concern has been satisfied I want you to get back into your carriage immediately and return to Brockle House,' Dominic instructed firmly.

'But—'

'Caro, do not argue with me over this, as you seem to feel you must argue every other point in our conversations.' Dominic's jaw was as tightly clenched as Drew's fists had been minutes ago. 'You can be of no possible help here,' he added.

'Might I suggest that you leave me to continue dealing with the situation here whilst you escort Caro home?' Drew quietly drew Dominic's attention, his pointed look in the direction of some activity at the side of the building enough to tell Dominic that Ben had been found; neither man believed he could have lived through the minutes he had spent trapped in that raging inferno…

'That is unnecessary—'

'It is very necessary.' Dominic easily cut across Caro's protest even as he gave a brief nod to the older man in recognition of their silent exchange.

'To you, perhaps—'

'To me, too, Caro.' Drew gently added his own weight behind the argument as he moved forwards so that he now stood beside Dominic. 'Do as his lordship advises and return to your carriage—'

'Why are you suddenly both in such a hurry for me to leave?' Caro eyed both men suspiciously as she realised they seemed to be crowding around her. Herding her, actually. Much like her father's estate workers when they were gathering the livestock together to house them in the huge barns over the winter. 'I—where is Ben?' Her gaze moved sharply to the left and then to the right, but with Drew and Dominic standing like two sentinels directly in front of her, she found that vision limited.

Deliberately?

'Caro—'

'Where is Ben, Dominic?' Caro lifted her hands and placed one against the chest of both men with the intention of pushing them aside, nimbly stepping around them when neither man was made to move. Just in time to see that several of the men who had been fighting the fire were now carrying something from the side of the building. Something heavy. A dead weight, in fact… 'Ben?' she gasped weakly.

'No, Caro!' Dominic reached out and grasped her by the shoulders as she would have run across to where the men were now placing that cumbersome burden down upon the ground.

Her gaze was frantic as she lifted her hands to fight against Dominic's hold upon her. 'Can you not see that it is Ben?'

'We know who it is, Caro.' Once again it was Drew who spoke gently. 'If there's anything that can be done for Ben, then you can be assured that it will be,' he added grimly. 'The best thing you can do for him now is to return home without any more fuss.'

Caro became very still in Dominic's grasp as she looked first at Drew and then back to Dominic, the latter giving a slight shake of his head as he turned back from looking at the frantic activity around that scorched bundled of rags that had obviously been Ben Jackson.

Because even from this distance Caro could see that his spirit was no longer there...

An anguished cry escaped her lips even as she felt her legs buckle beneath her and began to fall slowly to the ground.

'You are perfectly safe, Caro.' Dominic's voice sounded harsher than he had intended, in the otherwise silence of the moving carriage, as he tried to still her struggles to free herself from where he held her tightly against his chest. 'Please be still, Caro,' he urged more gently.

For once in their acquaintance she heeded him, unmoving in his arms as she looked up at him with huge sea-green eyes that were rapidly filling with tears. 'Is Ben really gone, Dominic?'

He drew in a ragged breath. 'If it is any consolation

then I believe he would have died from breathing in the smoke long before the fire ever came anywhere near him.' He sincerely hoped that was the case, at least.

Although the method of Ben's death did not change the fact he was indeed dead. And as a result of a fire both Drew and Dominic believed to have been deliberately set by Nicholas Brown.

'Truly, Dominic?'

He forced the rigidity from his expression at those grim thoughts of Brown's cowardly act before looking down at Caro, knowing that she needed to believe that Ben's death had been as painless as was possible given the circumstances. 'Truly.' Dominic nodded.

He had paused only long enough, after seeing the unconscious Caro into the safety of the carriage, to converse briefly with the men who had brought out Ben's body. It seemed they had found him collapsed in the hallway leading to Drew's office situated at the back of the club, where the fire itself was the least fierce.

'He was such a kind young man.' Caro's voice caught emotionally.

Dominic had seen Ben off and on for years on his visits to the gambling club; it had been impossible not to feel an affection for the younger man's almost childlike acceptance of his lot in life.

As such, Dominic knew that it was going to be hard for all of them to accept the death of such an affable and likeable young man. 'He was,' he acknowledged flatly.

Caro pulled out of his arms to slowly sit up. 'How could it have happened, Dominic?' She gave a slightly dazed shake of her head. 'I can hardly believe I was sitting drinking tea with him only hours ago…' The tears began to fall unchecked down her cheeks.

'Yes.' Dominic's mouth tightened as he easily recalled that Brown had been seated at that table, too. 'We may perhaps have more insight into how the fire began once the flames have died down and we are able to get back inside the building.' Although in his own mind—and undoubtedly that of Drew Butler—Brown, or one of his henchmen acting on instructions, was clearly to blame.

'Do you believe Nicholas Brown to be responsible?'

Dominic was not in the least surprised at the speed of Caro's astuteness. 'Undoubtedly,' he confirmed grimly.

'As just another deliberate act to cause you as much inconvenience as possible, or do you think he really meant either Ben or Drew—or possibly both—to die?' Her face had taken on a slightly green cast as she voiced that last possibility.

As far as Dominic was aware, he had never lied to Caro; in fact, his actions, especially this morning, had possibly been too honest where she was concerned. Possibly? The whole of his behaviour today, from making love to her to the crassness of his marriage proposal, had been honest to the point of self-destruction!

That she had allowed him to hold her just now, even briefly, Dominic knew was due only to her distress over Ben's death. Once she had recovered her senses they would no doubt be back to a state of daggers' drawn.

He drew in a deep breath as he chose his words carefully. 'I believe it was the former. At the same time, I also believe Brown did not care who, or if, anyone should be hurt in the fire,' he acknowledged heavily before taking the kerchief from his pocket and wiping the worst of the soot and grime from his face and hands.

Caro breathed shakily. 'Ben would not have hurt even a fly.'

Remembering those ham-sized fists, and the several occasions upon which he had witnessed the younger man wielding them, Dominic was not quite sure of the truth of that statement! Nevertheless, he took Caro's point; there had never been any malice in Ben's actions in doing his job defending the club.

'I am sure it was pure misfortunate that Ben perished in the fire.' Dominic was not as certain of that as he sounded, aware as he was that this morning Nicholas Brown had witnessed both Ben and Drew busily at work in the gambling club so that it might re-open as soon as was possible.

Caro looked up at him closely. 'Do you honestly believe that?'

'I...believe it is a reasonable assumption, yes,' he said carefully.

'I am neither a child nor an imbecile, Dominic, and after all that has happened, I do not expect you to treat me as such!' Caro's expression had become fierce as she obviously picked up on his evasion.

He had no doubts as to her maturity or intelligence; it was simply not in his nature to confide his thoughts and feelings to another person. 'I assure you it is not my intention to do either of those things, Caro. I simply feel it is better not to voice my concerns until I can be completely sure of my facts.'

He also had no intention of allowing her to become in the least involved in the reckoning that Dominic had every intention would shortly descend upon Nicholas Brown; Caro was impetuous enough, reckless enough, to place herself in danger if she believed it was necessary to avenge Ben.

No, Dominic had every intention of dealing personally with Mr Nicholas Brown...

Caro still looked slightly ill. 'I cannot conceive of anyone doing something so...so heinous, as to have deliberately started a fire.'

Dominic was only too aware that Brown was reputed to have done much worse things than that in the past. Just as Dominic was now aware—too late to save Ben, unfortunately—that after the attack on Osbourne two nights ago, and despite Drew's assurances that he was quite capable of taking care of himself and his own family, including Ben, Dominic should have insisted on more safeguards being put in place. The reason he had not was because he had been so distracted by the need to protect Caro that he had given little thought to anything else...

A danger that now seemed more immediate than ever; Dominic had thought to make Caro safe by offering her his protection, by moving her as quickly as he could to the obscurity of Brockle House. But Brown's visit to the gambling club this morning had exposed Caro, if not as the masked singer, then certainly as a closer acquaintance to Dominic than the cousins they claimed to be. Now he feared the man might even know that Caro resided at Brockle House as from this morning...

Dominic shared Drew's eagerness to confront Nicholas Brown, to ensure that he paid for his crimes—in fact, at that moment, he knew he would enjoy nothing more than personally strangling the man with his own bare hands—but his explanation to Caro, when she had previously dared to question his honour, was also true. A soldier, an officer, did not confront his enemy until he had all of his troops in place.

And Nicholas Brown was now most certainly Dominic's enemy!

'Caro, I believe it would be best if I were to stay at Brockle House tonight.' He looked at her from underneath lowered lids.

Her own eyes widened. 'I believed we had both made our feelings on that subject perfectly clear—'

'I did not say it was with any intention of sharing your bed,' Dominic cut in impatiently. 'Only that it might be…safer, perhaps, if I were to stay at Brockle House tonight.'

Caro's cheeks warmed as she realised her mistake. Of course Dominic did not intend sharing her bed again tonight; he did not intend sharing her bed ever again! Something she should feel grateful for. And yet somehow did not… 'Is it your belief that we are both now in mortal danger from Nicholas Brown?'

Dominic shrugged. 'Perhaps.'

Caro was consumed with annoyance at Dominic's reticence, his refusal to share his thoughts and feelings with her. He had to be the most self-contained man she had ever met—and that was including her father, who had become so shut inside himself after their mother had left them all to go and live in London ten years ago, that he had never mentally been completely with his three daughters again. As far as she could tell,

Dominic shared none of his thoughts and ideas with anyone.

Least of all a woman to whom he had only offered marriage if *by some mischance*, as he'd put it, she should find herself carrying his child!

'If you feel it is necessary, Dominic, then of course you have every right to spend the night in what is, after all, your own property.' She gave a cool inclination of her head.

Dominic breathed heavily through his nose. 'In that case, until this situation has been resolved to my complete satisfaction, I feel it best if I spend all of my nights at Brockle House.'

Caro's eyes widened. 'Are you not going to find that a little…restricting?'

He scowled darkly. 'In what way?'

She shrugged. 'Would such an arrangement not… limit your own freedom to come and go as you wished?'

Dominic drew in an angry breath. 'Caro, if you are once again suggesting that I might have a mistress set up in another house in London somewhere, and with whom I might wish to spend my nights, then let me state, once and for all, that I do not now, nor have I ever, had a mistress in the accepted sense of the word!' He eyed her coldly.

'No?' Her brows rose. 'I would be interested to know why not.'

'Then it is an interest I am afraid you will just have to continue to endure,' Dominic growled. 'After only a few days of having you as a permanent fixture in my life, of feeling responsible for you twenty-four hours a day, I am more convinced than ever that my decision never to be tied down by such an arrangement was the correct one.' He meant to be insulting, and he knew he had succeeded when he saw the sparkle of anger in the deep blue-green of Caro's eyes.

A spark of anger that Dominic had deliberately incited...

'That situation can be rectified any time you choose to let me leave both your home and your company,' she came back challengingly.

'Unfortunately, it cannot.' Dominic sighed. 'Not until Brown has been brought to justice. Never fear, Caro,' he added mockingly. 'I am sure that Brockle House is large enough for us to successfully avoid spending time in each other's company, if that is what you wish?'

'I wish it more than anything!' There was an angry flush to Caro's cheeks as she turned away from him to present him with her profile as she stared out of the carriage window.

Dominic accepted that it had been cruel of him to bedevil her in this way when their lovemaking had ended so disastrously earlier today. When she had been present as they pulled Ben's body from the burning building. His only excuse was that his baiting of her had briefly cast aside her bewilderment and pain over Ben's death, to be replaced by a little of the usual fiery spirit he so admired and which was such a large part of her nature.

A spirit Dominic dearly hoped would help see her through, what he was sure, were going to be several difficult days...

Chapter Fifteen

'Caro, when I said earlier that you might avoid my company as much as is possible for the duration of my stay here, it was not with any intention that you would eat your dinner in your bedchamber whilst I am left to dine downstairs alone.'

She was completely unmoved by the impatience in Dominic's tone as she turned to look at where he stood in the open doorway of her bedchamber.

It had been almost two hours since they had arrived back at Brockle House. Dominic appeared to have bathed and changed out of the soiled clothing of earlier into a black evening jacket and snowy white linen with a meticulously tied neckcloth. Evidence, perhaps, that in the interim he had sent to Blackstone House for both his valet and his clothes.

Caro had spent those same two hours trying to come to terms with the fact that Ben Jackson was dead. To accept that her friend had perished in a fire Dominic believed had been started deliberately by Nicholas Brown or one of his close associates.

For years she had chafed and fought against the sheltered life she had been forced to lead in Hampshire, with the result that she had not hesitated to put her plan into action once she had decided to run away to London as a means of avoiding the arrival of her guardian and his unwanted offer of marriage. She had believed herself to be thoroughly capable of taking care of herself, and that spending several weeks in London would be an exciting adventure she would remember for the rest of her life.

Nothing about her previous life could possibly have prepared her for such stark reality as she had witnessed today.

She gave a slight shake of her head. 'I have not eaten my dinner in my bedchamber.'

Dominic scowled darkly as he strode forcefully into the room. 'In that case, why haven't you?'

She gave a listless shrug. 'I am not hungry.'

'Caro—'

'Dominic, please!' She stood up restlessly, also having bathed and changed into the deep rose-coloured gown. 'How can I possibly eat when every time I so much as think of poor Ben's fate I feel utterly nauseous?'

Dominic's expression softened as he realised that, while he'd had some little relief from her tempting charms in the past couple of hours, suggesting they avoid each other's company had not been particularly beneficial to her; he could see the evidence of the tears she had obviously shed once she was alone in the slight redness about pain-darkened eyes and the pallor of her cheeks. 'It will not help anyone if you make yourself ill—'

'You cannot expect me to eat when Ben is lying dead in the morgue!' Caro's voice broke emotionally over the last, and she buried her face in her hands, her shoulders shaking, as she once again began to sob piteously.

Dominic felt a tightening in his chest as he witnessed her distress, taking the two steps that enabled him to reach out and take her into his arms, her head resting against his chest as she wept. He had never been at ease with a woman's tears, and, after the intimacies they had shared, he found Caro's especially difficult to bear. Her close proximity was even more difficult as he felt her arms move about his waist and the warm spread of her fingers across his back...

Dear Lord! Desire, arousal were the last things he should be feeling when she was obviously so distraught. And yet, try as he might, he could exert no control over the stirring, the hardening of his thighs, as Caro nestled the softness of her body against his. She rested so trustingly against him—for Dominic was sure that she shared none of those same thoughts of desire as she continued to sob quietly. His own physical response to that trust was as inappropriate as it would no doubt be unwelcome should she become aware of it, and he grimaced with annoyance at his own body's betrayal.

As Caro's tears slowly began to abate she sensed a change in the mood between herself and Dominic. A tension, an intimacy, that invaded her senses with a subtlety that was as insidious as it was undeniable. The very air around them seemed to thicken, to deepen, and she was suddenly completely aware of the tense heat of his body and the ragged unevenness of his breathing, as his chest rose and fell beneath the increasing warmth of her cheek. She was also aware of the thick length of his arousal as it continued to grow and press against the softness of her own thighs.

Her breath caught in her throat as she slowly raised her head to look up at him, knowing by the glittering intensity of the silver gaze that looked down and met hers that she was not mistaken concerning his present state of arousal.

She moistened dry lips before speaking. 'Dominic, how can it be that we feel this…this desire after all that has happened today?' She was utterly bewildered— almost ashamed—by the feelings now coursing hotly through her own body.

Dominic shook his head. 'I have seen it dozens of times in soldiers following a battle,' he recalled huskily. 'I believe it is a need, a desire, to reaffirm one's own place in the mortal world following confrontation with death.'

Caro breathed shallowly. 'Is it not shocking for me to feel this way now?'

His expression softened. 'Does it feel shocking to you?'

'No.' The pink tip of her tongue swept across her lips a second time. 'I— It feels as if, as you say, I have a need to know that we both still live.'

Dominic looked down at her searchingly, a gaze that she met unflinchingly. 'Will you allow me to make love to you, Caro?' he asked gently.

Her eyes widened. 'But I thought you had made it quite clear that we could not, must not, repeat the events of this morning?'

'Neither will we.'

Her frown was perplexed. 'I do not understand…'

Dominic gave a rueful smile. 'There are many ways in which to make love, my dear. Many of them do not involve the penetration that could so easily result in you becoming with child.'

Caro's cheeks felt hot. 'I see. And will you…will you show me these other ways?' Her cheeks were flushed, her eyes fever bright.

But not with awkwardness or discomfort, Dominic noted with admiration, but instead with a curiosity and underlying excitement. He knew he should not allow this to happen, that he should refuse to acknowledge the invitation in her eyes. But as he looked down at her, he clearly saw the same desire in her that now throbbed through his own body, and he knew he would not, could not, walk away from her as he surely should.

He, too, had had time to think since they had parted after arriving at Brockle House earlier. To realise that she could just as easily have gone to visit Drew and Ben at Nick's this afternoon rather than this morning. To acknowledge that she might have been inside the club with the other two men when the fire began, and easily envisage the nightmare of what might have been—Caro lying in the morgue rather than Ben Jackson…

Which perhaps explained why he had felt it so keenly when Denby had told him a short time ago that Caro had asked him to inform Dominic she would not be joining him downstairs for dinner. Whatever the reason, no matter how much more it might complicate matters if he were to make love with her again, he knew that it was something he urgently needed to do.

Caro pulled out of his arms to turn her back on him before looking at him over her shoulder. 'I believe we should start by removing my gown?'

He drew his breath in sharply as he looked at the calm determination in Caro's expression for several long seconds before raising his hands to begin releasing the buttons down the back of her gown. Only to falter slightly once he had unfastened a half-dozen of those tiny buttons. 'Are you *sure* you want to do this?'

'I am very sure, Dominic,' she murmured even as she tilted her head forwards to reveal the fragile vulnerability of her nape.

It was more than any man could bear—more, certainly, than he could at this moment—to resist Caro's absolute conviction in what they were about to do. And once he had unfastened the rose-coloured gown, allowing it to pool on the carpet at her feet, before she stepped free of its confinement and turned to face him wearing only a shift that nevertheless revealed the firm thrust of her breasts tipped by those darker nipples, and the silky thatch of golden curls between her thighs, Dominic had no room for thoughts of resistance. His desire blazed completely out of his control as she reached up to slip the thin straps of her last garment down over the slenderness of her arms, before allowing that, too, to fall at her feet and she stood before him completely naked.

Dominic meant to be gentle with her, out of consideration for the discomfort she must still feel following their lovemaking this morning. But it was a gentleness Caro firmly rejected as she stepped boldly into his arms before raising her head so that her lips might capture his. That kiss became wild, fiercely heated, as she dispensed with his jacket and waistcoat before unfastening his shirt and pushing her hands inside the silky material to caress his bared chest.

Dominic returned the heat of that kiss even as he reached up to rend the material of his shirt in two to allow her better access to his flesh. Caro's nails scraped over the hard nubbins nestled amongst the silky dark hair that covered his chest, the hard tips of her own breasts pressed against the muscled hardness of his abdomen. He gasped into her mouth as those caressing, confident hands moved slowly downwards to stroke the length of his erection as it jutted proudly against the confinement of his pantaloons.

It did not remain confined for long as Caro easily dispensed with the six buttons at the sides of his pantaloons before peeling that flap of material aside, the fingers of one hand curling about his engorged arousal even as she cupped him beneath with the other.

Dominic broke the kiss, his groan one of aching longing as he felt her dextrous fingers sweep across the sensitive tip before moving down along the length of him. 'Yes, Caro! Oh, God, yes!'

'Tell me how to give you pleasure, Dominic,' she encouraged softly.

His breath caught in his throat. 'Kiss me there, take me into the sweetness of your mouth!' His moan was heartfelt as Caro dropped softly to her knees in front of him, that sea-green gaze looking up to steadily meet his as she slowly and deliberately opened those kiss-swollen lips and took him into the fiery heat of her mouth.

Dominic's knees almost buckled completely as he looked down at her pleasuring him, his hands moving to become entangled in her golden curls as she continued her delicious ministrations until he knew he was going to lose control. He needed to taste her before that happened, wanted to pleasure her in the same way.

Dominic ignored her slightly reproachful look as he gently disengaged himself and pulled her back up on to her feet. He swung her up into his arms and carried her over to lie her down upon the bed, gently propping her head upon the pillows. She watched him as he first drew off his boots and then threw off the rest of his clothes before moving to kneel between her legs. The darkness of his gaze briefly held hers captive before he lowered his head between her parted thighs to run his own tongue along the length of her opening before rasping moistly over and around her sensitive bud, feeling it pulse with each rhythmic stroke. 'Watch me, Caro!' he urged.

She obeyed as he gently parted her golden curls and cried out as he lowered his head once again to stroke that pulsing bud with the hard tip of his tongue, and she felt the pleasure begin to build, to grow, deep inside her. Suffusing her with heat. Turning her limbs to water. Her head fell back against the pillows even as her thighs began to undulate against that marauding mouth and tongue.

That pleasure surged out of control as his hands moved up to cup and capture both her breasts before he rolled the nipples between finger and thumb,

Caro's release hitting with the force of a tidal wave as he squeezed those roused tips at the same time as his tongue thrust into her time and time again until she lay limply back against the pillows.

Dominic moved up on to his knees to look down at Caro as she lay there, replete and naked against the pillows. 'My turn now, love,' he said throatily.

Caro was completely focused on that jutting arousal as she came up on to her knees to move down the bed and kiss him slowly from base to tip, before then taking him fully into the heat of her mouth.

It was too much, Dominic already far too aroused from both the taste of her in his mouth and her earlier attentions, and his hands tightly gripped Caro's shoulders as he climaxed fiercely, hotly, triumphantly…

Caro's hand moved in a gentle caress against the unruly darkness of the hair at Dominic's nape, his head resting lightly against her breast as they lay naked together in the aftermath of their wild and satisfying lovemaking.

She felt no awkwardness, no shame; she knew that they had both needed what had just happened between them, that he had been correct in that they had both needed to reaffirm their precarious grip on mortality, and the silence between them now was companionable rather than uncomfortable.

Dominic raised his head slightly to look at her, that silver gaze guarded. 'I was not too rough with you?'

'Not at all,' she assured without hesitation. 'Was I too rough with you?' she added, aware that she had been somewhat less than gentle herself!

He smiled slightly before lowering his head back down on to her breast. 'Not in any way I would not like you to repeat if, or indeed whenever, the mood should take you.'

Caro's cheeks felt warm as she recalled the way in which she had caressed and kissed Dominic so intimately. She had no knowledge of lovemaking between a man and a woman other than the things he had shown her these past few days, and yet she had gloried in touching and kissing the beauty of his hard arousal.

'I no longer feel quite so…empty.' Her voice was husky with emotion.

'Nor I,' Dominic acknowledged softly.

She frowned as a thought occurred to her. 'Do you know whether or not Ben had any family?'

Dominic's shoulders tensed beneath the caress of Caro's fingers. 'He has a sister, I believe. A Mrs Grey.'

'She will be deeply saddened by his death.'

'As we all are,' Dominic said heavily. 'Drew was to go and see her as soon as he was able to get away. I have asked him to convey my regrets, and also to tell her that I will call on her tomorrow to discuss the funeral arrangements if that is what she wishes.'

'I would like to attend the funeral.'

The tension in Dominic's shoulders increased. 'I am not sure that is a good idea—'

'It was not a request, Dominic,' Caro insisted. 'Have you—have you seen much of death?' she asked before he could voice any more objections.

'More than I care to remember,' he admitted harshly.

Caro breathed a sigh. 'My own mother died when I was but ten years old, and she was not at home with us when it happened.' She gave a pained frown as she remembered the circumstances under which her mother had died. 'My father died only a few months ago, but he had been ill for some time, and in truth, it was more of a happy release for him than a shock to…to his family.'

Dominic was aware that the pieces that made up Caro's life were given rarely and sparingly, but she had said enough just now for him to know it was no more a father that she hid from than a husband.

He could not resist looking up at her and teasing her a little. 'I believe you told Drew that it was a maiden aunt who had died a few months ago, and in doing so left you homeless as well as penniless.'

Two bright wings of colour now brightened Caro's cheeks. 'I did say that, yes.'

'And…?'

She gave an irritated little snort. 'What difference does it make whether it was a father or a maiden aunt?'

'None at all—except maybe to that father or aunt.' Dominic placed a slow and lingering kiss upon the side of her breast in apology for his teasing of what they both knew to be a complete fabrication of her previous life. But he felt too relaxed, too satiated, to seriously question it at this moment. That relaxed contentment rendered him ill prepared for Caro's next question…

'Obviously you are the Earl, so your own father is no longer with us, but what of the rest of your family? Your mother, for instance?'

All relaxation fled, all contentment, as Dominic sat up sharply. 'Also dead. They both died when I was but twelve years old.'

Caro gasped. 'Both your parents?'

'Yes.'

'Together?'

'No. Caro—'

'Please do not go, Dominic!' She reached out to grasp his arm as he would have stood up, her gaze pleading as he paused to look down at her. 'If you do not wish to talk of your parents, then we will not do so,' she promised huskily.

Dominic concentrated on how her loosened curls looked, all spread out on the pillow behind her. Her eyes were a beautiful, luminous sea-green, her lips slightly swollen from the kisses they had shared. Her cheeks were flushed, as was the delicate skin of her breasts, the tips all pouting and rosy from his attentions. His expression softened as he slowly exhaled his tension away before once again lowering his head to rest against one of those kiss-reddened breasts, his hand moving to lightly cup its twin. 'There is nothing more to say about my parents other than that they are both dead.'

'But your mother, at least, must have been quite young when she died?'

Dominic sighed. 'She was but two and thirty at the time of the accident. My father was eight and thirty when he chose to follow her only days later.'

Caro stilled, her heart pounding loudly beneath Dominic's head. 'He *chose* to follow her?'

Dominic had learnt early on in their acquaintance not to underestimate Caro's intelligence, and with this question she once again proved he had been wise not to do so. 'Yes.'

Caro's throat moved convulsively as she swallowed

before speaking. 'Can you possibly mean that he took his own life?'

Dominic made no attempt to halt his movements a second time, instead sitting up and moving away from her. Caro was sensible enough—or too stunned still—not to try to stop him, either by word or deed. He shrugged. 'He loved my mother very much and obviously saw no reason to continue living without her.'

'But he had a young son to care for!'

'Obviously he did not feel I was reason enough to continue living.' Dominic stood up and began pulling on the pantaloons he had discarded so eagerly only minutes ago.

Caro reached down and pulled the bedsheet up to her chin as she watched him with huge, disbelieving eyes. 'My own father loved my mother very much, too, and was devastated when she died. But even so, I do not think he ever contemplated the idea of taking his own life; he accepted that he had other responsibilities—'

Dominic's scathing snort cut off her halting words. 'Obviously your father was made of sterner stuff than my own.'

'I do not believe it was a question of that—'

'And I believe we have talked of this quite long enough for one evening!' His eyes glittered a pale and dangerous silver.

Caro lowered her gaze. 'It is just that I do not understand how any man, no matter how devastated he is by loss, could deliberately take his own life at the cost of leaving his twelve-year-old son alone in the world.'

'I have *told* you why!' Dominic paused to glare across at her once he had pulled on the tattered remnants of his shirt. 'He loved my mother so much he had no desire to live without her.'

The compassion in her eyes as she looked up at him was almost his undoing. As it was, the painful memories this conversation evoked felt like a heavy weight bearing down upon him. 'I am sure my father felt justified in his actions, Caro,' he said.

Caro looked stubborn. 'I do not believe there can be any justification for leaving a twelve-year-old boy alone and without either of his parents.'

Dominic's dark brows lifted, his expression hard and uncompromising; eyes a steely grey, cheekbones as sharp as blades beneath the tautness of his skin, that vicious scar livid from eyes to jaw, and his mouth a thin line. 'Not even if you hold that twelve-year-old boy—your own son—responsible for the death of the woman you loved?'

Caro gave a shocked gasp, all the colour draining from her cheeks as she stared up at Dominic with those huge sea-green eyes.

Chapter Sixteen

Dominic knew that the look of horrified disbelief on Caro's face was perfectly justified; no doubt that was exactly the emotion she was feeling, at even the suggestion that a twelve-year-old boy could be responsible for killing his own mother. Let alone that it might actually be the truth…

Not that Dominic had caused his mother's coach to leave the road and plunge into the river. Nor had he wedged the door of that carriage shut so that it was impossible for her to escape when the carriage began to sink and the water to flood inside it. And neither had he physically held his mother's head beneath the water until she'd drowned.

No, he had not personally done any of those things. Nevertheless, he knew he was as much to blame for his mother's death as if he had done every one of them.

Caro shook her head. 'It is utterly ridiculous to even suggest you might have done such a thing.'

'Is it?'

'Utterly,' she spoke with conviction.

'You do not believe me capable of killing someone?' He eyed her tauntingly.

'Of course you have killed in the heat of battle,' she said. 'It is the way of things. But I do not believe you capable of harming any woman, let alone killing your own mother.'

'Come now, Caro, I am sure you must know me well enough by now to realise that I am capable of all manner of things. Seducing, not once, but twice, the young woman I have taken into my care is only one of them.' He looked disgusted with himself.

'I was as instrumental as you in both those seductions.' Caro's cheeks warmed with guilty colour as she quickly stood and collected her wrap, securing the belt of that robe around her waist. 'I also believe you are only saying these things about your mother in order to shock me.'

His mouth twisted. 'Am I succeeding?'

'I am more disappointed that you feel you have to say things that cannot possibly be true—'

'Oh, but they are true,' he cut in, his voice silkily soft, eyes narrowed to challenging slits as she looked across at him. 'I, and I alone, am responsible for the death of my mother.'

Once again Caro could see the ruthlessness in Dominic's expression; yes, she had no doubt that if he deemed it necessary for someone to die, then he would be cold and decisive, even savage, in the execution of that death. But the underlying edge of gentleness, of love, she had heard in his voice as he spoke of his mother told her that he could not have had a hand in her death. Besides which, what would a twelve-year-old boy know of killing anyone?

'Tell me how she died, Dominic,' she urged.

'What difference does the manner of her death make?'

'It makes all the difference in the world,' Caro said crossly. 'Why did you tell me these things if you did not wish me to question you?' Although she might take a guess on it having something to do with him thinking that he deserved to have people—women, most especially—feeling no affection for him.

But also an indication, perhaps, that he might also fear that she was falling in love with him? Caro winced inside. That he was determined to foil any such softness of emotion, if it existed, was humiliating. Worse than humiliating, if he'd guessed her feelings correctly.

In contrast, Dominic was a difficult man to read. That was deliberate, she felt sure. On the surface he was an arrogant, hard and uncompromising man, who outwardly scorned all the softer emotions. Yet, at the same time, he'd shown a deep concern over the attack on his friend, Lord Thorne. And instead of being furious earlier at the loss of his gambling club, as many gentlemen might have been, Dominic had instead only revealed a deep sorrow and anger at the death of poor Ben.

And Dominic's concern for Caro's own safety and welfare was just as undeniable, even though he took great pains to claim he had been forced into saving her from her own reckless behaviour!

He might give himself all sorts of reasons for his behaviour, but Caro had seen the man beneath and would have no part of it. 'I will know the truth, Dominic, if you please!'

He arched mocking brows. 'And will you then reveal to me the truth about yourself?'

Caro was in a quandary. No doubt he considered such an exchange of information fair. And it probably was. Except she could not confide her own situation to him, especially now when, having thought long and hard earlier this evening, Caro had decided that, guardian or not, she must return to Shoreley Hall as soon after Ben's funeral as possible.

Once back at Shoreley Hall she would assume the mantle of Lady Caroline Copeland. That being so, there was absolutely no reason for him to know anything further concerning Caro Morton, a woman who did not exist out of the small circle of acquaintances she had made in London.

She drew in a deep breath. 'I must refuse.'

Dominic's lip curled. 'Then it would seem we are at an impasse.'

'The two situations are completely different,' Caro snapped her impatience with his stubbornness. 'I have not just laid claim to killing someone!'

'How do I know that you did not see off this "maiden aunt" or your father before making your escape to London?' Dominic eyed her mockingly.

Because there was no maiden aunt, and of course Caro had not been involved in her father's death! But the second part of his statement, concerning her having made her escape to London, was too close to the truth for comfort...

'I believe you are merely trying to fudge the issue by making ridiculous accusations,' she said.

'You may think what you please,' Dominic retorted. 'As far as the subject of my mother, and the manner of her death, is concerned, I have no wish to discuss the matter further. With you or anyone else.' The finality in his tone did not allow for further argument. 'I believe I will wish you goodnight now, Caro.' He gave her a brief bow before striding across the room, pausing briefly when he reached the door. 'If you wish it, I will have some supper brought up to you.'

'That will not be necessary, thank you.' Caro felt even less like eating now than she had earlier. Ben was still dead, and contemplating food after the intimacies she and Dominic had just shared was impossible. Also, his refusal to further discuss his mother's death had left Caro with more questions than answers, especially as she now feared she might indeed have fallen in love with him!

Dominic's face darkened in fury when he returned to Brockle House late the following morning, accompanied by Drew, and was informed by a concerned Denby that Mrs Morton and Mr Brown were taking tea together in the Gold Salon.

The fact that Nicholas Brown had come here at all was disquieting. That Caro had chosen to receive him, knowing all that she did about the other man, was more disturbing still in view of what Dominic knew to be her often reckless and impulsive nature!

'Damn it, Denby.' He glared at the man who had once been his batman in the army but was now, for the sake of expediency, posing as his butler. 'What is the good of my installing you here to protect Caro when you then let the biggest threat to her calmly walk through the front door?'

The other man gave a pained frown. 'Mrs Morton had been for a walk in the park across the way—she was accompanied by my wife,' he added quickly as Dominic looked set for another explosion. 'It was apparently as she was returning to the house that she saw Mr Brown stepping down from his coach and stopped to engage him in conversation.'

Which sounded exactly the sort of thing Caro would do, Dominic realised frustratedly. He also realised that Brown must have had the two of them followed yesterday to know to find Caro at Brockle House at all. 'That still does not explain why you allowed the man to accompany her into the house?'

'I tried to prevent it from happening—'

'Obviously you did not try hard enough!'

'My wife is in the Gold Salon with them, my lord.'

'I am relieved to see that you have not completely lost your senses!' Dominic barked.

'We are wasting time here, my lord.' Drew put a steadying hand upon Dominic's arm. 'Brown can be a wily cur at the best of times, and I really don't think we should leave Caro to deal with him alone any longer. She is also likely to say more than she ought to him.'

'Caro has no more sense than a—'

'She is merely idealistically young,' the older man interrupted diplomatically.

'Nothing a sound beating would not cure!' Dominic assured the other man grimly as he strode across the entrance hall to thrust open the door to the Gold Salon, taking in at a glance the determined expression on Caro's face as she sat on the sofa looking up at a relaxed and nonchalant Nicholas Brown as he stood beside the unlit fireplace.

'I apologise for you having to receive our guest alone, Caro.'

She gave a self-conscious start at the icy coldness of Dominic's tone, one glance at the fury so clearly evident upon his face enough to show her how displeased he was at having returned to Brockle House to find that, despite all his warnings, she had chosen to invite Nicholas Brown inside when he'd had the audacity to arrive outside in his carriage some minutes earlier.

Dominic was no doubt perfectly aware that her sole purpose for inviting the other man to join her for tea, knowing him to be responsible for both Ben's death and the attack upon Lord Thorne, was to confront him with his perfidy! Something she had been just about to do when Dominic had arrived accompanied by Drew Butler.

In truth, Caro knew a certain relief in the timely arrival of the two men. Every attempt on her part to challenge the villain with his terrible deeds had been smoothly and charmingly foiled by him as he had kept up a stream of polite gossip and inanities from the moment they had entered the Gold Salon. Caro had even begun to doubt both her own and Dominic's conviction that Brown was responsible for anything more than having the misfortune to have gained a bad reputation!

'To what do we owe the pleasure of your visit, Brown?' Dominic obviously felt no such doubts as he kept the icy coldness of his gaze firmly fixed upon the older man.

Brown raised dark and mocking brows. 'I merely called to pay my respects to Mrs Morton.'

'Indeed?' Dominic's teeth showed in a predatory smile.

'I understand she was present when the fire occurred yesterday afternoon?' Brown said smoothly.

Dominic's jaw clenched. 'What of it?'

'I, of course, wished to assure myself of her good health.' Brown's smile was lazily confident. 'Women are such fragile creatures, are they not?'

It was impossible for Dominic to miss the underlying threat in that single remark. For him not to feel an icy chill in his veins at the thought of this man harming one golden hair upon Caro's head. His mouth thinned. 'Which is why men were, presumably, put on the earth to protect them.' Two could engage in this particular game of veiled threats. And when that game now so obviously involved Caro it was one that Dominic had every intention of winning.

As was to be expected, Caro was unable to stop herself from commenting on Dominic's remark. 'I am sure I am perfectly capable of protecting myself, Dominic.'

'All evidence to the contrary, my dear,' he said grimly.

Her cheeks flushed prettily. 'You—'

'I, too, am pleased to see that you are quite recovered from yesterday's ordeal, Mrs Morton,' Drew cut in tactfully.

Caro gave him a grateful smile. 'And I you.'

'Oh, I believe you will find that it's going to take

more than a fire to be rid of me,' he said, at the same time shooting a telling glance in Brown's direction.

'My compliments on your lucky escape, Drew,' the other man taunted.

'Would that Ben had been so lucky,' Drew said pointedly.

Hard brown eyes glittered with satisfaction. 'Such a waste of a young life...'

'A needless waste,' Drew agreed harshly.

'It would appear that you have had a busy morning, Brown?' Dominic felt it was time to intercede, before Drew's anger became such that he spoke or acted incautiously and this situation deteriorated whilst Caro was still present. Dominic and Drew had talked of this earlier and had agreed it must not be allowed to happen; if she were not present now, the conversation would no doubt have ceased being polite long ago!

Even the thought of Caro being anywhere near when that veneer of politeness was stripped from this situation, to reveal the ugly truth they all knew lurked beneath, was enough to send a cold rivulet of fear down Dominic's spine; he had no doubt, for all Brown looked so elegant in his perfectly tailored clothes, that the other man had a knife, or possibly even a small pistol, concealed somewhere about his person. Just as Dominic also believed that Caro would be Brown's target if this situation were to explode into violence now...

'Indeed?' Brown drawled.

Dominic nodded. 'I am informed by Ben's sister, Mrs Grey, that you have assisted her by financing tomorrow's funeral arrangements.'

He gave a dismissive shrug. 'It seemed the least I could do in the circumstances.'

'And what *circumstances* might they be?' Dominic asked.

Nicholas Brown met his gaze unblinkingly. 'Ben was my employee, and as such was loyal to me, for far longer than he was to you.'

It was tantamount to a declaration that it had been this change of loyalty on Ben's part—and no doubt on Drew's, too—which had ultimately brought about the young man's demise. That Brown would have been more than happy if both Drew and Ben had perished in yesterday's fire, as retribution for the fact that they had chosen to continue being employed by the new owner of Nick's rather than leave.

Just as Brown's visit to Caro was yet another veiled threat? That the villain had so clearly shown that he was fully aware of exactly where Caro resided now was, to Dominic's way of thinking, tangible evidence of that threat…

'I believe it is time you took your leave, Brown.' Dominic had had quite enough of even attempting to be polite to this man. 'Caro is looking a little pale. No doubt she is in need of rest following the events of yesterday and all this talk of death and funerals today.' He rang the bell for Denby.

Caro knew she might look less than perfect, but she had not, as yet, had the opportunity to say all that she wished to say to Mr Nicholas Brown! Added to which, she had been rendered almost speechless by the politeness—at least on the surface—of the conversation between the three men. Why did Dominic or Drew not just confront the man? Tell him of their suspicions and demand an explanation? It was what she had intended doing until she had found herself rendered tongue-tied by the man's smooth charm!

'Having now assured myself as to your welfare, Caro, I believe I will also take my leave,' Drew said smoothly.

But not smoothly enough that Caro was not aware of the hard edge beneath the blandness of his tone. 'No doubt I will see you again at Ben's funeral tomorrow.'

Brown raised surprised brows. '*You* will be attending?'

Caro looked at him coldly. 'But of course I shall—'

'It has yet to be decided.' Dominic was the one to cut in as he stepped forwards to lift one of Caro's hands and place it firmly in the crook of his arm so that the two of them now stood side by side as they faced Brown.

The gesture was so obviously one of possession that Caro could not help but be aware of it. Just as she was aware of the warning of Dominic's fingers firmly gripping her own as he kept her hand anchored in the crook of his arm. 'Dominic—'

'It is time to say goodbye to Mr Brown and Drew now, Caro,' he instructed her tautly.

Just as if she were a child who needed reminding of her manners! Or as if Dominic meant to silence her before she had the chance to do or say something that would totally strip away even this tense veneer of social politeness. Her mouth firmed determinedly. 'Perhaps before he leaves, I might ask Mr Brown—'

'I am sure, Caro, that whatever queries you might have for Mr Brown, they can surely wait until another day.' Those long fingers again pressed down on Caro's.

'Perhaps tomorrow at Ben's funeral?' she persevered.

Silver eyes glittered down at her in warning. 'Perhaps.'

Caro's cheeks flushed in temper. 'This is utterly ridiculous—'

'Ah, Denby.' Dominic turned to the butler as he quietly entered the room. 'Mr Brown and Mr Butler are leaving.'

'But—'

'Say goodbye to our guests, Caro.' The dangerous glitter in Dominic's eyes dared her to do anything more than that.

Much as she longed to accuse Nicholas Brown, Caro had enough wisdom to know when Dominic had been pushed to the limit of his patience. And the hard tension of his body as he stood next to her informed her that he had reached that limit some time ago.

Her parting comments to the other two men were made distractedly, her agitation now such that she could barely restrain herself.

It was a lack of restraint that Dominic clearly echoed, as he waited only long enough for Denby to close the door firmly behind himself, his wife and their departing visitors, before releasing Caro's hand and rounding on her furiously. 'What did you think you were doing by calmly inviting Brown in here? No, do not tell me, I know exactly what your intentions were!'

'Someone must confront Mr Brown—'

'And someone will,' Dominic assured her fiercely. 'But not you, Caro. *Never* you! And if you dare—so much as *dare*,' he grated, 'accuse me of behaving in a cowardly manner by not confronting him myself just now, then I must warn you, Caro, that I really will have no recourse but to administer the beating someone should have given you long ago!'

Her cheeks were pale. 'I had no intention of accusing you of being cowardly!'

'That is something, I suppose,' Dominic muttered darkly.

Caro knew him well enough now to know that he could be every bit as dangerous as Nicholas Brown if he chose to be. Nor had she missed the lethal purpose in the gaze Dominic had directed at Brown when he entered the salon a few minutes ago.

The difference between the two men was, of course, that Dominic was undoubtedly a man of honour. Of integrity. A gentleman. A gentleman who had caused her to behave as less than the lady she was from the moment they had first met!

Which thought had absolutely no place in their present conversation! 'That is not to say I understand why neither you nor Mr Butler did not challenge Mr Brown, both over the attack on Lord Thorne, and the setting of the fire that resulted in Ben's death.' A frown creased the creaminess of her brow.

'Perhaps because we were both endeavouring to protect *you*?'

'Me?'

Dominic gave a rueful shake of his head at the surprise in Caro's expression. Despite the week she had spent singing in a gentlemen's gambling club, and after all that had happened these past few days—including their lovemaking—she remained an innocent. She could not conceive, it seemed, that Nicholas Brown was more than capable of killing her where she stood, and to hell with the consequences.

Yet Dominic now feared that Brown's visit here today meant that he had decided, by implication, if not yet deed, to now turn the focus of his malevolent attentions upon Caro herself…

Chapter Seventeen

It was a threat Dominic intended taking very seriously indeed. 'I have decided, now that Brown has made it so obvious he knows of your whereabouts, that for your own safety it would be a good idea if I were to remove you immediately from London and place you at my estate in Berkshire.'

Caro's eyes widened, initially in shock, quickly followed by indignation. She had already spent a night at Blackstone House, followed by another in Brockle House, both properties owned by the Earl of Blackstone; for her to now be seen to move into his estate in Berkshire was unacceptable. Besides which, there was the added insult that Dominic had not even bothered to consult her before making this decision.

She gave a firm shake of her head. 'No.'

He became very still, his eyes narrowed to silver slits. *'No?'*

Caro shrugged her slender shoulders. 'No, Dominic. I must have a say in where I go and what I do—and this makes me feel like an unwanted relative you must needs move from house to house in order to avoid their company.'

If Caro really were a relative of his then Dominic would have put her over his knee and spanked her pretty bottom days ago. For the sheer stupidity, her complete lack of caution, in coming alone to London at all, and therefore placing herself firmly in the midst of this highly volatile situation. As it was, Dominic was currently perceived—by Brown, if by no other—as being Caro's protector. 'When it comes to the subject of your safety, Caro, I feel you must do as I ask.'

'No, Dominic, I must not.' Her unblinking gaze challenged him, her chin raised in haughty disdain. 'I have not had opportunity to tell you before this, but it is already my intention to leave London once I have attended Ben's funeral tomorrow.'

'To go where, may I ask?' Dominic glowered down at her.

'No, you may not ask—Dominic!' She protested as he reached out and took a tight grip of her wrist. 'You will not be able to force my compliance simply by the use of brute strength.' She spoke calmly and clearly, her gaze reproachful as she looked up at him.

Dominic had no wish to force her compliance or hurt her in any way. But just the thought of the likes of a man like Brown ever being in a position to cause her harm caused a painful tightening in his chest.

As did the thought of Caro leaving London. Leaving *him*…

He also wondered, if not for their present heated conversation, whether she would have even bothered to inform him of her intention to leave London, let alone confide where he might be able to find her if he wished to see her again.

If he wished to see her again?

Dominic released his grip on Caro's arm to step sharply away from her, a frown darkening his brow as he studied her between guarded lids. There was no doubting that she was a breathtakingly beautiful young woman. Or that just looking at her now in that green gown, and imagining the naked curves beneath, filled him with the need to once again make love to her. But surely that was all she was, or ever could be, to him? Just a beautiful young woman who—for the moment— he felt a need to protect? To imagine she might mean any more to him than that was unacceptable to a man who had long ago decided he did not want or need one particular woman in his life. Especially if that woman was one he might care for enough that her death would drive him to the same brink of madness his father had suffered after the death of Dominic's mother.

He shook his head. 'You know I cannot allow it, Caro.'

'Why not?' For Caro to dare to hope that he might feel some of her own regret at the thought of them parting would, she knew, be too much to ask.

He looked irritated now. 'Because Brown is still a threat.'

'To me?'

'Caro, how do you imagine Brown even knew to visit you here at Brockle House?'

Her eyes slowly widened. 'He had us followed yesterday?'

'Exactly,' Dominic bit out curtly. 'And until he is…
dealt with, I must insist, if you will not agree to go to
my estate in Berkshire, that you at least agree to remain
at Brockle House for now.'

Caro looked at him searchingly, noting the grim
determination of his expression, the light of battle in
his eyes. 'You intend to deal with Mr Brown yourself,
do you not?'

Dominic drew in a harsh breath, wishing not for
the first time that Caro were not as astute as she was
beautiful. Or so forward in voicing her shrewd opinions
and observations. 'It is for the law—'

'Dominic, I have asked several times that you not
treat me as a child or an imbecile!'

He sighed deeply at her obvious irritation. 'Very
well, then. Yes, if the law is not enough to bring Brown
to justice, then I will feel no hesitation in dealing with
him myself.'

'How?'

'I think it best if you do not know the details.'

'Dominic.'

'Caro!' he exclaimed in exasperation. 'Is it not
enough to know that I respect you, admire you, even
like you?' he added ruefully. 'And that it is because
I feel all of those things for you that I do not wish to
involve you any further in this mess than you already
are.'

Caro knew from the implacability of his tone that
Dominic really would tell her no more on that subject.
Just as she knew that having his respect, admiration and
liking, whilst being secretly cherished, could never be
enough for her. She wanted him to feel so much more

than that. Needed him to love her in the same way she had realised she loved him. Completely. Irrevocably.

Who could have ever known that, in coming to London in this way, she would meet the man she was to fall so deeply in love with? Certainly not Caro. She had thought only to avoid being coerced into a marriage she did not want. Instead she had met the man whom she would love for the rest of her life and *he* didn't want to marry *her*...

Caro stepped away from him, her trembling hands clasped tightly together in front of her, knowing that her pride would never allow her to let him see how deeply she had fallen in love with him. 'I accept that for the moment it is best that I remain here. But I do wish to leave as soon as you feel it is safe for me to do so,' she added firmly.

Dominic looked at her between narrowed lids. 'With the intention of returning to your family?'

'Yes. And please do not ask me where or who that family is,' she said ruefully as she could see that was exactly what Dominic was about to do. 'As with your own actions concerning Mr Brown, it serves no purpose for you to know the details of my destination.'

He straightened abruptly. 'And if you need to talk to me at some point in the future?'

If she found herself with child, he meant... 'Then I will know where to find you,' Caro dismissed evenly.

Dominic sighed. 'You know, Caro, I do not have so many people I consider friends that I can simply allow one of them to just up and leave London and for ever disappear.'

Dominic thought of them as being friends?

Knowing how and why, after hearing the sad tale of his parents' deaths, Dominic shunned emotional attachments of any kind, she could not help but feel flattered that he should think of her as a friend. Unfortunately, she wanted to be so much more to him than just a friend!

'I am sure that you have many more friends than Lord Thorne, Drew Butler and myself,' she said lightly.

'Perhaps,' Dominic conceded drily. 'Osbourne and I have just spent the past month in Venice with one of our oldest and closest friends.'

Venice?

Caro stiffened, barely daring to breathe as she looked searchingly at Dominic now. He had recently spent a month in Venice? Where Lord Gabriel Faulkner, Earl of Westbourne since the death of Caro's father, and now the guardian of all three sisters—the very same man who had sent his lawyer with the offer of marriage to one of the three Copeland sisters, without so much as having met any of them—had resided for the past two years, at least?

Caro was well aware that Venice was a large city with an even larger population, Venetians as well as other people simply visiting. Nevertheless, she could not help her feelings of disquiet at the knowledge that Dominic had just spent a month there. Where he had no doubt met and socialised with both the Venetian aristocracy and those members of English society currently residing there. Possibly including Lord Faulkner?

'Perhaps you will have the chance to meet him,' Dominic continued. 'Westbourne is due to arrive back in England himself in the next few days,' he explained at Caro's questioning glance.

Westbourne!

Caro's fears had just been realised!

Not only did Dominic know Lord Faulkner, but the two of them had obviously been close friends for a number of years. Worst of all, Dominic was expecting Westbourne to arrive back in England any day! No doubt one of the first things he would do was pay a visit to his friend, Lord Vaughn—and Dominic had just told her that he would introduce the two of them!

Caro moved carefully over to a chair and sat down, knowing her legs were in danger of no longer supporting her. What was she to do? If, as Dominic said, he was expecting the Earl of Westbourne to arrive in England within days—possibly even today—then Caro could not afford to linger in London any longer if she wished to avoid detection, no matter what she might have assured Dominic earlier.

Not that Lord Faulkner would recognise her as anyone other than Caro Morton here in London. But she had never intended her absence from Shoreley Hall, and the separation from her beloved sisters, to be a permanent one, which meant that Westbourne must one day be introduced to his ward, Lady Caroline Copeland. If he had already been introduced to Caro Morton, the repercussions to all of them when that happened would be great indeed!

Caro had dearly wanted to attend Ben's funeral before returning to Shoreley Hall, and the thought of leaving Dominic so soon was worse than painful, but the knowledge of her guardian's imminent arrival in England meant that she had no choice but to leave immediately.

Caro Morton must cease to exist forthwith.

'Caro?'

She straightened, schooling her features into the polite social mask recognisable as Lady Caroline Copeland as she looked up and saw the concern in Dominic's expression. 'Yes?'

'Will you promise me not to leave the house unaccompanied until this matter is settled?'

She could not give such a promise and mean it. Not now. 'I trust I am not so foolish as to even attempt it now that you have alerted me to the fact that Nicholas Brown is watching my every move,' she answered.

Dominic nodded, apparently sensing none of the evasion in her reply. 'I will be out for the rest of the day, but should hopefully be back in time for us to dine together this evening.'

'I will look forward to it.' They had become almost like strangers in these past few minutes, Caro recognised heavily, Dominic's friendship with Lord Faulkner, and her knowledge of her own imminent departure from London, seeming to have severed the tenuous bonds of their own friendship.

Caro could feel the hot burn of tears in her eyes. 'I believe I will go upstairs to rest.' Dominic must be made to leave. Now. Before those threatening tears started to fall and he demanded an explanation as to the reason for them. She doubted he would appreciate hearing that it was because her heart was breaking at the very thought of being parted from him.

Now that the time had come, Dominic felt an uncharacteristic reluctance to part from Caro, even for a few hours.

Damn it, apart from the friendship he had long held

with Osbourne and Westbourne, he had never been a man who allowed himself to become entangled in emotional attachments. And yet he was aware he had formed a friendship of sorts these past few days with both Drew Butler and Ben Jackson.

And he had formed a friendship with Caro, too…

A friendship that Dominic knew had come into being because he had ultimately been unable to deny the respect and admiration he felt for the courage and determination she had shown him from their very first meeting. He would feel Caro's loss all the more keenly once she was allowed to return to her home and family. But it was a friendship Dominic could not, would not, allow to control either his actions or his judgement.

He drew himself up stiffly. 'Until this evening, then.' He nodded to her before turning on his heel to stride determinedly from the room.

Caro waited only long enough to be sure that he had truly gone before she allowed the tears to fall. Hot and remorseless tears that almost brought her to her knees. At the thought of never seeing Dominic again. At the knowledge that she would never again know the warmth of being held in his arms. Kissed by him. Never again know the wonder, the beauty, of their lovemaking.

Caro cried until there were no more tears inside her to be shed. Until all that was left was the knowledge that she must leave this house immediately.

Must leave London.

And Dominic…

Once outside Dominic dismissed the carriage he and Butler had arrived in earlier, deciding that the walk to

Mrs Wilson's to check on Osbourne one last time before his aunt whisked him off to the country to recover from his injuries would be far more beneficial in helping to clear his head of the disturbed thoughts that had been plaguing him ever since he had realised how deeply he would feel it when Caro left London for good.

Except Dominic's thoughts remained distracted, for the duration of his walk, and whilst he chatted with the disgruntled but resigned Osbourne. And they continued to plague him after he had taken his leave and stood outside on the pavement outside Mrs Wilson's home.

He had intended lunching at his club, before returning to Blackstone House for the afternoon to deal with estate business, leaving him free to once again spend the night at Brockle House.

Yet he did none of those things, as instead, his feet took him back in the direction of Brockle House. Back to Caro.

His behaviour was totally illogical. Totally unprecedented. He felt a longing to be with her that he knew he should strongly resist. But could not…

Just as he could not believe his own eyes as he neared Brockle House and saw Caro hurrying towards him. Alone. Dressed in her dark cloak and that unbecoming brown bonnet, which should have been consigned to the incinerator along with those unbecoming gowns, but somehow had not. And carrying the bag in which her few belongings had been packed to transport them to Brockle House.

Caro came to an abrupt halt, her eyes widening in alarm, as she saw a furiously angry Dominic striding forcefully towards her. It could not be! Dominic had gone off for the day to see to other business. He was not really here at all, was a figment of her imagination, brought about by the chasm of misery Caro had fallen into at the thought of being parted from him.

'Where do you think you are going?' The grip of his hands on the tops of her arms felt real enough, as did the fierceness of his scowl as he glowered down at her. 'Answer me this instant, Caro!'

Dominic was real! He was really here!

Caro could not breathe. Could not think. Could only stare up into Dominic's face and know that she loved him past all bearing…

'You little fool!' He shook her, eyes glittering in the harsh handsomeness of his face as he glared down at her. 'Do you not realise the danger you have put yourself in by venturing out alone like this?'

'Why are you here?' She gave a dazed shake of her head. 'You told me you had other business to attend to for the rest of the day. You said—'

'I am well aware of what I said, Caro,' he grated. 'Just as I am aware that you *lied* to me when you said you would be resting in your rooms for the rest of the morning. You have obviously taken advantage of my absence to pack your bag and make your escape without so much as a word of goodbye!'

'I—' Caro moistened her dry lips.

'Where were you going?' Dominic demanded harshly as he shook her slightly again. 'What—?' He broke off abruptly, his eyes suddenly wide and staring.

'Dominic?' Caro could only look up at him uncomprehendingly as those silver-grey eyes turned up into his head before glazing over completely, his mouth becoming lax, and his hands losing their grip upon her arms as he began to sink slowly to the ground.

Revealing to her frightened gaze the hefty and brutish-looking man who stood behind him, some sort of cudgel raised in his hand, before something was thrown over her head to cut off all sight and she felt herself being lifted and carried away…

Chapter Eighteen

Caro had no idea how long she had been held a prisoner in this opulently furnished bedchamber. It had seemed like hours, and yet it could equally have been only minutes. Time had become unimportant to her since she had seen Dominic fall to the ground after receiving that blow to the back of his head.

None of her anguished thoughts since that time had been for herself; she was far too worried whether that blow to Dominic's head had been heavy and hard enough to kill him.

A world without Dominic was unthinkable. Unimaginable. Making a complete nonsense of any concerns Caro might have for her own welfare. She had become the prisoner of Nicholas Brown, of course. There could be no other possible explanation for what had occurred. But none of it mattered to Caro in the slightest if Dominic were now dead.

She stood up and moved restlessly around the room to end up standing in front of the window. It was barred on the outside and looked out over a walled and secluded garden, with a sheltering of surrounding trees that made it impossible for anyone in any of the neighbouring houses to see either into the garden or the house.

It was a seclusion she was already aware of, because the window had been the first place she had checked for escape, once she had managed to untangle herself from the blanket that had been kept about her as she was bundled inside a coach and transported to this house.

There had been two men inside the coach with her, and although the blanket did not allow her to see their faces, she could easily guess that one of them had struck Dominic, and the second was the man who had stood behind Caro and thrown the blanket over her head. Neither of them had deigned to answer her repeated demands during the journey to know whether or not they had killed Dominic.

So far she had seen nothing of Nicholas Brown…

Caro knew that she should be afraid of the man. That the men he employed were responsible for Ben's death and the severity of the injuries Lord Thorne had received several nights ago. That those same men might also have now slain Dominic…

And yet Caro felt too contemptuous and angry towards Brown to be in the least afraid of him. Contempt, because all of those acts had been cowardly, administered in such a way that neither Brown nor any of his men were ever in any real danger of injury themselves. Anger, because if Dominic did indeed lie dead somewhere, then Caro felt fully capable of administering that same fate to Brown, if she were given the slightest opportunity.

A choking sob rose in her throat. Dominic could

not be dead! It was a possibility too horrific to even contemplate—

Caro turned sharply as she heard the key turning in the lock of the door, her chin raised proudly high, sea-green eyes full of the contempt she felt as Nicholas Brown stepped into the room.

'Mrs Morton,' he greeted with his usual relaxed charm—for all the world as if they were exchanging pleasantries in a drawing room! 'You're comfortable, I hope?' he added courteously as he remained standing in the doorway of the bedchamber.

Her chin lifted disdainfully. 'I have witnessed a man being…felled before my eyes.' Caro gathered her courage after that slight falter as she talked of the attack on Dominic, determined to show this man no weakness whatsoever. 'I have suffered being covered in a rough and smelly blanket, abducted in a coach, and held a prisoner in this bedchamber for some time. Yes, Mr Brown, I am perfectly comfortable, thank you.'

Grudging admiration entered that calculating brown gaze. 'I understand now why Blackstone became so besotted with you,' he murmured.

It was an admiration Caro did not value in the slightest. Any more than she believed Dominic had ever been besotted with her. But the thought of it was enough to give her the courage to continue in the same vein. 'Unfortunately I consider you so far beneath contempt that you do not even have the right to breathe Lord Vaughn's name.'

A tightness appeared around those brown eyes as his gaze narrowed. 'We will see how wonderful you still consider him to be when he fails to rescue you in time from my "contemptuous" clutches.'

The only part of that statement that mattered to Caro was the indication it gave that Dominic was still alive! She sagged inside. If that could only be true, if Dominic could still but live, then whether or not he succeeded in rescuing her did not matter; Caro just wanted him to be safe.

She raised scornful brows. 'Dominic is worth a hundred—no, a thousand!—of you.'

Brown scowled darkly. 'Perhaps you should wait to make comparisons as to who is the better man until after I have bedded you?'

Caro's eyes had widened before she had a chance to control her reaction to this shocking statement. 'You will not find me a willing bed partner, Mr Brown,' she assured cuttingly, her chin still raised defiantly high.

His mouth twisted derisively. 'I am counting on it, Mrs Morton,' he drawled mockingly. 'Blackstone took my prized possession from me and now I am very much enjoying the anticipation of availing myself of his,' he jeered before stepping out of the room, and relocking the door behind him.

Caro sank weakly down on to the bed, wondering how she could ever have been deceived into thinking Nicholas Brown was anything other than what he was: a low, despicable man, with no honour, or, indeed, any virtues to recommend him.

She could only hope that, if Dominic truly were still alive, he would look for her—as he surely must?—and find her, before Brown decided to carry out his threat.

'Everyone is in position, my lord.' Drew Butler spoke softly at Dominic's side as the two men stood hidden in a doorway further down the road from the house in Cheapside belonging to Nicholas Brown.

The house where Dominic hoped and prayed that he would find Caro. Alive. And unharmed. Anything else was unacceptable to him.

What he would say and do to Caro once he had delivered her safely back at Brockle House, Dominic had not dared think of as yet. He had still not got over the shock of regaining consciousness earlier only to find Caro was nowhere to be found.

'Are you sure you are up to this, my lord?' Drew voiced his concern. 'The blow to your head was severe, and—'

'Let's get this over with, Drew,' he said grimly as he raised the two pistols in his hands ready for breaching Brown's front door. 'There will be time enough to worry about the blow I received to my head once we have found Caro and I am assured she has come to no harm at Brown's hands.' The expression on his face was enough to show what would happen to said man if Caro had been harmed in any way...

Dominic had downed a single glass of brandy earlier in order to put him back into his right senses, after which he had sent for Drew Butler, and then taken him and the men who had formerly been under his command into the study at Brockle House, in order that they might devise a plan to effect a rescue without injury to Caro.

Spending over two hours observing the comings and goings of Brown's men to his house in Cheapside, so that they might count the number of adversaries they would have to deal with once they were inside, had stretched Dominic's patience to breaking point. Enough so that now he could not wait to get inside the house and have this thing between himself and Brown over and done with once and for all.

And, far more importantly, to know that Caro was indeed safe and unharmed...

Caro felt both thirsty and hungry as she lay upon the bed, several more hours having passed without anyone offering her refreshment of any kind. Something she did not feel inclined to bring to anyone's attention when she had not seen Nicholas Brown again for that same length of time.

It was—

Caro sat up abruptly as she heard the sound of several unnaturally loud bangs, taking several seconds—and a few more of those loud bangs—before she realised that what she was hearing was gunfire.

Dominic!

She rose hastily from the bed to run across to the locked door, pressing her ear against it to see if she could hear anything of what was taking place on the other side. Men shouting. Feet running. More shots. And then an unnatural and eerie silence...

Caro stepped back from the door, unsure as to whether Dominic and the men who had accompanied him were the victors of the battle or whether it was the despicable Nicholas Brown and his men. If it was the latter—

The key was being turned in the lock!

The handle was turning.

The door being pushed open—

'Dominic!' Caro cried gladly as he stood so tall and

in command in the doorway, that gladness turning to horror, and her face paling, as Caro saw the blood staining the front of his jacket and shirt. She ran across the room. 'You are hurt!'

'It is not my blood, Caro,' he had time to reassure her before his arms wrapped about her and he held her tightly against his chest.

She leant back slightly to look up at him with wide, haunted eyes. 'Is it Nicholas Brown's?'

Dominic's jaw tightened. 'We struggled, and the gun between us went off. He is dead, Caro,' he added hoarsely.

'I am glad!' she assured him fiercely. 'He meant to—he threatened to—'

'Do not think of it again, my dear.' Dominic could not bear just now to know what Brown had threatened to do to Caro if she had not been rescued. Any more than he wanted to think of the battle, the deaths, that had just occurred.

All talk, explanations, could come later. It was enough for now that he held her safely in his arms...

'The physician would not approve of you imbibing brandy so soon after receiving that severe blow to your head!' Caro stood in the doorway of the study at Brockle House as she glowered at Dominic disapprovingly.

In truth, his head was pounding worse than it had this morning. But whether the physician who had been called would have approved of his actions or not, Dominic knew that a glass of best brandy, his first since returning Caro back to Brockle House two hours earlier, was necessary if he was to get through the necessary conversation with her. Indeed, that he might need more of it before the evening was through…

It had been a difficult afternoon for all of them—explanations to be made to the representatives of the law, arrangements made for the removal of Brown's body and those of his men.

With so many witnesses to what had taken place, and Caro's own testimony of her abduction and Brown's intentions towards her, it had not been too difficult to persuade the authorities that Brown and his men were the guilty parties, and Dominic and his men merely effecting a rescue. In truth, he had a suspicion that certain members of the law were pleased to be relieved of the presence of the troublesome Nicholas Brown, once and for all.

Caro, as Dominic might have expected, had stood up wonderfully well under all the strain!

'Come in and close the door, Caro,' Dominic requested softly now as he leant back against the front of the leather-topped desk.

She stepped lightly into the study and closed the door behind her, disturbed by how ill Dominic now looked; there was a grey cast to his skin, his eyes sunken in the dark shadows above the high blades of his cheekbones. His mouth was a grimly thinned line and his jaw was clenched tensely.

'Did…the events of this afternoon disgust you?' he asked huskily.

She raised startled eyes to look at him searchingly, but was unable to read anything of his mood from his expression. 'How could I possibly feel disgust when I know that if you had not succeeded in killing Brown then it would be you and I who now lay dead?'

His mouth quirked. 'There have been several occasions when you have given me the impression you would not consider my own death to be such a bad thing.'

'I was young and silly—'

'And now you are mature and so much wiser?' he teased.

Caro felt the warmth of the colour that entered her cheeks. 'I feel...older than I was this morning, certainly.'

Dominic's frown was pained. 'I am sorry for that.'

'Why should *you* be sorry?' She looked at him quizzically. 'It is Nicholas Brown who is responsible for my new maturity, Dominic, and not you. He—if you had not rescued me, he told me that he intended to—'

Dominic stepped forwards and took her firmly into his arms. 'I have already told you that it will do you no good to think of that any more,' he urged. 'Bad enough that I have to think of it, imagine it, without knowing it hurts you, too.' His arms tightened almost painfully about her.

Caro raised her head to once again look up at him. 'Does the thought of it hurt you so badly, Dominic?'

His eyes glittered a pale silver. 'Almost as much as the knowledge that you were leaving me.'

'I was not leaving you, Dominic.' She sighed. 'I merely thought it best that I return home—'

'Without so much as a goodbye? Giving me no idea how I would ever find you again?' His expression had become fierce, those silver eyes glowing with repressed emotion as he looked down at her.

Caro swept the tip of her tongue lightly over the dryness of her lips, a hope, a dream, starting to build and grow inside her. 'Would you ever have wanted to find me again?'

'How can you even ask me that?' Dominic shook her slightly in exasperation. 'Do you not know—have you not guessed yet how much I love you?'

'What did you say?' Caro hardly dared to believe the emotions she could now read in those glowing silver eyes. Warmth. Admiration. Love!

'I love you, Caro,' he repeated huskily. 'Do you think, after all that has happened, that if I were to get down on my knees and beg, you might one day be able to love me in return and consider becoming my wife?'

Her cheeks warmed as she remembered the occasion upon which she had said those words to him. 'As I recall, you had just finished telling me that our love-making was a mistake—'

'Then it was a most wonderful, glorious mistake!' he assured her fiercely as he cupped the sides of her face between gentle hands. 'I have been a fool, Caro. An arrogant fool. My only excuse—if there can ever be one!—is that I have never met a woman like you before. Never known any woman with your courage, your generosity of spirit, your honesty. I love you truly, Caro, and if you could one day learn to love me in return, I promise you I will love you for the rest of our lives together. Will you, Caro? Will you give me the chance to show you how much I love you? A chance to persuade you into learning to love me?' he added less certainly.

It was that uncharacteristic uncertainty that convinced Caro she could not be dreaming, after all; even in a dream she would not have bestowed uncertainty upon a man she knew to be always confident and sure, of both his own emotions and those around him!

And yet Dominic was not sure of her and seemed to have no idea that she had fallen in love with him, too. 'My dear...' her voice was gentle, tentative '...I am already in love with you—'

'My darling girl!' Dominic swept her ecstatically up into his arms before claiming her mouth with his.

Caro was still so overwhelmed by his declaration of love and his proposal of marriage, that for several long and pleasurable minutes all she could do was return the passion of his kisses.

It was some time later before her sanity returned. 'I realise that the Earl of Blackstone could not possibly marry a woman such as Caro Morton—'

'I can marry whom I damned well please,' he told her with a return of his usual arrogance. 'And I choose to marry you, if you will have me,' he added determinedly. 'I do not care who or what you are, Caro. Or what you are running away from. I love you. And it is my dearest wish—my only wish—to make you my wife.'

This, more than anything else, finally convinced Caro of the depth of Dominic's love for her. He was a lord, an Earl, and yet he was proposing marriage to a woman he had only known as a singer in a gambling club. A woman he had already made love to. Twice!

She chewed briefly on her bottom lip. 'I should tell you that my mother ran away with her lover when I was a child, and was later shot and killed by him when he caught her in the arms of yet another lover.'

Dominic's thumb moved lightly across her bottom lip, his eyes ablaze with the love he claimed to feel for her. 'I have said I do not care about your past, my love, and I truly do not,' he vowed. 'Besides, you are not responsible for your mother's actions.'

'Any more than you are to blame for the death of your own mother.'

Dominic released his breath in a deep sigh. 'I have always felt responsible...'

Caro gently touched his cheek with her fingertips. 'Tell me what really happened.'

He gave a pained wince. 'I do not believe I could bear it if, once I have done so, you decided you did not love me, after all.'

'It will not happen,' she vowed with certainty. 'Dominic, I know you to be a man who is honest and true. A man who cares deeply for others in spite of himself— Lord Thorne, Drew, Ben, myself, to name only four. I absolutely refuse to believe that you would ever have harmed your own mother.'

'I hope you still think that once I have told you what happened.' Dominic kissed her slowly and lingeringly before speaking again. 'I went away to school when I was twelve years old. I was not a good pupil. I resented being sent away, and got into all manner of scrapes in an attempt to be sent home again. I do not even remember what the last one was.' He grimaced. 'Only that it resulted in my mother having to travel to the school shortly after the Christmas holidays in order to stop the headmaster from expelling me.'

Caro could hear his heart beating rapidly in his chest, the harshness of his breathing as he was obviously beset by the memories that had haunted him into adulthood. 'I love you, Dominic,' she encouraged gently.

His arms tightened about her as he continued. 'Her coach slipped on the icy roads and into an even icier river. The doors became stuck fast and she could not get out as the water—'

'Do not say any more!' Caro sat up and placed her fingertips over his lips as she gazed down at him. 'You were a child, Dominic. A child who felt hurt and rebellious because he felt he had been sent away from those he loved. You were no more responsible for the death of your mother or your father than—than I am.'

Strangely, as Dominic looked up into Caro's compassionate and love-filled eyes, all of the guilt, the feeling that he was unworthy of being loved, quietly and for ever slipped away.

She shook her head. 'It is sad that your father felt he could not go on living without her but—loving you as I do, I believe I know something of how he must have felt,' she added shyly; if Dominic really had been killed earlier today, then Caro knew she would have found it difficult to go on living, too...

He gave a choked groan as he pulled her tightly against him and buried his face in her hair. 'How was I ever lucky enough to find you, Caro? How?'

Caro did not want him to be sad any more; he had already suffered enough, believed himself unworthy of love for long enough. 'But you do not know yet whom you have found,' she reminded him teasingly.

He raised his head to smile at her. 'First tell me that you will marry me, whoever you are.'

'I will.'

'Caro...' Dominic kissed her for several more love-filled minutes, the happiness on his face when he at last raised his head, making him look almost boyish as he grinned down at her.

'But before that can happen,' Caro murmured ruefully, 'you will have to obtain the approval of my guardian.'

Dominic's smile faded slightly. 'Your guardian?'

'I am afraid so.'

He frowned. 'Tell me who this guardian is and I will go to him immediately, assure him that I am a reformed character since meeting you and solicit him for his permission to marry you.'

'It is not necessary for you to go to him.' Caro's eyes glowed with laughter. 'I believe that he is coming to you.'

'To me?' Dominic frowned his confusion. 'But how——?' His eyes widened as he became still. *'Westbourne?'* he breathed in disbelief.

'I am afraid so,' Caro admitted.

Dominic stared down at her, absolutely dumbstruck for several long seconds, and then he began to smile, and then finally to laugh. 'Westbourne!' He sobered suddenly. 'It is because I had told you I was expecting him to arrive in England any day that you were leaving London so hurriedly earlier,' he realised incredulously.

'Yes.'

'What I should have added is that Gabriel does not intend to remain in London, but travel almost immediately to Shoreley Hall.'

'Oh dear!' Caro cringed now at the thought of what her sister Diana would have to say to Dominic's friend when he arrived.

Dominic seemed to suffer no such worries as he

chuckled, once more diverted by the thought that he had stolen a march on his friend and whipped one of his possible choices of bride out from under his nose. 'And which Lady Copeland will I have the pleasure of making my wife?'

'Caroline—I am the second daughter.'

'And you decided to run away to London after refusing to even contemplate becoming Westbourne's bride?'

She gave a delicate shudder. 'I could not possibly marry a man I do not love.'

'And your sisters? Have they run away, too?'

'Oh, no, I am sure they have not.' Caro shook her head, firmly pushing away the flicker of doubt in her mind about that girl in the park who had looked so like Elizabeth. 'I am the rebellious one, I am afraid.'

'Something I will be grateful for until the day I die,' Dominic assured her lovingly.

Dominic loved her just as much as Caro loved him— and she was blissfully certain that he would obtain his friend's permission for the two of them to marry as soon as it could be arranged.

She wound her arms about his neck as she arched up into him. 'Would you care to show me how much you are grateful, Dominic?'

'Gladly!' he groaned as his head lowered and his mouth once again captured hers, the two of them quickly forgetting everything and everyone else but the love they felt for one other, now and for always.

* * * * *

HISTORICAL

Where Love is Timeless™
HARLEQUIN® HISTORICAL

COMING NEXT MONTH
AVAILABLE NOVEMBER 22, 2011

THE MARSHAL AND MISS MERRITT
Cahill Cowboys
Debra Cowan
(Western)

COMING HOME FOR CHRISTMAS
Carla Kelly
(19th century)

UNMASKING THE DUKE'S MISTRESS
Gentlemen of Disrepute
Margaret McPhee
(Regency)

THE LADY FORFEITS
The Copeland Sisters
Carole Mortimer
(Regency)

You can find more information on upcoming
Harlequin® titles, free excerpts and more
at www.HarlequinInsideRomance.com.

HHCNM1111

REQUEST YOUR
FREE BOOKS!

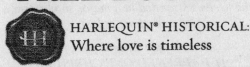

HARLEQUIN® HISTORICAL:
Where love is timeless

2 FREE NOVELS PLUS 2 **FREE GIFTS!**

YES! Please send me 2 FREE Harlequin® Historical novels and my 2 FREE gifts (gifts are worth about $10). After receiving them, if I don't wish to receive any more books, I can return the shipping statement marked "cancel." If I don't cancel, I will receive 6 brand-new novels every month and be billed just $5.19 per book in the U.S. or $5.74 per book in Canada. That's a savings of at least 17% off the cover price! It's quite a bargain! Shipping and handling is just 50¢ per book in the U.S. and 75¢ per book in Canada.* I understand that accepting the 2 free books and gifts places me under no obligation to buy anything. I can always return a shipment and cancel at any time. Even if I never buy another book, the two free books and gifts are mine to keep forever.

246/349 HDN FEQQ

Name	(PLEASE PRINT)	
Address		Apt. #
City	State/Prov.	Zip/Postal Code

Signature (if under 18, a parent or guardian must sign)

Mail to the Reader Service:
IN U.S.A.: P.O. Box 1867, Buffalo, NY 14240-1867
IN CANADA: P.O. Box 609, Fort Erie, Ontario L2A 5X3

Not valid for current subscribers to Harlequin Historical books.

Want to try two free books from another line?
Call 1-800-873-8635 or visit www.ReaderService.com.

* Terms and prices subject to change without notice. Prices do not include applicable taxes. Sales tax applicable in N.Y. Canadian residents will be charged applicable taxes. Offer not valid in Quebec. This offer is limited to one order per household. All orders subject to credit approval. Credit or debit balances in a customer's account(s) may be offset by any other outstanding balance owed by or to the customer. Please allow 4 to 6 weeks for delivery. Offer available while quantities last.

Your Privacy—The Reader Service is committed to protecting your privacy. Our Privacy Policy is available online at www.ReaderService.com or upon request from the Reader Service.

We make a portion of our mailing list available to reputable third parties that offer products we believe may interest you. If you prefer that we not exchange your name with third parties, or if you wish to clarify or modify your communication preferences, please visit us at www.ReaderService.com/consumerschoice or write to us at Reader Service Preference Service, P.O. Box 9062, Buffalo, NY 14269. Include your complete name and address.

HH11B

*Lucy Flemming and Ross Mitchell shared a magical,
sexy Christmas weekend together six years ago.
This Christmas, history may repeat itself when they find
themselves stranded in a major snowstorm...
and alone at last.*

Read on for a sneak peek from
IT HAPPENED ONE CHRISTMAS
by Leslie Kelly.

Available December 2011, only from Harlequin® Blaze™.

EYEING THE GRAY, THICK SKY through the expansive wall of
windows, Lucy began to pack up her photography gear.
The Christmas party was winding down, only a dozen or so
people remaining on this floor, which had been transformed
from cubicles and meeting rooms to a holiday funland. She
smiled at those nearest to her, then, seeing the glances at her
silly elf hat, she reached up to tug it off her head.

Before she could do it, however, she heard a voice. A
deep, male voice—smooth and sexy, and so not Santa's.

"I appreciate you filling in on such short notice. I've
heard you do a terrific job."

Lucy didn't turn around, letting her brain process what
she was hearing. Her whole body had stiffened, the hairs on
the back of her neck standing up, her skin tightening into
tiny goose bumps. Because that voice sounded so familiar.
Impossibly familiar.

It can't be.

"It sounds like the kids had a great time."

Unable to stop herself, Lucy began to turn around,
wondering if her ears—and all her other senses—were
deceiving her. After all, six years was a long time, the mind

could play tricks. What were the odds that she'd bump into *him,* here? And today of all days. December 23.

Six years exactly. Was that really possible?

One look—and the accompanying frantic thudding of her heart—and she knew her ears and brain were working just fine. Because it was *him.*

"Oh, my God," he whispered, shocked, frozen, staring as thoroughly as she was. "Lucy?"

She nodded slowly, not taking her eyes off him, wondering why the years had made him even more attractive than ever. It didn't seem fair. Not when she'd spent the past six years thinking he must have started losing that thick, golden-brown hair, or added a spare tire to that trim, muscular form.

No.

The man was gorgeous. Truly, without-a-doubt, mouth-wateringly handsome, every bit as hot as he'd been the first time she'd laid eyes on him. She'd been twenty-two, he one year older.

They'd shared an amazing holiday season.

And had never seen one another again.

Until now.

Find out what happens in
IT HAPPENED ONE CHRISTMAS
by Leslie Kelly.
Available December 2011, only from Harlequin® Blaze™

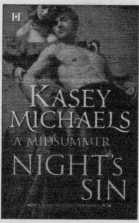

A Ph⊂*tographic Guide to*

BIRDS

⊂F AUSTRALIA

Peter Rowland
The Australian Museum

NEW HOLLAND

*Dedicated to my friend
and teacher, Walter.*

Published in Australia in 1999 by
New Holland Publishers (Australia) Pty Ltd
Sydney • Auckland • London • Cape Town
14 Aquatic Drive Frenchs Forest NSW 2086 Australia
218 Lake Road Northcote Auckland New Zealand
Garfield House 86 Edgware Road London W2 2EA United Kingdom
80 McKenzie Street Cape Town 8001 South Africa

First published in 1995
Reprinted in 1996, 1997, 1999, 2001, 2003, 2004

National Library of Australia Cataloguing-in-Publication Data

   Rowland, Peter, 1967–
   A photographic guide to birds of Australia
   Bibliography
   Includes index.
   Birds--Australia--Identification.
   Birds--Australia--Pictorial works.
   Also Titled: Birds of Australia

ISBN 1 85368 5992

Edited by Louise Egerton
Typeset by Anaconda Graphic Design
Reproduction by Hirt & Carter
Printed and bound by Times Offset (M) Sdn Bhd

Front cover: Australian King-Parrot (M. Prociv)
Back cover: Silvereye (G. Weber)
Spine: Laughing Kookaburra (P. German)
Title page: White-bellied Sea-Eagle (R. Brown)

Contents

Introduction

The function of this guide is to give the novice Australian birdwatcher the basic information necessary to identify the more commonly encountered species: concise texts and descriptive photographs are provided in a format that fits the pocket.

About 750 species of birds can be found in Australia. Many are migrants that appear only at certain times of the year; some are rare vagrants, with only a few sightings. Others have very limited distribution or live in areas that are difficult to access. Probably only a little more than half of the total are likely to be encountered on a regular basis by people who keep to the easily-travelled parts of Australia. This book deals with these species.

With the aid of this guide, you will probably be able to identify most species that you encounter – or at least reduce the possibilities and place an unidentified bird in a particular family. You can then consult a more comprehensive book to make your identification.

Most Australian birds occur nowhere else. Some birdwatchers are driven to make confirmed sightings of as many as possible of these in a lifetime. Others are concerned to understand the biology and behaviour of birds and study relatively few in depth. This book has been written for the less motivated reader, who simply wants to identify a bird seen in a suburban garden or in the course of a walk through a national park. Be warned, however: birdwatching is addictive.

How to use this book

The text for each species account has been kept as concise as possible. Size (as total length and in some cases wingspan) is given beside the name of each species. Within the accounts, reference has been made to other species that may be confused with the species in question, or have such minute and obvious differences that they do not warrant an account of their own. Distribution maps show currently known ranges within Australia.

Classification of Australian birds

The classification of birds (like that of all animals) is an ongoing process, always subject to revision. Taking a reasonably modern view but avoiding major controversy, we can recognize 82 bird families in Australia. Several of these are of Australasian origin and either occur nowhere else or have their centre of distribution on the Australian subcontinent. Several families (e.g. ostriches and bulbuls) are exotic groups introduced to the subcontinent by Europeans.

ORDER STRUTHIONIFORMES

The Struthioniformes evolved on the ancient Gondwana supercontinent, and many species are still found in the southern hemisphere. All lack a keel on the sternum and all are flightless. Australia's native representatives are the Emu and Southern Cassowary (Casuariidae). The African Ostrich (Struthionidae) has been released from captive populations. All have strong legs, and have long loose (barbless) feathers. The body feathers of these species are double-shafted. All lack a hind toe, the Emu and Cassowary retaining three toes, the Ostrich simply two. Males undertake nesting duties away from their polygamous mates.

ORDER GALLIFORMES

Of the ground-frequenting specialists, the best known group includes the pheasants and quails. Their wings are rounded and they often have a large, heavy body and therefore have poor or limited flight. The beak is short and stout. Large feet, toes and claws are used to scratch for food on the ground, and strong legs contribute to rapid running. All have precocial young. Three families are represented in Australia. The mound builders (Megapodiidae) are large and best known for the construction, by males, of huge mounds of soil and fermenting vegetation in which the eggs are incubated. The true quails (Phasianidae) occupy open areas, and are usually gregarious. A third family (Odontophoridae) is represented by a single introduced species, the Californian Quail.

ORDER ANSERIFORMES

Members of this order have partially or fully webbed toes (with an associated swimming capability), a broad, flattened beak, and strong flight. The Magpie Goose (Anseranatidae) occurs only in Australia and New Guinea: it is long-legged, and has partially webbed toes. The swans and ducks (Anatidae) are short-legged, have fully webbed toes and are strong swimmers. They feed by grazing, dabbling at the water's edge or diving. All have precocial young.

ORDER PODICIPEDIFORMES

Grebes (Podicipedidae) are a cosmopolitan group of waterbirds. They are both swimmers and divers with legs placed well back on the body. The legs are laterally flattened and the toes are lobed (not webbed). The wings are reduced in size, restricting flight.

ORDER SPHENISCIFORMES

Penguins (Spheniscidae) are medium to large birds, with bold black and white plumage, confined to the southern hemisphere. Penguins swim well but cannot fly. The forelimbs are modified as flippers, with which the birds swim at speed both on and below the ocean surface.

ORDER PROCELLARIIFORMES

This order comprises the "true" seabirds, characterized by possession of long, thin wings adapted for continuous flight and webbed toes for swimming. It includes albatrosses, petrels, shearwaters and storm-petrels. Albatrosses (Diomedeidae) are the largest, their huge bodies having long plated beaks with basal nostril openings on the side of the bill. Smaller than these are the petrels and shearwaters (Procellariidae), in which the nasal cavities open at the top of the beak. Storm-petrels (Hydrobatidae) are the smallest and daintiest of the group, with longer and more delicate legs. Storm-petrels are similar to petrels in having the nasal opening on the top of the beak.

ORDER PELECANIFORMES

Members of this order have all four toes connected by webbing; all possess a throat-pouch (enormous in pelicans); and all have altricial young. Six families are represented in Australia. Tropicbirds (Phaethontidae) are pelagic by nature and gull-like in appearance: their distinguishing character is extremely long central tail feathers. Gannets and boobies (Sulidae) are oceanic, adapted to capture food by diving, often from great heights, into the sea. The Darter (Anhingidae) is remarkably like the cormorant, but differs in having a long, very thin neck, head and bill and a long tail; it also differs in behaviour. Cormorants (Phalacrocoracidae) are found in both salt and fresh water. Because the feathers lack the water-proofed capability of those of other aquatic birds, cormorants must spend time with their wings spread to dry. Food is captured underwater, the birds commencing the chase from a surface swimming position. Pelicans (Pelecanidae) are the largest members of the order: they have the longest beak and biggest throat pouch and, proportionately, the shortest legs. Food collection is done by dipping below the water surface. Frigatebirds (Fregatidae) are oceanic species possessing long thin wings, a strongly forked tail and heavily hooked bill. They take food from the surface and rob other species of their prey.

ORDER CICONIIFORMES
Herons and their allies are a group of long-legged, long-necked, wading birds. The young are all semi-altricial. Three families are represented in Australia. Herons (Ardeidae) have long legs and a long (often slender) beak. The neck has a spring-like action. In flight, the neck is normally held in a characteristic tight 'S' shape. Ibises and spoonbills (Threskiornithidae) have long legs and neck: the beak in the former is down-curved; in the latter, it is spatular. Ibisis and spoonbills fly with the head and neck outstretched. Storks (Ciconiidae) are long-legged, have a long stocky beak and fly with the neck outstretched.

ORDER FALCONIFORMES
Eagles, hawks and their kin are of cosmopolitan distribution. The beak is short, strongly hooked, and has a fleshy cere. The toes have sharp talons. Most are diurnal. The hawks and eagles (Accipitridae) generally possess rounded wings and fly relatively slowly. Falcons (Falconidae) have long, pointed wings and are fast fliers. They have a notched cutting edge on the maxilla.

ORDER GRUIFORMES
This diverse group is cosmopolitan: some possess, some lack, a hind toe. Cranes (Gruidae) are large and long-legged, with the hind toe raised above the others. Cranes are found in grassland and marsh. Rails (Rallidae) vary considerably in size: all have very slimly built bodies, and exhibit a hind toe. Many are aquatic and swim well; some are flightless. The plains-dwelling Bustard (Otididae) is bulkily built and spends most of its time on the ground, but is able to fly: it lacks a hind toe.

ORDER TURNICIFORMES
This small group comprises one family of button-quails (Turnicidae). These small, short-legged birds have a superficial resemblance to true quails but, among many differences, lack a hind toe and have many reversed sexual roles.

ORDER CHARADRIIFORMES
This large assemblage of varying sized wading, swimming and

flying birds contains many that are migratory. The young are either precocial or semi-precocial. There are ten Australian families, many with cosmopolitan affiliations. Uniquely Australian is the Plains Wanderer (Pedionomidae). Once thought to be allied to the button-quails, it is now recognized to be a wader. It has a hind toe and is sexually dimorphic: the male incubates the eggs and rears the chicks. Sandpipers, snipes and godwits (Scolopacidae) are common migrants, varying in size from diminutive to moderate. Most are cryptically coloured. Identification often depends on the relative lengths of beak and legs. All have unwebbed feet.

The Painted Snipe (Rostratulidae), which superficially resembles true snipes, is a cryptic species in which the male incubates the eggs and rears the chicks. Jacanas (Jacanidae) are rail-like and inhabit lily-covered lagoons and waterholes. Here their distinctive long toes allow them to walk across floating vegetation on the water's surface with ease. Stone-curlews or thick-knees (Burhinidae) are long-legged and nocturnal: they are accomplished runners, and often congregate in numbers during cooler months.

Oystercatchers (Haematopodidae) are moderately sized, with brightly coloured legs and colourful beaks: they haunt beaches and rocky headlands. Stilts and avocets (Recurvirostridae) are delicate, long-legged birds with beaks that are, respectively, needle-thin and straight; or thin and upcurved. Moderate to small sized waders are the widespread plovers, dotterels and lapwings (Charadriidae). These have a short beak, round head and short neck. They are often gregarious.

Pratincoles (Glareolidae) possess long streamlined wings and a short tail. One species has short legs, in the other they are long and thin. Pratincoles feed from the ground and on the wing. Terns and gulls (Laridae) are characterized by having webbed toes on short legs, and long pointed wings. They are gregarious, swim and obtain food from the surface of the water by diving (terns) or by scavenging (gulls).

ORDER COLUMBIFORMES

This order is cosmopolitan but only one family (Columbidae) is represented in Australia. Pigeons are both terrestrial and arboreal. Many species exhibit brilliantly coloured plumage, either completely or as iridescent patches. All construct a fragile nest and lay white eggs. The young are altricial and are fed on a liquid 'pigeon milk' produced by the parent.

ORDER PSITTACIFORMES

Parrots are easily recognized by their bright colours; short, hooked beak; and a foot with two toes directed forward and two to the rear. All parrots use the beak in climbing. Two families of parrots are readily distinguished: the cockatoos (Cacatuidae), and the lorikeets and typical parrots (Psittacidae). The former are large crested parrots restricted in distribution to Australia and the south-west Pacific. The remaining parrots may have brush-like tongues (lorikeets) or typical thick, horny tongues. Most are gregarious and noisy. A number have fleshy ceres, or colourful areas of bare skin.

ORDER CUCULIFORMES

Most Australian cuckoos are nest parasites, laying eggs in the nests of other birds, which incubate and feed the intruders. All cuckoos have slightly decurved beaks and short legs; two toes point forward and two back. Two families occur in Australia: the typical nest-usurping cuckoos (Cuculidae) and the nest-constructing and parentally inclined coucal (Centropodidae).

ORDER STRIGIFORMES

Like the diurnal raptors, many nocturnal owls possess strong legs and talons. They differ from Falconiformes in the structuring of the feathers that ensure silent flight and the feet, which have two toes directed forward and two to the rear. Their eyes are directed forward and are adapted for nocturnal vision. Hawk owls (Strigidae) have rounded heads and short legs. Barn owls (Tytonidae) have large facial disks and long legs. Both families vary from moderately sized to large birds.

ORDER CAPRIMULGIFORMES

Nightjars, owlet-nightjars and frogmouths are nocturnal. They lack the talons and associated actions of the Strigiformes, and most have frail legs. They hunt by pouncing on prey and swallowing it whole. Three families occur in Australia. The largest birds are the frogmouths (Podargidae), characterized by their size, wide beaks and choice of retiring to rest on a branch of a tree. The nightjars (Caprimulgidae) are long-winged and feed by aerial pursuit. Their feet are weak, and they possess large eyes and are ground-nesters. One owlet-nightjar (Aegothelidae) occurs in Australia. It is small, has a wide beak, soft plumage and big bulbous eyes. It nests and roosts in hollow limbs.

ORDER APODIFORMES

Swifts and swiftlets are long-winged and extremely weak-legged. There is one family in Australia (Apodidae). The tail of the two larger species is spiny. They are aerial feeders capturing flying prey in the short, very wide, beak. Saliva is used in their nest construction, which is undertaken in caves and crevices.

ORDER CORACIIFORMES

Kingfishers, bee-eaters and rollers are brightly coloured birds, all with weak legs and syndactyl toes. Members of the four Australian families have a large head and a heavy beak. The water-kingfishers (Alcedinidae) nest in hollows along waterways and feed principally by diving into water. The terrestrial kingfishers (Halcyonidae) nest in hollow trees and earthen banks and characteristically feed by securing prey from trees or the ground. The long-winged bee-eaters (Meropidae) have long central tail feathers. The slender and slightly decurved beak is employed in aerial feeding. The single Australian species nests in an earthen burrow. Rollers (Coraciidae) have long, pointed wings and a short but wide beak. They are aerial feeders and nest in tree hollows.

ORDER PASSERIFORMES

Song- or perching birds make up the remaining (34) families of Australian birds belonging in one immense order. Anatomically, they all display a distinctive palate and have three toes forward and one to the rear. The young are altricial. Gaudily coloured pittas (Pittidae) are very distinctive. They have short, rounded wings, long legs, and are generally terrestrial. Lyrebirds (Menuridae) and scrub-birds (Atrichornithidae) are also largely terrestrial: both have short, rounded wings. Lyrebirds have stout legs and feet. A long tail on the male is used in elaborate displays. The closely related scrub-birds are known for their loud, ringing song and proficient mimickry. They are cryptic and elusive birds, secreting themselves in dense understorey.

Treecreepers (Climacteridae) have a long, decurved beak and feed principally from limbs and trunks of trees. Fairy-wrens (Maluridae) are small birds and, generally, adult males are the brightest coloured. Both sexes have a short, weak beak, a long tail and short and rounded wings. Pardalotes (Pardalotidae) differ in being arboreal, choosing to nest in hollows of trees or those evacuated in the soil. Also included in the family is a number of small species commonly called 'little brown birds': gerygones, thornbills and scrubwrens, which can be terrestrial or arboreal. All have thin beaks and short, weak, rounded wings.

A large songbird family, the honeyeaters (Meliphagidae), is characteristic of Australia; nearly all species have slender, decurved beaks. Related to honeyeaters are the Australian chats, which are mainly ground-haunting. In all species the tongue is bifurcate and brush-tipped, the wings short and rounded. Another family of Australasian origin comprises the robins (Petroicidae). These are best characterized by their small size, often colourful plumage, rictal bristles, short, weak legs and beaks. Logrunners (Orthonychidae) are also a group of ancient Australian origin. They are terrestrial and have short, rounded wings and long, stout legs.

Babblers (Pomatostomidae) are gregarious, have a long, strong and decurved beak, short and rounded wings, and short and stout legs. Quail-thrushes and whipbirds (Cinclosomatidae) are typically ground-dwelling. Some have a long, pointed beak; all have stout legs and rounded wings. Among the arboreal groups are the minute sittellas (Neosittidae) with a beak that is thin, short and gently upcurved. They climb and feed from limbs and trunks of trees.

Superficially resembling the robins (but larger) are the whistlers and shrike-thrushes (Pachycephalidae). These have a rounded head, a stout, hooked beak and short, pointed wings. Another flycatching group includes the fantails, Magpie-lark and drongos (Dicruridae). These have a broad head; a long, hooked, but sometimes weak, bill; long wings; and short legs. All possess rictal bristles. The Magpie-lark is the only member of this family to construct a nest of mud. Cuckoo-shrikes (Campephagidae) have a stout beak, which is slightly decurved. The nostrils are partly hidden by short bristles. The wings are pointed and the legs short and weak.

Orioles (Oriolidae) are widespread through Africa to Asia and Australia. Two genera occur in Australia, the Figbird being restricted to Australia, New Guinea and eastern Indonesia. All orioles have a long bill and long, pointed wings. The legs are short and stout. Figbirds are similar to orioles but have a broader bill. Woodswallows, butcherbirds, magpies and currawongs are now placed in the same family (Artamidae). Woodswallows are typical aerial feeders, spending much time on long, pointed wings. The tail and legs are stout, the bill is short and stout, and the tongue is brush-tipped. Butcherbirds, magpies and currawongs all have stout, hooked beaks. Bright iridescent colours dominate in male birds-of-paradise (Paradisaeidae).

Within the bowerbirds and catbirds (Ptilonorhynchidae) the brightly coloured males construct bowers of sticks, which may be decorated by coloured ornaments. Crows and ravens (Corvidae) are large birds, with black iridescent feathering. Their legs are stout and they have long, feathered rictal bristles. Mud-nesting is a characteristic of a very small family (Corcoracidae): both species are gregarious and terrestrial. Larks (Alaudidae) possess pointed wings, a long hind claw and a distinctive display flight. Pipits and wagtails (Motacillidae) are terrestrial and have long pointed wings, a beak that is thin and pointed, and an elongated hind toe.

An introduction of sparrows (Passeridae) in the 19th century has caused these birds to be well-distributed throughout eastern Australia. Their short, conical beak and short legs are very distinctive. The native grass finches are related. Several species of true finches (Fringillidae) have been introduced from Europe: these have rounded wings, a short, conical bill and short legs. Sunbirds (Nectariniidae) are represented by one small but brightly coloured species with a long decurved beak and partly tubular tongue. Another family with only one Australian representative comprises the flowerpeckers (Dicaeidae). Typically, these have short legs and short and pointed beaks but the wings of the Australian species are long and pointed.

Swallows and martins (Hirundinidae) are aerial-feeding species with long pointed wings and weak legs. The beak is short and wide, bordered by rictal bristles. Bulbuls (Pycnonotidae) are exotic birds introduced by Europeans. They possess rictal bristles and short wings, the legs are short and weak. Smaller-sized birds with remarkably melodious songs include the cosmopolitan old-world warblers (Sylviidae) which have a slender beak, and wings that are short and usually rounded. Silvereyes or white-eyes (Zosteropidae) are widespread from Africa, Asia and the south Pacific islands to Australia. Apart from a ring of white feathering about the eyes, these small birds are generally grey or yellow in colour. They have straight, slender bills. The legs are short, and the wings are rounded.

Australian species of thrushes and thrush-like birds (Muscicapidae) are generally terrestrial in habit. They have long slender beaks, the legs are stout, and the wings rounded or pointed. Introductions from Europe and Asia are the gregarious Common Myna and Common Starling (Sturnidae). They, and the native species, have straight, pointed bills and strong legs.

Bird habitats and distribution

Australia comprises a wide variety of environments, ranging from the tropical rainforests of northern Queensland to the alpine scrubs of Mount Kosciusko. This has encouraged the evolution of a rich diversity of birds.

Grassland is the most extensive environment, followed by scrubland and woodland, then dry and wet eucalypt forests. There are relatively small areas of rainforest, wetlands, heathland, coastal mudflats and mangroves.

The habitats of most birds are restricted to one or a few of these environments – usually to particular components of them. Most environments are shared by a number of species that exploit different resources of food and shelter. Many species may appear to share the same habitat but close examination usually reveals that they are separated by behaviour: one may feed on the ground, another in mid-level vegetation, another in the tree canopy. Some species are sedentary, spending their entire lives in one area. Others move nomadically between similar habitats in response to the availability of food, or migrate very great distances

– sometimes from one hemisphere to the other. As a general rule, better watered environments are home to a greater number of sedentary species than those with lower or less regular rainfall. Arid grasslands have the lowest proportion of resident species.

Whether sedentary or mobile, every species has habitat requirements that are limited by available environments. It is self-evident that if the extent of a particular environment (such as tropical rainforest or temperate wetland) is diminished, certain habitats will decrease, leading to reduction in the population of birds that depend upon these habitats – a process that can lead to extinction. It is equally self-evident that agriculture, forestry and urbanization have led – and continue to lead – to destruction of most natural environments, except where areas have been set aside as national parks or similar reserves. Rather surprisingly, no mainland bird species has yet become extinct but a number are very vulnerable and may not persist long into the 21st century.

Bird biology

Parts of a bird

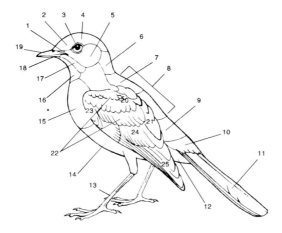

1 lores	10 uppertail coverts	19 upper mandible
2 forehead	11 tail	20 scapulars
3 eye-ring	12 undertail coverts	21 tertials
4 crown	13 tarsus	22 wing coverts
5 ear coverts	14 belly	23 alula
6 nape	15 breast	24 secondaries
7 mantle	16 throat	25 primaries
8 back	17 malar region	
9 rump	18 lower mandible	

Emu *Dromaius novaehollandiae* Up to 2m

R.W.G. Jenkins

This bird's grey-brown body feathers consist of two long plumes which are attached at the base of each black feather shaft. The male and female have similar plumage. The black upper-neck feathers are thinly scattered and allow the blue skin to show through, this is slightly darker in female birds. Emus pair for about five months of the year and egg-laying commences in April or May. The 7 to 20 dark green eggs are hatched solely by the male. Found in all but the densest forests and most heavily populated areas, this large, flightless bird is a common sight over much of Australia.

Southern Cassowary *Casuarius casuarius* 1.5-2m

Dick Whitford

The prominent greyish casque and red wattle hanging from the neck, make the Southern Cassowary easily identifiable. The feathers of the body are black and hair-like, becoming more rufous toward the tail. The bare skin of the head and fore-neck is blue, while the hind-neck is red. The female is generally taller than the male and has a taller casque. Calls consist of a variety of guttural rumblings and grunts. Uncommon and wary. Attacks on humans have been recorded, especially during the breeding season, June to October. The elusive Southern Cassowary inhabits the dense rainforests of northern Queensland.

Hoary-headed Grebe *Poliocephalus poliocephalus* 27-30cm

R. Drummond

The upperparts of the Hoary-headed Grebe are generally grey and underparts are white. During the breeding season the throat turns black and the head becomes dark grey with numerous overlying white plumes. The male is slightly larger than the female and has a pale golden-yellow eye, speckled with black. When observed in the field, a bird seldom allows close approach and generally flies off at the sight of an intruder. Prey consists mainly of aquatic insects and crustaceans, caught in underwater dives. Probably the most gregarious of the grebe family, it is often seen nesting and roosting in groups on unsheltered areas of fresh and brackish waterways.

Australasian Grebe *Tachybaptus novaehollandiae* 25-27cm

G. Little

Outside of the breeding season, this species is often confused with the **Hoary-headed Grebe** but can be distinguished by its yellow eye. During the breeding season, September to March, both sexes attain a rich chestnut facial stripe that extends from just behind the eye through to the base of the neck. The remainder of the head becomes glossy black and the oval patch of bare skin at the base of the bill becomes pale yellow. Food, which consists mainly of small fish and water insects, is normally caught during deep underwater dives but some prey is taken on the surface.

13

Great Crested Grebe *Podiceps cristatus* 46-50cm (Females smaller than males)

P. Slater

When in breeding plumage, November to February, this large grebe is resplendent with its beautiful chestnut and black tippets and glossy black crest. Outside of the breeding season it has a black crown with a reduced crest, dark brown upperparts and white underparts, tinged with rufous on the flanks. During the breeding season both sexes perform an elaborate mating display, in which both birds face each other and rear up on their tails, becoming almost vertical out of the water. Found on extensive, open waterways, it feeds on a wide variety of aquatic animals and plants.

Little Penguin *Eudyptula minor* 32-34cm

R.L. Smith

The smallest of the penguins found in Australian waters and the only species to breed on the Australian mainland. At rest, the bird lies on the surface of the water with its flippers outstretched. The underparts, including the underside of the flippers, are white and the upperparts are dark blue, camouflaging it against the surrounding water. The eye is silver-grey and the bill is black. Food, which consists of fish and squid, is caught by skilful underwater pursuits. Unlike other penguins, it waits for the cover of night before coming ashore to roost. It occurs throughout southern Australia.

Wandering Albatross *Diomedea exulans* 80-135cm; Wingspan 260-325cm

G. Robertson

Often seen scavenging from fishing boats, the Wandering Albatross appears entirely white at a distance. Closer inspection reveals fine black wavy lines on the breast neck and upper back. The white tail is occasionally tipped with black and the back of the wings change from black to white with age. The female is slightly smaller than the male and has brown speckles on the crown. The Wandering Albatross spends most of the year roaming the southern parts of the globe in an effortless glide, resting occasionally on the water's surface to feed on squid, fish and waste from boats. It occurs in Australian waters between June and September.

Black-browed Albatross *Diomedea melanophris* 85-88cm; Wingspan 220-240cm

G. W. Johnstone

The slate-black back and upper wing of the Black-browed Albatross is very striking against the contrasting white of its head, neck and underparts. This, combined with the bird's 'smudged' grey-black eyebrow, makes it instantly recognizable. The bill is yellow-orange, becoming more red at tip, and the feet are grey-blue. Sub-adult birds have more black on the underwing. For most of the year this is the most commonly seen albatross off the southern Australian coastline. Although recorded in Australian waters in all months of the year it is most common between May and October, arriving a few weeks ahead of the **Wandering Albatross**.

15

Southern Giant-Petrel *Macronectes giganteus* 85-90cm; Wingspan 200-220cm

C. Gill

The distinctive tube-nosed bill, which is rather pale and finishes in a pale green bulbous tip, distinguishes this bird from the **Northern Giant-Petrel**, which has a dark pink-brown tip. The most common colour for birds found in Australia is dark brown, adults having a white head and upper neck. The white form of this species is mostly confined to areas around the Antarctic Circle. Superficially resembling an albatross in size and shape, the immature Southern Giant-Petrel is a regular visitor to coastal areas of southern Australia. Common in offshore areas and harbours.

White-headed Petrel *Pterodroma lessonii* 40-46cm (Females smaller than males)

T. Palliser

The white head, breast and belly, with contrasting mottled grey-black upperparts and black wings, distinguish this bird from other petrels found in Australian waters. Spending much of its time at sea, it feeds at night on squid and fish, plucked from the surface of the water. The White-headed Petrel is mainly solitary, pairing

only for the breeding season, August to May. Although birds are usually silent when at sea, breeding colonies are quite noisy, uttering a variety of high-pitched 'wik-wik-wik' and braying 'oooo-er' calls. It occurs off the southern Australian coastline in late summer and winter.

Great-winged Petrel *Pterodroma macroptera* 40-42cm

This uniformly blackish-brown petrel is easily identified by its large size and absence of pale markings on the body. Normally solitary, it pairs only for the breeding season, from January to October. Outside the breeding season it spends its time at sea, hunting by night for krill and squid, which it scoops from the surface of the water. It is usually silent at sea but breeding colonies are noisy places, with a variety of staccato 'kik-kik-kik' or 'si-si-si' calls being uttered in the air and at the nest. It is common on offshore islands and open ocean off the southern Australian coast.

N. Kolichis

Fairy Prion *Pachyptila turtur* 23-25cm

M. Carter

With the exception of the **Fulmar Prion**, which is not found in Australian waters, the Fairy Prion is the 'bluest' of its family. Chiefly blue-grey above and white below, it can also be distinguished from other prions by its short dark blue bill. It has a robust hook on the tip of the upper mandible, leaving only a short space between it and the nasal tubes. A dark black 'M' is visible on the back of the wings when in flight. The Fairy Prion is the only prion to breed in Australia. It is common in offshore and coastal areas of southern Australia.

Wedge-tailed Shearwater *Puffinus pacificus* 42-47cm

T. Lindsey

The diagnostic long, wedge-shaped tail clearly distinguishes this species from other shearwaters. After moult, the plumage is a dark glossy black but soon turns to the usual dark brown with wear. The Wedge-tailed Shearwater has a less common pale morph, in which the underparts are white, as are the centres of the underwings. The upperparts are pale brown with a faint 'M' visible on the wings and back, when in flight. Immatures resemble adults in both forms. The Wedge-tailed Shearwater usually occurs alone or in small groups. It is found on both the eastern and western coastlines of Australia.

Short-tailed Shearwater *Puffinus tenuirostris* 40-43cm

J.R. Napier

The Short-tailed Shearwater is dark brown in plumage, the underwing occasionally having traces of white in the centre. The tail is rounded and, when in flight, the dark grey feet trail slightly behind. This species should not be confused with the **Sooty Shearwater**, which is larger with a longer bill. Immature birds are similar in plumage to the adults. During summer, this is the most common shearwater along the south and south-eastern coasts of Australia: at this time many dead and dying birds may be found washed up on beaches.

Wilson's Storm-Petrel *Oceanites oceanicus* 15-19cm

P. Morris/Ardea

This sooty black bird, with a square tail and white rump, does not resemble any other storm-petrel found off the Australian coast. The underside of its feet are yellow and, in flight, protrude beyond the end of the tail. When feeding, its flight resembles that of a butterfly, wings held high, bouncing erratically above the surface of the water as it collects whale oil and blubber and small crustaceans. It is the most common storm-petrel found on Australia's continental shelf, particularly along the east and west coasts.

White-faced Storm-Petrel *Pelagodroma marina* 18-20cm

G. Robertson

As its name suggests, this species is easily distinguished by its conspicuous white face pattern. The upperparts are almost entirely dark grey, with a paler grey rump; underparts are white. It feeds on krill and small squids, taken from the surface of the water. Breeding takes place in small colonies on offshore islands, between September and April. The White-faced Storm-Petrel is the most common storm-petrel found in Australian waters, occasionally sighted off Tasmania and the coastline of mainland south-eastern Australia.

19

Australian Pelican *Pelecanus conspicillatus* 160-180cm

D. & M. Trounson

With its enormous pouched bill and bulky frame, the pelican is unmistakable when fishing or at rest on land. The female is slightly smaller than the male, but both share the characteristic black and white plumage. Immature birds are brown where adults are black. When soaring high (up to 3000m) on thermal currents, it is often confused with the **White-bellied Sea-Eagle**. Breeding is opportunistic, and commences when there is sufficient rain or available ground water. Pelicans are found on rivers, lakes and coastal mudflats throughout all but the most arid areas of Australia.

Australasian Gannet *Morus serrator* 84-95cm

J.R. Napier

The male and female are similar in plumage: most of the body is white with darkened tips to the major wing feathers and the inner tail feathers. The head is buff-yellow and the bill is pale blue-grey with striking black borders to the bill sheaths. In immature birds the head and upperparts are mostly brown with inconsistent amounts of white spotting. Familiar off the southern coast of Australia, the Australasian Gannet forms small flocks that soar ten or more metres above the surface of the water, then fold their wings back and dive into the water in pursuit of fish.

Darter *Anhinga melanogaster* 85-90cm

B. Chudleigh

Male Darters are predominantly glossy black with buff-cream streaks on the upper wing. The bill is yellow and sharply pointed, and a white stripe extends from below the eye to the first curve of the neck. Females are light grey brown where the males are black and the white eye-stripe is bordered with black. Young birds resemble the female in plumage but lack the eye-stripe. Sitting quietly in the water with its body submerged and only its head and neck visible, the Darter will sink silently under water to pursue fish, insects and small turtles for up to a minute at a time.

Little Pied Cormorant *Phalacrocorax melanoleucos* 50-60cm

G. Little

The Little Pied Cormorant is entirely black above and white below. The face is dusky and, in adult birds, the white of the underside extends above the eye. It is easily distinguished from the larger **Pied Cormorant**, which has an orange-yellow face patch. One of the more common Australian waterbirds, the Little Pied Cormorant is at home on virtually any body of water, fresh or saline, throughout Australia. It is often seen in large flocks on open waterways and on the coast, especially where large numbers of fish are present. On inland streams and dams, however, it is often solitary.

Great Cormorant *Phalacrocorax carbo* 70-90cm

G. Little

This is the largest of the Australian cormorants and one of the largest in the world. It is almost entirely black in plumage, apart from a small white patch on each thigh (absent in winter), and can be distinguished from the **Little Black Cormorant** by its larger size and by the white chin and yellow throat. In spite of its preference for extensive areas of permanent fresh water, the Great Cormorant is by no means confined to these and is often observed on coastal inlets and estuaries. It occurs throughout most of Australia but is more numerous in the south-east and south-west.

Little Black Cormorant *Phalacrocorax sulcirostris* 60-65cm

M. Carter

This common cormorant is easily distinguished from the **Great Cormorant** by its entirely black plumage, including the face and bill, and its smaller size. The feathers of the back have a faint green gloss, which is not always visible. Where food is abundant it often forms large flocks. It is a familiar sight on farm dams and small ponds (often in the company of the **Little Pied Cormorant**) and is a regular visitor to the flood waters of the interior. Its preference for fresh water, especially small lakes and ponds, and its tolerance of salt water environments make it a common sight throughout most of Australia.

White-necked Heron *Ardea pacifica* 76-105cm

Hans & Judy Beste

Its large size and distinct white head and neck, with a double row of brown-black spots on the front, distinguish the White-necked Heron from any other Australian heron or egret. The lower breast and belly are grey-brown, streaked with white, while the back and wings are chiefly grey-black (with long maroon plumes on the back in the breeding season). In flight, a conspicuous white patch is visible on the bend (elbow) of each wing. It is largely nomadic, favouring wet grasslands, freshwater wetlands and, less commonly, coastal waters over much of Australia. It is common throughout its range.

White-faced Heron *Egretta novaehollandiae* 60-70cm

G. Hoye

The most familiar heron in Australia, it is easily identified by its primarily blue-grey plumage and a characteristic white face. When disturbed it rises to the air in a slow bouncing flight with its long neck outstretched, croaking in alarm as it goes. In flight the darker flight feathers are contrasted against the paler grey plumage, making it easily identifiable when viewed from below. This species feeds on a wide variety of prey, including fish, insects and amphibians. It is found on any suitable body of water throughout the mainland and Tasmania, from tidal mudflats to moist grasslands.

23

Cattle Egret *Ardea ibis* 48-53cm

K. Ireland

Smallest of the Australian egrets, this bird should not be confused with the larger **Intermediate Egret**, which occasionally occupies similar habitat. Both species have a yellow bill (unlike the **Little Egret**, which has a predominantly black bill). The Cattle Egret walks with a very obvious back-and-forth head movement. For most of the year it has almost entirely white plumage but, during the breeding season (October to January), it is distinguished by long, dark golden plumes on the head, neck, breast and mantle. It is commonly seen in small flocks, opportunistically feeding on grasshoppers, and other insects, that are disturbed by grazing cattle.

Great Egret *Ardea alba* 41-49cm

G. Weber

This is the largest of the Australian egrets. The plumage is white and, for most of the year, the bill and facial skin are yellow. During the breeding season (October to December) long nuptial plumes hang from the mantle and at this time the bill is mostly black and the facial skin is green. The length of its neck is greater than the length of its body. The Great Egret usually feeds alone but roosts at night in groups and breeds in colonies, usually in association with cormorants and ibises, as well as other egrets. Common throughout most of Australia, and indeed the world.

24

Nankeen Night Heron *Nycticorax caledonicus* 55-65cm

L.F. Schick

Quite distinct from other herons in Australia, the Nankeen Night Heron has rich cinnamon-rufous upperparts and a black crown. Three long white plumes which cascade from the back of the head are retained throughout the year, unlike some other herons. Young birds are often confused with bitterns, especially the **Australasian Bittern**, due to their streaked plumage. However, the narrower streaking of the heron's underparts and the regular 'tear-drop' spotting on its wings and back should distinguish it in the field. It frequents shallow, sheltered waterways and flooded grasslands where it feeds on fish, aquatic insects, small crustaceans and amphibians. It is nocturnal.

Black-necked Stork *Ephippiorhynchus asiaticus* 129-137cm

C. Andrew Henley/Larus

The only member of the stork family found in Australia. The black and white body plumage, glossy dark green and purple neck and massive black bill distinguish this bird from all other Australian birds. The female has yellow eyes. In flight, the long coral-red legs trail behind the body and the long neck and bill are held outstretched. Immature birds resemble adults, but the black plumage is brown and the white plumage is more grey-brown. Mostly restricted to coastal and near-coastal areas of northern and eastern Australia, it feeds on fish, small crustaceans and amphibians in lagoons, swamps and tidal mudflats.

25

Australian White Ibis *Threskiornis molucca* 69-76cm

The Australian White Ibis is identified by almost entirely white body plumage and black head and neck. The head is featherless and its black bill is long and down-curved. During the breeding season the small patch of skin on the under-surface of the wing changes from dull pink to dark scarlet. Adult birds have a tuft of cream plumes on the base of the neck. Frequenting swamps, lagoons and floodplains, as well as urban parks and gardens, it feeds on a wide variety of foods, from aquatic insects and crustaceans to human refuse. Well adapted to all but the most arid habitats, it is common and widespread.

Straw-necked Ibis *Threskiornis spinicollis* 59-76cm

The commonest and most striking of the Australian ibises, this species is identified by its iridescent purple-green back and wings and snow-white underparts. The down-curved bill is black, as is the bare skin of the head and neck; the lower neck is covered with short feathers. Long 'straw-like' plumes cascade from the fore-neck (these are absent on young birds). During the breeding season the bare yellow skin of the underwing becomes bright red. It often occurs in large flocks in wet or dry grasslands over much of Australia, feeding on terrestrial invertebrates.

Glossy Ibis *Plegadis falcinellus* 48-61cm

D. & M. Trounson

This is the smallest ibis found in Australia and has an unmistakable colouration. It is entirely dark chestnut with an iridescent purple and green sheen, darker green on the wings. When not breeding the head is dull brown with some white streaking. The male has a slightly longer bill than the female.

Mostly inhabiting shallow freshwater lagoons and flooded pastures, it is also found in mangroves and on estuarine mudflats, feeding on insects, fish and crustaceans. The Glossy Ibis is very nomadic, foraging in groups, often quite large ones, and over a wide area. It occurs over much of the Australian mainland.

Royal Spoonbill *Platalea regia* 75-80cm

D. & M. Trounson

The Royal Spoonbill is easily identified by its white plumage and black spatulate bill (in contrast to the pale yellow bill of the **Yellow-billed Spoonbill**). The Royal Spoonbill feeds in shallow lagoons and swamps, catching small fish and crustaceans by sweeping its head from side to side. During the breeding season long white plumes descend from the nape; these are lacking in young birds. It usually occurs alone or in small groups but breeds in colonies which can be quite large. It is almost silent. Of the two Australian spoonbills, the Royal Spoonbill is the more common and is found extensively throughout the northern and eastern parts of Australia.

Magpie Goose *Anseranas semipalmata* 71-92cm (Females smaller than males)

C. Andrew Henley/Larus

This large, noisy goose is readily recognized. The head and neck are black and there is a characteristic knobbed crown. The underparts are white, with contrasting black margins on the underwing. The legs, feet and bill are orange. It frequents flood-plains and wet grasslands from Fitzroy River, Western Australia, through northern Australia to Rockhampton, Queensland, and occasionally south to the Hunter River, New South Wales. The Magpie Goose is a specialised feeder, with wild rice *Oryza, Panicum, Paspalum* and spike-rush *Eleocharis* forming the bulk of its diet. It is gregarious, often forming vast, noisy flocks.

Black Swan *Cygnus atratus* 120-142cm (Females smaller than males)

Dick Whitford

This is the only black swan found anywhere in the world. In flight the neck is held outstretched and the broad white wing tips contrast against the otherwise black body. The bill is a deep orange-red with a distinct narrow white band and paler white nail at the tip of the upper mandible. Introduced into several countries and a vagrant to New Guinea, the Black Swan favours extensive waterways and permanent wetlands where it feeds mainly on algae. It can be observed throughout Australia, with the exception of Cape York Peninsula, but is more common in the south.

Plumed Whistling-Duck *Dendrocygna eytoni* 44-62cm

K. Ireland

The Plumed Whistling-Duck is paler than its close relative the **Wandering Whistling-Duck**. Mostly brown above, paler yellow-brown on head and neck, and pale brown below, it has a rufous breast, conspicuously barred with black. The long flank plumes are cream with black margins. In flight, its speckled underwing, white belly and pink legs make it easily identifiable. Rarely observed in the water, it feeds on grasses, herbs and sedges on the margins of swamps and lagoons or open pastures often far from water. It is found in dense flocks throughout much of eastern and northern Australia.

Pacific Black Duck *Anas superciliosa* 50-60cm

Dick Whitford

The dark brown line through the eye, bordered with cream above and below, and a dark brown crown make this duck easily distinguishable at a distance. The upper body feathers are mid-brown, each feather being edged with buff, and the underparts are mottled brown. Upperwing colour is the same as the back, with a bright green sheen on the secondaries. The white underwing is conspicuous in flight. One of the most versatile of the Australian ducks, it frequents all types of water, from isolated forest pools to tidal mudflats. It is found in all but the most arid regions of Australia.

Grey Teal *Anas gracilis* 40-48cm

D. Hadden

At rest, this duck is easily overlooked. It is almost entirely grey-brown, each feather of the body being edged with buff, except on the rump. The chin and throat are white, (distinguishing it from the female **Chestnut Teal**, which has a pale brown chin and throat). The eye is red and the bill is dark blue-grey. The secondary wing feathers are glossy black (with a blue sheen) above, tipped with white, and have broad white bases. In flight these white bases form a horizontal white stripe which becomes wider towards the body. It is common in all sheltered aquatic habitats throughout Australia.

Chestnut Teal *Anas castanea* 38-48cm

L. Robinson

The endemic Chestnut Teal is most common throughout the southern parts of its range. The male is easily identified by its green head, dappled chestnut breast and belly, brown back and diagnostic white flank patch. The female is quite drab in comparison, with predominantly grey-brown plumage, darker on the back, crown and hind-neck, and is generally darker than the similar **Grey Teal**. It is sedentary, in small flocks, often with **Grey Teal** and occurs in coastal areas and inland waterways, from about Innisfail, Queensland, south through Tasmania and South Australia, to about Geraldton, Western Australia.

Hardhead *Aythya australis* 41- 55cm

Dick Whitford

The male Hardhead, or White-eyed Duck, is easily identified by its overall dark brown plumage, white-tipped bill and conspicuous white eyes. The female's eyes are brown. Food, mostly molluscs, crustaceans and aquatic insects, is caught during deep underwater dives, which may last some time. The Hardhead is mostly silent, the only sounds uttered being a few soft whistles or croaks. It is nomadic and gregarious, forming small flocks on deep permanent swamps and lakes, as well as other wetland areas. It is most common in eastern and western Australia, occurring only as vagrants in the interior.

Australian Wood Duck *Chenonetta jubata* 42-60cm (Females smaller than males)

Peter Rowland

The Australian Wood Duck is identified by its brown head, grey and black back and wings, and speckled underparts. The male has a black mane, and the female has two pale lines passing through the eye. The bill is short and blackish. The call of the female is a drawn-out nasal 'gnew'; that of the male is shorter and higher pitched. A 'perching' duck, it seldom takes to the water except for bathing or mating. Most often observed grazing on a river bank or perched in a tree, this duck is a common sight in well-watered wooded swamps over much of Australia.

Green Pygmy-goose *Nettapus pulchellus* 30-36cm (Females smaller than males)

D. & M. Trounson

This is a beautiful little duck. The male is easily identified by its glossy green head, neck and upperparts, ornately barred green and white underparts and large white cheek patch. The female is somewhat duller, and can be distinguished from the similar female **Cotton Pygmy-goose** by its darker eyebrow and throat, and barred underparts. (The male **Cotton Pygmy-goose** has an almost entirely white head and neck.) It frequents deep lagoons and swamps, where it feeds on a variety of vegetable matter, often at night. A common sight throughout northern Australia.

Musk Duck *Biziura lobata* 47-73cm (Females much smaller than males)

C. Andrew Henley/Larus

The male Musk Duck has the unfortunate reputation of being the most grotesque bird in Australia. Both sexes are sooty-brown in plumage, paler below and becoming whiter towards the abdomen. The male is decorated with a large bulbous lobe of skin hanging from the lower mandible. The common name refers to the strong musk odour produced from a gland on the rump. It is usually silent outside the breeding season. Found in deep freshwater lagoons, interspersed with dense reedbeds, where it feeds on a variety of animals, from aquatic insects to fish and frogs.

Osprey *Pandion haliaetus* 50-65cm (Females larger than males)

G.B. Baker

A skilled fisher, the Osprey is predominantly dark brown above, apart from the white crown. The underparts are white, with a brown band across the upper breast and a brown eye-stripe, more noticeable on female. The undersides of the wings and tail are barred with brown and white. In flight, the wings are bowed and only slightly angled. The Osprey inhabits mangroves, estuaries and rivers, on or near the coast, where it feeds on fish, birds, mammals and amphibians. It is found throughout the coastal regions of Australia, except southern Victoria and Tasmania, and is most abundant in the northern part of its range.

Black-shouldered Kite *Elanus axillaris* 33-38cm

C. Todd

This is a small raptor. The upperparts are grey, with the exception of a large black patch on the upperwing; the underparts and head are white. When perched, the Black-shouldered Kite appears almost identical to the less common **Letter-winged Kite** but can be distinguished by a small patch of black feathers which extends slightly past the eye. In flight, it shows only a small amount of black on the underwing. It frequents woodlands and grasslands, where it feeds on small mammals, reptiles and insects. It is common in all but the more arid areas of the Australian mainland.

Black Kite *Milvus migrans* 47-55cm

R. Brown

The Black Kite is a large dark brown raptor. The tail is forked and barred with darker brown. The call is a descending whistle 'psee-err' followed by a staccato 'si-si-si-si-si'. The Black Kite is found in a variety of habitats throughout mainland Australia, and is often observed in and around outback towns. It is rarely seen singly and often congregates in flocks of several hundred, especially during grasshopper plagues. A bushfire is often the ideal place to observe the Black Kite, as it preys on lizards, small mammals and insects fleeing the flames.

Whistling Kite *Haliastur sphenurus* 50-60cm

G. Chapman

Although it feeds on live prey, the Whistling Kite resembles other kites in its scavenging behaviour and can often be seen feeding on animals killed on the road. Chiefly brown, paler and more streaked on the head, neck and underparts. In flight, the margins of the wings are darker, with a pale grey-brown wedge towards the tip of each wing. The underside of the tail is also pale

grey-brown. The call, a descending whistle 'psee-err' followed by a staccato 'si-si-si-si-si', is similar to that of the **Black Kite**. The Whistling Kite is most common in open wooded habitats near permanent water.

Brahminy Kite *Haliastur indus* 45-51cm

This beautiful chestnut and white raptor is unmistakable. It is easily recognized by its white head, neck and breast and contrasting chestnut belly and upperparts. First-year birds resemble the **Whistling Kite**, but lack pale wedges on the underwing, and have a shorter tail. The call is a drawn-out 'pee-ah-ah-ah' or 'keee-e-yah'. The Brahminy Kite is solitary and pairs only during the breeding season. It inhabits coastal areas of northern Australia, from about Carnarvon, Western Australia to Hastings River, New South Wales, where it feeds on fish and other marine animals, normally stranded or washed up by the tide.

C. Andrew Henley/Larus

Brown Goshawk *Accipiter fasciatus* 37-55cm

This beautiful, slender bird of prey, should not be confused with the smaller and squarer-tailed **Collared Sparrowhawk.** Adults are identified by their grey-brown upperparts, finely barred russet and cream underparts and rufous collar. Immature birds are brown above, with broader brown and cream barring and spotting below. The Brown Goshawk feeds on a variety of prey, including birds, mammals and reptiles. It is generally solitary in behaviour. Although it is normally silent, some harsh chattering is emitted when alarmed. Found in most timbered areas around Australia, it is fairly abundant throughout its range.

Hans & Judy Beste

White-bellied Sea-Eagle *Haliaeetus leucogaster* 75-85cm

R. Brown

This unmistakable large bird of prey is a common sight in coastal and near coastal areas of Australia. Adults have white on the head, rump and underparts and dark grey on the back and wings. In flight the contrasting black flight feathers are easily visible from below. Young birds may be confused with the **Wedge-tailed Eagle**, but differ in having a paler head and tail and more steeply upswept wings when soaring. Food consists mainly of fish, turtles and nestlings from seabird colonies. The call is a loud 'goose-like' honking. Sea-Eagles form permanent pairs that inhabit permanent territories.

Wedge-tailed Eagle *Aquila audax* 87-105cm (Females larger than males)

R. Brown

With a wingspan that exceeds two metres, the beautiful Wedge-tailed Eagle is the largest of Australia's raptors. The plumage is chiefly black, with paler brown on the wings, nape and undertail coverts. In flight the wings are held upswept and the characteristic wedge-shaped tail is clearly visible. Pair-bonds are permanent and territories are permanent. It is normally silent, except for occasional whistles and screeches. Found in most Australian environments except dense forests, it spends most of the day soaring on thermal currents in search of live prey or carrion.

Peregrine Falcon *Falco peregrinus* 35-50cm (Females larger than males)

Reaching speeds in excess of 300 km/h, the Peregrine Falcon is the fastest falcon in the world. Superficially resembling the smaller **Australian Hobby**, the Peregrine Falcon can be distinguished by its blue-grey upperparts, black head, white throat and finely barred buff and black underparts; the underparts are more rufous in the female. The Peregrine Falcon is a swift and deadly raptor, feeding on small to medium-sized birds and, occasionally, some much larger than itself. Although it is found in most mainland and island environments, it is most common around coastal cliffs and rocky outcrops.

R. Brown

Australian Hobby *Falco longipennis* 30-35cm (Females larger than males)

This is a stocky falcon with long wings, dark blue-grey upperparts and streaked rufous underparts. The sides of the head are black, as is the crown in some individuals. In flight, the streaked half-rufous and half-white underwings are clearly visible and the tail is seen to be long and square (unlike that of the **Nankeen Kestrel**). Hobbies feed almost exclusively on small birds which they kill and carry off to be consumed either on the wing or on an exposed perch, high in a treetop. Hobbies are found in wooded areas throughout Australia, and are a common sight around urban areas.

L.F. Schick

37

Brown Falcon *Falco berigora* 41-51cm (Females larger than males)

R. Brown

The Brown Falcon exhibits a variety of colour phases. Generally, the upperparts are dark brown and the underparts are pale buff or cream. The sides of the head are brown with a characteristic tear-stripe below the eye. Birds from the tropical north are very dark, while those from central Australia are paler. The Brown Falcon is normally silent at rest, but utters some cackling and screeching notes when in flight. It is found in all but the densest forests, feeding on small mammals, insects, reptiles and, less often, small birds. Locally common throughout Australia.

Nankeen Kestrel *Falco cenchroides* 31-36cm (Females larger than males)

G. Threlfo

This is a slender falcon. The upperparts are predominantly rufous, with some dark streaking. The wings are tipped with black. The underparts are pale buff, streaked with black, and the undertail is finely barred with black and a broader black band towards the tip. The Nankeen Kestrel feeds on small mammals, reptiles and a variety of insects. Prey is located by hovering a short distance above the ground on rapid wing-beats, the head and body kept perfectly still. It is found in most environments throughout Australia, but is absent from dense forests and most common in lightly wooded areas and open agricultural regions.

Australian Brush-turkey *Alectura lathami* 70cm

G. Little

The mainly black body plumage, laterally flattened tail, bare red head and yellow wattle around the neck readily distinguish the Brush-turkey from all other Australian birds. It inhabits rainforests and, occasionally, drier inland areas, feeding on insects and seeds and fruits, which it finds by raking the leaf litter with the large feet. Eggs are laid by several females in a single, large mound, approximately four metres by one metre, which is maintained solely by the male. This large, ground-dwelling megapode is found in eastern Australia from Cape York Peninsula, Queensland, south to about Manning River, New South Wales.

Orange-footed Scrubfowl *Megapodius reinwardt* 40-60cm

B.J. Coates

This large, mainly terrestrial bird is easily identified by its bright orange legs and feet, brown back and wings, and dark slate-grey head, neck and underparts. The head has a small brown crest. Calls consist of a combination of loud clucks and screams. Although it is the smallest of the megapodes found in Australia, the Orange-footed Scrubfowl builds the largest incubation mound, up to three metres high and seven metres wide. Inhabiting rainforests and dense vine forests, individuals defend exclusive feeding territories but several pairs may use the same incubation mound.

Stubble Quail *Coturnix pectoralis* 18-19cm

P.D. Munchenberg

Most widespread and well-known of the Australian quails, this small, mainly terrestrial bird is fawn-brown above, conspicuously streaked with pale cream, and has a bright red eye. It is paler below, blotched and streaked with darker brown. The male has a chestnut throat and a black centre to the breast. The Stubble Quail is much larger than the female **King Quail**, which it superficially resembles in plumage. The call is a clear, three-syllable whistle, 'cuck-u-wit'. The Stubble Quail is abundant in dense grassland throughout much of Australia but seldom observed unless flushed out.

Red-chested Button-quail *Turnix pyrrhothorax* 13-15cm (Females larger than males)

A. Young

This is a small, mainly terrestrial bird. It is grey-brown above with black mottling and conspicuous buff-white centres to the feathers. The female has a rich rufous throat, chest and belly; this is paler in the male and confined to the chest and flanks. In flight, two rufous patches are visible at the sides of the tail. A whistling 'churrp' is uttered when flushed. The Red-chested Button-quail is found in grasslands in eastern and northern Australia, from the Kimberleys, Western Australia to Adelaide, South Australia, and as far inland as Alice Springs. It is locally abundant, numbers fluctuating with food availability.

Buff-banded Rail *Gallirallus philippensis* 29-33cm

C. Seller

Generally observed singly or in pairs, the Buff-banded Rail is distinguished from other Australian rails by its conspicuous white eyebrow. It has mottled brown and white upper-parts, banded black and white underparts and a narrow buff breast-band. Like other rails it is a ground-dweller and is generally quiet and unobtrusive. The call is a loud 'sswit sswit', usually heard at dusk. The Buff-banded Rail is found in coastal and near coastal areas over much of Australia. Favouring thickly vegetated areas, such as mangroves, tussock grassland and reedbeds, normally near water, it feeds on insects and other invertebrates, seeds and some vegetable matter.

Australian Spotted Crake *Porzana fluminea* 18-21cm

R. Drummond

This large Crake can be distinguished from the smaller **Baillon's Crake**, by its all-white undertail and two-tone bill, which is olive-green with a red base to the upper mandible. Both Crakes are, however, mottled brown and black above, spotted with white, and have black and white barring on the belly. (The **Spotless Crake** is chiefly grey-brown with bright orange-red legs and feet. The **White-browed Crake** has no black barring on the underparts and has a conspicuous white eyebrow.) Crakes inhabit thickly vegetated swamps and lagoons, usually around inland rivers and estuaries.

41

Black-tailed Native-hen *Gallinula ventralis* 33-36cm

M. Seyfort

Bright orange-red legs and large, flattened, black tail distinguish the Black-tailed Native-hen from other rails found in Australia. The upper mandible is bright green, while the lower mandible is red. The upperparts are olive-brown, and the underparts are dark grey, tinged with blue. Some large white spots are visible on the flanks. It usually is silent, but will utter a short loud call if alarmed. Found over much of Australia, the Black-tailed Native-hen often occurs in moderately large groups, in open areas with nearby water and shelter.

Dusky Moorhen *Gallinula tenebrosa* 34-38cm

R. Drummond

Most of this bird's plumage is sooty-grey, browner on the back and wings. The feet and lower legs are green; the upper legs and knees are orange-red. The bill and frontal shield is orange-red, with a prominent yellow tip. Like other members of the rail family, the Dusky Moorhen is a ground-dweller, feeding on both terrestrial and aquatic vegetable matter, insects, molluscs and small fish.

The call consists of a variety of raucous squawks and whistles. It is common in freshwater swamps and urban parklands throughout eastern Australia and the far western corner of Western Australia.

Purple Swamphen *Porphyrio porphyrio* 44-48cm

T. Lindsey

This large rail is unmistakable. Predominantly black above, with a broad dark blue collar, it is generally dark blue below, with a white undertail (birds in south-west Western Australia are more purple below). The robust bill and frontal shield are deep red. The call is a loud 'kee-ow'; some softer clucking occurs between members of a group while feeding. The Purple Swamphen is mostly found around freshwater swamps, streams and marshes, where it feeds on terrestrial and aquatic vegetable matter, seeds, fruit and insects. It is common throughout eastern and northern Australia, with an isolated population in the extreme south-west of the continent.

Eurasian Coot *Fulica atra* 32-39cm

Dick Whitford

The Eurasian Coot cannot be confused with any other rail found in Australia. The plumage is entirely slate-grey; the white bill and frontal shield is diagnostic. Immature birds are generally paler than adults and have a white wash on the throat. Nestlings are downy, with fine, yellow-tipped black plumage, the head is orange-red and the bill is red with a cream-white tip. In Australia, Coots feed almost entirely on vegetable matter, supplemented with only a few insects, worms and fish. The most familiar call is a single, loud 'kowk'. Coots commonly inhabit vegetated lagoons and swamps.

Brolga *Grus rubicunda* 1-1.25m

I.R. McCann

Superficially similar to the **Sarus Crane**, the Brolga is a large grey crane, with a featherless red head and grey crown. Unlike the **Sarus Crane**, the red of the head does not extend down the neck, the legs are grey, (not fleshy pink) and there is a black dewlap under the chin. The call is a loud trumpeting 'garooo' or 'kaweee-kreee-kurr-kurr-kurr-kurr-kurr-kurr'. The Brolga frequents open wetlands, swamps and grassy plains throughout eastern and northern Australia. (The **Sarus Crane** is less common and restricted to northern Queensland.)

Australian Bustard *Ardeotis australis* M 100-120cm; F 70-80cm

Hans & Judy Beste

No other Australian bird resembles the Bustard. The back and wings are brown; black and white spotting in the front of the wings is most extensive in the male. The head and neck are grey-buff, except for the black crown, eye-stripe and breast-band (browner and less prominent in the female). The remainder of the underparts are white. If alarmed, a Bustard tends to crouch down on the ground with wings out-stretched. When courting, the male's throat-sac inflates until it touches the ground. The Bustard inhabits open wooded grasslands, pastoral lands and shrub steppes over most of the Australian mainland.

Comb-crested Jacana *Irediparra gallinacea* 19.5-23cm

G.B. Baker

This striking bird gives a casual observer the impression that it can walk on water. In fact, it walks on floating vegetation, with the aid of its grotesquely elongated toes. It is identified by the red fleshy forehead comb; black crown, back and breast; brown wings; and contrasting white belly, face and throat. A faint yellow tinge can be seen around the eye and throat. Calls consist of a mixture of high-pitched squeaks. It is found in tropical and sub-tropical freshwater wetlands, from the Kimberleys, Western Australia, through northern Australia to about Grafton, New South Wales, being more abundant in the north of its range.

Bush Stone-curlew *Burhinus grallarius* 52-58cm

Hans & Judy Beste

The Bush Stone-curlew's small black bill, large yellow eye, conspicuous white eyebrow and grey-brown plumage, heavily streaked with black, distinguish it from all other birds. (The related **Beach Stone-curlew** has a much larger bill and has little or no black streaking on the plumage.) The Bush Stone-curlew is mainly nocturnal and reluctant to fly during the day. The voice is a characteristic drawn-out, mournful 'wer-loooo', often heard at dusk and during the night. Although more abundant in the north, the Bush Stone-curlew can be found in open wooded country, scrubs and even golf courses over much of Australia.

Pied Oystercatcher *Haematopus longirostris* 48-51cm

G. Threlfo

All oystercatchers have a bright orange-red bill, eye-rings and legs. The white breast and belly distinguishes the Pied Oystercatcher from the closely related **Sooty Oystercatcher** (which is all black in plumage). Oystercatchers feed on bivalve molluscs, which are prised apart with their specially-adapted bills; worms, crustaceans and insects are also taken. It is mostly silent when feeding, but may utter a whistled 'peepapeep' or 'pleep-pleep', when in flight. Commonly found in coastal areas throughout the Australian continent, the Pied Oystercatcher is rather shy of humans and seldom allows close approach.

46

Masked Lapwing *Vanellus miles* 33-38cm

K. Ireland

Unmistakable in both appearance and voice, this bird has predominantly white underparts, brown wings and back and a black crown. Prominent yellow wattles cover the face. Southern birds are black on the hind-neck and sides of breast, and have smaller facial wattles. (The **Banded Lapwing** is much smaller, and has a predominantly black head and upper breast, with a distinct white eyestripe and bib and a red patch at the base of the bill.) The voice is a staccato 'kekekekekekekek'. The Masked Lapwing inhabits grasslands, marshes and mudflats and, although common around urban areas, it is wary of people and seldom allows close approach. It is common throughout northern, central and eastern Australia.

Red-capped Plover *Charadrius ruficapillus* 14-16.5cm

M. Seyfort

This is a small wader. Brown above, reddish on the crown and nape, and with a white face and underparts, the Red-capped Plover cannot be confused with any other wader found in Australia. It feeds mainly on insects, which are caught on the drier shores of lakes, estuaries, marshes and beaches: it seldom wades for food. While feeding, a Red-capped Plover runs rapidly along the ground, stopping suddenly to snatch prey from the surface. The call is a faintly trilled 'tik' or 'twink'. It is a common sight throughout coastal and inland Australia.

47

Black-fronted Dotterel *Elseyornis melanops* 16-18cm

M. Seyfort

This small wader is readily recognised by its white underparts with a distinct black band which extends across the chest, around to the base of the neck and through the eye to the forehead. The upperparts, including the crown, are mottled brown. The bill is orange-red with a black tip and a conspicuous orange ring surrounds the eye. Juvenal birds lack the black breast-band. A metallic 'tip' is uttered in flight. The Black-fronted Dotterel inhabits margins of lakes, swamps and dams, feeding on aquatic insects, crustaceans and seeds. Found throughout the mainland and Tasmania, it usually occurs in pairs or small groups.

Black-winged Stilt *Himantopus himantopus* 35.5-39cm

M. Wright

The Black-winged Stilt is a large black and white wader with long orange-red legs and a straight black bill. It differs from the **Banded Stilt** in having black on the back of the neck and a thin white collar. The Black-winged Stilt feeds on aquatic insects, molluscs and crustaceans. Unlike the **Banded Stilt** and **Red-necked Avocet** it seldom swims for food, preferring to wade in shallow water, and seize prey on or near the surface. The Black-winged Stilt is gregarious and usually found in small groups on freshwater and saltwater marshes throughout mainland Australia.

48

Red-necked Avocet *Recurvirostra novaehollandiae* 40- 45cm

W. Labbett

Among the Australian waders, the Red-necked Avocet is distinguished by its russet-red head and neck, and thin upturned black bill. The body is white below, with black and white upperparts. The legs are long and pale blue-grey. The Red-necked Avocet feeds on aquatic insects, crustaceans, molluscs, worms and some seeds, which it obtains by wading in the shallows, sweeping its bill through the water in a scythe-like manner. It frequents shallow marshes and mudflats in both salt- and freshwater environments, throughout much of mainland Australia (absent only from the north-east).

Eastern Curlew *Numenius madagascariensis* 53-62cm

D. & M. Trounson

This is a large wader. The plumage is chiefly mottled buff and brown, paler below and on the rump; the legs are grey. The long sickle-shaped bill is brown with a pinkish base to the lower mandible. It can be distinguished from the **Little Curlew** and **Whimbrel** by its much larger size and longer bill (the Little Curlew is the smallest of the three). Curlews and Whimbrels inhabit mudflats, mangroves and swamps where they feed on molluscs, crustaceans and worms by probing their bills into the soft mud. The Eastern Curlew is a common sight around the Australian coast.

49

Common Greenshank *Tringa nebularia* 30-35cm

L. Pedler

This inconspicuous wader is a non-breeding migrant, mainly visting Australia from September to April. The upper back and wings are mottled olive-brown, paler on the head and neck; the underparts are white. The lower back and tail are white with pale brown barring on the edges of the tail. The legs are olive and the bill is dark olive-brown. The Common Greenshank's most common call is a ringing 'tiu-tiu-tiu'. It frequents inland and coastal lakes, feeding on insects and small fish, with a characteristic head-bobbing motion and is found throughout Australia (except the harsh interior of Western Australia).

Latham's Snipe *Gallinago hardwickii* 23-29cm (Females larger than males)

Hans & Judy Beste

Latham's Snipe is difficult to distinguish from other snipes that may visit Australia. The bill is long and straight, fading from black at the tip to brown at the base. The crown and back are mottled black and brown, with distinct pale cream markings. The underparts are buff-cream with distinct black barring. Its common call is a rasping 'khreck'. More widely distributed than other visiting snipes and thought to be the only snipe to visit southern Australia and Tasmania, it can be seen between August and April inhabiting dense, tussock grasslands or reedbeds in the margins of swamps and marshes.

50

Bar-tailed Godwit *Limosa lapponica* 37-45cm (Females larger than males)

D. & M. Trounson

This non-breeding migrant is mainly mottled brown above, lighter and more uniform buff below. The dull white rump and underwing, and long, slightly upturned bill distinguish it from the **Black-tailed Godwit**. Calls include a rapid 'tititi' and a sharp 'kuwit' in alarm. Godwits inhabit estuarine mudflats, beaches and mangroves, where they feed on molluscs and aquatic insects. Food is found by wading through the shallows or over exposed mud and probing the long bill rapidly into the bottom. This bird is common in coastal areas of Australia and Tasmania from August to May each year.

Sharp-tailed Sandpiper *Calidris acuminata* 18-24cm

C. Andrew Henley/Larus

The Sharp-tailed Sandpiper is a small shorebird. The bill is straight, dark-grey to black, with a paler olive base. The upperparts are mottled black and brown, with clear buff edges to the feathers, and the underparts are white, darker and heavily streaked on the breast. It is difficult to distinguish from the less numerous **Pectoral Sandpiper**, which has a more distinct separation between the breast markings and white belly. This Sandpiper inhabits shallow freshwater lagoons, estuarine mudflats and beaches in all but the most arid areas of Australia and Tasmania. It is one of the most abundant of the migrant waders found in Australia between August and March.

51

Curlew Sandpiper *Calidris ferruginea* 18-21cm

B. Chudleigh

The relatively long down-curved bill, grey upperparts, with white eye-stripe, and white underparts make this wader easily identifiable. In flight, its solid white rump, rounded tail and white-edged flight feathers distinguish it from other sandpipers. It feeds on molluscs, crustaceans, worms and insects, which it catches by pecking and probing in shallow waters. The most common call is a soft 'chirrup'. Although found in some inland areas, the Curlew Sandpiper favours estuarine mudflats, beaches and wetlands, and is one of the commonest waders to visit the Australian coast, mainly from August to April.

Red-necked Stint *Calidris ruficollis* 13-16cm

T.G. Lowe

This beautiful bird is one of the smallest and most numerous migratory waders to winter in Australia. The non-breeding plumage is mottled grey-brown above, white below. In flight the rump is white with a broad black stripe extending from the lower back to the tip of the tail. The Red-necked Stint is very difficult to distinguish from other stints, but has a comparatively shorter bill and is generally plumper. The most common call is a faint 'chip-chip'. This stint frequents mudflats and beaches in both coastal and inland areas, where it feeds on molluscs and crustaceans.

Australian Pratincole *Stiltia isabella* 19-23cm

Hans & Judy Beste

This species is similar in size and shape to the **Oriental Pratincole** which breeds in Asia and visits northern Australia between October and December. The Australian Pratincole is distinguished by its dark buff-red breast and longer legs. The upperparts are generally light brown, paler on face, and the wings are edged with black. The black-tipped bill is orange-red at the base. In flight, the underwing is seen to be dark grey, lighter on the flight feathers: the feet trail behind the square tail. Most active at dusk and dawn, it feeds on insects. It lives and breeds in the arid plains of central Australia.

Silver Gull *Larus novaehollandiae* 40-45cm

K. Ireland

This is a small gull. Its white head, tail and underparts, grey back and black-tipped wings, easily distinguish it from any other gull found in Australia. The bright orange-red bill, legs and eye-ring are present only in adults. Juvenals can be distinguished from the immatures by a varied amount of brown on the upperparts. The Silver Gull has a varied diet, ranging from worms, fish, insects and crustaceans to human refuse. The most frequently-heard call is a harsh 'kwee-aarr'. It is common in watered areas over much of Australia, and is rarely observed far from land.

Pacific Gull *Larus pacificus* 60-65cm

T. & P. Gardner

This is large gull. The back and wings are black, and the head, neck and underparts are white. The white tail, with a broad black band towards the tip, and the large yellow bill with red tip, distinguish it from the otherwise similar **Kelp Gull**. Young birds are predominantly dark brown and buff in plumage, the yellow bill and white rump becoming visible after the first year. It often occurs in small flocks, feeding on a variety of foods, including fish, molluscs and human refuse. The most common call is a loud 'oww, oww'. It is a common sight in coastal areas of southern and south-western Australia.

Caspian Tern *Sterna caspia* 50-56cm

G. Chapman

The largest tern found in Australian waters. The massive, bright red bill, with dusky black tip, and its large size easily identify the Caspian Tern. The body plumage is chiefly grey and white, with a conspicuous black crown, extending down the hind-neck. Food, mainly fish, is caught by spectacular plunging dives into the water, often from as high as 15 metres. Common calls include a deep, barking 'kaah' or 'kraah'. It occurs along the coast, as well as in wetland and riverine areas, throughout inland Australia (except the more arid areas of Western Australia). Most breeding takes place on offshore islands.

Whiskered Tern *Chlidonias hybridus* 24-26cm (Females smaller than males)

B. Chudleigh

In the non-breeding season this graceful predominantly grey and white tern can be identified by its short, shallow-forked tail, red bill and black crown, faintly streaked with white. During the breeding season, generally September to December, the underparts become dark grey, with the exception of the undertail which remains white. The Whiskered Tern is often encountered in small flocks, hunting for small fishes, frogs and insects over brackish or freshwater swamps, sewage farms and well-watered grasslands throughout much of the Australian mainland.

Crested Tern *Sterna bergii* 44-49cm

K. A. Hindwood

The Crested Tern is the second largest of the terns found in Australia and one of the most common. Its pale yellow bill and scruffy black crest distinguish it from the smaller **Lesser Crested Tern**, which is found only in the northern parts of Australia, and has a bright orange bill in the breeding season. Although often observed on its own, the Crested Tern is gregarious and often forms mixed flocks with other terns or gulls. Breeding is colonial, on offshore islands. Most common calls are a raspy 'kirrick' or 'krrow'. Inhabiting coastal areas throughout Australia and Tasmania, it feeds mainly on fish.

55

Common Noddy *Anous stolidus* 40-45cm

N. Chaffer

Largest of Australia's noddies, the Common Noddy is identified by its dark brown plumage with paler grey crown. It is distinguished from the **Lesser Noddy** and **Black Noddy** by its thicker bill, two-toned upper wing and wedge-shaped tail, which is slightly notched in the centre. Noddies feed on fishes and squids, which they snatch from the surface of the water in a series of swooping dives. Common calls of the Common Noddy include a harsh 'karrk' and lower 'kuk-kuk-kuk'. This bird is found along the Australian coastline from Geraldton, Western Australia, north to Rockhampton, Queensland.

Rose-crowned Fruit-Dove *Ptilinopus regina* 22-24.5cm

G. Threlfo

Although seasonally abundant and beautifully coloured, this small dove often goes unobserved in the densely vegetated areas that it inhabits. The rich rose-coloured crown, edged with yellow, and orange-yellow belly distinguish it from the **Superb Fruit-Dove**, which has a predominantly white belly. The female is duller than the male. The Rose-crowned Fruit-Dove is nomadic and gregarious, occasionally forming large flocks where fruit is abundant. The main call is a loud 'coo-coo-coo-coo-coo', becoming faster at the end. It is found in a broad coastal strip from the Kimberleys, Western Australia, across northern Australia to just north of Sydney, New South Wales.

Wompoo Fruit-Dove *Ptilinopus magnificus* 35-50cm

M. Seyfort

Perhaps the most beautiful of all the doves found in Australia, the Wompoo Fruit-Dove is distinguished by its large size, rich purple throat, chest and upper belly, and yellow lower belly. It has predominantly green upperparts, with a paler grey head and a conspicuous yellow wing-bar. Birds in the north are smaller. It feeds on a variety of fruits. The call is a deep resonant 'wollack-a-woo' and, occasionally, a more abrupt 'boo'. It is found in densely vegetated forests along the east coast of Australia, from Cape York, Queensland, to just south of Dorrigo, New South Wales, being more abundant in northern parts of its range.

Spotted Turtle-Dove *Streptopelia chinensis* 29-32cm

L. Robinson

The upperparts of the introduced Spotted Turtle-Dove are predominantly brown, with darker centres to the feathers of the back and wings. The head is grey, and the neck and underparts are grey-brown, tinged with pink. In flight the white-tipped tail is conspicuous. Its large black and white patch found at the base of the hind-neck is absent on the **Laughing Turtle-Dove** of Western Australia. The most common call of the Spotted Turtle-Dove is a musical 'cocoo, crooor'. It is a common sight in cities, parks and agricultural areas of eastern, southern and south-western Australia.

Rock Dove *Columba livia* 33-36cm

D. & M. Trounson

Commonly referred to as the Feral Pigeon, this species is descended from the Rock Dove found in Europe and Asia. Many plumage variants have been developed by selective breeding over the years, the most common being a mixture of grey, black, white and brown, with purple and green sheens. The most common call is a moaning 'cooo'. The common and familiar Rock Dove is closely associated with human settlement in many countries throughout the world. In Australia it is found in large numbers in capital cities and larger towns, with the exception of Darwin. Birds have also been observed in many other areas of Australia.

Brown Cuckoo-Dove *Macropygia amboinensis* 30-43cm

N. Chaffer

The Brown Cuckoo-Dove is easily identified by its chiefly brown plumage, paler and more pink-grey on the underside, and long, wide tail. Females have black mottling on the throat and upper breast. Food consists mainly of fruits from trees and shrubs, such as mistletoes. It seldom visits the ground except to drink and consume small stones to aid its digestive processes. The contact call is a 'whoop-a-whooop', the last note higher pitched than the first. Although the Brown Cuckoo-Dove has been the victim of much habitat loss and widespread hunting, it is still common in rainforest and dense shrubbery along the east coast of the mainland.

Peaceful Dove *Geopelia striata* 20-23cm

M. Wright

The beautiful Peaceful Dove is easily identified by its plump stature, grey-brown upperparts, barred with black, pink-buff underparts and pale blue eye-ring. The black barring is more concentrated at the neck, forming a broad collar. The Peaceful Dove is common and nomadic, moving around in response to the availability of food and water. The call is a distinctive 'doodle-doo'. These doves are normally found in pairs or small groups, in lightly timbered grasslands close to water. Although absent only from the south-west of the Australian mainland, they are generally uncommon in the more arid inland.

Bar-shouldered Dove *Geopelia humeralis* 27-31cm

T. & P. Gardner

This slender dove is easily identified by its blue-grey face, throat and upper breast; its brown upperparts, heavily barred with black; and its rufous hind-neck. The remainder of the underparts are white, tinged with pink on the breast. Mainly sedentary, it moves around within a small area in search of seeding grasses and herbs. Feeding takes place on the ground. Its common call is a triple 'coo' or 'kook-a-wook'. This dove has declined in numbers following the introduction of the **Spotted Turtle-Dove** in 1870. It is found in coastal and near-coastal eucalypt woodlands and fringes of scrubs and mangroves, from the Pilbara, Western Australia, through northern Australia to Goulburn River, New South Wales.

Common Bronzewing *Phaps chalcoptera* 30-36cm

R. Drummond

The Common Bronzewing can be distinguished from the similar **Brush Bronzewing** by its pinkish-grey breast and paler brown back. Bronzewings get their name from the iridescent patches of green, blue and red in the wing. The male Common Bronzewing has a yellow-white forehead and darker pink breast. Both sexes have a conspicuous white line below and around the eye. Food consists of seeds and other vegetable matter, consumed on the ground. The common call is a deep 'oom', repeated several times. Found in all but the most barren areas and densest rainforests, the Common Bronzewing is one of the most abundant pigeons in Australia.

Emerald Dove *Chalcophaps indica* 23-28cm

Hans & Judy Beste

This beautiful dove is distinguished by emerald-green wings and dull purple-brown head, neck and underparts. Juvenal birds are darker brown, heavily barred with black on the head, neck and underparts. Although primarily a bird of the forest floor, the Emerald Dove often perches on the thicker branches of trees, where it feeds on accessible fruits. The common call is a repeated low-pitched 'coo'. Found in dense forests, mangroves and dense thickets, in a broad coastal and sub-coastal band from the Kimberleys, Western Australia, to near Bega, New South Wales, it is absent only from the Gulf of Carpentaria.

60

Crested Pigeon *Ocyphaps lophotes* 30-35cm

G.K. Taylor

This is a stocky pigeon with a conspicuous black crest. Most of the plumage is grey-brown, becoming more pink on the underparts. The wings are barred with black, and are decorated with glossy green and purple 'patches'. The head is grey, with a tall, dark crest and an orange ring around the eye. It is usually found in the vicinity of water, where it feeds on seeds of crops and weeds. If disturbed, it flies off with rapid whistling wing-beats, interspersed with short glides on slightly downturned wings. The common call is a wavering 'coo'. The Crested Pigeon is a common sight in lightly wooded grasslands in both rural and urban areas.

Spinifex Pigeon *Geophaps plumifera* 19-23cm

R. Brown

This curious little pigeon with a tall chestnut crest is distributed in two isolated populations within Australia. Both are predominantly chestnut, with conspicuous black and grey barring on the back and wings, and a black and grey line across the breast. The face is red, bordered with black, grey and white. Birds found in the Pilbara region of Western Australia have all chestnut underparts; those from central and northern Australia have a white belly. The most common call is a soft 'oom'. Both races inhabit arid grasslands and open stony deserts, usually in the vicinity of permanent water.

61

Pied Imperial-Pigeon *Ducula bicolor* 35-44cm

This is a beautiful black and white pigeon. The black flight feathers, lower half of tail, and spotting on the thighs and ventral area mar the otherwise snow-white plumage. Its food consists of fruits, plucked from the trees. In the late afternoon, continuous streams of birds descend to drink at nearby waterholes. The most common call is a deep 'coo-hoo',

which can be heard from quite a distance. This pigeon is found in coastal and sub-coastal rainforests and mangroves from near Rockhampton, Queensland, through coastal Northern Territory, to the Kimberleys, Western Australia, being more common in the north of its range.

Red-tailed Black-Cockatoo *Calyptorhynchus banksii* 50-63cm

This is a large, black cockatoo. The male is easily identified by its dense crest of black feathers, almost entirely black plumage, and bright red undertail. The female is duller grey-brown, barred and spotted with yellow, and has a diagnostic whitish bill. The **Glossy Black-Cockatoo** of south-east Australia and Kangaroo Island, South Australia, has a paler head and breast and is much smaller. The contact call of the Red-tailed Black-Cockatoo is a rolling, metallic 'kreee' or 'krurr', usually given in flight. Commonly found in scattered groups and in a variety of habitats, it favours lightly timbered country along watercourses over much of Australia.

D. & M. Trounson

62

Yellow-tailed Black-Cockatoo *Calyptorhynchus funereus* 55-65cm

This cockatoo is easily identified by its predominantly black plumage, the feathers of the body edged with yellow, and its yellow cheek patch and yellow on the underside of the tail. (Until recently the **Short-billed Black-Cockatoo**, found in south-western Western Australia and having white tail panels instead of yellow, was considered a subspecies of the Yellow-tailed Black-Cockatoo rather than a distinct species.) The Yellow-tailed Black-Cockatoo's contact call is a drawn-out 'kee-ow'. Often seen in small to large flocks, flying on slowly flapping wings, it is a common sight in the eucalypt woodlands and pine plantations of south-eastern Australia.

D. & M. Trounson

Cockatiel *Nymphicus hollandicus* 30-33cm

The plumage of this atypical member of the cockatoo family is chiefly grey, paler below, with a white wing patch, orange cheeks and a distinctive crest. The male can be distinguished by its bright yellow forehead, face and crest. The Cockatiel is usually seen in pairs or small flocks, in most types of open country, near water. It feeds on a variety of grass seeds, nuts, berries and grain, obtained either from the ground or from trees. Mostly silent, it utters a prolonged 'queel-queel' in flight. It is widespread and common throughout mainland Australia, especially in northern areas.

P.D. Munchenberg

Gang-gang Cockatoo *Callocephalon fimbriatum* 34-35cm

The Gang-gang Cockatoo can be identified by its general grey plumage, each feather edged with greyish-white, and its short, square tail. The male has a conspicuous red, curly crest. It is almost completely arboreal, venturing to the ground only to drink or to pick up fallen food. It is easily overlooked when feeding. The most common call is a prolonged creaky screech. It inhabits the eucalypt forests of south-eastern mainland Australia and northern Tasmania, being common in certain areas, but less numerous towards the boundaries of its range. It has an annual migration, moving to higher altitudes in summer.

Galah *Cacatua roseicapilla* 35-36cm

The Galah can be easily identified by its rose-pink head, neck and underparts, with paler pink crown, and grey back, wings and undertail. It has a bouncing acrobatic flight, but spends most of the day sheltering from heat in the foliage of trees and shrubs. The voice is a distinctive high-pitched screech, 'chi-chi'. The Galah is one of the most abundant and familiar of the Australian parrots, found in large flocks, in a variety of timbered habitats, usually near water. It occurs over most of Australia and is becoming more abundant in areas of human habitation, where it is commonly seen swinging upside-down from utility wires.

Little Corella *Cacatua sanguinea* 35-42cm

M. Unkovich

Several races are found in Australia and are distinguished by bill length and body size. All are generally white in plumage (some tinged with pink), and have a conspicuous fleshy blue eye-ring, and a pale rose-pink patch between the eye and bill. In flight, a bright sulphur-yellow wash can be seen on the underwing and undertail. Birds from the south-west have a larger white crest. (The similar, but less abundant, **Long-billed Corella** has an orange-scarlet band across the throat.) Often forming vast flocks in trees along watercourses and where seeding grasses are found, the Little Corella is common and widespread.

Major Mitchell's Cockatoo *Cacatua leadbeateri* 35-36cm

D. & M. Trounson

This is a beautiful salmon-pink and white cockatoo. When the crest is erected it reveals a dark pink-red colouration with a broad yellow band running through the centre. In flight, the dark pink of the underwings is clearly visible. It feeds on a variety of seeds, nuts, fruits and insects, both in trees and on the ground. Forming small flocks, occasionally in the company of Galahs, the Major Mitchell's Cockatoo inhabits a variety of wooded habitats, especially mallee and acacia. The normal contact call is a quavering two-syllable screech. It is found in the arid and semi-arid areas of inland Australia.

Sulphur-crested Cockatoo *Cacatua galerita* 45-50cm

D. Greig

The white plumage, black bill and distinctive sulphur-yellow crest of the common and familiar Sulphur-crested Cockatoo distinguish it from all other cockatoos found in Australia. Although the normal diet consists of berries, seeds, nuts and roots, the Sulphur-crested Cockatoo has become a pest around urban areas, where it uses its powerful bill to destroy timber decking and panelling on houses. It is a noisy and conspicuous cockatoo, both at rest and in flight. The most common call is a distinctive loud screech, ending with a slight upward inflection. It is found in a variety of timbered habitats throughout northern and eastern Australia.

66

Rainbow Lorikeet *Trichoglossus haematodus* 28-32cm

This striking bird has one of the most beautiful plumage patterns of all Australian parrots. There are two distinct plumage variations. Birds in eastern Australia have all green upperparts, with a dark blue head, streaked with paler blue, and a pale green collar. The breast is mottled orange and yellow, the belly is dark blue, and the undertail coverts are green, edged with yellow. Birds in Western Australia and the Northern Territory have a dark orange-red collar and breast, and a dark blue patch on the upper back. It frequents open forests, rainforests and urban parks and gardens.

D. & M. Trounson

Scaly-breasted Lorikeet *Trichoglossus chlorolepidotus* 22-24cm

T. & P. Gardner

This medium-sized lorikeet is the only one to have an all-green head. The rest of the body plumage is green, with the exception of the throat and breast, which are scalloped with yellow, hence the name. The bill is orange and, in flight, the red-orange colouration of the underwing is clearly visible. It often associates in mixed flocks with the **Rainbow Lorikeet** and is common in open woodland and heathland throughout eastern Australia, from Cape York Peninsula, Queensland, to the Illawarra District of New South Wales. A small population of escaped or liberated aviary birds also exists near Melbourne.

Australian King-Parrot *Alisterus scapularis* 41-43cm

G. Little

The beautiful male King-Parrot is unmistakable with a bright crimson head, neck and underparts, green back and wings, and dark blue rump and tail. The female is somewhat duller and has a green head, neck and upper breast. The King-Parrot feeds on fruits, berries, nuts and seeds. The most common call is a shrill 'crassak-crassak'. It is commonly observed in moist and dry forests, open woodlands, orchards and suburban gardens. It is found in a coastal and sub-coastal belt throughout eastern Australia, from the Atherton Tableland, Queensland, to southern Victoria.

Red-winged Parrot *Aprosmictus erythropterus* 30.5-33cm

Hans & Judy Beste

The male Red-winged Parrot is one of the most spectacularly coloured of Australia's parrots. The head, neck and underparts are bright green, darker on the back, wings and tail, with a large rich-red patch on the upper wing. The lower back is bright blue, turning to pale green on the rump. The female is generally green all over, with a smaller red wing patch. The most common call is a metallic 'crillik-crillik'. The Red-winged Parrot is usually found in small family groups in open eucalypt and casuarina woodland, and acacia scrub.

Budgerigar *Melopsittacus undulatus* 17-18cm

Although cagebirds have been breed in a variety of colours, the natural colour of the Budgerigar is green and yellow, with conspicuous black barring above, and a small blue cheek patch. The male has a darker blue cere. The Budgerigar is nomadic, taking to the air in a characteristic undulating flight. It is most active in the morning, drinking at waterholes and feeding on grass seeds, mostly on the ground. The contact call is a warbling 'chirrup', also 'zit' in alarm. It is found in most open habitat types, but seldom far from water, throughout most of mainland Australia.

W.A. Worrad

Crimson Rosella *Platycercus elegans* 32-36cm

This beautiful parrot is easily identified by its predominantly rich crimson plumage and bright blue cheeks. The back and wings are black, each feather broadly edged with red, the wings having a broad blue patch along the edge. The tail is blue-green above, pale blue below. Young birds are largely green with varying amounts of red on the underparts. It has various calls, the most common being a disyllabic 'cussik-cussik', also a variety of harsh screeches and metallic whistles. Two separate populations exist within Australia: the one in northern Queensland is smaller and darker; the other occurs from southern Queensland to South Australia.

K. Stepnell

Eastern Rosella *Platycercus eximius* 28-32cm

C. Andrew Henley/Larus

This striking parrot should not be confused with any other parrot in south-eastern Australia. The head, neck and upper breast are red, with conspicuous white cheeks. The remainder of the underparts are yellow, washed with green on the abdomen, and red on the vent and undertail coverts. The wings and back are black, each feather broadly edged with yellow-green; a broad dark blue patch is present on the front of each wing. The Eastern Rosella's most common call is a staccato 'chut-chit'. It is found in a variety of open wooded habitats.

Australian Ringneck *Barnardius zonarius* 34-38cm

T. Howard

The most well-known and widely distributed form of the Ringnecks is the **Port Lincoln Ringneck**. Found in western and central Australia, it is identified by its green upperparts, black head, with dark blue cheeks, yellow collar and belly. The **Twenty-eight Parrot**, confined to the extreme south-western corner of Western Australia, has a splash of red above the bill and a green belly. The smaller **Mallee Ringneck** and **Cloncurry Parrot** are found in central and eastern Australia; both lack the black head and blue cheeks. The **Cloncurry Parrot** is confined to a small area between the Mackinlay and Gregory Rivers of northern Queensland, and has a yellow belly.

Red-rumped Parrot *Psephotus haematonotus* 26-27cm

R. Drummond

This small parrot, subtly coloured with greens, blues and yellows is a common sight throughout much of the southeast. The male is generally green above, washed with turquoise on the head, paler green on the breast and yellow on the belly. In flight the red rump is strikingly obvious. The female is duller than the male, being generally olive in plumage, with a bright green rump and yellowish-white belly. Although generally observed in pairs or small groups, large flocks often form during the winter. It is commonly found in lightly-timbered and cultivated areas of south-eastern Australia, normally in the vicinity of water.

Blue Bonnet *Northiella haematogaster* 26-32cm

M. Seyfort

The beautifully decorated Blue Bonnet cannot be confused with any other parrot found in Australia. The breast, neck and upperparts are grey-brown, the belly and ventral area are yellow, with varying amounts of red, and the fore-crown, face and chin are blue. When walking on the ground or perched, the stance is very upright. The contact call is a harsh 'cluck-cluck', often repeated. Common and familiar, it is found in lightly-timbered grasslands and arid shrublands in southern and eastern Australia. Small parties are often flushed from the roadside, where they forage for seeds.

Pallid Cuckoo *Cuculus pallidus* 28-33cm

G. Chapman

The Pallid Cuckoo is easily identified by its grey plumage, darker on the wings and back; and broadly barred black and white undertail. Immature birds are heavily mottled with brown and buff above, grey-brown below, with a darker breast band. The similar sized **Oriental Cuckoo** has conspicuous black and white barring on the lower breast and belly, and is generally darker in plumage. The Pallid Cuckoo lays its eggs in the nests of honeyeaters, woodswallows and flycatchers. The call is a loud, ascending whistle 'too-too-too...', repeated several times. This is the most common and widely distributed of the cuckoos.

Fan-tailed Cuckoo *Cacomantis flabelliformis* 24.5-28.5cm

R. Shepherd

The Fan-tailed Cuckoo is identified by its dark grey upperparts, pale rufous underparts and black and white barred undertail. The yellow eye-ring distinguishes it from the paler and smaller **Brush Cuckoo**, which has a grey eye-ring. (The **Chestnut-breasted Cuckoo** has dark chestnut underparts and less conspicuous barring on the undertail.) Eggs are laid in the nests of numerous other birds, including thornbills, flycatchers and scrubwrens. The common call is a descending trill, normally by the male in advertisement. This beautiful, slender cuckoo is often seen perched on an exposed branch in open forest or woodland, throughout eastern and south-western Australia.

Shining Bronze-Cuckoo *Chrysococcyx lucidus* 17-18cm

The beautiful bronze-cuckoos get their name from their metallic bronzed-green upperparts. The Shining Bronze-Cuckoo is identified by its white underparts with complete copper-bronze bars and copper-coloured head. It differs from **Horsfield's Bronze-Cuckoo**, which has rufous on the undertail and is duller above; and the **Little Bronze-Cuckoo**, which has narrow, incomplete bars on the underparts and a red eye-ring (males only). The contact call is a series of high-pitched whistles, often ending with a longer descending note. The Shining Bronze-Cuckoo is common in forests of eastern and south-western Australia and Tasmania.

G. Chapman

Common Koel *Eudynamys scolopacea* 39-46cm

D. & M. Trounson

This migrant cuckoo is often the cause of many sleepless nights and early awakenings. Arriving in September each year from New Guinea, the Koel advertises its presence by a loud ascending whistle 'coo-ee', monotonously repeated. The male is easily identified by its entirely glossy black plumage, tinged with blue and green, and striking red eye. The female has glossed brown upperparts, heavily spotted with white, and a black crown. The underparts are generally buff-cream with numerous fine black bars. Young birds resemble the adult female, but have a dark eye. It is found in tall forests and suburbs throughout northern and eastern Australia in the warmer part of the year.

Channel-billed Cuckoo *Scythrops novaehollandiae* 58-65cm

Hans & Judy Beste

Visiting Australia from New Guinea and Indonesia between August and October each year, this large cuckoo parasitizes the nests of several species, including the **Australian Magpie** and **Pied Currawong**. Its massive, pale, down-curved bill, grey plumage, darker on the back and wings, and long barred tail, make it impossible to confuse it with any other bird. It is found in tall open forests, generally where host species occur. The young birds do not evict the host's young or eggs from the nest, but simply grow faster and demand all the food, thus starving the others. The call is a loud 'kawk' followed by a more rapid, and fainter 'awk-awk-awk...'.

Pheasant Coucal *Centropus phasianinus* 50-70cm (Females larger than males)

C. Webster

Unmistakable. In breeding plumage, the head, neck and underparts are black, and the back, wings and tail are generally rufous, with black and buff mottling. The long, pheasant-like tail is duller and more brown in colour. Outside of the breeding season, the head and neck are straw-coloured, with paler feather shafts. Unlike other Australian cuckoos, the Pheasant Coucal builds its own nest and rears its own young. Its flight is clumsy and limited. The call is a distinctive 'oop-oop-oop-oop-oop...', descending in the middle and then ascending at the end. This large, mainly ground-dwelling, cuckoo is found in thickly vegetated areas of northern and eastern Australia.

Southern Boobook *Ninox novaeseelandiae* 25-35cm

The smallest and most common owl in Australia, it is identified by its dark chocolate-brown plumage above and rufous-brown below, heavily streaked and spotted with white. Young birds are almost entirely buff-white below, with conspicuous dark brown facial discs. The Tasmanian race is smaller and more heavily spotted with white, while birds of the Cape York rainforests are slightly larger and darker. The Southern Boobook is often observed perched on an open branch or tree-top, emitting a distinctive 'boo-book' or 'mo-poke'. It is found Australia-wide in a variety of habitats, from dense forest to open desert.

J. Hicks

Barking Owl *Ninox connivens* 35-45cm

This owl's plumage resembles a large **Southern Boobook**, although it is less rufous and more heavily streaked (rather than spotted) on the underparts. The eyes are large and yellow. The Barking Owl (or Screaming Woman, as it is often called) has two main calls, both distinctive and unmistakable. The first is a double-noted, dog-like 'wook-wook', the second a wavering human-like scream (seldom heard outside winter). Most common in savanna woodland, it is also found in well-forested hill and riverine woodlands. It is widely distributed and moderately common, although more often heard than seen.

F. Kristo

75

Barn Owl *Tyto alba* 28-39cm

Dick Whitford

Most widespread and familiar of the owls, the Barn Owl is medium-sized, with a 'heart-shaped' face, sandy-orange upperparts and white to cream underparts; both the back and breast are evenly spotted with black. By day it roosts in hollow logs, caves or thickly foliated trees, usually alone or in pairs. When threatened, it crouches down and spreads its wings. It is generally quiet, the common call being a 1-2 second rough, hissing screech. Found in open, often arid, country, such as farms, heath and lightly wooded forest, throughout Australia, it is moderately common but generally unobtrusive.

Masked Owl *Tyto novaehollandiae* 35-50cm (Females larger than males)

Jiri Lochman

Larger and generally darker than the Barn Owl, this species occurs in three basic plumage phases: pale, intermediate and dark. Upperparts vary from blackish-brown to grey-white, liberally spotted with grey and white. Underparts are rufous to white, speckled with dark brown. The facial disc is rounded and slightly more rufous than the underparts. It is bordered with dark brown, and the large black eyes are bordered with dark chestnut-brown. The call is a deep, rasping screech. The Masked Owl inhabits forests and woodlands in a broad coastal band around most of Australia, seldom more than 300 kilometres from the coast.

Tawny Frogmouth *Podargus strigoides* 34-53cm

N. Chaffer

When roosting during the day, the Tawny Frogmouth is easily overlooked. The general plumage of the common phase is silver-grey, slightly paler below, streaked and mottled with black and rufous. Another plumage phase is russet-red instead of grey. The eye is yellow in both forms. The **Papuan Frogmouth** is confined to Cape York Peninsula, and is larger, with an orange-red eye.

The **Marbled Frogmouth** is similar in size to the Tawny Frogmouth but is found only in rainforests, and has an orange-yellow eye. The Tawny Frogmouth is nocturnal and common in wooded areas throughout Australia. It is larger in the south east than in the north.

Australian Owlet-nightjar *Aegotheles cristatus* 21-25cm

Dick Whitford

This delicate little bird with large brown eyes, is common throughout Australia. The Owlet-nightjar is the smallest nocturnal bird found in Australia, but, unlike other nocturnal species, its eyes are non-reflective to lights. There are two plumage phases: one russet-brown, the other grey, both paler below, and faintly barred with black. The wide black stripes on the head meet on the nape. By day the Owlet-nightjar roosts in hollow branches and tree trunks. Its call consists of a loud grating churr of either two or three notes, typically 'chir-chir-chir'. It is found in eucalypt forests and woodlands with suitable tree hollows.

Spotted Nightjar *Eurostopodus argus* 29-31cm

G.A. Hoye

The Spotted Nightjar is the only nightjar with an all-white throat. The plumage is largely grey, darker above, and spotted with buff, black and white. In flight the two large white wing spots are obvious. The smaller **Large-tailed Nightjar** of northern Australia also has white spots on its wings, but can be distinguished by its white outer tail feathers. Like other nightjars, the Spotted Nightjar is nocturnal, roosting by day on the ground, and resembling a piece of fallen wood or bark. Absent only from eastern coastal areas, it is common and widespread.

White-throated Nightjar *Eurostopodus mystacalis* 32-37cm

K. Ireland

Largest of Australia's nightjars, the plumage is grey-brown, more black above, and spotted with buff, black and white. The white throat is broken in the centre by a distinct black line. Unlike other nightjars, the White-throated Nightjar has no white markings on the underside of the wings or tail. It is generally abundant but difficult to see. The contact call is a laugh-like 'wook-wook-wook-wook-wook-ko-ko-ko-ko-ko-ko-ko', becoming more rapid and higher-pitched at the end. It is nocturnal and inhabits woodlands and forests throughout eastern Australia.

White-throated Needletail *Hirundapus caudacutus* 20-22cm

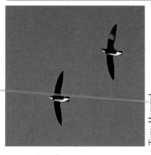

Tony Howard

This large swift is often mistaken in flight for a small bird of prey. Its grey-brown plumage, glossed with green, long pointed wings, short square tail, and diagnostic white throat and undertail, distinguish it from other Australian swifts. The much smaller **House Swift**, a rare vagrant to Australia's Top End, has a white rump and darker grey plumage. The **Fork-tailed Swift** has a dusky white rump and throat, but is otherwise uniform dark grey, with a long forked tail. Needletails often occur in large numbers over eastern and northern Australia, where they feed on flying insects.

White-rumped Swiftlet *Collocalia spodiopygius* 11-12cm

A.V. Spain

The most abundant swiftlet in Australia, this species is distinguished from martins by its reduced grey-white rump and more slender wings: the White-rumped Swiftlet is the only Australian swiftlet with a grey-white rump. The plumage is predominantly grey-brown, slightly glossed black on the wings. Both the **Uniform Swiftlet** and the **Glossy Swiftlet** are rare vagrants in Australia. The **Uniform Swiftlet** is grey-brown, slightly paler on the throat and vent, whereas the **Glossy Swiftlet** has a white breast and belly. Swiftlets are aerial birds, rarely landing, except when at the nest or roosting.

Azure Kingfisher *Alcedo azurea* 17-19cm

R. Drummond

This beautiful small kingfisher has resplendent violet-blue upperparts, rufous-orange underparts, paler on the throat, and bright red-pink legs and feet. A large buff-white spot is visible on the side of the neck. The long black bill is ideally suited to catching fishes, crustaceans and aquatic insects. The Azure Kingfisher is the second smallest of Australia's kingfishers, and is easily distinguished from the slightly smaller **Little Kingfisher**, which has white underparts and black legs. The Azure Kingfisher is found in stream-side vegetation and mangrove swamps throughout eastern and northern Australia.

Laughing Kookaburra *Dacelo novaeguineae* 40-45cm

G. Weber

This Kookaburra is generally white below, faintly barred with dark brown; brown on the back and wings. The tail is more rufous, broadly barred with black, and a conspicuous dark brown eye-stripe distinguishes it from the **Blue-winged Kookaburra** of the north; the latter having a blue tail and a large amount of blue in the wing. The chuckling voice that gave this bird its name is a raucous 'koo-koo-koo-koo-koo-koo-kaa-kaa-kaa', which is often sung in a chorus with other birds; also a shorter 'koooaa'. The Laughing Kookaburra is common in wooded areas throughout eastern and south-western Australia.

Forest Kingfisher *Todiramphus macleayii* 17-23cm

Usually seen sitting motionless on an open branch or telegraph wire, the Forest Kingfisher is easily identified by its deep, royal blue head and upperparts and striking white underparts. Male birds have a broad white collar. Birds in eastern Australia are more turquoise and have a smaller white wing spot. A harsh repetitive 't'reek t'reek' can be heard throughout the breeding season, August to December. Forest Kingfishers are found in woodlands and open forests in a broad coastal and near inland band from the Kimberleys, Western Australia through Queensland to Taree, New South Wales. It is more common in the north.

C. Webster

Red-backed Kingfisher *Todiramphus pyrrhopygia* 20-24cm

Babs & Bert Wells

The blue-green upperparts, white collar and broad black eye-stripe may confuse this species with the **Sacred Kingfisher** or the **Collared Kingfisher**, but a closer inspection will reveal the distinct red back and rump that gives this beautiful bird its name. The underparts are white, thus distinguishing it from the **Sacred Kingfisher**, and the crown is streaked with white. It is generally silent for much of the year, but utters some drawn-out whistles and harsh chattering during the breeding season. Unlike the mangrove-dwelling **Collared Kingfisher**, the Red-backed Kingfisher is found in dry woodlands throughout most of Australia.

Sacred Kingfisher *Todiramphus sanctus* 19-23.5cm

The Sacred Kingfisher is easily recognised by its blue-green back and crown, buff-cream collar and cinnamon-buff underparts. The upperparts are generally duller in the female and the underparts lighter. A broad black stripe extends from the back of the eye around the nape of the neck, in both sexes. The Sacred Kingfisher inhabits woodlands, mangroves and paperbark forests, feeding on crustaceans, beetles, reptiles and insects. The

call is a loud, staccato 'ek-ek-ek-ek', repeated continuously at the commencement of the breeding season. This bird is common and familiar in all but the most arid areas.

Buff-breasted Paradise-Kingfisher *Tanysiptera sylvia* 29-35cm (Including tail)

Early in November this beautiful kingfisher arrives in Australia from New Guinea to breed. Its blue, black and white upperparts, orange-buff breast and long white tail distinguish it from any other kingfisher. The bill is bright orange-red, as are the legs and feet. The **Common Paradise-Kingfisher**, with its white underparts and blue tail, is somewhat misnamed for Australia, with only one recorded sighting to date. The Buff-breasted Paradise-Kingfisher's presence is betrayed by a constant trilling call or a repeated 'chuga-chuga-chuga'. Within Australia, it is confined to lowland tropical rainforest in northern Queensland.

82

Rainbow Bee-eater *Merops ornatus* 21-28cm

Hans & Judy Beste

This brilliantly coloured bird is unmistakable in both plumage and voice. Both sexes have beautiful blue-green body plumage, a rufous crown, a yellow throat, and conspicuous black lines through the eye and on the lower throat. At a certain time of the year the two central tail feathers extend beyond the rest of the tail; these are longer on the male. In flight the wings are bright rufous-orange below. The call is a high-pitched 'trrrrp-trrrrp', mainly in flight. Bee-eaters are abundant in open, lightly timbered areas throughout Australia, migrating north outside of the breeding season.

Dollarbird *Eurystomus orientalis* 26-31cm

J. Bell

The conspicuous Dollarbird gets its name from the pale blue coin-shaped patches towards the tips of its wings. The plumage is generally dark brown, glossed heavily with blue-green on the back and wing coverts. The underparts are brown, glossed lighter with green, and the throat and undertail coverts are glossed with bright blue. The short, thick-set bill is orange-red, finely tipped with black. The Dollarbird's call is a harsh 'kak-kak-kak', repeated several times. It breeds in northern and eastern Australia during spring each year, migrating northwards to New Guinea and adjacent islands in February and March.

Noisy Pitta *Pitta versicolor* 17-20cm

A. Young

The Noisy Pitta can be difficult to see, despite its combination of chestnut cap, green back, iridescent blue wing patch, buff-yellow underparts, black belly patch, red undertail coverts, and tailless profile. In flight, it reveals large white wing patches. More often heard than seen, a Noisy Pitta can be attracted by imitating its 'walk to work' call. It will call in response or silently approach an observer and perch in a nearby tree. Various terrestrial invertebrates are eaten, snails being a particular favourite. It lives in east coast rainforests, spending much of its time on the ground.

Superb Lyrebird *Menura novaehollandiae* 80-100cm (Females smaller than males)

C. Andrew Henley/Larus

A lyrebird looks like a large brown pheasant. Only the adult male has the ornate tail, with special curved feathers that, in display, assume the shape of a lyre. The tails of females and young males are long, but lack the specialised feathers. The Superb Lyrebird occurs in wet forests of south-eastern Australia. The male's courtship display involves spreading its tail across its back while singing and dancing. The voice is powerful, and remarkable for its mimicry of a wide variety of other birds. **Albert's Lyrebird**, restricted to far north New South Wales and south Queensland, is more reddish, and the male's tail is less elaborate.

Welcome Swallow *Hirundo neoxena* c.15cm (Outer tail feathers longer in males than females)

D. & M. Trounson

One of several common Australian swallows, the Welcome Swallow can be recognised by its long forked tail, dark rump, rusty forehead and throat and light grey underparts. The **Barn Swallow**, an uncommon visitor to parts of northern Australia, has a black breast band and white underparts. The Welcome Swallow is frequently seen around buildings and other human structures, where it may nest colonially in open mud cups attached to a vertical wall. The voice consists of a variety of soft twittering notes. The Welcome Swallow is widespread in the south and east except for heavily forested regions and drier inland regions.

Fairy Martin *Hirundo ariel* 11-12cm

M. Seyfort

Both of Australia's martins have a short, square tail and pale rump. The Fairy Martin has a rusty-pink forehead and crown. The widespread **Tree Martin** has the top of the head dark blue-black except for a small rusty forehead. The Fairy Martin is gregarious, gathering in flocks to feed on fly-ing insects. A colonial breeder, it crowds large bottle-shaped mud nests together on vertical surfaces, such as the inside of bridges and culverts. The call consists of a few soft churring notes. The Fairy Martin can be found in open country almost anywhere on the mainland.

85

Singing Bushlark *Mirafra javanica* 12-15cm

M. Seyfort

Australia's only native lark, is distinguished from other small brown ground birds by its short tail with white edges, chestnut wing patch and thick, sparrow-like beak. Its considerable variation in colour across its range is often correlated with soil colour. Eastern birds are dark brown, while northwards and westwards there are increasing amounts of cinnamon in the plumage. The introduced **Common Skylark** is larger and has a small crest and longer tail. An inhabitant of grasslands, the Singing Bushlark is frequently seen sitting on some prominent perch or performing its courtship flight, in which a bird hovers on quivering wings, singing loudly.

Richard's Pipit *Anthus novaeseelandiae* 16-18cm

A. Foster

Australia's only pipit differs from other small brown ground birds in its combination of prominent white edges to its tail, slender, pale bill, long, pale eyebrow and two thin dark streaks on the sides of the throat. It characteristically bobs its tail when walking. It is usually seen alone on the ground or perched along sides of roads, in paddocks and other areas with low ground cover. The usual calls are a trill given in flight and chirruping notes. This is one of Australia's most common birds, found throughout the mainland and Tasmania in grassland and other open country.

Black-faced Cuckoo-shrike *Coracina novaehollandiae* 32-34cm

R. Brown

Cuckoo-shrikes are slender, attractive birds, with the curious behavioural trait of shuffling the wings upon landing. As indicated by its name, this species has a black face and throat, contrasting with its blue-grey back, wings and tail; and white underparts. In young birds, black plumage is restricted to a mask through the eyes to the ear coverts. The call most often heard is a soft churring. The nest, a small cup, is remarkably small for the size of the bird. This species is widespread and common, and can be found in almost any wooded habitat and in many suburban situations.

White-bellied Cuckoo-shrike *Coracina papuensis* 26-28cm

J. Purnell

The most common of several colour phases can be confused with a young **Black-faced Cuckoo-shrike** but its black mask does not extend behind the eye. Less commonly, the face, throat and often much of the head are black, extending onto the breast as a series of broken bars. The voice is a churring, similar to that of the **Black-faced Cuckoo-shrike** but higher pitched. The **Cicadabird** utters a strange insect-like buzzing: the male is slate-grey, the female brown with a prominent eyebrow. The White-bellied Cuckoo-shrike inhabits woodlands from the south-east and east through to the tropical north.

White-winged Triller *Lalage sueurii* 16-18cm

I.L. Morgan

The adult male White-winged Triller is unusual in having two annual plumages. During breeding, it has a black crown, back and tail, and grey rump; the wings are black with white shoulders and white-edged coverts. The wings, tail and rump are similar in non-breeding plumage but the rest of the upperparts are brown. Females resemble non-breeding males but are browner on the wings and tail. The **Varied Triller** has a white eyebrow, black eye-stripe and light orange undertail coverts. The White-winged Triller's song is a clear 'ch-ch-ch-joee-joee-joee', ending with a trill. It frequents lightly wooded open country.

Red-whiskered Bulbul *Pycnonotus jocosus* 20-22cm

J.D. Waterhouse

In identifying the Red-whiskered Bulbul, the red whisker mark is diagnostic, but not easily seen. More helpful are the pointed black crest, white cheek, reddish undertail coverts and white-tipped tail. It is commonly encountered in parks, gardens and other suburban areas, feeding on native or exotic fruits, as well as insects. The Bulbul is not timid around humans, perching prominently on the top of bushes or on lines, from which sites it gives its characteristic descending musical whistle. In winter, birds may congregate at a food source. A native of southern Asia, this introduced species has become familiar in urban areas near Sydney.

Bassian Thrush *Zoothera lunulata* 25-28cm

G. Weber

Although common, this native thrush can be difficult to see. Its plumage, bronze above with white underparts, is boldly marked with dark scalloping, helping it to blend into the forest background: when disturbed, it stands motionless on the ground or a branch. In flight, it displays a prominent white wingbar. The **Russet-tailed Thrush** is slightly smaller with more rusty upperparts, and has a shorter tail. Shyer than the **Common Blackbird**, the Bassian Thrush prefers sheltered areas of moist forest, only occasionally entering suburban areas. The song is somewhat like the Blackbird: a series of pleasant warbling notes.

Common Blackbird *Turdus merula* 25-25.5cm

T.A. Waite

First introduced in 1862, this thrush has established itself in urban areas of the south-east. The all black adult male, with its orange bill and eye-ring, is unmistakable. Young males and females are less obvious: mostly shades of brown, with a paler, lightly streaked throat and a yellowish brown bill. The **Song Thrush**, also introduced, has a brown back and dark spots on its underparts. Not shy, the Blackbird is commonly seen on lawns and in parks. It is an accomplished singer, uttering a series of melodious phrases. Usually seen in urban areas, it also enters wetter timbered areas.

89

Flame Robin *Petroica phoenicea* 12.5-14cm

M. Seyfort

The orange breast and throat of the male of this aptly named species, and the grey back and white wing-bar, separate it from other robins. The female is largely warm grey-brown; however, the wing-bar is pale buff, and only the outer tail feathers are extensively white. Flame Robins pounce on prey from prominent lookouts in the open, returning to a perch to eat. The attractive song has been interpreted as 'you may come if you wish to the sea'. In summer they occur in forests and woodlands to 1800 metres, dispersing in winter to lower altitudes.

Scarlet Robin *Petroica multicolor* 12-13.5cm

C. Andrew Henley/Larus

The male Scarlet Robin differs from the male **Flame Robin** in having a red breast, and black back and throat (both have a white wing-bar). A pale reddish wash on the breast of the female distinguishes it from other brown robins. The male **Pink Robin** is pink below and has no white in the wing; the female has a double wing-bar and lacks white in the tail. Like other species, the Scarlet Robin pounces on its prey. Its song has been rendered as 'wee-chee-dalee-dalee'. It spends much of its time in woodland and forest, moving into more open country in winter.

Red-capped Robin *Petroica goodenovii* 11-12cm

M. Seyfort

This is the smallest of Australia's robins. The male resembles the **Scarlet Robin** in its black back, white wing-bar and red front but is distinguished by the red forehead. The otherwise light brown female also has a red forehead. The **Rose Robin**, a bird of moist forests, is pink below, grey above, and lacks white in the wing. The voice of the Red-capped Robin is a pleasant trill, rather insect-like in nature. This is one of the most wide-spread of the robins, preferring more open, drier wooded country than other 'red-breasted' species. It can be found in much of subtropical Australia, reaching the coast in many areas.

Hooded Robin *Melanodryas cucullata* 14.5-17cm

R.G. Palmer

The boldly marked black and white male can be confused with few other Australian birds. Any uncertainty is resolved by the black hood which extends onto the breast, the prominent white wing-bar and the white panels in the tail. The mostly grey female lacks contrasting body plumage but shares the male's wing and tail patterns. In flight, both sexes display a white wing-stripe. The male calls most frequently before dawn, giving a piping whis-

tle. The Hooded Robin prefers open, lightly wood-ed country across the continent. In Tasmania, it is replaced by the **Dusky Robin**, with plumage in shades of brown.

Eastern Yellow Robin *Eopsaltria australis* 15-17cm

N. Chaffer

Both sexes of this common bird are easily recognised by the yellow underparts and grey faces and lores. Southern birds have an olive-yellow rump; in northern birds it is brighter yellow. The **Western Yellow Robin** has a grey breast. The **Pale Yellow Robin** is smaller, and has pale lores and lighter underparts. The voice of the Eastern Yellow Robin includes high bell-like piping, a repeated 'chop chop' and scolding notes. Its habitat extends from dry woodlands to rainforests, and it is often seen in parks and gardens. It is approachable, and often perches on the side of tree trunks.

Jacky Winter *Microeca fascinans* 12.5-14cm

G. Chapman

Although drab, this flycatcher is an attractive bird, with plain brownish upperparts, pale underparts, a slight eyebrow and prominent white edges to the black tail. The **Lemon-bellied Flycatcher** of tropical Australia is yellower below, lacks white in the tail and spends less time on the ground. From conspicuous perches, it watches for prey, catching it in the air or pouncing on it. While at rest, a Jacky Winter wags its tail from side to side. The song is a sweet, continuous 'peter-peter-peter'. It inhabits open woodland, paddocks and parkland.

Golden Whistler *Pachycephala pectoralis* 16-17.5cm

D. Val

True to its name, the Golden Whistler is an extroverted songster and the adult male is bright yellow on the underside and nape. This contrasts strikingly with the black head and breast band and white throat. Females and young birds are strong singers but lack bright plumage, being shades of grey-brown with washes of olive-green or buff. The voice is strong, musical and varied, including a 'we-we-we-whit', the last note strongly emphasised, and a rising 'seep'. The Golden Whistler can be found in almost any wooded habitat, from rainforest to mallee, including parks and orchards.

Rufous Whistler *Pachycephala rufiventris* 16-18cm

N. Chaffer

The adult male Rufous Whistler resembles the **Golden Whistler** in its white throat and black mask and breast band; it is distinguished by rufous underparts and a grey crown and upperparts. Females and young birds are greyer on the back, usually with a pale rufous wash on the streaked underparts. The Rufous Whistler is a spirited songster, producing a loud 'ee-chong', a repeated 'joey-joey-joey-joey', and other musical notes. Rufous and Golden Whistlers can be found together but the former generally prefers more open habitats. Both species are inquisitive and can be attracted by squeaking.

Grey Shrike-thrush *Colluricincla harmonica* 22.5-25cm

M. Seyfort

Plain grey, with pale lores and underparts in the southern part of its range, it becomes increasingly brown northwards. Adult males are browner on the mantle. Young birds have varying amounts of rufous on the lores and wings. What it lacks in colour, this species makes up for in voice which is rich and melodious, exhibiting considerable variation across the country. Typical phrases include 'pip-pip-pip—pip-hoee', 'pur-pur-pur-kwee-yewl', and a sharp 'yorrick'. This shrike-thrush searches for food on the ground and on limbs and trunks. It can be encountered in most forests and woodlands.

Crested Shrike-tit *Falcunculus frontatus* 15-19cm

M. Wright

The laterally flattened bill of this species is used for prising off bark and opening leaf galls. The bright yellow underparts are like a **Golden Whistler's**, but the crest and boldly marked black and white head are unlike any other Australian bird. The black throat of the male is replaced by olive-green in the female. Shrike-tits search for insects by noisily removing the bark; the sound of this action is a clue to their presence, as is the chuckling 'knock-at-the-door' call and a drawn out, plaintive whistle. They are birds of eucalypt forests and woodlands and some drier inland scrubs.

Crested Bellbird *Oreoica gutturalis* 21-23cm

The ringing voice of the Bellbird, is heard more often than the bird is seen. The male looks like a shrike-thrush with an orange eye, and white face and throat, bordered with black from the crest to the upper breast. The female lacks the white front and black band, but is recognized by the black crest and orange eye. The males call prominently, but, because the voice is ventriloquial, they are often difficult to locate. The cowbell-like notes increase in volume, 'pan-pan-panella'. Bellbirds are to be found in drier inland woodlands and some coastal regions.

A. Selby

Black-faced Monarch *Monarcha melanopsis* 14.5-16.5cm

N. Chaffer

The prominent black face and throat, sharply demarcated orange belly, and grey wings and tail identify this species. Immatures lack the black face. The Black-faced Monarch's presence is betrayed by its distinctive 'why-you-which-yew' call. It can be seen foraging among the foliage or sallying out for passing insects. Migratory over most of its Australian range, the Black-faced Monarch spends its summers in rainforest and wet sclerophyll forests. In the **Spectacled Monarch**, also a rainforest species, the black extends through the face, the orange reaches the sides of the throat and the tail is black, with white tips.

Leaden Flycatcher *Myiagra rubecula* 14.5-16cm

J. Gray

The male Leaden Flycatcher differs from other flycatchers in its leaden blue-grey upperparts. Females are duller and have a light buff-orange throat and upper breast. The male **Satin Flycatcher** is darker and glossy blue-black above; the female is slightly darker on the upperparts and throat. When not actively chasing flying insects, the Leaden Flycatcher sits on a branch, rapidly quivering its tail up and down. Its calls include a harsh 'zzrip' and a whistled 'zoowee zoowee'. The species is found in a variety of habitats, from open eucalypt forests and woodlands, to coastal scrubs and mangroves.

Restless Flycatcher *Myiagra inquieta* 19-21.5cm

E. Zillmann

This striking flycatcher is known more for its behaviour than its appearance. Its glossy blue-black upperparts contrast with the white throat and underparts: the breast is often washed with a dark buff. It hunts insects in sallies from a branch and by pouncing. This latter action consists of hovering while producing an unusual grinding noise, like scissors being sharpened on a stone wheel. Another call often heard is a musical 'chewee, chewee, chewee'. It is at home in open forest and woodlands, often near water. Northern birds are smaller, and frequently inhabit paperbark swamps.

Grey Fantail *Rhipidura fuliginosa* 14-16.5cm

G. Little

Fantails are great aerial acrobats when they chase flying insects. When perched, the characteristic fan-shaped tail is held slightly up and alternately spread and folded. The Grey Fantail is dark grey above, with white wing-bars, broken eyebrow and throat, and a dark breast band. The amount of white in the tail varies regionally. The song is a thin but attractive rising whistle. This species can be found in almost any habitat. The rump, base of the tail and eyebrow of the **Rufous Fantail**, is bright rufous. It looks and behaves like the Grey Fantail but usually prefers thicker, wetter vegetation.

Willie Wagtail *Rhipidura leucophrys* 18.5-21.5cm

G. Little

Superficially like the **Restless Flycatcher**, this black and white species is distinguished by the black throat and white eyebrow. It chases flying prey in the air and can be seen darting around lawns as it hunts for insects on the ground. As it does so, the tail is wagged from side to side. Willie Wagtails are fearlessly aggressive towards larger birds. The song, often given throughout a moonlit night, has been rendered as 'sweet pretty creature'. Widely distributed in Australia, the Willie Wagtail is found in almost any habitat except the densest forests; it is common around habitation.

Eastern Whipbird *Psophodes olivaceus* 26.5-30.5cm

N. Chaffer

Although usually secretive, this bird is also curious, and with patience, the observer can obtain a view. Adults are olive-green, boldly marked with a black head and breast and a broad white patch on the side of the face. The head bears a crest, the eye is pale and the tail is long. The Eastern Whipbird is more often heard than seen. Its explosive whipcrack call is one of the most characteristic of the Australian bush. The male gives a long whipcrack, usually followed quickly by a sharp 'choo-choo' from the female. This whipbird occupies dense vegetation near the ground in wetter habitats.

Logrunner *Orthonyx temminckii* 17-20cm

T. & P. Gardner

The plumage of this elusive ground-dwelling bird is mottled rufous-brown and olive-grey, streaked with black on the wings, back and sides of the throat. The face is grey, as are the sides of the breast, and the belly is white. The female is distinguished from the male by the cinnamon, instead of white, throat and upper breast. Food is found by raking through leaf-litter on the forest floor, while the bird supports itself on its spiny-tipped tail. The common call is a repeated piercing 'weet'. The Logrunner is found in temperate and subtropical rainforests from Gympie, Queensland to Illawarra, New South Wales.

Spotted Quail-thrush *Cinclosoma punctatum* 25-28cm

M. Seyfort

Quail-thrushes are ground-dwelling birds. Within Australia there are four species, the largest of them being the Spotted Quail-thrush. The male is identified by its black face, grey neck and throat and white eyebrow and cheek-patch. The body is largely brown, conspicuously spotted with black. The female lacks the black face and white cheek-patch, having instead a white chin and buff-orange throat. The call is an almost inaudible series of high-pitched whistles, also some louder double whistles. It is found mostly in drier sclerophyll forests from southern Queensland to eastern South Australia and Tasmania.

Grey-crowned Babbler *Pomatostomus temporalis* 25-29cm

G. Weber

This social bird is the largest of the four Australian babblers, and is the only one without a dark crown. Sexes have the same plumage colouration but the male can be separated by its slightly longer bill. The plumage is largely brown, more chestnut on the breast, with a white throat and cream crown. The tail is tipped with white. The **Chestnut-crowned Babbler** has a rich chestnut crown and white wing-bars, while both the **White-browed Babbler** and **Hall's Babbler** have brown crowns; **Hall's Babbler** is darker with less white on the throat.

99

Clamorous Reed-Warbler *Acrocephalus stentoreus* 16-17cm

This slender warbler can be distinguished from similar warblers by its uniform tawny-brown upperparts, paler buff underparts and eyebrow, and cream-white throat. The **Great Reed-Warbler**, a rare migrant to northern Australia, is almost identical in the field, the only difference being its slightly thicker bill. The call is a loud, clear 'chut'. Both the **Tawny Grassbird** and **Little Grassbird** are heavily streaked above; the **Tawny Grassbird** has an unstreaked rufous crown. Moving south in spring to breed, the Clamorous Reed-Warbler is a common sight in dense vegetation around freshwater swamps.

Golden-headed Cisticola *Cisticola exilis* 10-11cm

Cisticolas are distinguished by their rich golden plumage and pale pink-yellow legs. During the breeding season the male Golden-headed Cisticola attains a beautiful, unstreaked, golden crown. The female retains a streaked crown, similar to that of the non-breeding male. The song is a drawn-out 'zzzzt', also a repeated metallic 'link-link' and a harsh 'zeep' in alarm. The **Zitting Cisticola**, an uncommon resident of Australia's north coast, differs from the Golden-headed Cisticola in having a white-tipped tail. Cisticolas, like reed-warblers and grassbirds, inhabit grasslands, normally in the vicinity of water.

Hans & Judy Beste

N. Chaffer

Brown Songlark *Cincloramphus cruralis* 19-26cm

G. Little

Adult male Brown Songlarks have a very distinctive plumage. The general brown feathering is deepest on the face and breast, the crown is greyer. There is a great difference between the sexes of this insectivorous species, females being considerably smaller and of paler colouration. When maintaining a breeding territory, males utilize distinctive song flights, the loud notes of the song being uttered while the male flies high overhead with wings held upswept from the body. The song is also performed as he floats down to earth and may also be given while perched on a stump, post or similar object. The Brown Songlark frequents open country and is migratory.

Rufous Songlark *Cincloramphus mathewsi* 16-19cm

R. Brown

Although smaller than its near relative, the **Brown Songlark**, a pale eye-stripe and tawny-rufous rump colouration assist identification of this species. Dark breast streaks are evident in younger birds. The adult male has a dark bill; this is paler in the female and immatures. The Rufous Songlark maintains a strong song, the consistent notes being uttered when perched or while in flight. Perches include the upper limbs of isolated trees or the top of a post. Also like its near relative, it has a distinctive song flight but the outstretched wings are held in a lower attitude.

Superb Fairy-wren *Malurus cyaneus* 13-14cm

C. Andrew Henley/Larus

It is fascinating to watch a family group of these diminutive, gregarious birds. Adult males are the most vibrantly coloured of the family group. Their rich blue, black and grey plumage distinguishes them from the browner females and immatures. Displaying males may erect their back feathers over the wing coverts creating a blue and black appearance. Calls consist of a series of high-pitched trills uttered by both species, the males often extending these trills into song. The species occurs south of the Tropic of Capricorn through eastern Australia and Tasmania to the south-eastern corner of South Australia.

Variegated Fairy-wren *Malurus lamberti* 12-14cm

Males of this species are the brighter coloured individuals: blue colouration is restricted to the crown and sides of the head, and there is a rich chestnut shoulder patch. Immatures and females are brownish grey. All have a longer tail than the **Superb Fairy-wren**. Females of Northern Territory and Western Australian populations exhibit a blue-grey (not brown-grey) plumage. The call is

a high-pitched trill. Habitats include forest, woodland and shrubland. The species is widespread throughout the continent, being absent only from Cape York Peninsula, Tasmania and the extreme south-western corner of Western Australia.

White-winged Fairy-wren *Malurus leucopterus* 11-13cm

The male is spectacularly coloured, even more so when assessed against the backdrop of reddish soil in the interior. The cobalt blue mixed with white and brown is very distinctive. Females and immatures are less colourful. Like many other birds, it can be attracted to the observer if he or she produces a high pitched squeaking. On two offshore islands of Western Australia the male's rich blue colour is replaced by black. The call is a high-pitched trill. The species inhabits areas of lignum, saltbush, and other low shrubs.

Southern Emu-wren *Stipiturus malachurus* 18-20cm

The sombre colour, streaked darker, is broken only on the male, which has a powder blue throat. A unique character of emu-wrens is the tail: the six tail feathers are barbless and their loose emu-like arrangements has given rise to the common name of these birds. Trilling calls are very low in volume and pitch, being difficult to hear, even when in very close proximity.

J. Purnell

This heath-frequenting wren is occasionally found away from these haunts, sometimes even in forest areas. Its range extends from south-eastern Queensland to Victoria, Tasmania, South Australia and south-western Western Australia.

White-browed Scrubwren *Sericornis frontalis* 11-13cm

C. Andrew Henley/Larus

The white eyebrow is characteristic: otherwise it is fuscous-brown with slightly paler underparts. Subtropical and tropical populations are more yellow underneath, males having an almost black facial mask. Other populations along the southern coastline have dark streaking on the throat. The call is an almost persistent chattering of notes uttered as if being disturbed. It is an accomplished mimic. This insectivorous species usually occurs in pairs low down in thick vegetation. It is common and widespread, inhabiting rainforest, open forest, woodland and littoral scrub.

Yellow-throated Scrubwren *Sericornis citreogularis* 12-14cm

Dick Whitford

The yellow throat and dark mask, fringed with white or yellow, are distinctive characteristics, easily seen in the darkness of the forest floor, where this bird moves about in pairs or small family groups. It seldom ascends high into the vegetation. The nest is a large pendulous structure suspended from a branch over a stream within the rainforest. The call is a pleasant series of ticking notes and the song includes

melodious whistles, interspersed with excellent mimicry of the vocalizations of other birds. An inhabitant of many forest types, the Yellow-throated Scrubwren occurs in two isolated populations. One is found about the Atherton Tableland, Queensland, the other extends from southern Queensland to just south of the Illawarra region of New South Wales.

Large-billed Scrubwren *Sericornis magnirostris* 11-13cm

G. Little

The light brown plumage of this bird is almost uniform but the large black bill is distinctive. It feeds in mid-level vegetation, higher than other species of scrubwrens, moving about as individuals or small family groups. It does not build a nest but expropriates one built by a **Yellow-throated Scrubwren**. This plain, unmarked species inhabits the interior and edges of rainforest along the east coast from Cooktown (where it has a white wing-spot) to southern Victoria.

Speckled Warbler *Chthonicola sagittatus* 11-12cm

N. Chaffer

The Speckled Warbler is cryptically coloured. Bold speckling over the body, in combination with the deeper intensity of marking on the head, adds to its beauty. Sexes may be distinguished by the colour of the eyebrow, females having a chestnut colour mixed into the black eye-stripe (this colour is often hidden). The Speckled Warbler lives close to the ground. Its nest, built on the ground, is difficult to locate. The egg is a rich reddish brown. A strong mimic that often confuses an unobservant watcher, it frequents areas of drier forest, woodland and shrubs on the eastern side of the continent.

Weebill *Smicrornis brevirostris* 8-9cm

M. Seyfort

Weebills of northern Australia are the country's smallest birds. The name refers to the very short, stubby, pale beak. Combined with a pale eye, slight eyebrow, and unmarked crown and breast, this separates it from thornbills, which it resembles and with which it often associates. In the south and east of the country, birds are light brown; northwards and inland they become increasingly yellow and paler. It moves in active flocks, feeding mainly by gleaning insects from leaves. The voice is 'wee bit' or 'wee willy weetee'. The Weebill is found in wooded areas throughout mainland Australia except the wettest forests.

Brown Gerygone *Gerygone mouki* 9.5-11cm

N. Chaffer

The Brown Gerygone is like other gerygones in that it lacks the coloured rump and marked forehead or breast of thornbills but it differs from other gerygones by its olive-brown upperparts, white eyebrow, grey face, buff flanks and black subterminal tail band. The **Western Gerygone** has a smaller eyebrow and white at the base of the tail. The Brown Gerygone is a small active bird that forages among the foliage of trees and shrubs. As it moves through the foliage, it repeatedly gives a 'what is it, what is it' call. Its habitat is rainforest and wet eucalypt forest.

White-throated Gerygone *Gerygone olivacea* 10-11.5cm

G. Little

Many gerygones are sombre brown birds. Not so this species, with its white throat and bright yellow underparts. This colouration, plus the white-tipped tail and white undertail coverts, separate it from its relatives. The **Fairy Gerygone** has yellow undertail coverts and no white in the tail and northern males have black throats and white whisker stripes. The White-throated Gerygone's voice has given rise to the nickname 'Bush Canary': one of its special sounds is its musical descending song. It is often found gleaning insects while hovering outside the foliage in open forests and woodlands.

107

Yellow-rumped Thornbill *Acanthiza chrysorrhoa* 10-12cm

W. Taylor

A pleasant musical call combined with jerking flight, black forehead with white spots and prominent yellow upper-tail coverts identify this species. It is invariably found on the ground, moving in small parties. Areas frequented include open forest, shrub, pasture and grassland. Unlike many endemic Australian birds, it shows a fondness for introduced pines. A nest is constructed in the outer limbs of hanging branches. The bulky structure often has a second, unused, nest on top, the significance of which is not understood. The nest is entered by a side entrance formed under a protruding canopy or overhang. The song is a tinkling whistle. The Yellow-rumped Thornbill ranges over most of the mainland and Tasmania.

Brown Thornbill *Acanthiza pusilla* 9-10cm

G. Little

This is one of Australia's many small brown birds. Characters useful in identifying this insectivorous species include the well-scalloped forehead, streaked throat, and dark eyes. The call is a pleasant 'tchit! tchit!', uttered when disturbed. It lives in a variety of habitats, varying from rainforests to woodlands, where it moves in pairs or small active family groups, usually frequenting the lower limbs and canopy, only occasionally feeding on the ground. The nest is constructed low down in thick vegetation.

108

Striated Thornbill *Acanthiza lineata* 9-10cm

The distinctive features of this small brown bird include a strongly streaked crown, face and throat. It has a more greenish tinge and paler eye than the **Brown Thornbill**. In open forest and woodland, it frequents the outer canopy and limbs and is often seen on branches, moving in small flocks or feeding parties. Like many other thornbills, it mixes freely with other small insectivorous species when feeding. The call is a soft 'zit' and the song is a high-pitched trill. Its distribution extends from near Gladstone, Queensland, to south-eastern South Australia.

G. Little

Southern Whiteface *Aphelocephala leucopsis* 10-12.5cm

Hans & Judy Beste

Whitefaces are somewhat like thornbills, to which they are related, but they have much stouter bills. The face pattern, from which they receive their name, consists of a white forehead extending to below the eye, bordered by black. The body is a drab light grey-brown. In flight, the broad black tail band and lighter rump are somewhat reminiscent of thornbills. The Southern Whiteface feeds on the ground in small parties, hunting for insects and seeds. Soft twittering notes and a 'tik tik tik' are the most usually heard calls. It prefers open, often dry, country with scattered shrubs, in which it takes refuge if disturbed.

Varied Sittella *Daphoenositta chrysoptera* 10-13cm

R. Brown

This species shows considerable plumage variation across its range. Depending on its location, a bird can have a combination of white, black, grey or mottling on the head; white or orange wing-stripe; and plain or streaked underparts. All have yellow upturned bills with a black tips, short tails and legs, and large feet. The Varied Sittella feeds on the trunks of trees and has the remarkable ability of walking along the underside of branches. The commonly heard call is a high-pitched 'chip chip'. It is usually found in active flocks of up to 20 birds, in most eucalypt forests, woodlands and inland scrubs.

White-throated Treecreeper *Cormobates leucophaeus* 13-17cm

K. Ireland

Like sittellas, treecreepers forage on the bark of trees but they cannot walk on the underside of branches. The common species of the east coast, the White-throated Treecreeper, has dark brown upperparts, white throat and upper breast, and flanks with white streaks edged with black. In flight, a buff wingbar is displayed. The **Red-browed Treecreeper** is similar but has a prominent rusty eyebrow. The White-throated Treecreeper's repeated, high-pitched piping is a common sound of forests. It can be found in rainforest, eucalypt forest and woodland, working its way up the sides of trees in search of insects.

Brown Treecreeper *Climacteris picumnus* 16-18cm

R. Drummond

This is lighter brown above than the **White-throated Treecreeper**. Its head, throat and upper breast are light brownish grey, the remaining underparts have buff streaks bordered with black, prominent buff eyebrow and, in flight, a buff wing-bar. It prefers drier, more open country than the **White-throated Treecreeper**. It works up trees in the same manner, but also feeds on the ground. The 'spink' call is uttered singly or in series. In the west it is replaced by the rusty

orange **Rufous Treecreeper**; in the northwest by the much darker brown **Black-tailed Treecreeper**.

Red Wattlebird *Anthochaera carunculata* 33.5-36cm

G. Chapman

The name refers to the fleshy reddish wattle on the side of the neck. Although diagnostic, it is often not easily seen, and identification relies on the grey-brown body with prominent white streaks, yellow belly, pale facial patch and long, white-tipped tail. It has several distinctive but unmusical calls, including coughs, a harsh 'yac a yac' and loud 'chok'. The Red Wattlebird occurs in forests, woodlands and gardens around flowering trees and shrubs. It is aggressive to smaller honeyeaters, driving them from food sources. In Tasmania, it is replaced by the larger **Yellow Wattlebird**, which has a longer, yellow wattle.

111

Little Wattlebird *Anthochaera chrysoptera* 26-30cm

D. & M. Trounson

As indicated by its name, this is the smallest of the wattlebirds; however, it lacks a cheek wattle. It is much the same colour as the **Red Wattlebird**, but is distinguished by the white facial patch that extends down the sides of the neck, finer white streaking on the body and, in flight, a conspicuous rufous patch in the wings: the belly is never yellow. Not as raucous as the **Red Wattlebird**, its voice is a mixture of notes, including a loud 'quok' and 'kokay kok'. It tends to prefer drier and often scrubbier habitats than does the **Red Wattlebird**.

Spiny-cheeked Honeyeater *Acanthagenys rufogularis* 23-26cm

M. Seyfort

Looking like a small wattlebird, this species replaces wattlebirds throughout much of the drier mainland. The unusual spines appear as a white patch on the side of the face; however, the dark buff throat and upper breast and bicoloured bill (dark pink base, black tip), are better clues to identification. In flight, it shows a white rump.

The voice is an amazing collection of odd sounds: a sharp 'kwok', an ascending then descending whistle, and liquid bubbling notes. It can be found in a wide range of timbered habitats, where it is often common and conspicuous.

112

Noisy Friarbird *Philemon corniculatus* 32-35cm

C. Andrew Henley/Larus

Friarbirds are large, ungainly, grey-brown honeyeaters with large amounts of bare (usually black) skin on the head. The Noisy Friarbird has a completely naked head apart from a small patch of feathers under the chin and a line over the eye. The base of the upper bill is adorned with a knob and the upper breast is covered with long, pointed silver-white feathers. When calling, it throws its head back, giving a raucous array of notes. A loud 'four-o-clock' is one of the more familiar. It aggressively contests insects, soft fruits, flowers and other food sources in open forests, woodlands and gardens.

Little Friarbird *Philemon citreogularis* 25-29cm

C. Andrew Henley/Larus

Smallest of the friarbirds, this species lacks a knob at the base of the bill. The skin on the face is blue-grey and there are grey-brown feathers on the crown: younger birds have yellow on the chin and throat. Less noisy than other species, it utters a curious 'arcoo'. It has the widest Australian distribution of the friarbirds, inhabiting a range of open forests, woodlands, scrubs and gardens. In northern Australia are two black-faced friarbirds with low rounded knobs. The **Silver-crowned Friarbird** has a silvery crown and throat. The **Helmeted Friarbird** is much larger with a brownish nape ruff.

Blue-faced Honeyeater *Entomyzon cyanotis* 24-32cm

N. Chaffer

Adults are aptly named for the large blue patch of naked skin on the face. In young birds this area is yellow-olive. At all ages the Blue-faced Honeyeater is distinguished by yellow-green upperparts, black nape, crown, throat and bib, and white nape band. Northern birds have a prominent white wing patch, obvious in flight. This honeyeater is a noisy, active inhabitant of woodlands and open forest. It also associates with human-modified habitats, and can become bold around camping areas and picnic grounds. The call is also distinctive: a loud 'quoit quoit quoit', with each note rising at the end.

Noisy Miner *Manorina melanocephala* 24-29cm

G. Little

A colonial species, the Noisy Miner is by turns aggressive, approachable or curious. Its bold demeanour is complemented by a 'cocky' appearance: black crown and cheeks, and yellow bill, legs and skin behind the eye, contrasting with the mostly grey body. The **Yellow-throated Miner** has a grey crown, white rump, and line of yellow skin on the sides of the throat. The Noisy Miner's name is well deserved: among the calls are a loud 'pwee pwee pwee' and piping 'pee pee pee' when alarmed. Frequenting woodland and open forests, it has also become well adapted to suburban situations.

Bell Miner *Manorina melanophrys* 17-20cm

N. Chaffer

More frequently called the Bellbird, this species is better known to most people by sound than sight. The olive-green plumage conceals it in the foliage, despite the contrasting yellow-orange bill and legs, and small scarlet patch of skin behind the eye. Uttering the familiar and persistent bell-like 'tink', Bell Miners also have a loud, harsh alarm call, given when they are disturbed. A squeaking noise by the observer will draw calling birds to within a few metres, permitting a good view. It is usually found in tall open forest with scrubby understoreys, where it forms colonies.

Lewin's Honeyeater *Meliphaga lewinii* 20-22cm

Dick Whitfort

This honeyeater has dark greenish grey colouration, interrupted only by the creamy yellow of a gape and the yellowish crescentic ear coverts. The sexes are similar in appearance. It is mostly frugivorous, eating berries and small fruits, but also taking insects and some nectar. The strong rattling notes of Lewin's Honeyeater carry long distances and instantly confirm its presence in an area. It is common in the wetter parts of eastern Australia, frequenting both rainforest and wet sclerophyll forest, often wandering into more open woodland. Similar species found in tropical Queensland may be distinguished by size and voice: ear covert shapes are also distinctive.

Yellow-faced Honeyeater *Lichenostomus chrysops* 16-17cm

M. Seyfort

This is a medium-sized, grey-fuscous honeyeater. Adult males and females are similar in appearance: young birds have buff rumps. A yellow facial stripe between two black ones, and light blue eyes are useful identification characteristics. A species with similar facial markings, and with which it may be confused, is the **Singing Honeyeater**. Size and vocalizations are handy clues to identification. Noisy flocks fly high over a variety of habitats. At other times the birds are found singly or in small groups. It's call is a 'chick-up', usually uttered from the canopy or limbs in forest or woodland. Migrations of the Yellow-faced Honeyeater occur through eastern Australia.

Yellow-tufted Honeyeater *Lichenostomus melanops* 19-22cm

G. Little

The general yellowish colouration enhanced by the bright yellow of the elongated ear tufts of this medium-sized honeyeater aid its identification. A distinctive black line from the lores to the front of the ears is characteristic. Southern populations have a crest on the crown. There are no sexual differences in plumage. It is gregarious by nature but occasionally moves about singly. In groups, it is quite vocal, uttering a series of single notes sounding like 'quirk': at other times it may be silent. The preferred habitat is riparian forest but some birds wander in the post-breeding period.

White-eared Honeyeater *Lichenostomus leucotis* 20-21cm

The overall olive-green colouration of both sexes of this medium sized honeyeater is washed yellow on the underparts. In combination with the grey crown, black face and distinct white ear coverts, the plumage is attractive and distinctive. In immatures the crown is more similar in colour to the back. Although of similar size to many other honeyeaters, the plumage pattern helps identification, as does the repetitive 'chock-chock-chock' calls. Solitary by nature, the White-eared Honeyeater is found in habitats ranging from heath and woodland to forest. When lining its nest, the adult female will often take hair or wool from other animals (including humans).

J. Handel

Singing Honeyeater *Lichenostomus virescens* 18-22cm

G. Taylor

The drab grey-fuscous plumage of this widespread honeyeater lacks sexual differences. Immatures are duller in colour and possess a buff rump. The dark facial stripe over a pale yellow one is a useful identification character. Like most honeyeaters it shows a preference for nectar and insects, often taking the latter in aerial pursuit. Despite its name, it is not a great songster but it has distinctive calls, one of which is a pleasant, repetitive 'prit-prit-prit'. It inhabits semi-arid to arid woodland and scrubland.

White-plumed Honeyeater *Lichenostomus penicillatus* 15-17cm

D. & M. Trounson

Like many honeyeaters this is a medium-sized bird. Both sexes have a pale yellow-olive colour combined with an almost unmarked face: a narrow white plume about the ear coverts not only lends a name to the bird but assists identification. Western populations are much paler than those from the south-east. Breeding and non-breeding birds differ in bill colour: black (breeding), and dusky with a yellow base (non-breeding). A gregarious species, the White-plumed Honeyeater moves in groups that freely disperse when feeding. The voice is a pleasant repeated 'chickawee', frequently uttered about a main food source. It is widely distributed throughout Australia.

White-naped Honeyeater *Melithreptus lunatus* 13-15cm

L. Robinson

This is one of several birds with olive-green upperparts, black head, white nape band and a coloured area of bare skin above the eye. This species has red eye-skin (white in the western population), the black of the face extending under the bill and nape band. The **White-throated Honeyeater** has blue eye-skin, white under the bill and nape band almost reaching the eye. The **Brown-headed Honeyeater** has a brownish head, yellow-ish eye-skin and cream nape band. The White-naped Honeyeater is common in forests and woodlands, where its sharp 'scherp scherp' call reveals its presence.

118

New Holland Honeyeater *Phylidonyris novaehollandiae* 17.5-18cm

J. Handel

This attractive bird is rarely still for very long, usually busily feeding at a flowering shrub or noisily interacting with others of its species. When it perches long enough, the black and white plumage, yellow wing patch, small white ear tuft, thin white whisker and white eye ensure identification. Found with this species is the very similar **White-cheeked Honeyeater** which has a single large cheek patch and a dark eye. The New Holland Honeyeater's voice comprises a loud 'chik', thin 'pseet' and chattering. It is common in heath, forests, woodland and gardens, particularly if grevilleas and banksias are present.

Eastern Spinebill *Acanthorhynchus tenuirostris* 15-16.5cm

N. Chaffer

This bird is unlikely to be confused with any other species. The orange-centred white throat, black crescent on the sides of the chest and orange belly are unmistakable, as is the long, fine curved bill. The **Western Spinebill** has an entirely orange throat, white belly and white eyebrow. Spinebills are active birds, and often hover when feeding on nectar. In flight, the outer white tail feathers are prominent and the wingbeat is noisy. The most frequently heard call is a high staccato piping. The Eastern Spinebill occurs around flowers in forests, woodlands, heaths and gardens.

Scarlet Honeyeater *Myzomela sanguinolenta* 10-11cm

G.A. Hoye

This bird is diminutive in size but not in colour or voice. The male has a vibrant scarlet head and central back over a black back, breast and tail: the female and young are brown. Its decurved bill helps identification. It feeds on nectar, insects and fruits and is attracted to flowering urban shrubs. The voice is a pleasant high-pitched warble, short in duration, often heard in forest or riparian situations. Ranging from north Queensland to Victoria, it is resident in the north and an irregular visitor in the south.

White-fronted Chat *Epthianura albifrons* 11-13cm

R. Drummond

This small bird has black and white colouration. Especially characteristic of the male chat is the black cap over a white facial area and a black breast-band. Females and immatures are a grey-fuscous colour with a reduced breast-band. It differs from the smaller **Double-barred Finch** in having a longer, finer bill, and a single breast-band (not double). In flight it shows a distinctive dark tail, edged with white. The quiet 'tang' call is characteristic of the species. The White-fronted Chat inhabits open areas of low vegetation, especially about wetlands. Although widely distributed, it appears to be declining.

120

Crimson Chat *Epthianura tricolor* 10-12cm

M. Willis

The brilliant crimson, white, and black plumage of this male chat is diagnostic. Females and immatures are drab in comparison, being brownish and having a washed out redness on the rump and breast. Another red-coloured bird with which it could be confused is the **Red-capped Robin**. Much time is spent feeding on the ground and in low shrubbery. It is frequently seen in loose flocks, and often in smaller groups. Vocalizations vary from simple single notes to a repetitive 'dik-it' or trills. The species is nomadic, inhabiting dry open environments throughout most of Australia.

Yellow-bellied Sunbird *Nectarinia jugularis* 10-12cm

K. Ireland

Australia's only sunbird is a familiar bird of the tropical north-eastern coast. The long curved bill resembles that of some honeyeaters but the bright yellow underparts prevent any confusion. Yellow colouration extends to the throat and upper breast of the female but is replaced in the adult male by glossy blue-black feathers. The Sunbird hovers to take nectar from flowers and shows a liking for spiders. High-pitched notes are given in flight and display. It can be found along the edges of rainforests and in suburban parks and gardens. Nests are often built round houses, where individuals become less wary of humans.

121

Mistletoebird *Dicaeum hirundinaceum* 10-11cm

This is one of the country's smallest birds. The adult male's glossy blue-black upperparts and wings, red throat and undertail coverts, and black stripe down the centre of the belly are diagnostic. The drably coloured female and young birds are less obvious but can be identified by the pink undertail coverts. The food is mostly mistletoe berries. The Mistletoebird's sticky droppings, containing seeds of this parasitic plant adhere to tree branches and help to spread it. The most commonly heard call is a short 'wit' given while in flight. This bird is found in any habitat throughout mainland Australia where mistletoes are present.

R. Brown

Spotted Pardalote *Pardalotus punctatus* 8-9.5cm

T. & P. Gardner

Although common, this species frequently passes unnoticed because it spends most of its time near the tops of trees. Seen closely, it is a striking bird. The male has fine white spots on the black crown and wings, a yellow throat and undertail coverts, and a reddish chestnut rump. The female is duller, with an off-white throat and cream spots on the crown. The most obvious indication of its presence is the frequently repeated, somewhat bell-like 'sleep babee'. This pardalote can be found in most wooded habitats, including suburban parks. The nest is made in a tunnel in an earthen bank.

Striated Pardalote *Pardalotus striatus* 9.5-11cm

G. Little

Like the **Spotted Pardalote**, this species is more common than is usually realized. Across Australia, it has white eyebrow with a yellow spot in front of the eye, an olive-grey back and a white stripe in the wing. Other colouration is very variable. The wing stripe may be narrow or wide, with a red or yellow spot at the front end of it. The crown is black, with or without fine white stripes. A frequent call is a sharp 'tchip tchip'. This pardalote can be found in almost any habitat with trees or shrubs.

Silvereye *Zosterops lateralis* 9.5-12cm

D. & M. Trounson

This is one of a group of birds known as white-eyes because of the conspicuous ring of white feathers around the eye. The Silvereye exhibits interesting plumage variations across its range. The grey back and olive-green head and wings are found in birds throughout the east; western birds have the back uniformly olive-green. Breeding birds of the east coast have yellow throats, pale buff flanks and white undertail coverts. During winter, these are replaced by southern birds, which have grey throats, chestnut flanks and yellow undertail coverts. The contact call, a thin 'psip', is given continually. Silvereyes may occur in almost any wooded habitat.

House Sparrow *Passer domesticus* 14-16cm

Following its introduction between 1863 and 1870, the House Sparrow quickly established itself in urban settlements throughout eastern Australia. The male is conspicuous with its grey crown, black face and throat and dark black and brown upperparts. The remainder of the underparts are pale grey-brown. The female is slightly paler and lacks the grey crown and black face, instead having a pale buff eye-stripe. Both the male and female **Tree Sparrow**, found only in south-eastern Australia, are similar to the male House Sparrow, but they have an all-brown crown and black ear patch. The call is a harsh 'cheer-up'.

Goldfinch *Carduelis carduelis* 12-15cm

This small, brightly-coloured finch, with a striking red facial disc, was introduced into Australia in the 1850s and quickly became established in the south-east. A few isolated populations in areas around Perth and Albany, Western Australia, are descended from escaped or liberated aviary birds. The plumage is largely buff above with a white rump, and black and golden-yellow wings. The underparts are white with varying amounts of buff, and the crown to nape is black. Goldfinches are gregarious, found throughout the year in small groups called 'charms', but occasionally flocks of 500 or more birds are seen. The common call is a repeated 'swilt-witt-witt'.

124

Red-browed Finch *Neochmia temporalis* 10-12cm

N. Chaffer

Like a fiery dart as it flies, this medium-sized finch is distinguished from other Australian finches, by its bright red rump and eyebrow. The remainder of the upperparts are olive-green, and the underparts and head are grey. The bill is red with a broad black wedge on the top and bottom mandible. The call is a high-pitched 'seeee' or 'ssitt'. It is found in a variety of habitats, especially shrublands with open grassy areas. The Red-browed Finch is distributed in a broad coastal band along the east coast, from Cape York, Queensland, to Adelaide, South Australia. A small population also exists near Perth, Western Australia.

Zebra Finch *Taeniopygia guttata* 10-11.5cm

Hans & Judy Beste

Generally associated with the more arid areas of Australia, the Zebra Finch is the most common and widespread of Australia's finches. The plumage is generally grey, with characteristic black 'tear-drop' eyestripes and 'zebra-like' black and white barring on rump and uppertail. The male is distinguished from the female by its conspicuous chestnut cheeks. The most common calls are a loud nasal 'tiah', often given in flight, and a soft 'tet-tet' in close contact. Zebra Finches live year round in social flocks of 10 to 100 birds in a variety of habitats, mainly dry wooded grasslands, bordering watercourses.

Double-barred Finch *Taeniopygia bichenovii* 9.5-11.5cm

N. Chaffer

Double-barred Finches need to drink regularly and are seldom found far from permanent water. Both sexes have a white face and cheeks, bordered with a broad black line. The white upper-breast is separated from the buff-white belly by another broad black line, and the upperparts are generally brown, heavily spotted with white on the wings. Birds from west of the Gulf of Carpentaria have a black, instead of white, rump. Double-barred Finches inhabit grassy thickets in open woodland and forest, from the Kimberleys, Western Australia, across the north, then south to Victoria. They usually occur in flocks of up to 30 or 40 birds.

Crimson Finch *Neochmia phaeton* 12-14cm

D. & M. Trounson

This large finch with a long, tapered red tail and red face cannot be confused with any other Australian finch. The upperparts are brown, washed with grey and red. The underparts are pale brown on the female, crimson on the male. Birds from Cape York Peninsula have a white belly. The Crimson Finch is not especially gregarious, usually occurring alone or in family groups, but will mix with other finch flocks. The call, a loud, penetrating 'tsee-tsee-tsee-tsee-tsee', can be heard over several hundred metres. It inhabits pockets of tall grassland and pandanus.

Chestnut-breasted Mannikin *Lonchura castaneothorax* 10-12.5cm

This beautiful, thick-set finch, with a powerful bill, is highly social, often forming vast flocks of several hundred birds. The upperparts are rich chestnut, with a grey crown. The underparts are generally white, with a broad chestnut breast-band, bordered below with black, and a conspicuous black face and throat. The call, 'teet' or 'tit', which may be either bell-like or long and drawn-out, is used in a variety of situations. The song, however, is long and high-pitched, often lasting up to 12 seconds. It is common in rank grasses and reeds, from the Kimberleys, Western Australia, to Sydney, New South Wales.

Hans & Judy Beste

Metallic Starling *Aplonis metallica* 21.5-24cm

Australia's only native starling lacks the disagreeable habits of its introduced relatives. Adults are entirely glossy oily black with long pointed tails and large bright red eyes. Young birds are similar except for the white throat and underparts, streaked with black. This species is colonial, and birds of different ages are seen together, particularly at nest trees, where their hanging nests are clustered in the outer branches. Food includes insects and introduced fruits. The voice includes chattering notes and a canary-like song. It is a bird of rainforests, mangroves and developed areas, where it becomes tame, often nesting in towns.

Hans & Judy Beste

127

Common Starling *Sturnus vulgaris* 20-22cm

Babs & Bert Wells

Introduced in the 1860s, this species has become well established and is expanding its range. When the plumage is fresh, the tips of the glossy purple-black body feathers sport large white spots. At this time the bill is dark. With wear, the white spots are lost, producing an unmarked plumage, and the bill turns yellow. Young birds are dull brown. The song is an unmusical collection of wheezy whistles, clicks, scratching notes and some mimicry. It is usually found near human habitation and most often seen when searching for seeds and insects on lawns and in paddocks. It also raids fruit crops.

Common Myna *Acridotheres tristis* 23-25.5cm

K. Griffiths

This bird, which was introduced in the 1860s and is now a serious pest, could be confused with the Noisy Miner, a native honeyeater. Both have yellow bills, legs and bare eye skin, but the Myna is brown with a black head. In flight, it shows large white wing patches. It is aggressive towards other species, bullying them around food sources and usurping nesting recesses. The voice is unpleasant: a collection of growls and other harsh notes. It is closely associated with towns and cities, rarely moving far from habitation, where it searches for natural food and human scraps.

Olive-backed Oriole *Oriolus sagittatus* 26-28cm

C. Andrew Henley

Although similar in size to several other species that gather together in fruiting trees, the Olive-backed Oriole is recognized by the combination of olive-green upperparts, white underparts with dark teardrop-shaped streaks and, in particular, the salmon-coloured bill. The red eye is a further clue. The **Yellow Oriole** of tropical Australia is yellow-green and more finely streaked below. The Olive-backed Oriole's pleasant 'olly ole' call is a feature of its habitats. It feeds on insects and a variety of soft fruits, which it finds in wooded areas from rainforest to some drier inland scrubs and in orchards and gardens.

Figbird *Sphecotheres viridis* 27.5-29cm

Hans & Judy Beste

Frequently associating with the **Olive-backed Oriole**, the Figbird can also be confused with it. Females are superficially oriole-like but have dark brown upperparts, more heavily streaked underparts, a short dark bill and dark eye. Males present no difficulties. The back is olive-green, head black and the eye is surrounded by naked red skin. Southern birds have grey underparts and collar; northern ones are bright yellow below and lack the grey collar. Females are similar throughout their range. As its name suggests, the Figbird largely eats soft fruits. It lives in flocks in rainforest and eucalypt forest, where its downwardly inflected 'tcher' is a characteristic background sound.

Spangled Drongo *Dicrurus bracteatus* 28-32cm (Females smaller than males)

R. Viljoen

The glossy black plumage and blood-red eye are striking, but the characteristic long, forked 'fish' tail confirms the identification of this species. The Spangled Drongo is noisy and conspicuous, usually active, and frequently aggressive to other species. It sits on a prominent perch, from which it dashes out to capture passing insects. It also gleens insects from bark and foliage, and will take nectar from flowers. The voice comprises a variety of sounds, including some distinctive metallic notes like a stretched wire being plucked. Although preferring wetter forests, it can also be found in other woodlands, mangroves and parks.

Satin Bowerbird *Ptilonorhynchus violaceus* 27-33cm

L.F. Schick

The adult male takes seven years to acquire its glossy blue-black plumage, pale bill and violet-blue iris. Younger males resemble the female in being olive-green above, off-white with dark scalloping below, with brown wings and tail: the bill and iris are dark brown. While adult males are solitary, 'green' birds frequently form large flocks. There is an amazing variety of calls, some mechanical in nature, as well as mimicry. The male gives a loud 'weeoo'. The bower, consisting of two parallel walls of sticks, is built on the ground in wetter forests and woodlands. In winter, birds move to more open country.

Regent Bowerbird *Sericulus chrysocephalus* 24-28cm

G. Threlfo

Few birds can compare with the adult male: its golden wings, shoulders, nape, crown, iris and bill contrast strikingly with the otherwise black plumage. Females and young males are mainly brown but nonetheless distinctive, with a black crown patch, heavily mottled back and scalloped underparts: the bill and iris are dark brown. The Regent Bowerbird feeds mainly on native fruits but may enter orchards and gardens for cultivated species. The voice, which is seldom heard, includes harsh or chattering notes and some mimicry. It occurs largely in rainforest and neighbouring habitats, where the male constructs a bower of parallel stick walls.

Spotted Bowerbird *Chlamydera maculata* 25-31cm

M. Seyfort

Although boldly marked with dark buff spots on the upperparts, this bowerbird is not colourful, except for the iridescent pink nape crest, which may not be visible unless the bird is in display. Sexes are similar but females may lack the crest.
The **Western Bowerbird** is darker and more richly coloured. The **Great Bowerbird** is larger, greyer and fairly uniform, lacking the prominent spots. The bower of the Spotted Bowerbird is a platform with two parallel walls of sticks, adorned with bones and snail shells. The voice includes harsh notes and mimicry. It occurs in a range of dry inland woodlands.

Great Bowerbird *Chlamydera nuchalis* 34-38cm

M. Seyfort

The male is a dull fawn coloured bird with darker mottling on the upperparts. The magnificent lilac nuchal crest is usually covered and revealed only during courtship display. The sexes are similar but the female often lacks the coloured nape. Using sticks, the male constructs a large avenue bower that is decorated with a variety of objects, including bones and shells. Other species of the genus are smaller and more distinctively marked. The species is found across Australia north of the Tropic of Capricorn, mostly in tropical woodland.

Green Catbird *Ailuroedus crassirostris* 24-33cm

D. Val

The name of this stocky bird refers to its appearance and its voice. The body is bright green above and on the white-tipped wings and tail, paler below, with a pale bill and red iris. Of its various calls, the most easily recognized is a cat-like yowling, frequently heard in rainforests. Although a bowerbird, it does not build a display area. Northwards, it is replaced by the **Spotted Catbird** which has a paler head with black patches on the sides of the face and around the bill; and the **Tooth-billed Bowerbird**, which is brown above and heavily streaked below.

Paradise Riflebird *Ptiloris paradiseus* 25-30cm

L.F. Schick

Riflebirds are unlike any other Australian bird. Both sexes have long, slender, decurved bills and short tails. The adult male is velvet black above and oily green below; the crown, throat, breast and central tail feathers are iridescent. The female is brown and lacks iridescence but the white eyebrow, reddish wings and arrow-like scalloping on the underparts are distinctive. A loud, explosive 'yas', sometimes given twice, is a characteristic sound in this bird's rainforest habitat. In flight, the male's wings sound like rustling silk. **Victoria's Riflebird**, which replaces it in the north-east, is similar.

White-winged Chough *Corcorax melanorhamphos* 43-47cm

R. Brown

The Chough is extremely sociable, almost always seen in groups of up to ten. The curved beak and red iris are unlike any other all black birds. Not visible at rest, the large white wing patch is obvious in flight. The Chough feeds primarily on the ground, moving in groups and raking through the litter. Its presence is often first detected by a mournful, descending whistle. If disturbed, it gives a ratchet-like call. The nest is a large bowl of mud. Members of a group cooperate in caring for their young. Primarily a bird of open forests and woodlands, it also enters modified habitats if not disturbed.

Apostlebird *Struthidea cinerea* 29-33cm

T. & P. Gardner

It is smaller than the **White-winged Chough**, and quite different in appearance but the two species are similar in habits. The Apostlebird has a grey body, dusky brown wings, a black tail and a short stout bill. It travels in troops of 10, occasionally up to 20, individuals, feeding on the ground, searching for food among leaf litter. The nest is a mud bowl, smaller than that of the Chough. The voice is characteristic: a variety of harsh, grating notes, usually uttered when a bird is disturbed. It also occurs in drier forests, woodlands and sometimes near human habitation.

Magpie-lark *Grallina cyanoleuca* 26-30cm

M. Seyfort

Like the **Apostlebird** and **White-winged Chough,** this species builds a mud nest but has little in common with these birds otherwise. Boldly marked black and white, it can be confused with few other birds. The thin whitish bill and pale iris are unlike other similarly coloured species. Adult males have black foreheads and throats; in females these are white; in juveniles, black and white respectively. The 'pee-o-wit' or 'pee-wee' call is frequently given as a duet, each bird raising its wings in turn. Magpie-larks may be found in almost any habitat except rainforest and the driest deserts. They are familiar urban birds.

White-breasted Woodswallow *Artamus leucorynchus* 17-18cm

C. Webster

With its boldly contrasting plumage, this is one of the most easily identified of the woodswallows. A large white rump patch interrupts the dark grey upper wings, tail and upperparts, which are sharply demarcated from the white underparts. This is the only species of Australian woodswallow with no white in the tail, a useful character when viewed from below. The **Masked Woodswallow** has a distinct mask (males black, females grey), a dark rump and white in the tail. From perches and in flight, White-breasted Woodswallows utter their 'pert pert' notes. They are usually found near water, from inland lakes and rivers to coastal mangroves.

Dusky Woodswallow *Artamus cyanopterus* 17-18cm

M. Seyfort

Woodswallows are attractive, sociable birds, often forming mixed flocks of several species. The white wing-stripe separates the Dusky Woodswallow from all others, particularly in combination with its brown body, dark blue-grey wings and white tail tip. The **Little Woodswallow** of northern Australia is smaller, much darker brown and lacks the white wing-stripe. When perched, Dusky Woodswallows have a peculiar habit of wagging their tails side to side. One call has been rendered as a pleasant 'vut vut'. Inhabitants of forests and woodlands, they catch flying insects with graceful swoops from a branch, returning to eat their prey.

135

White-browed Woodswallow *Artamus superciliosus* 19-21cm

G. Little

This is the most colourful of the woodswallows. The male is dark grey above, with a chestnut breast and belly and a conspicuous white eyebrow. In the female, the underparts are paler and the eyebrow smaller. The **Black-faced Woodswallow** is mainly dusky grey except for a small black facial patch. When overhead, the White-browed Woodswallow frequently gives a musical 'chep chep'. It is highly nomadic and can appear in large numbers after rains in a range of timbered habitats, particularly drier inland woodlands. Like other woodswallows, it feeds mainly on insects, but readily takes nectar when available.

Grey Butcherbird *Cracticus torquatus* 24-30cm

G. Weber

Somewhat incongruously, butcherbirds are excellent songsters but fearsome predators on small animals. The latter practice is indicated by the large, hooked grey and black bill. The adult Grey Butcherbird is attractively plumaged, with a black crown and face, grey back and white throat, underparts and partial collar. Younger birds are largely olive-brown. Its song, a lovely rich piping, makes it welcome around houses, while its predation on small birds has the opposite effect. This species may occur in a variety of wooded habitats, as well as suburban areas. In rainforests and mangroves of the north lives the all-black **Black Butcherbird**.

Pied Butcherbird *Cracticus nigrogularis* 33-37.5cm

L.F. Schick

Larger and more boldly marked than the **Grey Butcherbird**, this species shares that bird's predatory habits and vocal abilities. It is best distinguished from other black and white birds by its black head and upper breast, separated from the black back by a complete white collar, and its large white wing-stripe and robust bill. In flight, the black tail with white corners is conspicuous. Possibly the best singer of all Australian birds, its voice is a beautiful, melodious fluting, sometimes given in alternation by several individuals. It inhabits drier forests and woodlands and will often approach parks and houses.

Australian Magpie *Gymnorhina tibicen* 36-44cm

C. Andrew Henley

The plumage of this large black and white bird varies across its range. Throughout, its nape, upper tail and shoulders are white. Across most of Australia, the remainder of the body is black. In the south-east, centre, extreme south-west and Tasmania, the back and rump are entirely white. The song is a loud musical caroling, often given as duets or by groups. The Magpie is often quite tame but can be aggressive when nesting. It is a common and conspicuous bird usually found where there is a combination of trees and adjacent open areas, including parks and playing fields.

Pied Currawong *Strepera graculina* 44-51cm

G. Little

One of several large black and white birds, this common species is recognized by the white base and tip of the tail, a white patch in the wing, a black bill and yellow iris. The **Grey Currawong** exhibits considerable geographical variation in the amount of white in the wing but none have white at the base of the tail. The name comes from the 'currawong' call. Other frequent vocalisations of the Pied Currawong include guttural croaks and a wolf whistle. A bird of forests and woodlands, it has become well adapted to suburban areas. Large flocks form in winter.

Ravens and Crows *Corvidae* 48-54cm

C. Andrew Henley

Although all are black, the five species of ravens and crows can be separated on a combination of characters. Ravens have grey bases to the neck feathers and crows, white. When calling, the **Australian Raven** raises its long throat hackles and holds its body and head in a horizontal position; the wings are not flicked. The territorial call is a slow 'ah-ah-ah-aaaah' with the last note drawn out. It usually occurs in pairs.

The **Little Raven** has medium length hackles, which are not extended during calling, and the wings are flicked with each note. This species is quite sociable, sometimes forming large flocks. Its call is a much quicker 'kar-kar-kar'. The **Forest Raven** has a proportionally large bill and short tail, and utters a deep 'kor-kor-kor-kor', drawing the last note out. Both crows have more nasal voices and shorter hackles than ravens, and form large flocks. The call of the **Torresian Crow** is 'uk-uk-uk-uk'. Although not flicking its wings when calling, it repeatedly shuffles them after landing. The hackles are raised when calling. The **Little Crow** has a bill shorter than the head and gives a 'nark-nark-nark' call; it does not flick its wings.

138

Glossary

Adult. A bird that has attained its final plumage form (not including breeding variations) and which is capable of breeding.

Arboreol. Tree dwelling.

Casque. A raised, helmet-like, structure on the head or bill.

Cere. An area of bare skin surrounding the nostrils, at the base of the upper mandible.

Coverts. Feathers that overlap and cover the bases of larger feathers.

Crepuscular. Active in the twilight.

Crest. Long feathers attached to part of the head.

Culmen. The ridge along the length of the upper mandible.

Diagnostic. Individual characteristic used as an aid to identification.

Endemic. Native to the region under consideration.

Eyebrow. A horizontal line above the eye.

Eye-ring. A circle of naked skin or feathers surrounding the eye.

Eye-stripe. A horizontal line that passes from the bill through the eye.

Facial disc. A well-defined and flat area of the face, as in owls.

Family. A category into which an order is divided.

Flush. The act of disturbing a bird and encouraging its flight.

Frontal shield. An unfeathered, horny or fleshy forehead, continued from the base of the upper mandible.

Gape. The unfeathered fleshy area at each corner of the beak.

Genus. A category into which a family is divided.

Hackles. Long throat feathers.

Immature. A bird in the plumage that follows the first moult. Not yet capable of breeding.

Juvenal. A bird in its earliest full-feathered plumage.

Lores. A patch of feathers, often coloured, between base of bill and eye.

Mandible. The upper or lower half of the bill.

Migrant/Migratory. Undertaking regular geographical movement, e.g. from wintering grounds to breeding grounds.

Morph. An alternative plumage colouration possessed by some members of a species.

Nail. A hooked tip of the upper mandible (as in albatrosses, petrels and waterfowl).

Nape. The back of a bird's neck.

Nomadic. Of erratic and changeable movements.

Nuchal Crest. The crest of feathers at the base of the nape.

Nuptial. Pertaining to breeding condition.

Order. One of the major groups into which birds are classified.

Parasitism. The laying of an egg in the nest of another species, which incubates and rears the parasitic young.

Plumage. The layer of feathers or down on the body.

Plume. Long feather used for display.

Primaries. Outer flight feathers.

Rictal bristles. Hair-like structures surrounding the base of the bill.

Roost. A perching place for observation, resting or sleeping.

Secondaries. Inner flight feathers.

Sedentary. Spending the entire life in a relatively restricted region.

Shaft. The main stem of a feather.

Species. The category into which a genus is divided.

Tear-stripe. A vertical marking below the eye.

Territory. An area defended by an individual bird and its family.

Vent. The area from the belly to the undertail coverts.

Further reading

Blakers, M., Davies, S.J.J.F. & Reilly, P.N. (1984) *The Atlas of Australian Birds* Royal Australasian Ornithologists Union, Melbourne University Press, Carlton, Victoria.

Boles, W.E. (1988) *The Robins and Flycatchers of Australia* HarperCollins, Sydney.

Bransbury, J. (1992) *Where to Find Birds in Australia* Waymark Publishing, Fullerton, South Australia.

Cayley, N.W. (1984) (Revised by T.R. Lindsey) *What Bird is That?* HarperCollins, Sydney.

Crome, F. & Shields, J. (1992) *Parrots and Pigeons of Australia* HarperCollins, Sydney.

Forshaw, J.M. and Cooper, W.T. (1984) *Australian Parrots* (Third edition) Lansdowne, Sydney.

Garnet, S. (Ed) (1992). *Threatened and Extinct Birds of Australia* Royal Australasian Ornithologists Union and Australian National Parks and Wildlife Service. RAOU Report 82.

Lindsey, T.R. (1986) *The Seabirds of Australia* HarperCollins, Sydney.

Longmore, W. (1987) *Honeyeaters and their Allies of Australia* HarperCollins, Sydney.

Olsen, P, Crome, F. & Olsen, J. (1993) *Birds of Prey and Ground Birds of Australia* HarperCollins, Sydney.

Pizzey, G. (1991) *Field Guide to the Birds of Australia* (Second edition) A & R Bookworld, Sydney.

Pringle, J.D. (1987) *The Shorebirds of Australia* HarperCollins, Sydney.

Reader's Digest Complete Book of Australian Birds (1993) (Second edition) Reader's Digest, Sydney.

Roberts, P. (1993) *Birdwatcher's Guide to the Sydney Region* Kangaroo Press, Sydney.

Simpson, K. and Day, N. (1993) *Field Guide to the Birds of Australia* Viking O'Neil, Melbourne.

Trounson, A.D. and M. (1994) *Australian Birds Simply Classified* National Book Distributors and Publishers, Sydney.

INDEX (Common Names)